WITHDRAWN

ChiMiChaNga

™

THE SORROW OF THE "WORLD'S WORST FACE!

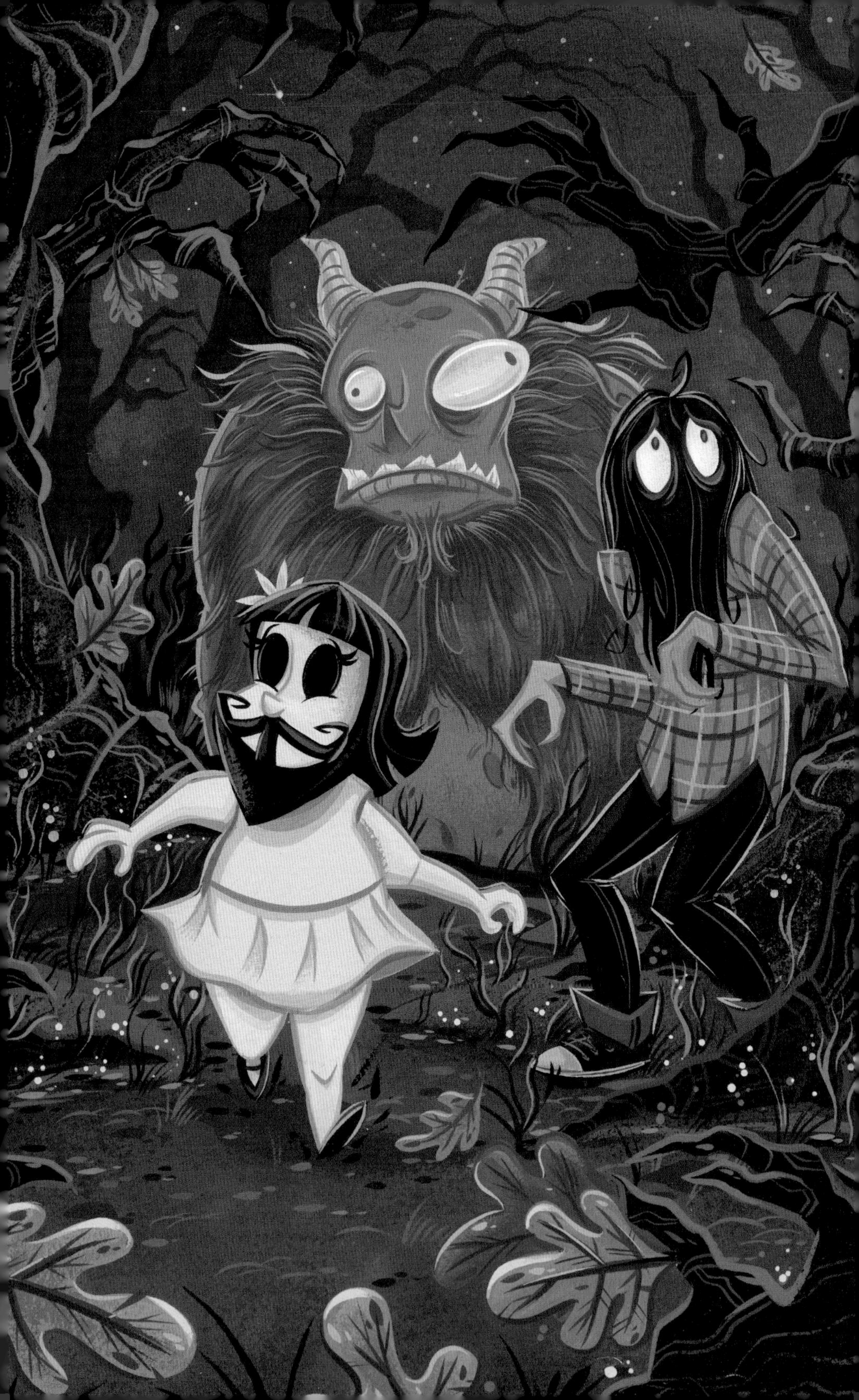

Chimichanga™

The Sorrow of the World's Worst Face!

SCRIPT BY ERIC POWELL

ART BY STEPHANIE BUSCEMA

LETTERING BY NATE PIEKOS
OF BLAMBOT®

DARK HORSE BOOKS

President and Publisher MIKE RICHARDSON

Editor SHANTEL LaROCQUE

Assistant Editor KATII O'BRIEN

Collection Designer ETHAN KIMBERLING

Digital Art Technician ALLYSON HALLER

Published by Dark Horse Books
A division of Dark Horse Comics, Inc.
10956 SE Main Street
Milwaukie, OR 97222

First edition: March 2018
ISBN 978-1-61655-902-1

1 3 5 7 9 10 8 6 4 2
Printed in China

International Licensing: (503) 905-2377
Comic Shop Locator Service: comicshoplocator.com

Neil Hankerson, Executive Vice President • Tom Weddle, Chief Financial Officer • Randy Stradley, Vice President of Publishing • Nick McWhorter, Chief Business Development Officer • Matt Parkinson, Vice President of Marketing • Dale LaFountain, Vice President of Information Technology • Cara Niece, Vice President of Production and Scheduling • Mark Bernardi, Vice President of Book Trade and Digital Sales • Ken Lizzi, General Counsel • Dave Marshall, Editor in Chief • Davey Estrada, Editorial Director • Chris Warner, Senior Books Editor • Cary Grazzini, Director of Specialty Projects • Lia Ribacchi, Art Director • Vanessa Todd-Holmes, Director of Print Purchasing • Matt Dryer, Director of Digital Art and Prepress • Michael Gombos, Director of International Publishing and Licensing Kari Yadra, Director of Custom Programs

Library of Congress Cataloging-in-Publication Data

Names: Powell, Eric, author. | Buscema, Stephanie, artist. | Piekos, Nate, letterer.
Title: Chimichanga : the sorrow of the world's worst face / script by Eric Powell ; art, cover, and chapter break art by Stephanie Buscema ; lettering by Nate Piekos of Blambot.
Description: First edition. | Milwaukie, OR : Dark Horse Books, 2017. | "This volume collects Chimichanga: The Sorrow of the World's Worst Face #1–#4." | Summary: "The story of a bizarre monster and the little bearded girl who guides him through life in the sideshow. Now they have met another misfit—a boy so ugly he hides behind the world's longest bangs!"—Provided by publisher.
Identifiers: LCCN 2016054361 | ISBN 9781616559021 (hardback)
Subjects: LCSH: Graphic novels. | CYAC: Graphic novels. | Sideshows—Fiction. | Monsters—Fiction. | Carnivals—Fiction. | Self-Esteem—Fiction. | BISAC: JUVENILE FICTION / Comics & Graphic Novels / General.
Classification: LCC PZ7.7.P68 Ch 2017 | DDC 741.5/973—dc23
LC record available at https://lccn.loc.gov/2016054361

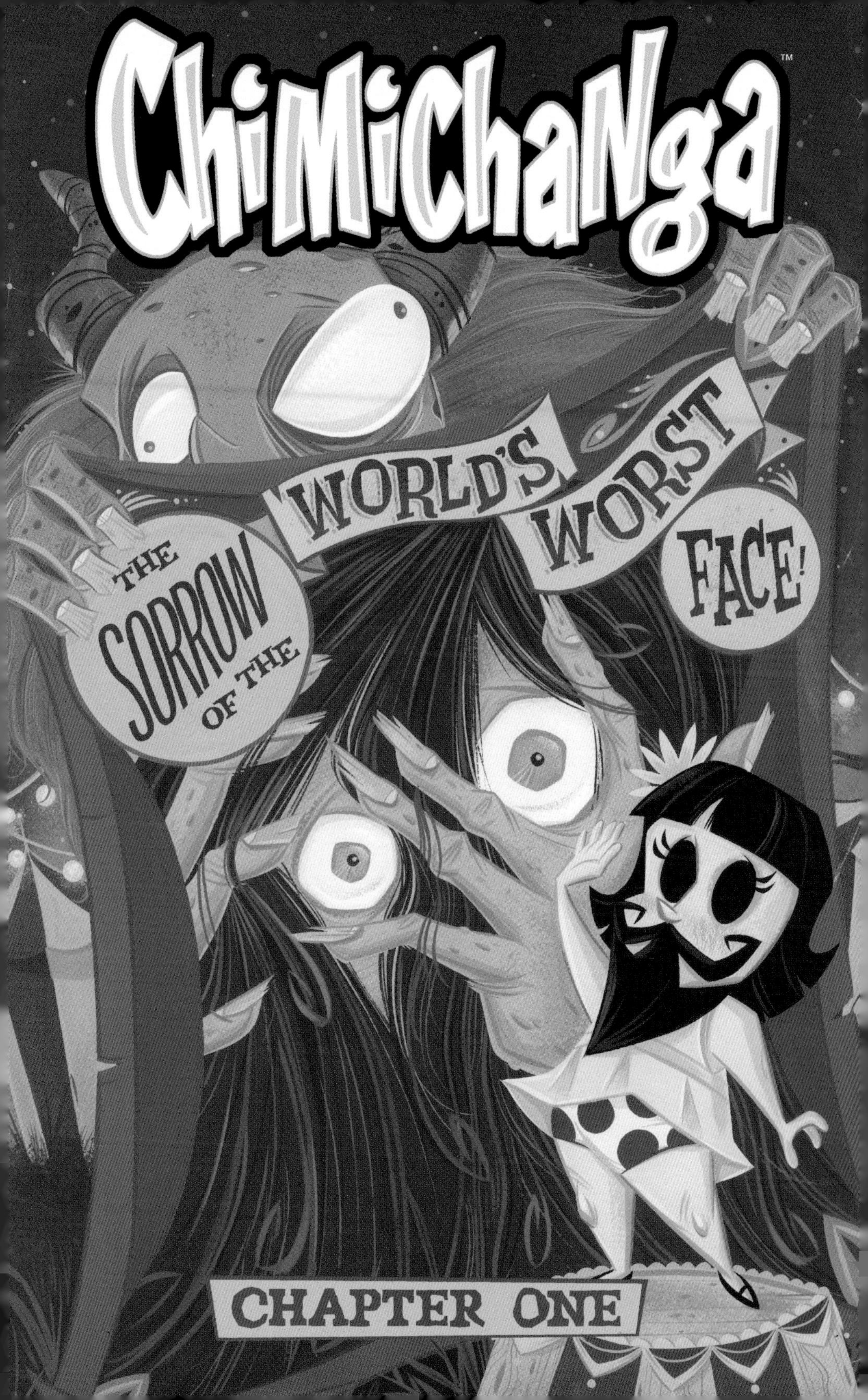
ChiMiChaNga™
THE SORROW OF THE WORLD'S WORST FACE!
CHAPTER ONE

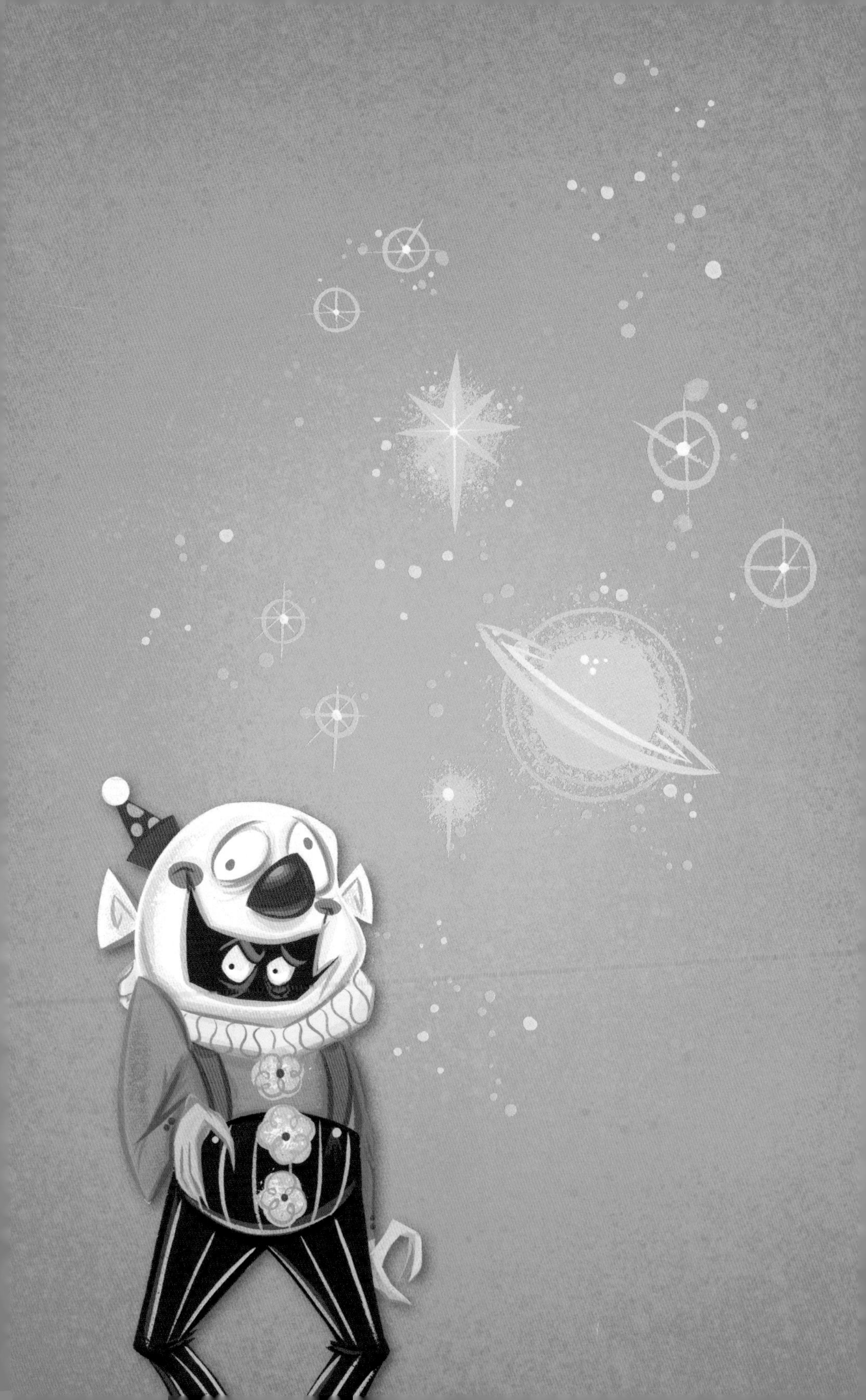

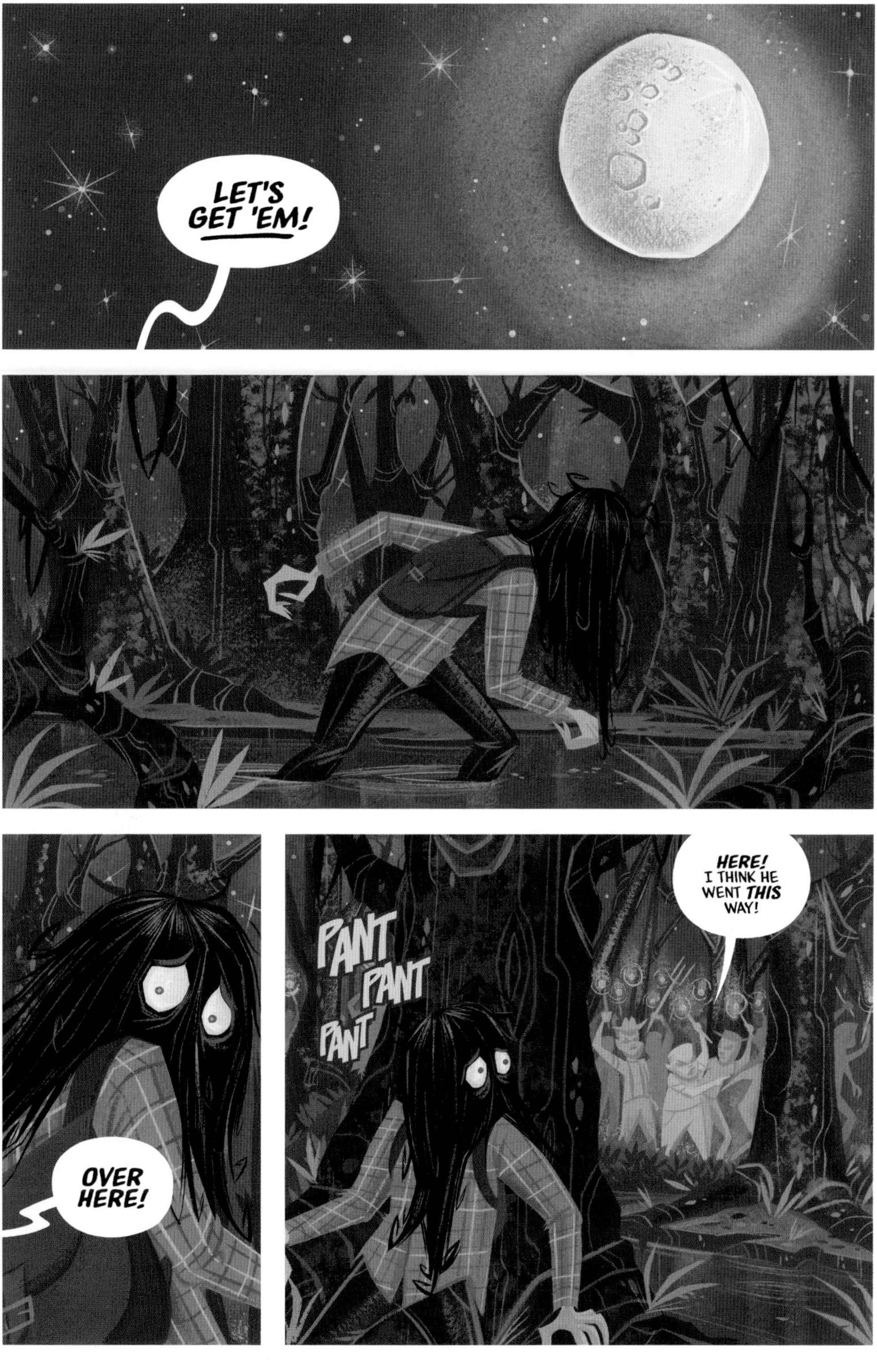

LET'S GET 'EM!
OVER HERE!
PANT PANT PANT
HERE! I THINK HE WENT THIS WAY!

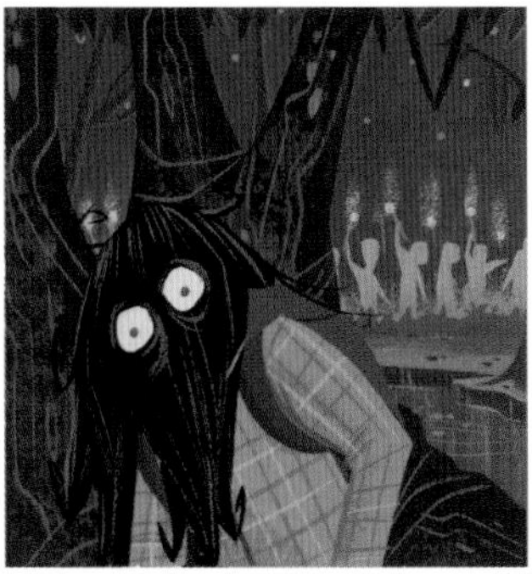

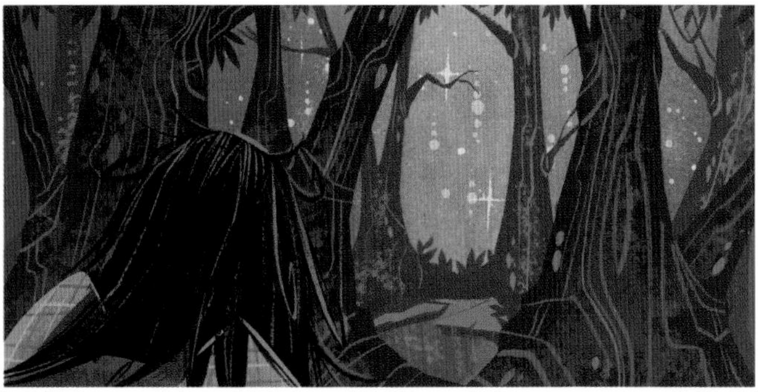

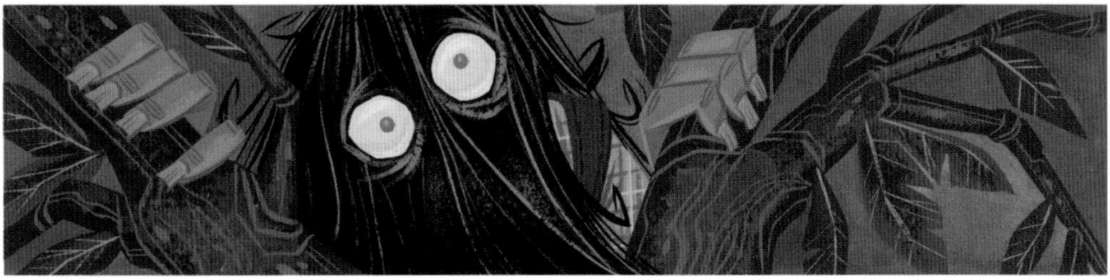

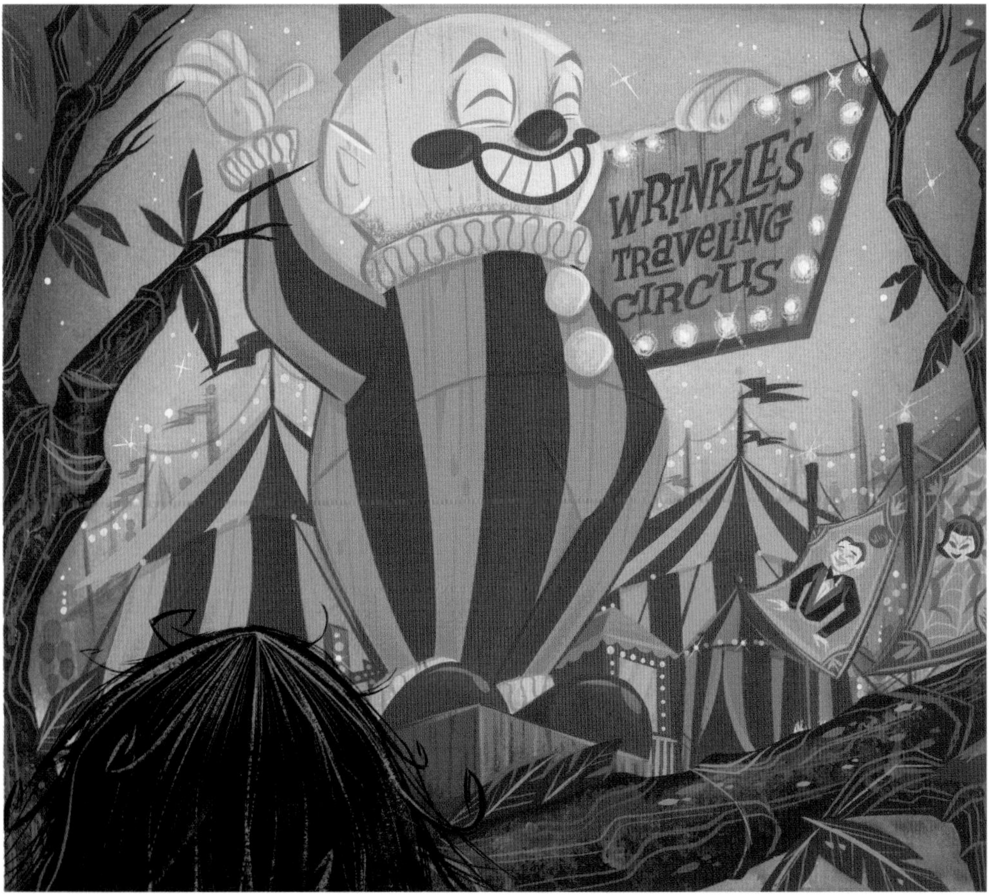
WRINKLE'S TRAVELING CIRCUS

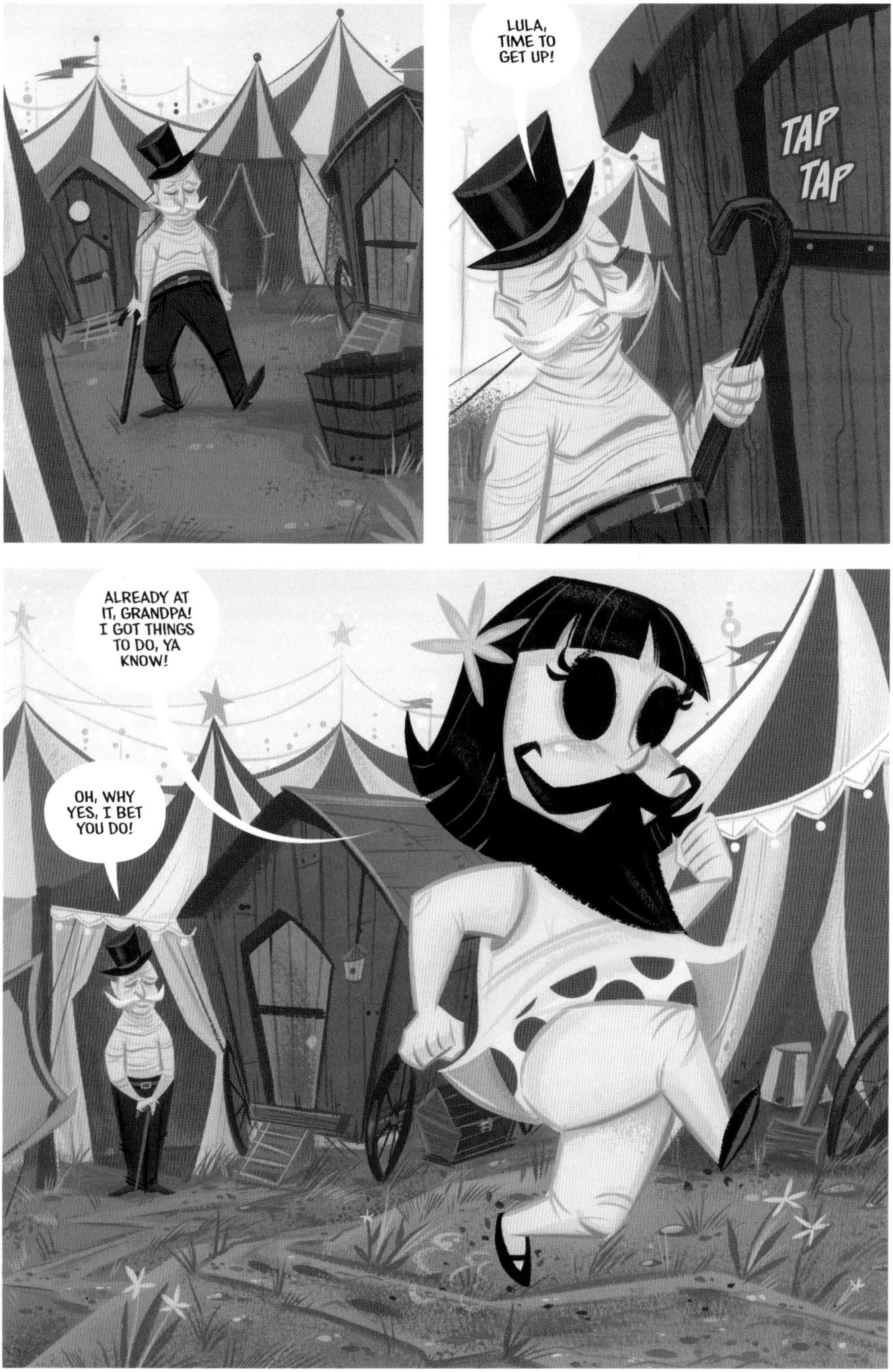
LULA, TIME TO GET UP!
TAP TAP
ALREADY AT IT, GRANDPA! I GOT THINGS TO DO, YA KNOW!
OH, WHY YES, I BET YOU DO!

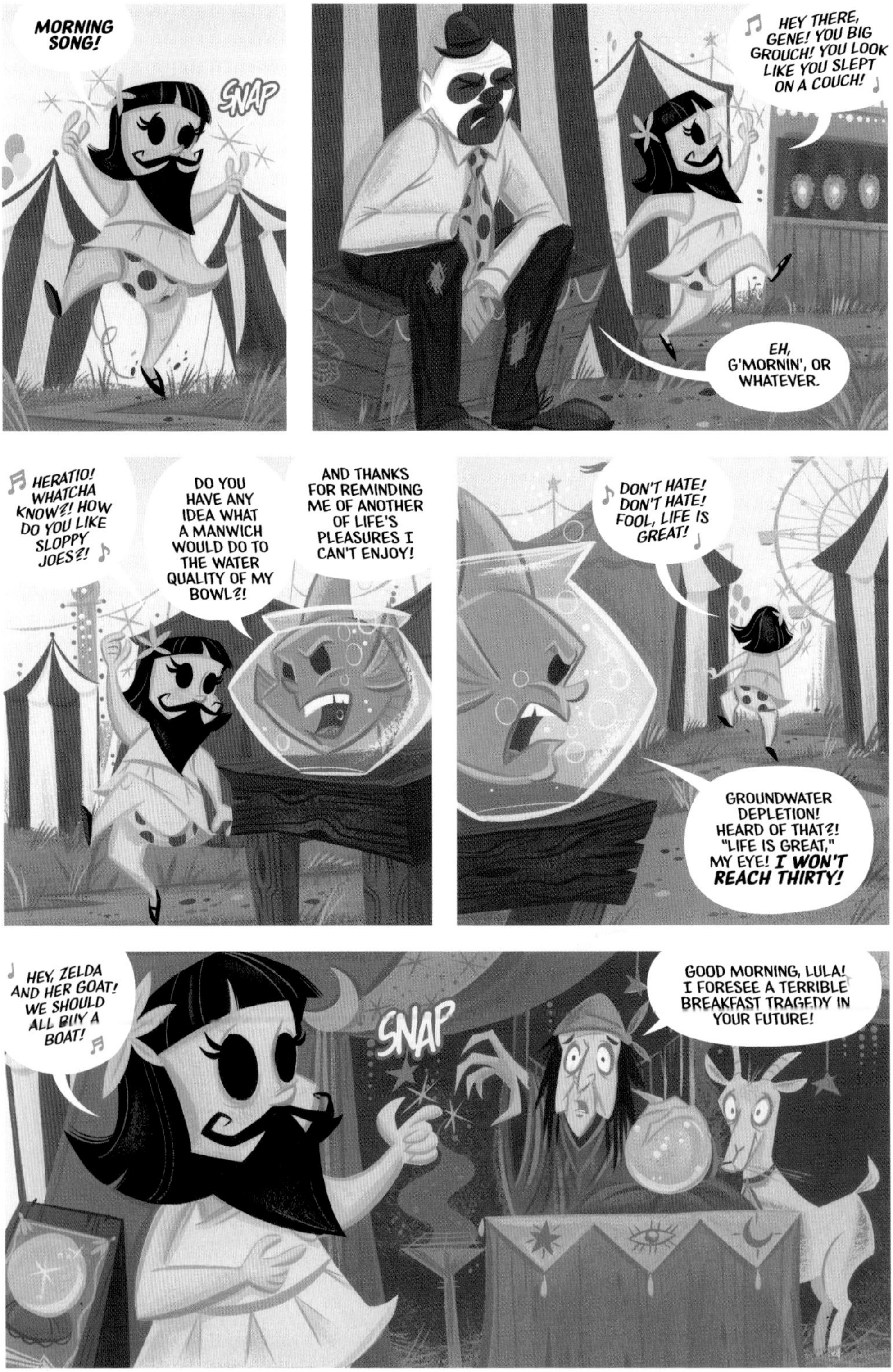
MORNING SONG!
SNAP
HEY THERE, GENE! YOU BIG GROUCH! YOU LOOK LIKE YOU SLEPT ON A COUCH!
EH, G'MORNIN', OR WHATEVER.
HERATIO! WHATCHA KNOW?! HOW DO YOU LIKE SLOPPY JOES?!
DO YOU HAVE ANY IDEA WHAT A MANWICH WOULD DO TO THE WATER QUALITY OF MY BOWL?!
AND THANKS FOR REMINDING ME OF ANOTHER OF LIFE'S PLEASURES I CAN'T ENJOY!
DON'T HATE! DON'T HATE! FOOL, LIFE IS GREAT!
GROUNDWATER DEPLETION! HEARD OF THAT?! "LIFE IS GREAT," MY EYE! I WON'T REACH THIRTY!
HEY, ZELDA AND HER GOAT! WE SHOULD ALL BUY A BOAT!
SNAP
GOOD MORNING, LULA! I FORESEE A TERRIBLE BREAKFAST TRAGEDY IN YOUR FUTURE!

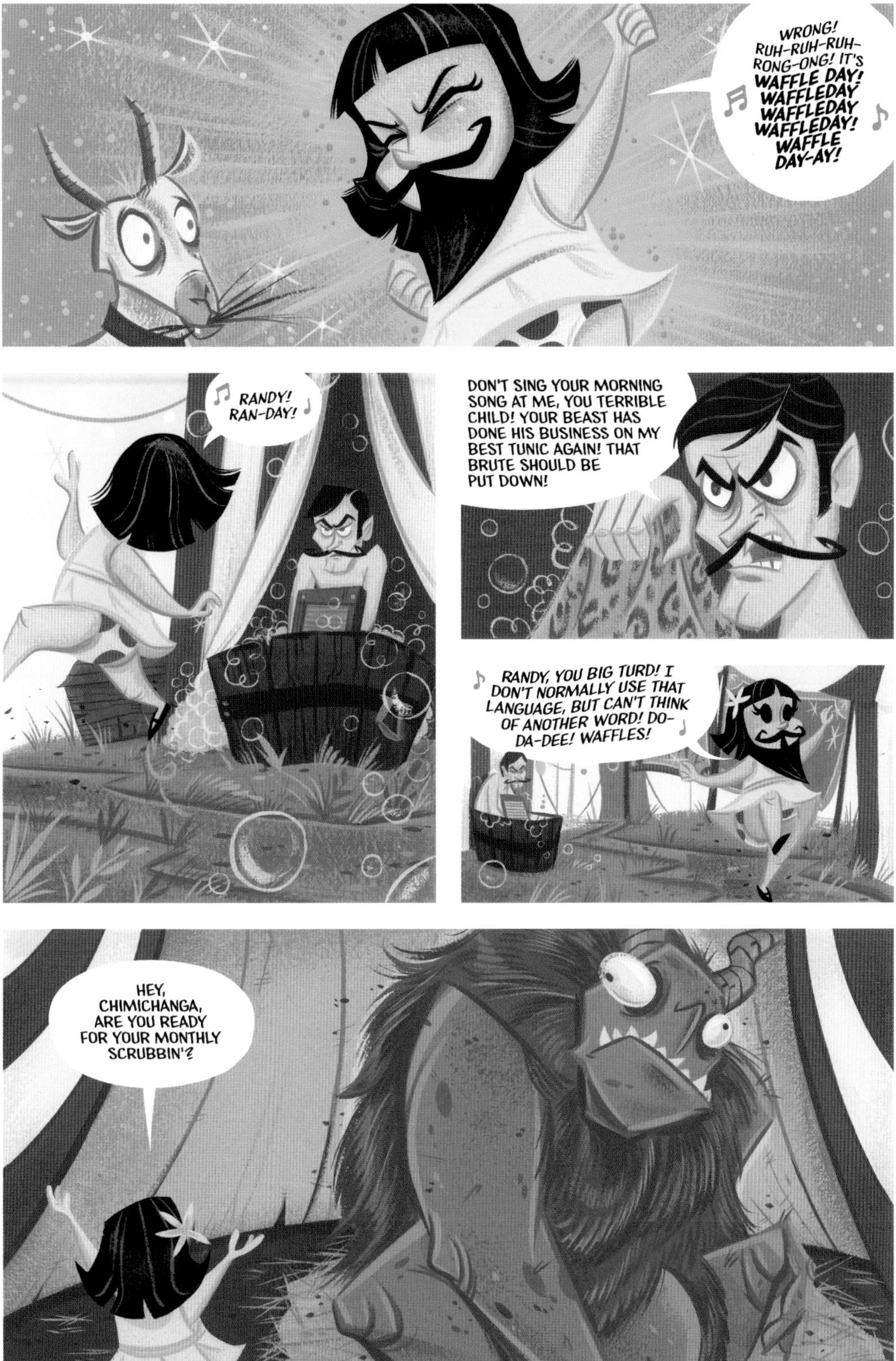
WRONG! RUH-RUH-RUH-RONG-ONG! IT'S WAFFLE DAY! WAFFLEDAY WAFFLEDAY WAFFLEDAY! WAFFLE DAY-AY!
RANDY! RAN-DAY!
DON'T SING YOUR MORNING SONG AT ME, YOU TERRIBLE CHILD! YOUR BEAST HAS DONE HIS BUSINESS ON MY BEST TUNIC AGAIN! THAT BRUTE SHOULD BE PUT DOWN!
RANDY, YOU BIG TURD! I DON'T NORMALLY USE THAT LANGUAGE, BUT CAN'T THINK OF ANOTHER WORD! DO-DA-DEE! WAFFLES!
HEY, CHIMICHANGA, ARE YOU READY FOR YOUR MONTHLY SCRUBBIN'?

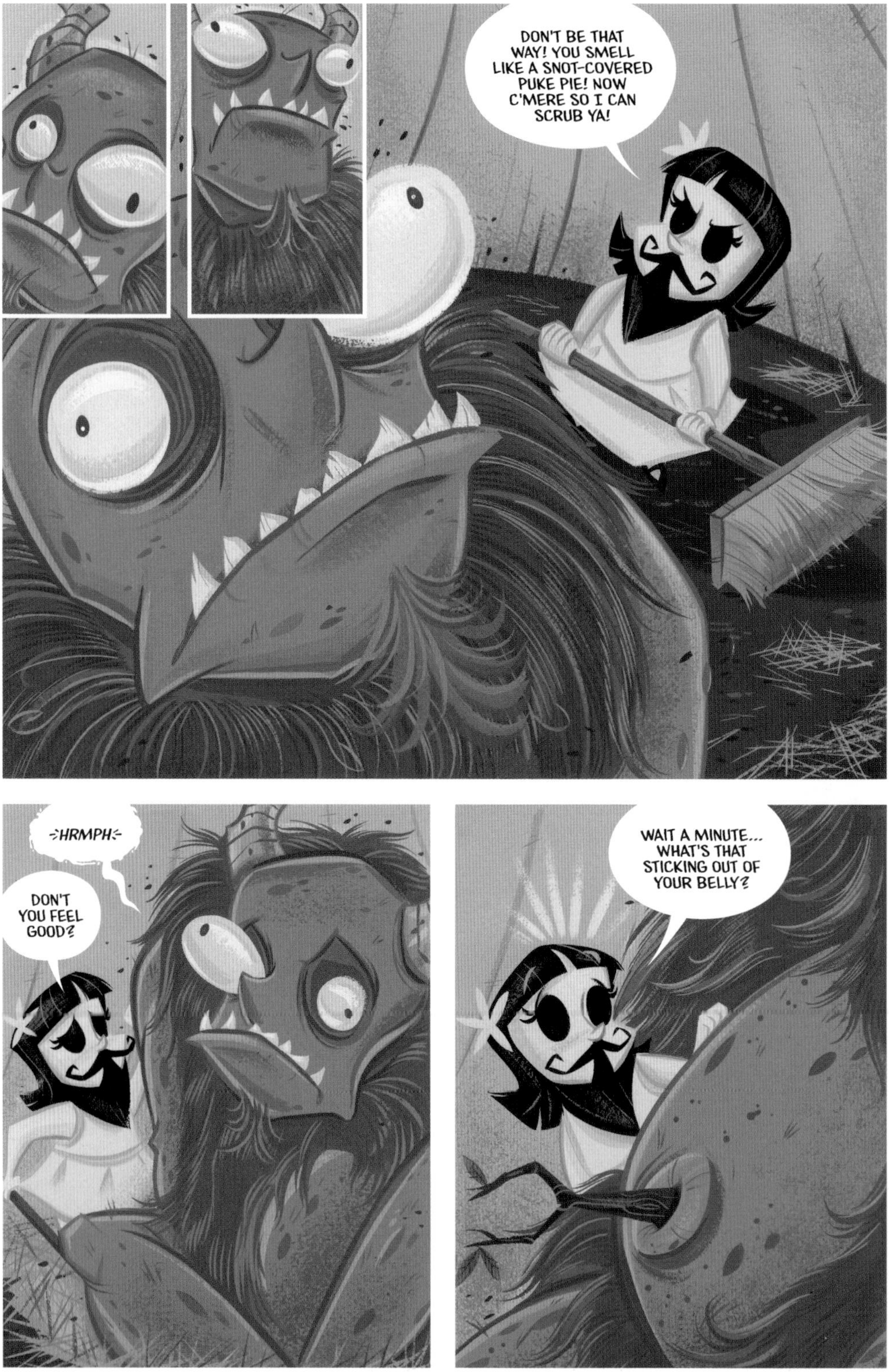
DON'T BE THAT WAY! YOU SMELL LIKE A SNOT-COVERED PUKE PIE! NOW C'MERE SO I CAN SCRUB YA!
HRMPH
DON'T YOU FEEL GOOD?
WAIT A MINUTE... WHAT'S THAT STICKING OUT OF YOUR BELLY?

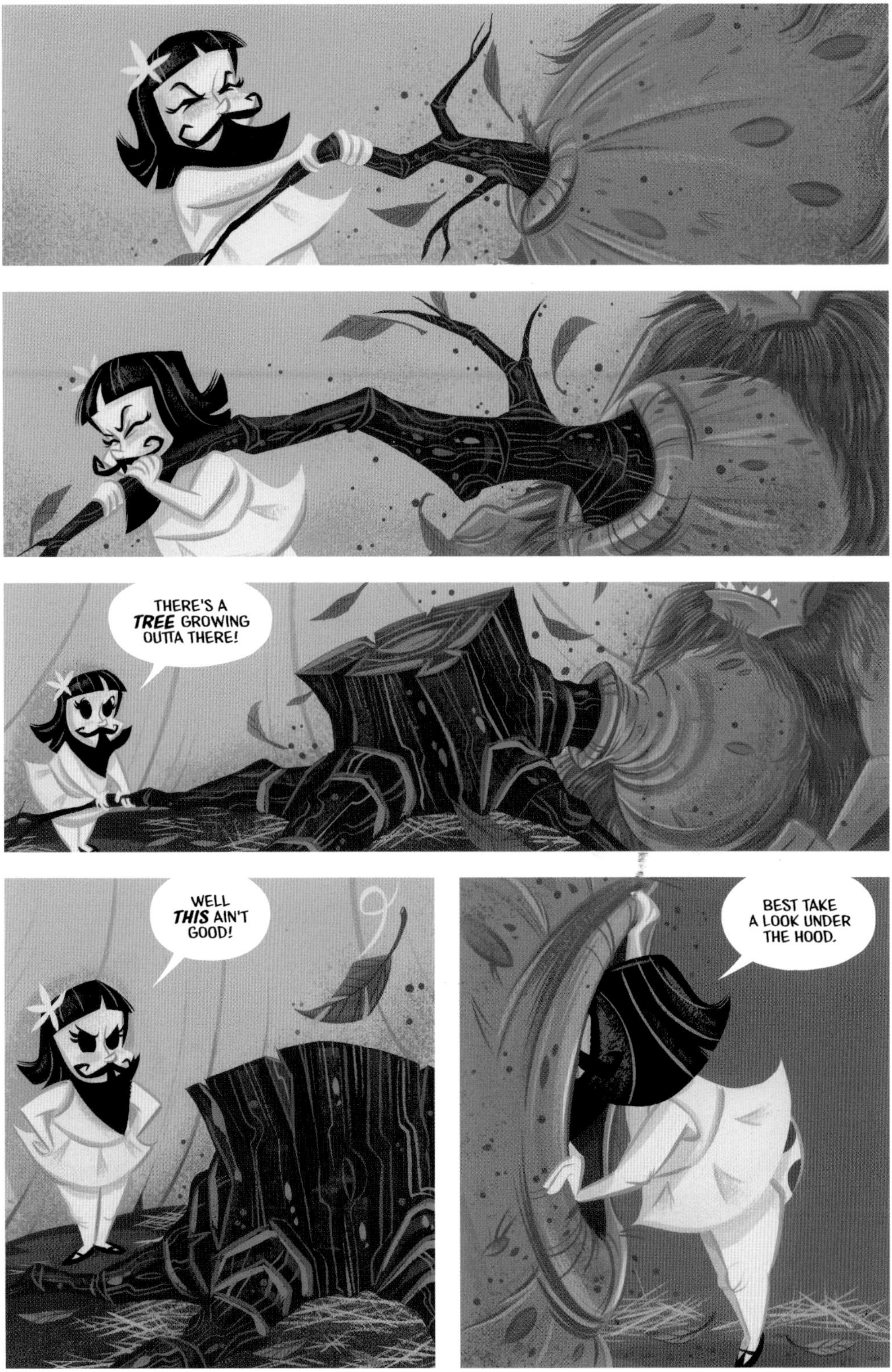
THERE'S A TREE GROWING OUTTA THERE!
WELL THIS AIN'T GOOD!
BEST TAKE A LOOK UNDER THE HOOD.

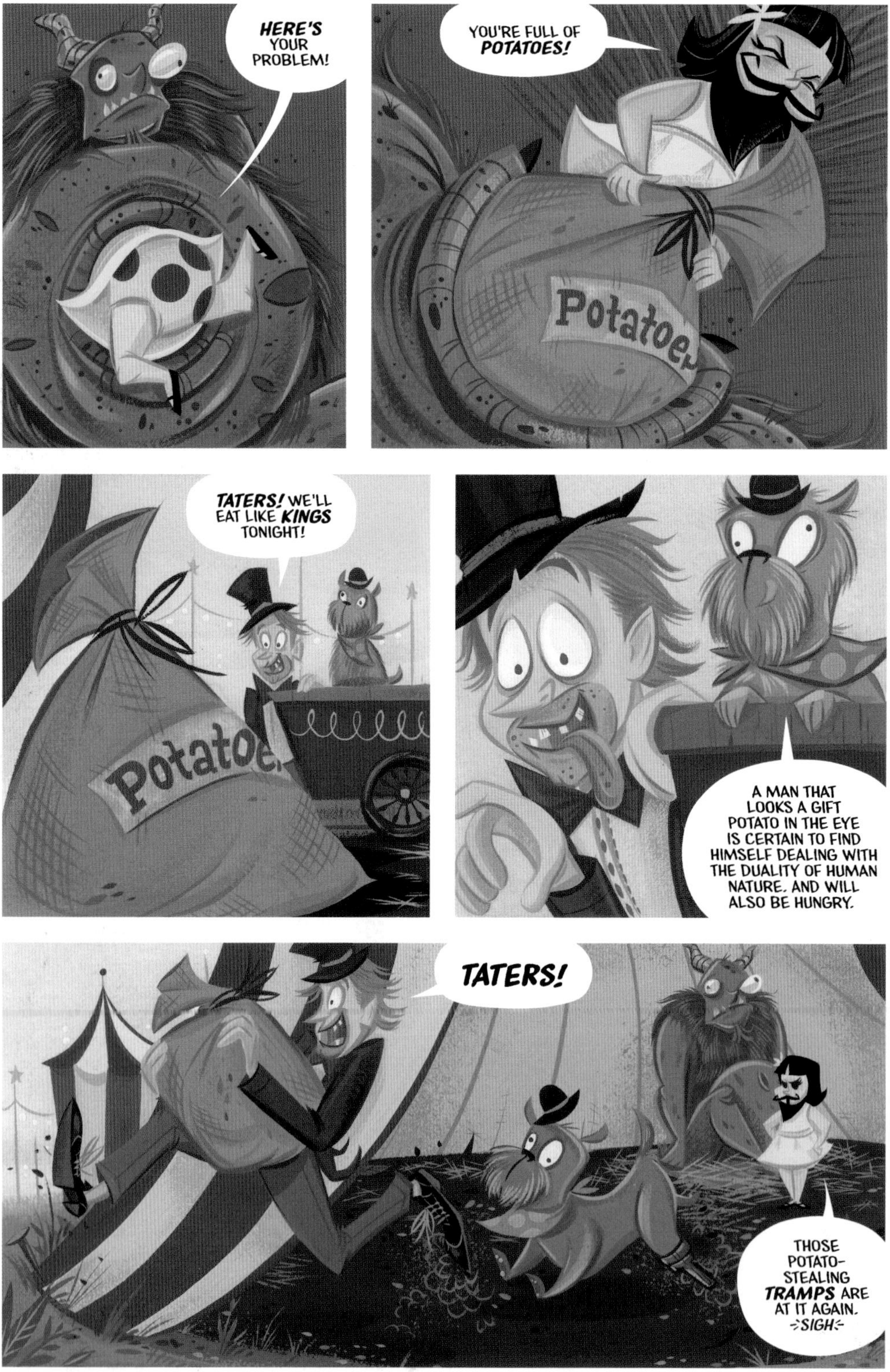
HERE'S YOUR PROBLEM!
YOU'RE FULL OF POTATOES!
Potatoe
TATERS! WE'LL EAT LIKE KINGS TONIGHT!
Potatoe
A MAN THAT LOOKS A GIFT POTATO IN THE EYE IS CERTAIN TO FIND HIMSELF DEALING WITH THE DUALITY OF HUMAN NATURE. AND WILL ALSO BE HUNGRY.
TATERS!
THOSE POTATO-STEALING TRAMPS ARE AT IT AGAIN. -SIGH-

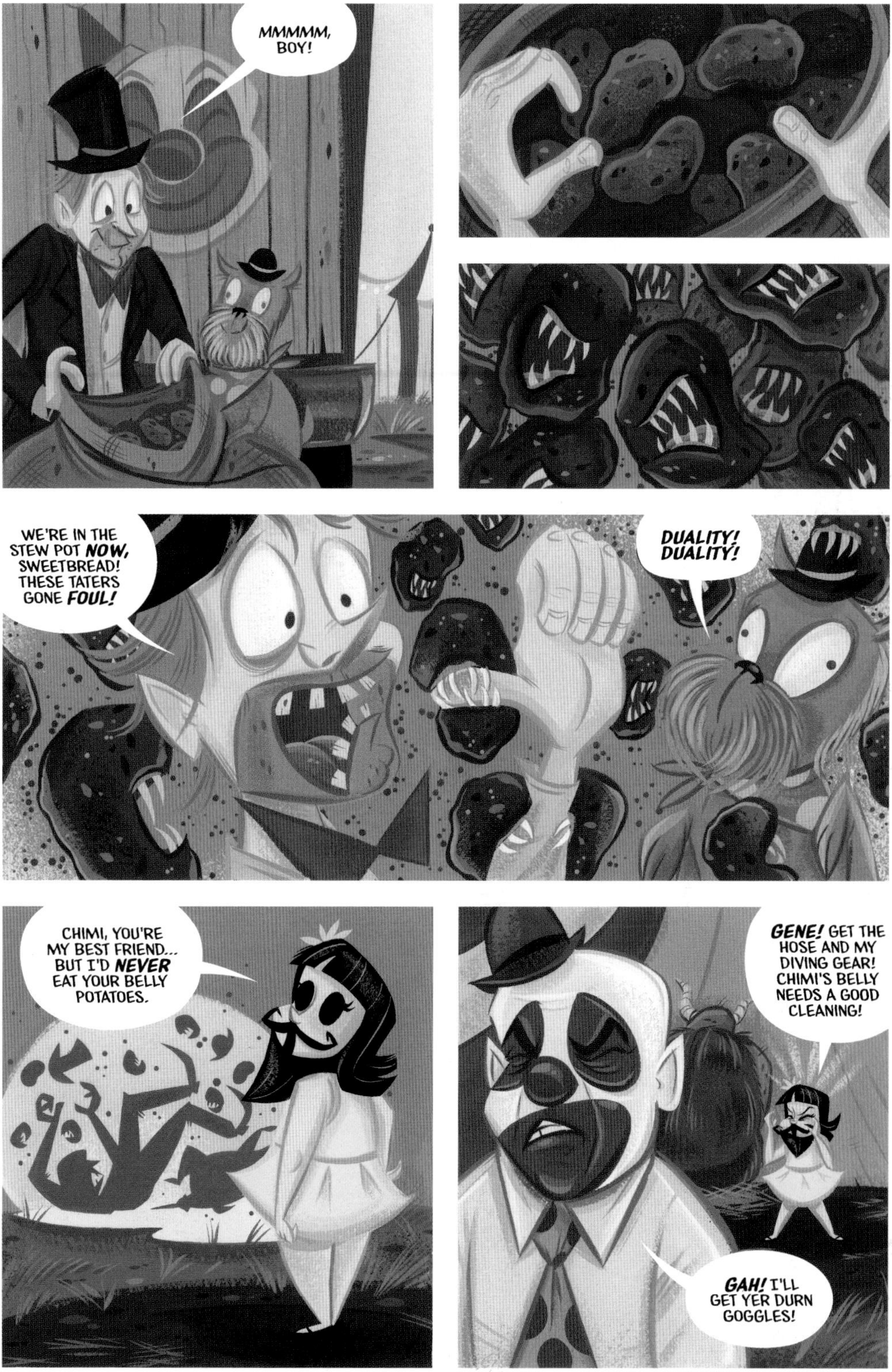
MMMMM, BOY!
WE'RE IN THE STEW POT NOW, SWEETBREAD! THESE TATERS GONE FOUL!
DUALITY! DUALITY!
CHIMI, YOU'RE MY BEST FRIEND... BUT I'D NEVER EAT YOUR BELLY POTATOES.
GENE! GET THE HOSE AND MY DIVING GEAR! CHIMI'S BELLY NEEDS A GOOD CLEANING!
GAH! I'LL GET YER DURN GOGGLES!

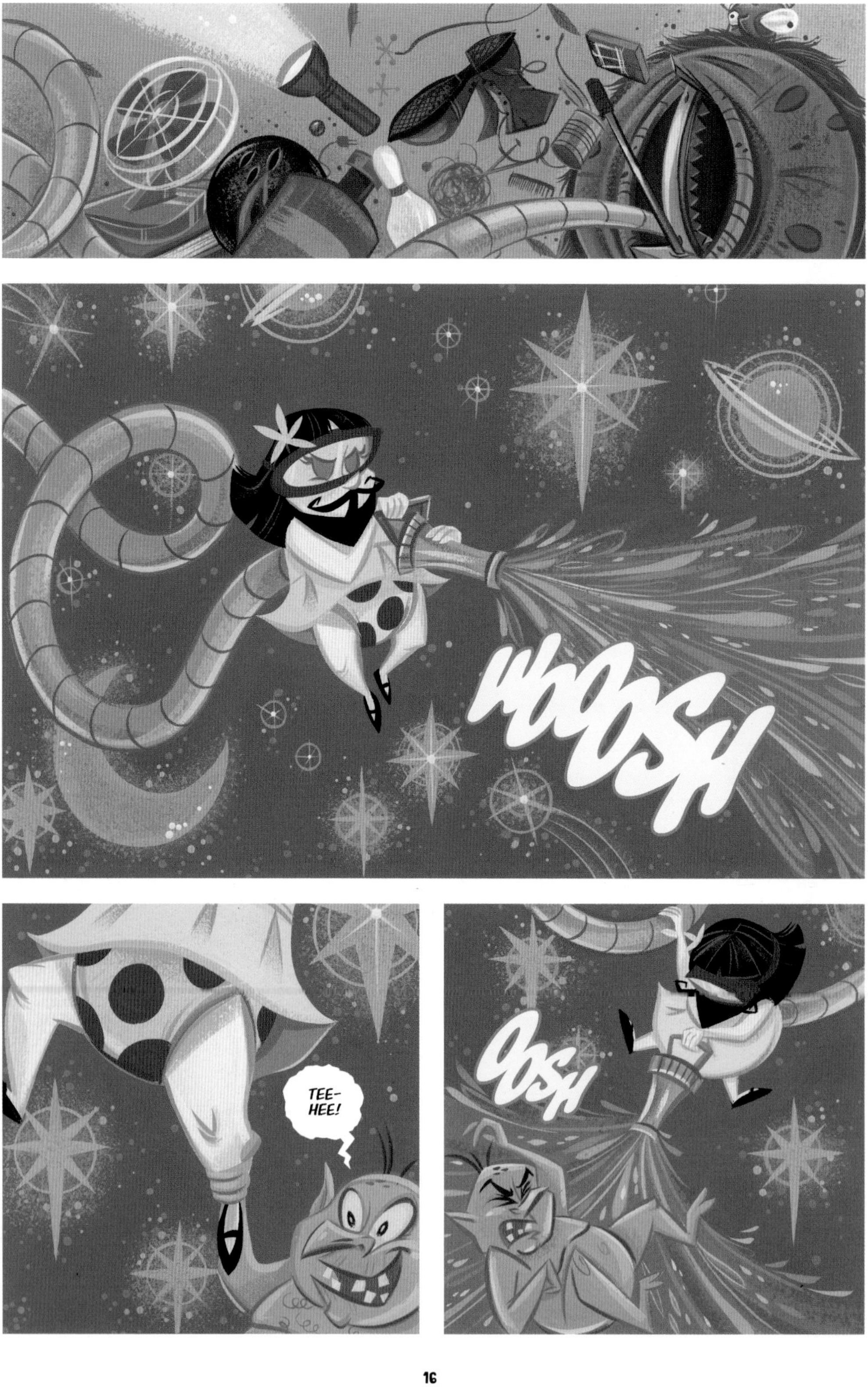
WOOOSH
TEE-HEE!
OOSH

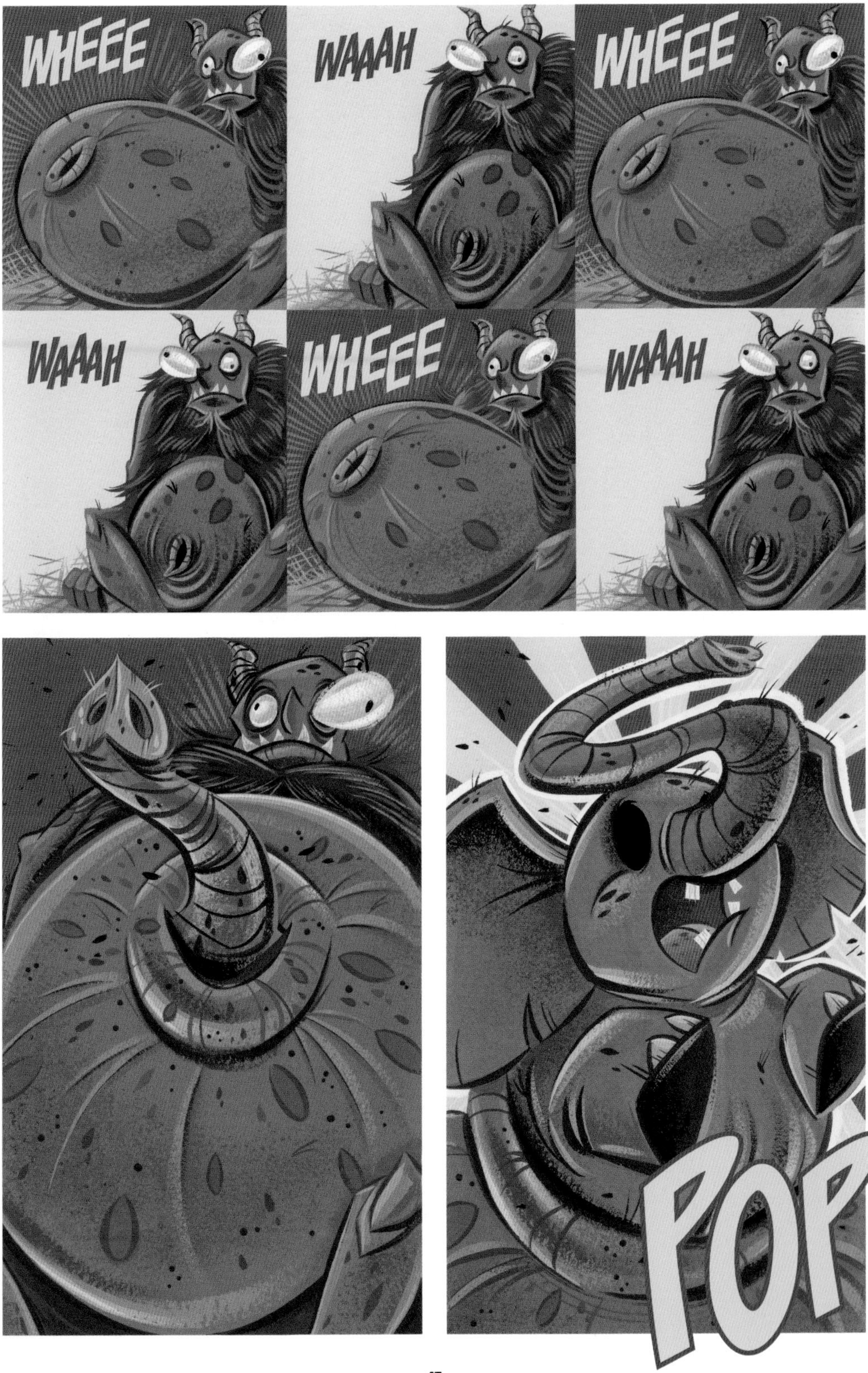
WHEEE
WAAAH
WHEEE
WAAAH
WHEEE
WAAAH
POP

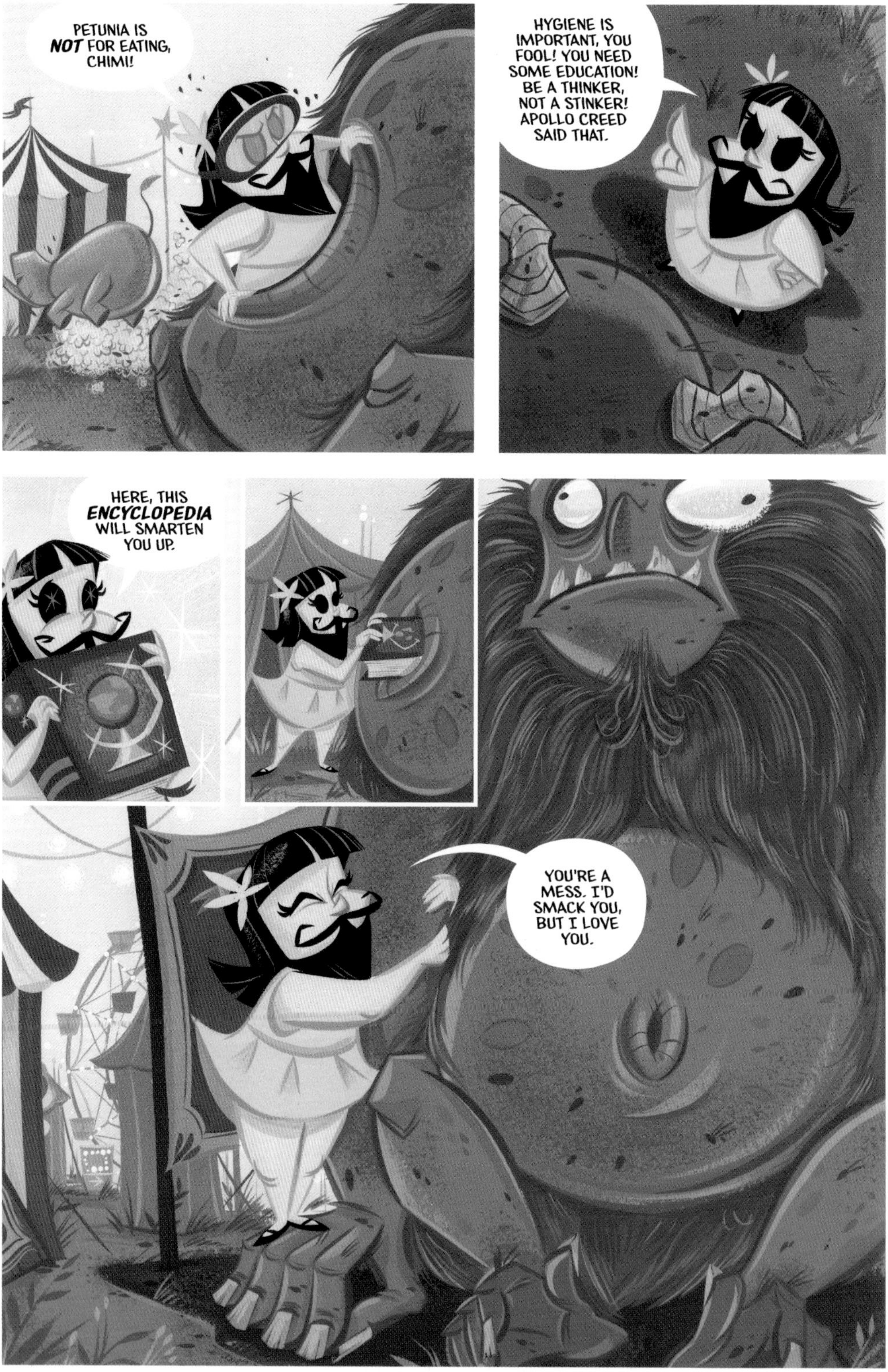
PETUNIA IS NOT FOR EATING, CHIMI!
HYGIENE IS IMPORTANT, YOU FOOL! YOU NEED SOME EDUCATION! BE A THINKER, NOT A STINKER! APOLLO CREED SAID THAT.
HERE, THIS ENCYCLOPEDIA WILL SMARTEN YOU UP.
YOU'RE A MESS. I'D SMACK YOU, BUT I LOVE YOU.

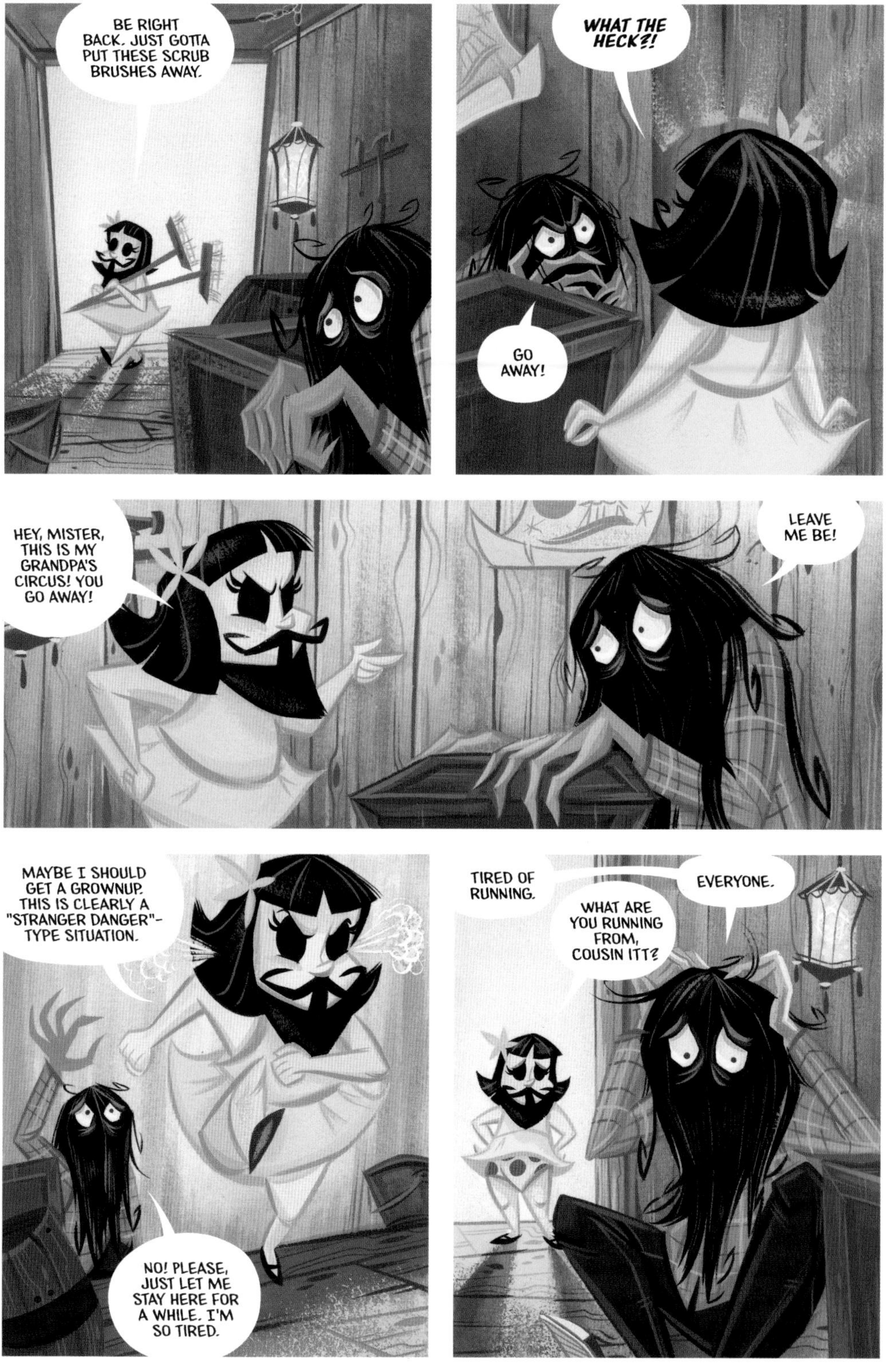
BE RIGHT BACK. JUST GOTTA PUT THESE SCRUB BRUSHES AWAY.
WHAT THE HECK?!
GO AWAY!
HEY, MISTER, THIS IS MY GRANDPA'S CIRCUS! YOU GO AWAY!
LEAVE ME BE!
MAYBE I SHOULD GET A GROWNUP. THIS IS CLEARLY A "STRANGER DANGER"-TYPE SITUATION.
NO! PLEASE, JUST LET ME STAY HERE FOR A WHILE. I'M SO TIRED.
WHAT ARE YOU RUNNING FROM, COUSIN ITT?
TIRED OF RUNNING.
EVERYONE.

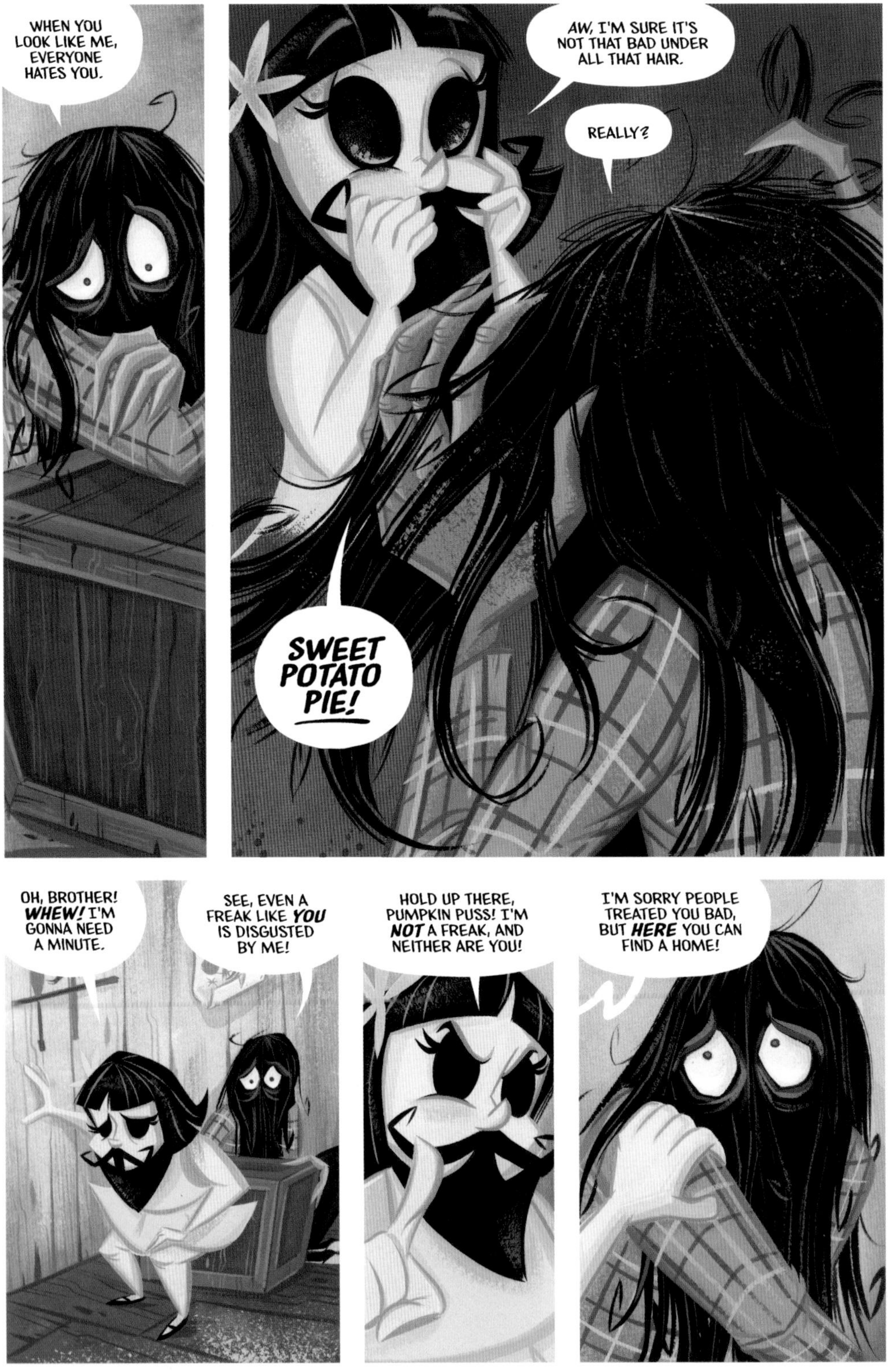
WHEN YOU LOOK LIKE ME, EVERYONE HATES YOU.
AW, I'M SURE IT'S NOT THAT BAD UNDER ALL THAT HAIR.
REALLY?
SWEET POTATO PIE!
OH, BROTHER! WHEW! I'M GONNA NEED A MINUTE.
SEE, EVEN A FREAK LIKE YOU IS DISGUSTED BY ME!
HOLD UP THERE, PUMPKIN PUSS! I'M NOT A FREAK, AND NEITHER ARE YOU!
I'M SORRY PEOPLE TREATED YOU BAD, BUT HERE YOU CAN FIND A HOME!

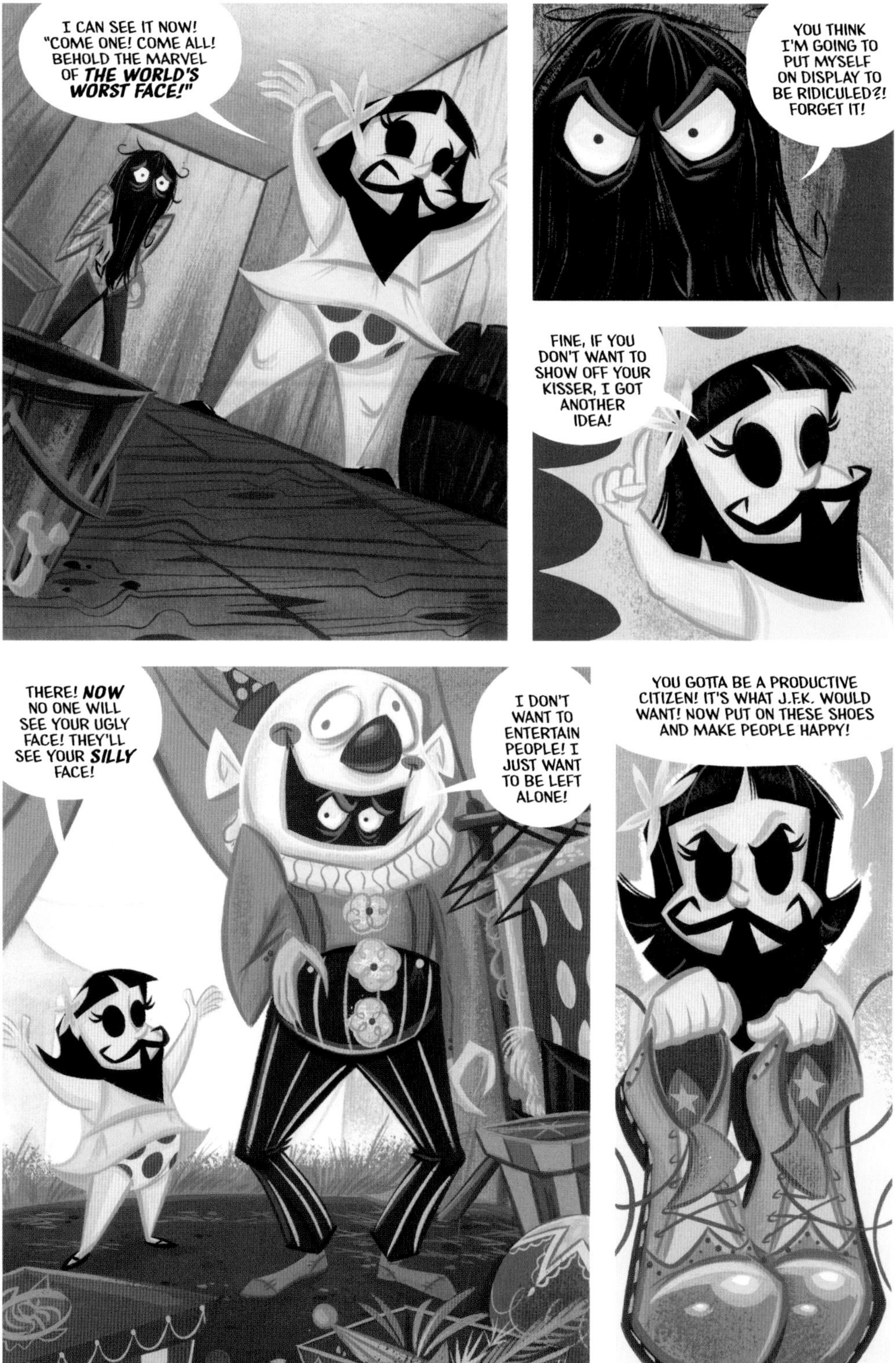

I CAN SEE IT NOW! "COME ONE! COME ALL! BEHOLD THE MARVEL OF ***THE WORLD'S WORST FACE!***"
YOU THINK I'M GOING TO PUT MYSELF ON DISPLAY TO BE RIDICULED?! FORGET IT!
FINE, IF YOU DON'T WANT TO SHOW OFF YOUR KISSER, I GOT ANOTHER IDEA!
THERE! ***NOW*** NO ONE WILL SEE YOUR UGLY FACE! THEY'LL SEE YOUR ***SILLY*** FACE!
I DON'T WANT TO ENTERTAIN PEOPLE! I JUST WANT TO BE LEFT ALONE!
YOU GOTTA BE A PRODUCTIVE CITIZEN! IT'S WHAT J.F.K. WOULD WANT! NOW PUT ON THESE SHOES AND MAKE PEOPLE HAPPY!

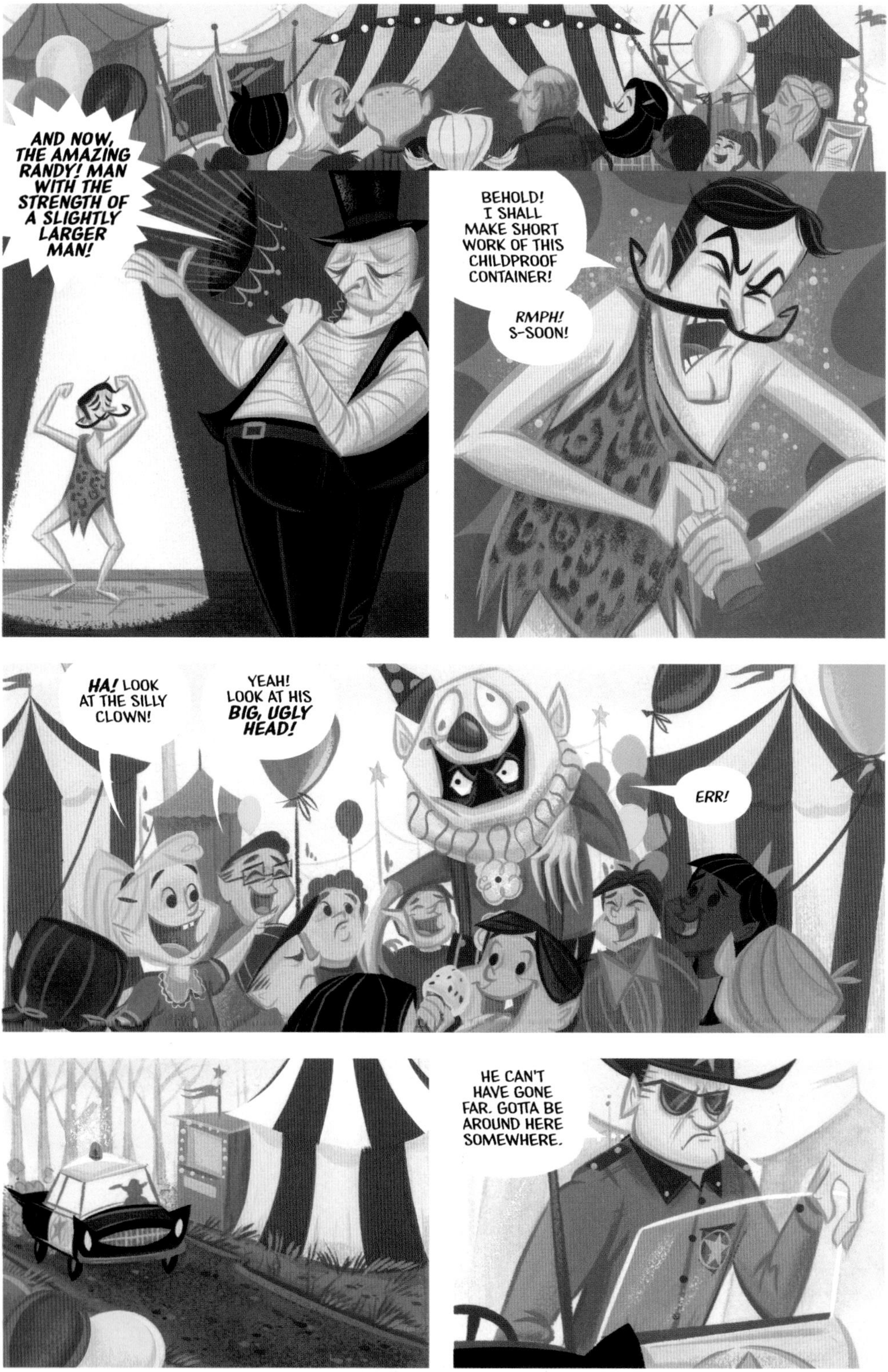
AND NOW, THE AMAZING RANDY! MAN WITH THE STRENGTH OF A SLIGHTLY LARGER MAN!
BEHOLD! I SHALL MAKE SHORT WORK OF THIS CHILDPROOF CONTAINER!
RMPH! S-SOON!
HA! LOOK AT THE SILLY CLOWN!
YEAH! LOOK AT HIS BIG, UGLY HEAD!
ERR!
HE CAN'T HAVE GONE FAR. GOTTA BE AROUND HERE SOMEWHERE.

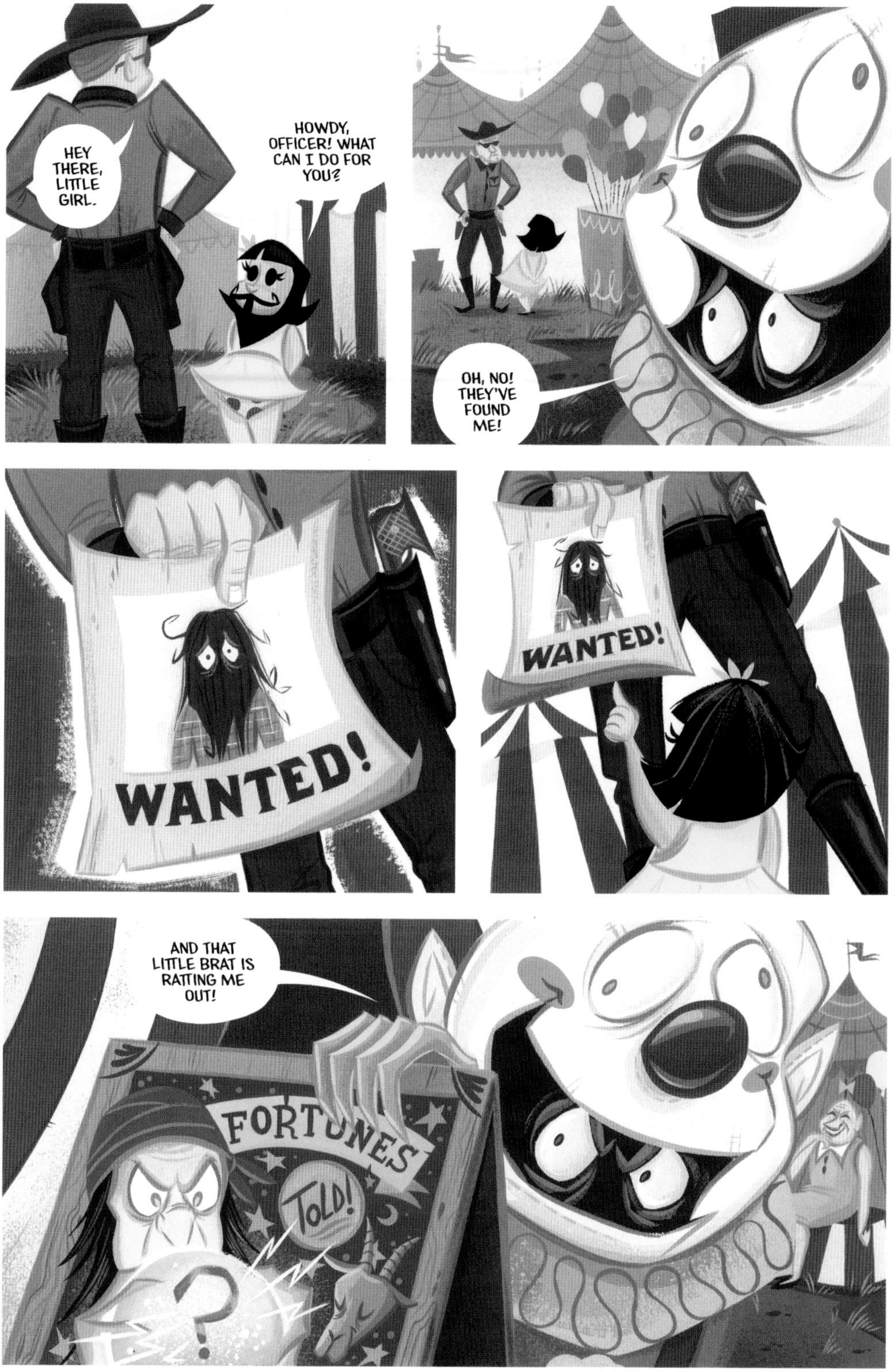
HEY THERE, LITTLE GIRL.
HOWDY, OFFICER! WHAT CAN I DO FOR YOU?
OH, NO! THEY'VE FOUND ME!
WANTED!
WANTED!
AND THAT LITTLE BRAT IS RATTING ME OUT!
FORTUNES
TOLD!

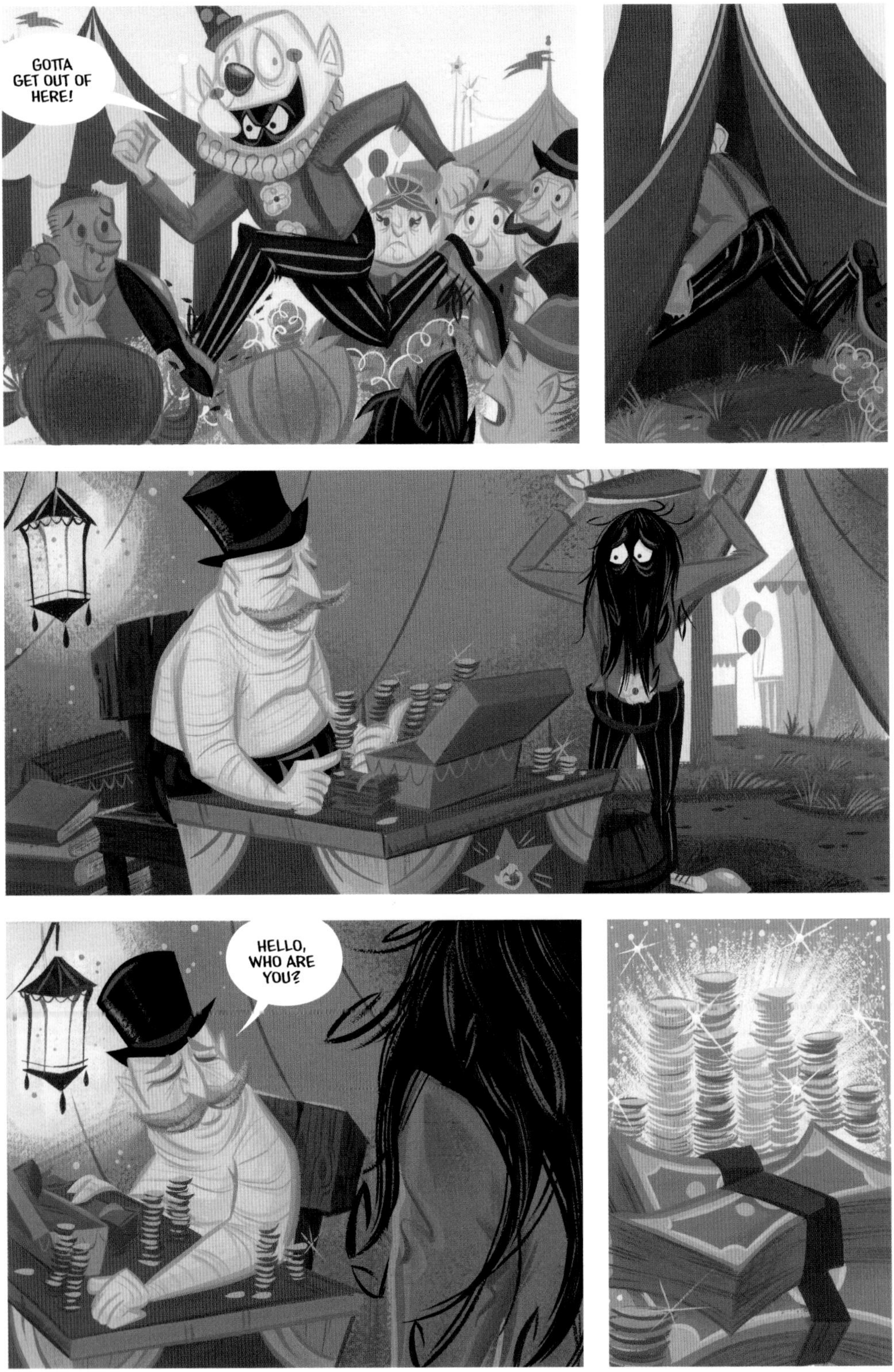
GOTTA GET OUT OF HERE!
HELLO, WHO ARE YOU?

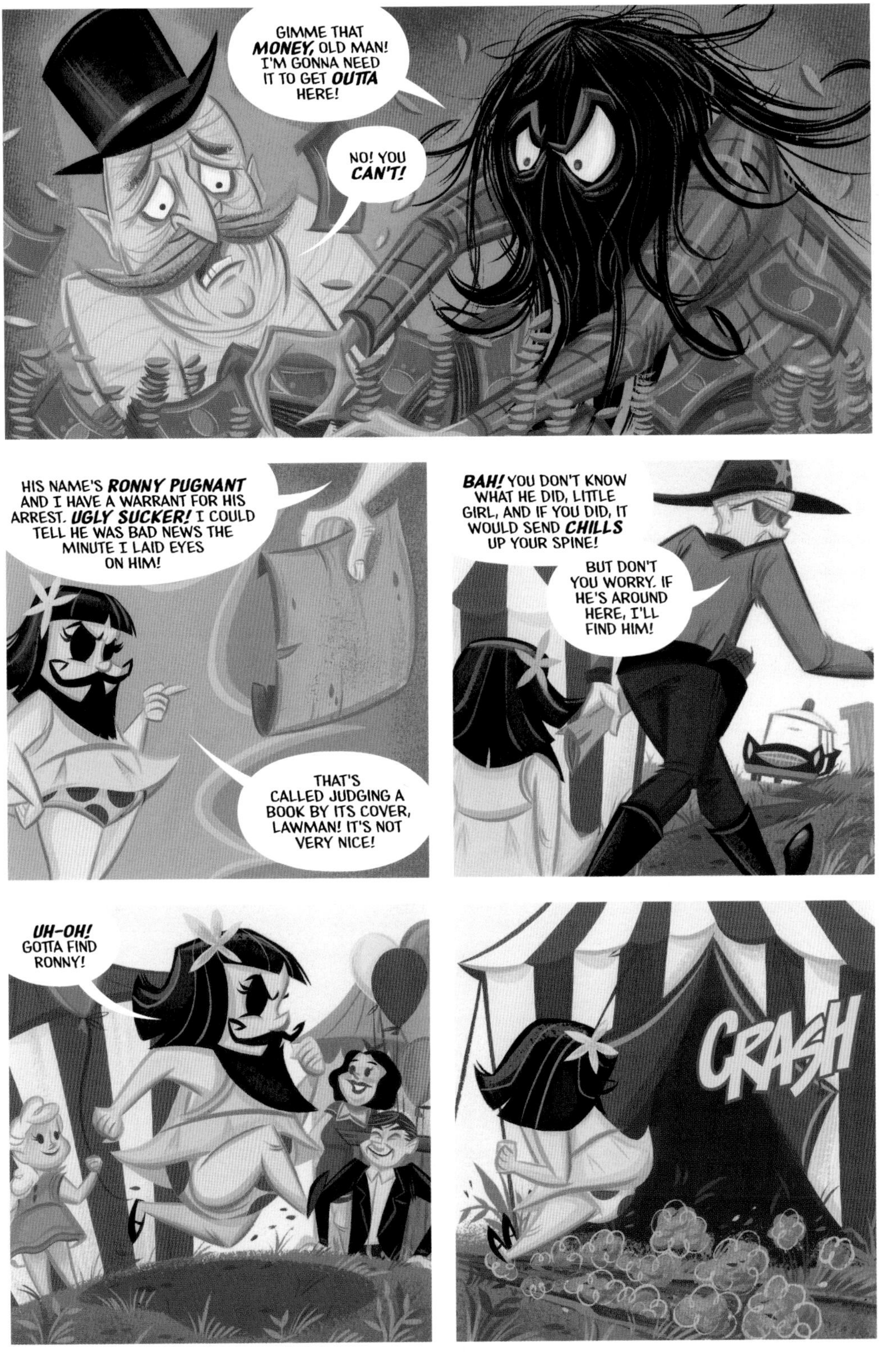
GIMME THAT MONEY, OLD MAN! I'M GONNA NEED IT TO GET OUTTA HERE!
NO! YOU CAN'T!
HIS NAME'S RONNY PUGNANT AND I HAVE A WARRANT FOR HIS ARREST. UGLY SUCKER! I COULD TELL HE WAS BAD NEWS THE MINUTE I LAID EYES ON HIM!
THAT'S CALLED JUDGING A BOOK BY ITS COVER, LAWMAN! IT'S NOT VERY NICE!
BAH! YOU DON'T KNOW WHAT HE DID, LITTLE GIRL, AND IF YOU DID, IT WOULD SEND CHILLS UP YOUR SPINE!
BUT DON'T YOU WORRY. IF HE'S AROUND HERE, I'LL FIND HIM!
UH-OH! GOTTA FIND RONNY!
CRASH

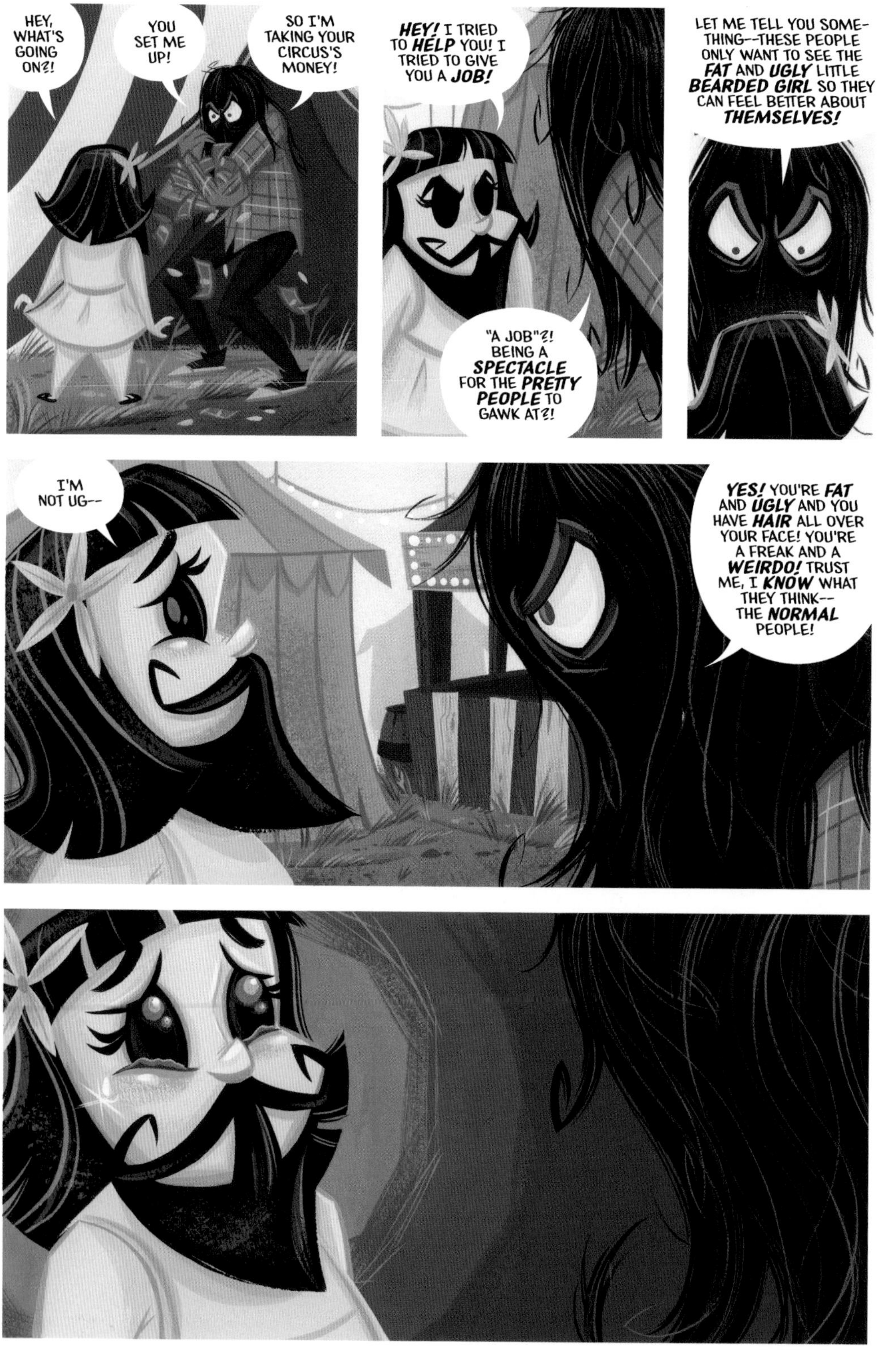
HEY, WHAT'S GOING ON?!
YOU SET ME UP!
SO I'M TAKING YOUR CIRCUS'S MONEY!
HEY! I TRIED TO HELP YOU! I TRIED TO GIVE YOU A JOB!
"A JOB"?! BEING A SPECTACLE FOR THE PRETTY PEOPLE TO GAWK AT?!
LET ME TELL YOU SOME-THING--THESE PEOPLE ONLY WANT TO SEE THE FAT AND UGLY LITTLE BEARDED GIRL SO THEY CAN FEEL BETTER ABOUT THEMSELVES!
I'M NOT UG--
YES! YOU'RE FAT AND UGLY AND YOU HAVE HAIR ALL OVER YOUR FACE! YOU'RE A FREAK AND A WEIRDO! TRUST ME, I KNOW WHAT THEY THINK-- THE NORMAL PEOPLE!

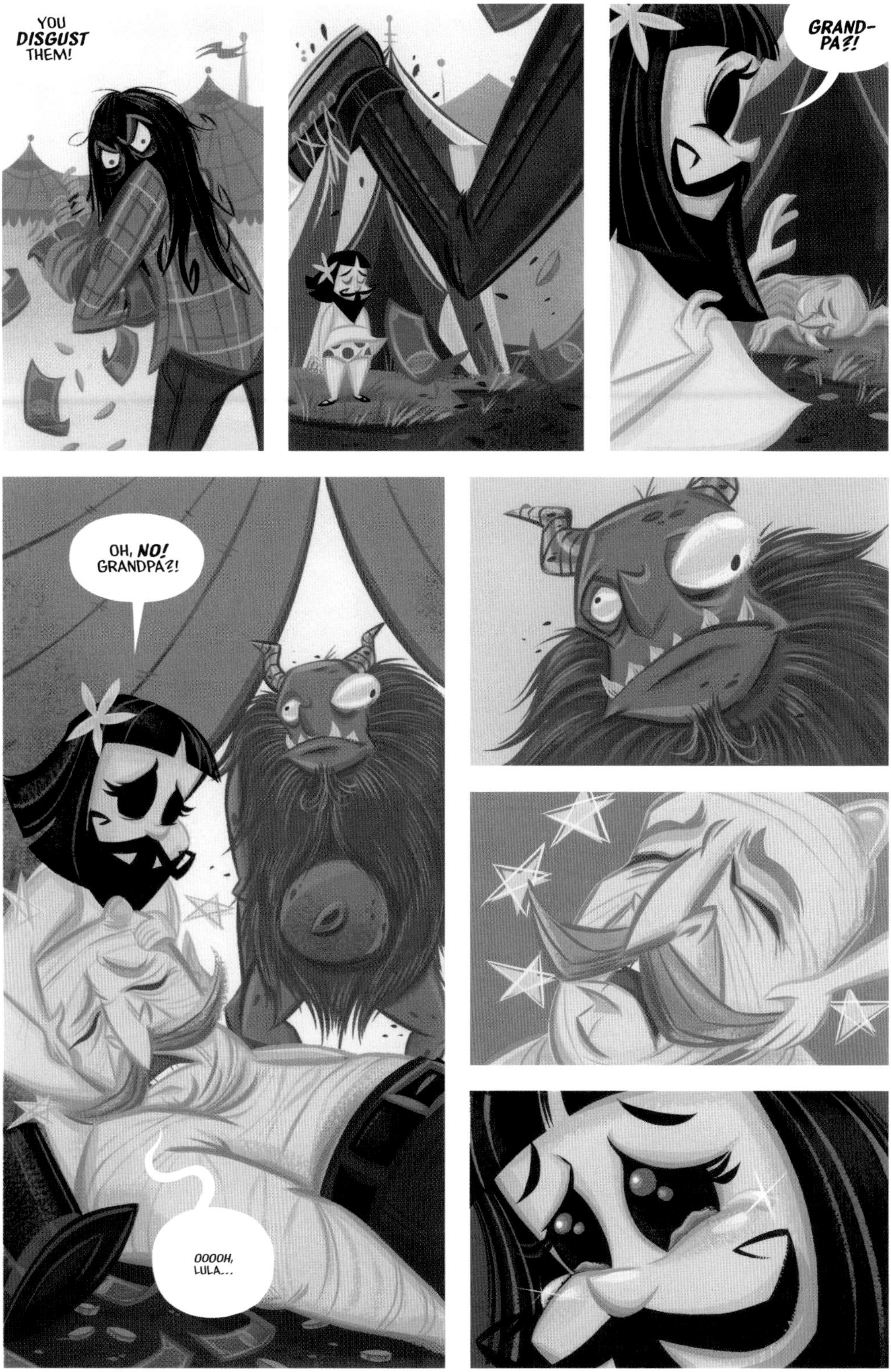

YOU *DISGUST* THEM!
GRAND-PA?!
OH, *NO!* GRANDPA?!
OOOOH, LULA...

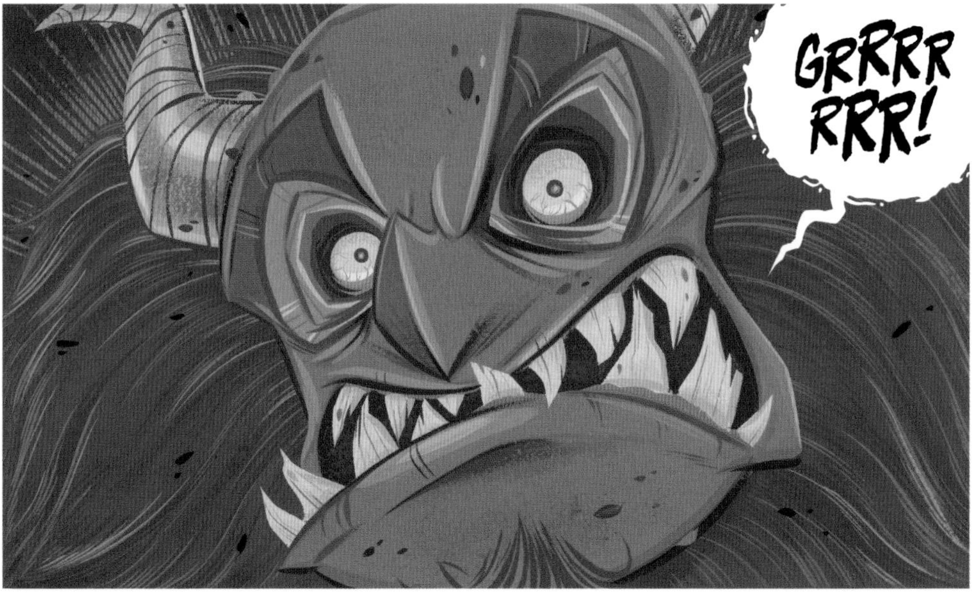
GRRRR RRR!

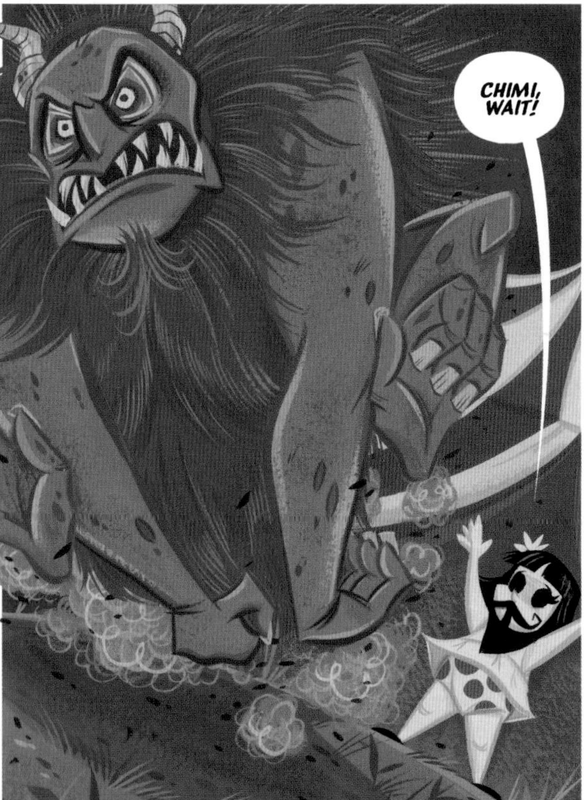
CHIMI, WAIT!

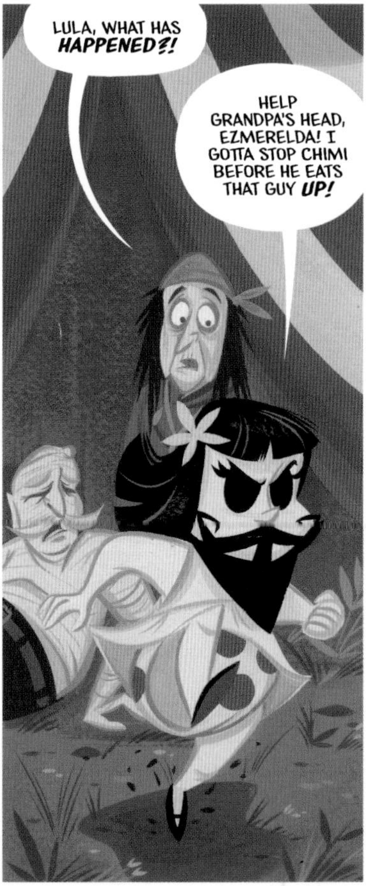
LULA, WHAT HAS HAPPENED?!
HELP GRANDPA'S HEAD, EZMERELDA! I GOTTA STOP CHIMI BEFORE HE EATS THAT GUY UP!

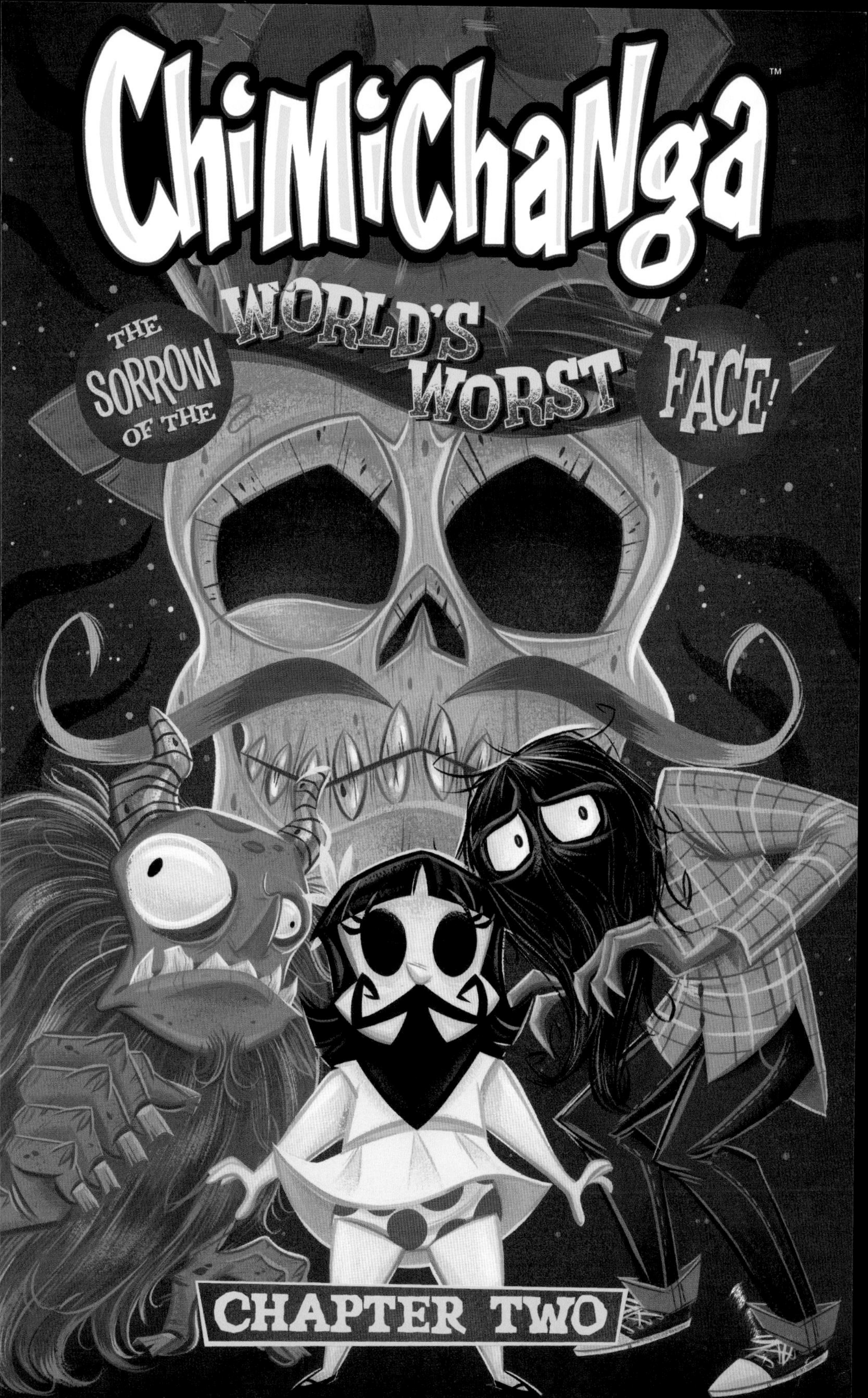

ChiMiChaNga™
THE SORROW OF THE WORLD'S WORST FACE!
CHAPTER TWO

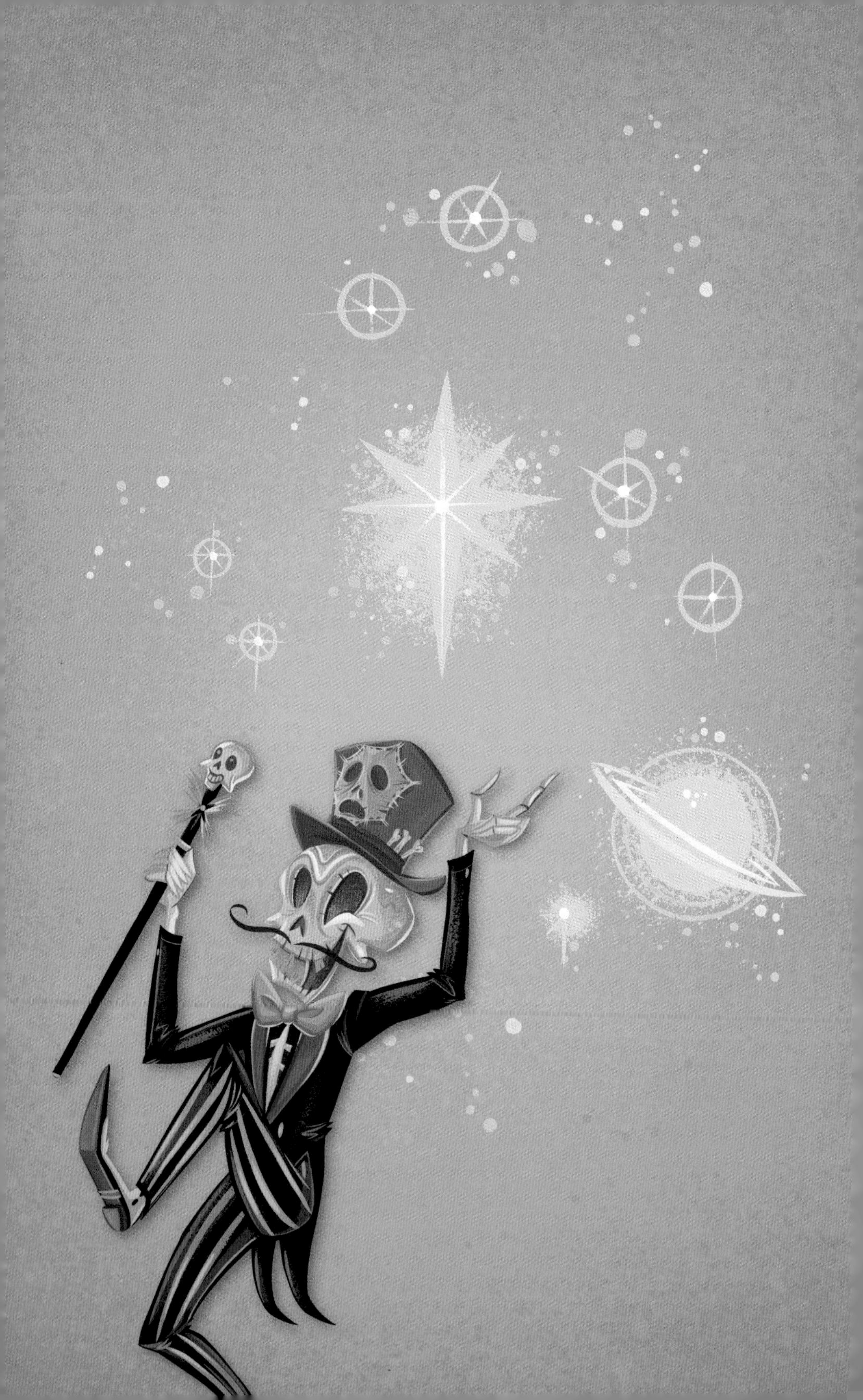

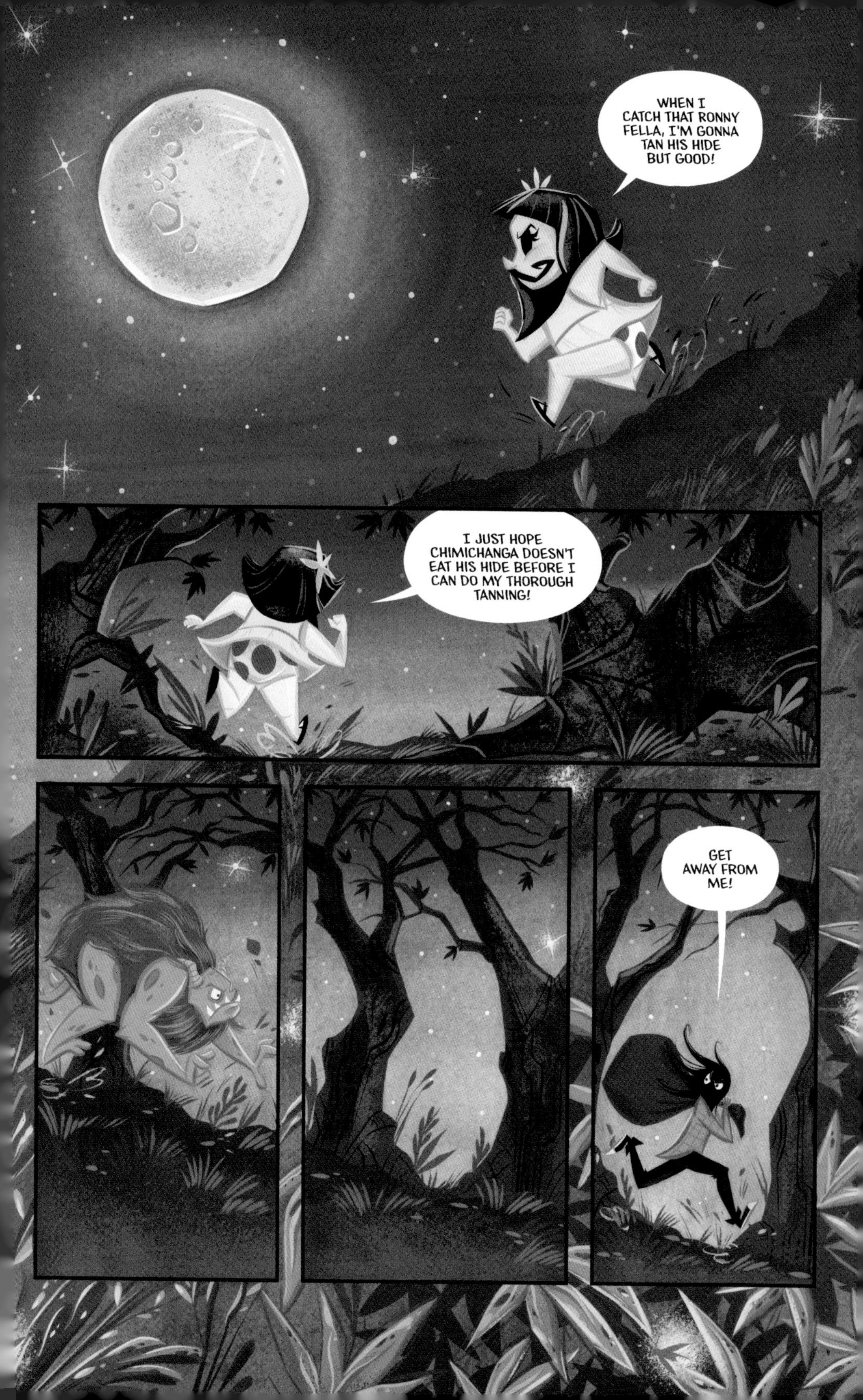
WHEN I CATCH THAT RONNY FELLA, I'M GONNA TAN HIS HIDE BUT GOOD!
I JUST HOPE CHIMICHANGA DOESN'T EAT HIS HIDE BEFORE I CAN DO MY THOROUGH TANNING!
GET AWAY FROM ME!

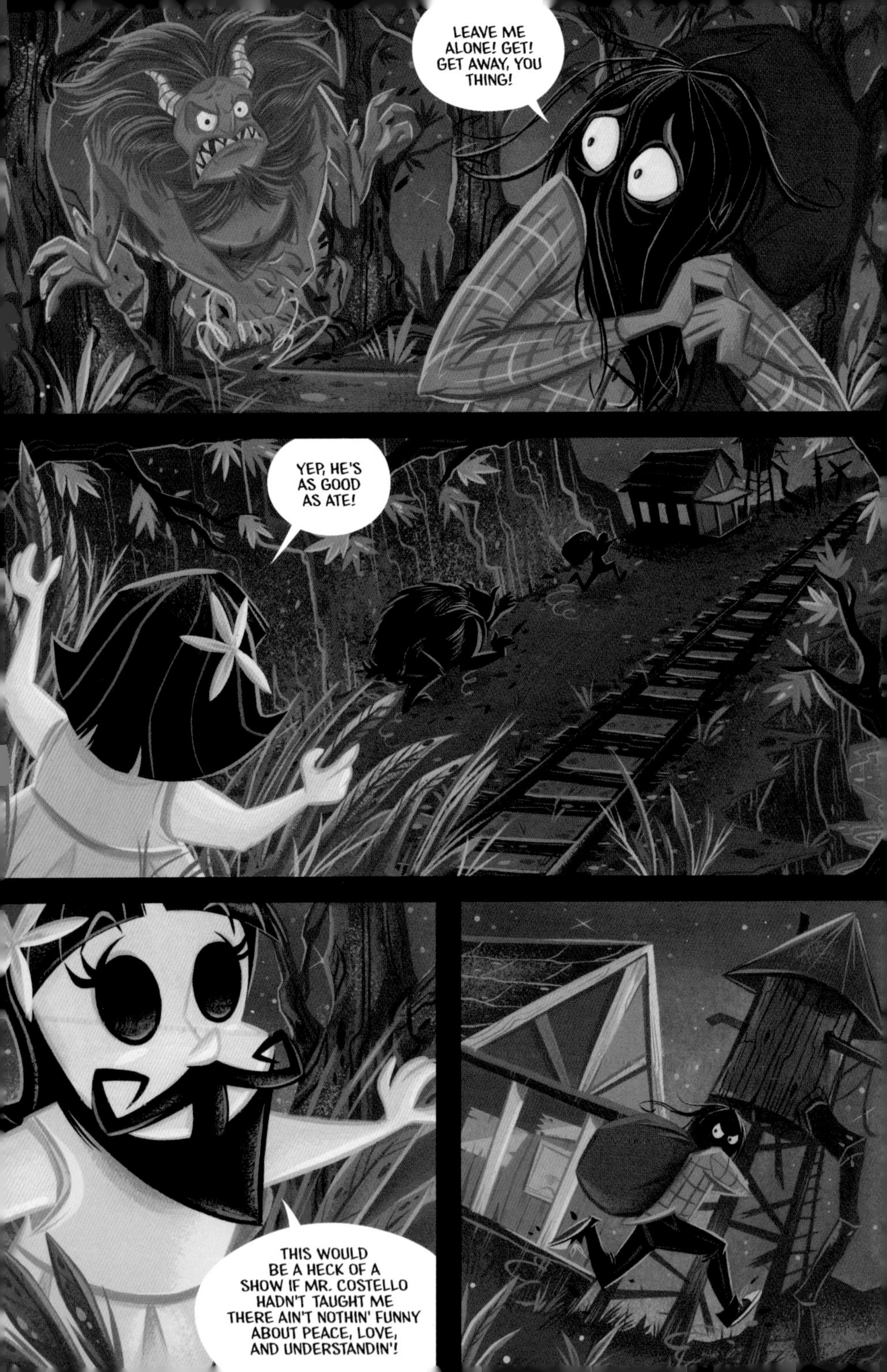
LEAVE ME ALONE! GET! GET AWAY, YOU THING!
YEP, HE'S AS GOOD AS ATE!
THIS WOULD BE A HECK OF A SHOW IF MR. COSTELLO HADN'T TAUGHT ME THERE AIN'T NOTHIN' FUNNY ABOUT PEACE, LOVE, AND UNDERSTANDIN'!

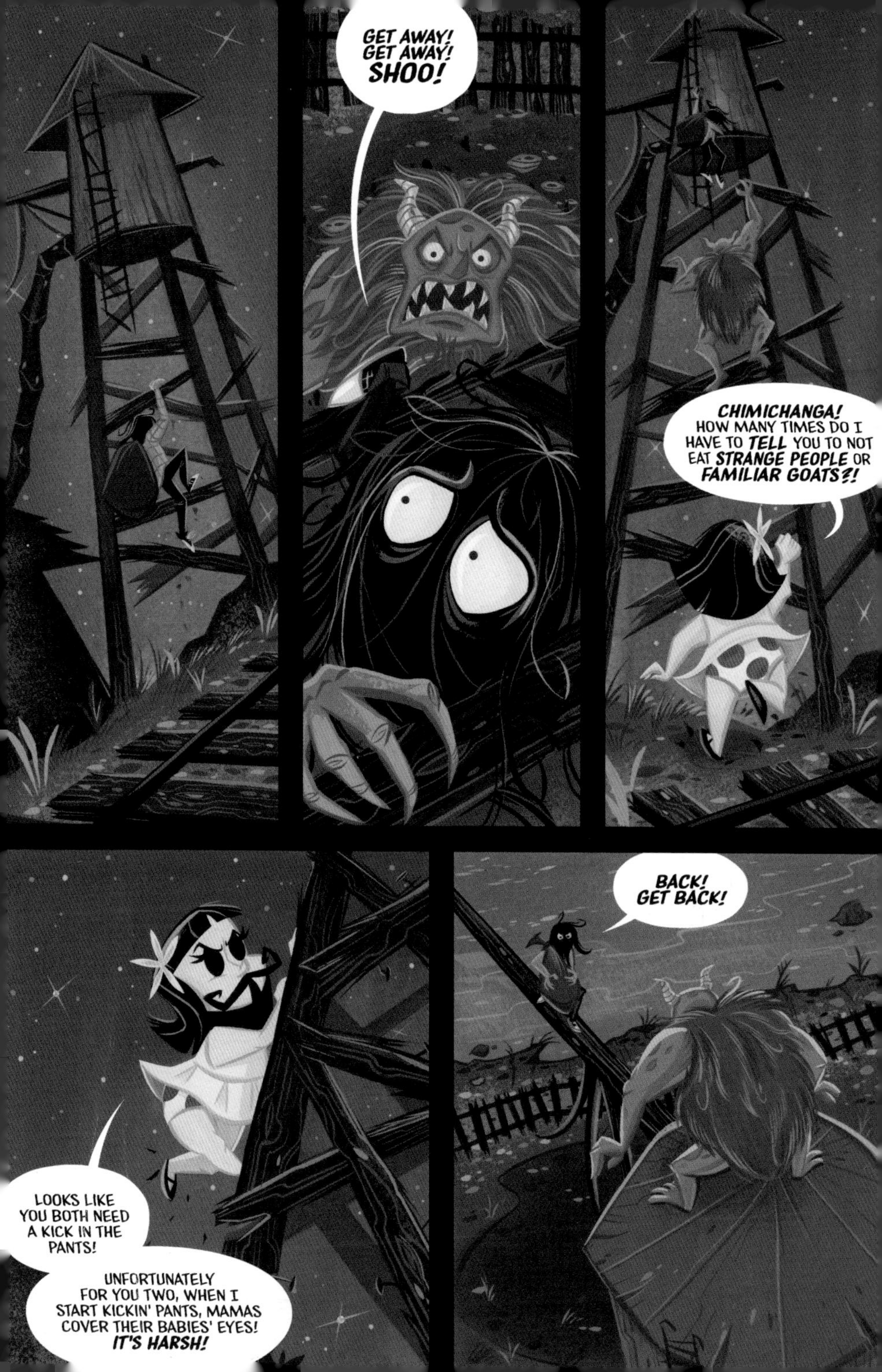
GET AWAY! GET AWAY! SHOO!
CHIMICHANGA! HOW MANY TIMES DO I HAVE TO TELL YOU TO NOT EAT STRANGE PEOPLE OR FAMILIAR GOATS?!
LOOKS LIKE YOU BOTH NEED A KICK IN THE PANTS!
UNFORTUNATELY FOR YOU TWO, WHEN I START KICKIN' PANTS, MAMAS COVER THEIR BABIES' EYES! IT'S HARSH!
BACK! GET BACK!

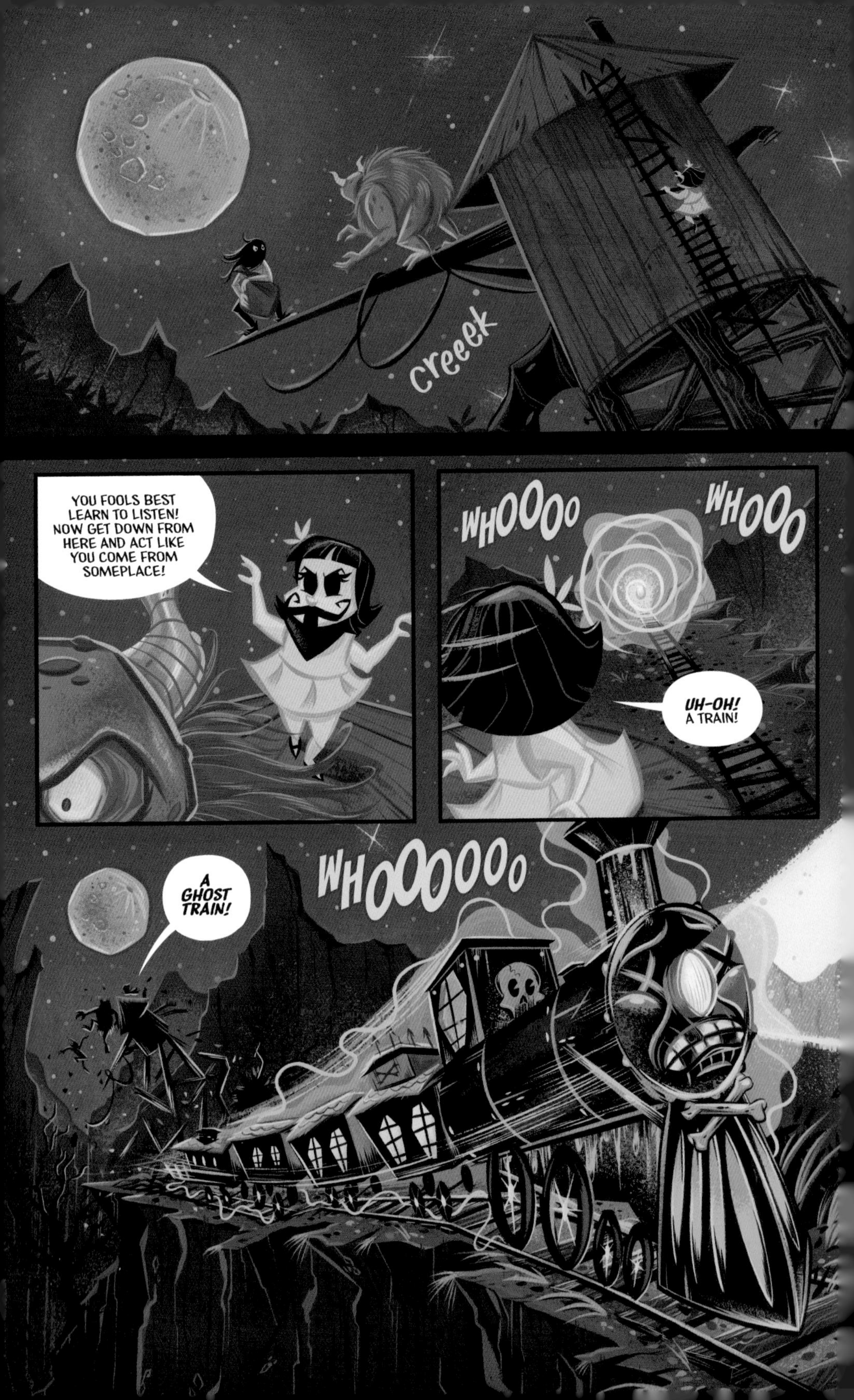
creeek
YOU FOOLS BEST LEARN TO LISTEN! NOW GET DOWN FROM HERE AND ACT LIKE YOU COME FROM SOMEPLACE!
WHOOOO
WHOOO
UH-OH! A TRAIN!
WHOOOOOO
A GHOST TRAIN!

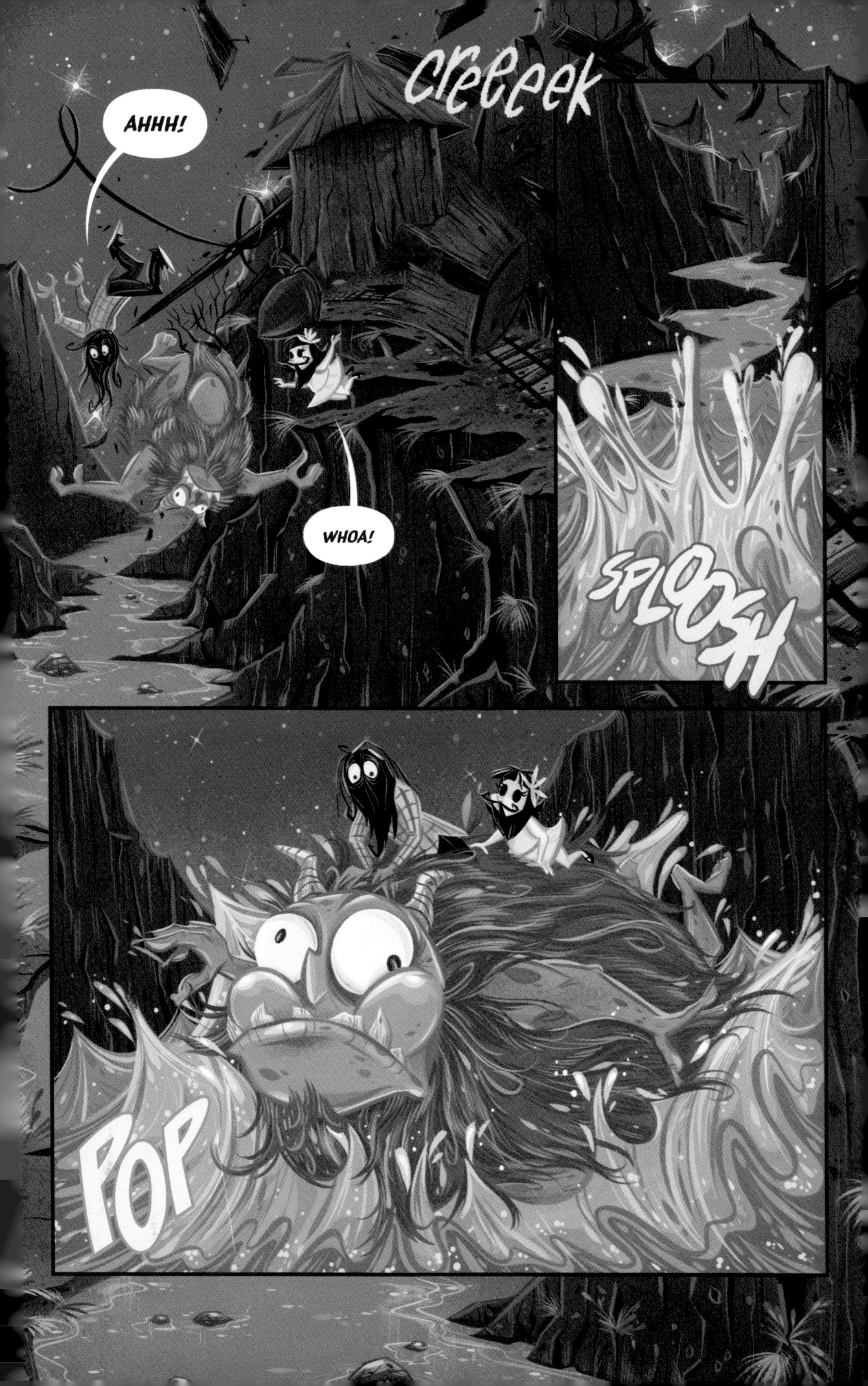
CREEEEK
AHHH!
WHOA!
SPLOOSH
POP

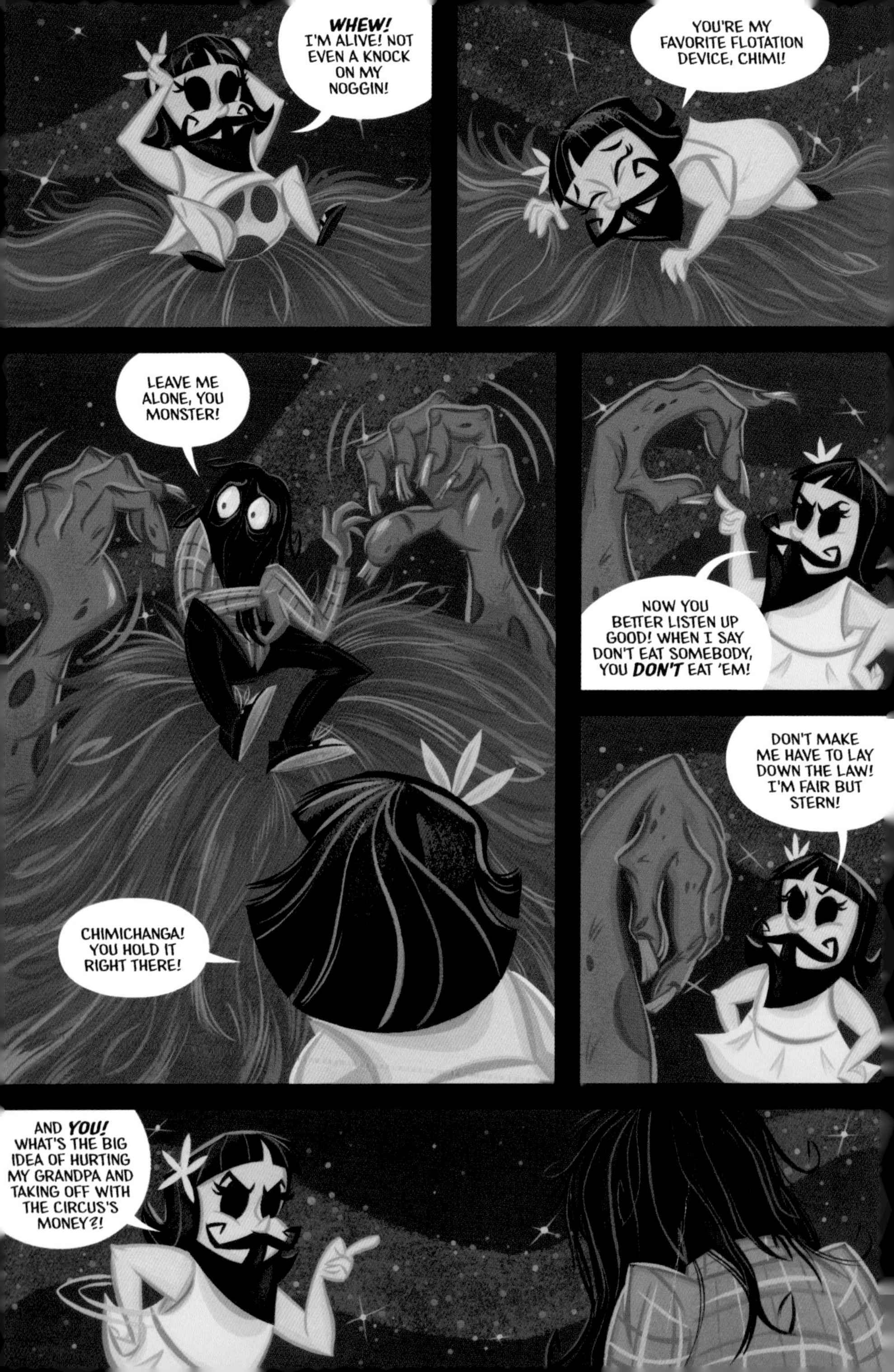

WHEW! I'M ALIVE! NOT EVEN A KNOCK ON MY NOGGIN!
YOU'RE MY FAVORITE FLOTATION DEVICE, CHIMI!
LEAVE ME ALONE, YOU MONSTER!
CHIMICHANGA! YOU HOLD IT RIGHT THERE!
NOW YOU BETTER LISTEN UP GOOD! WHEN I SAY DON'T EAT SOMEBODY, YOU DON'T EAT 'EM!
DON'T MAKE ME HAVE TO LAY DOWN THE LAW! I'M FAIR BUT STERN!
AND YOU! WHAT'S THE BIG IDEA OF HURTING MY GRANDPA AND TAKING OFF WITH THE CIRCUS'S MONEY?!

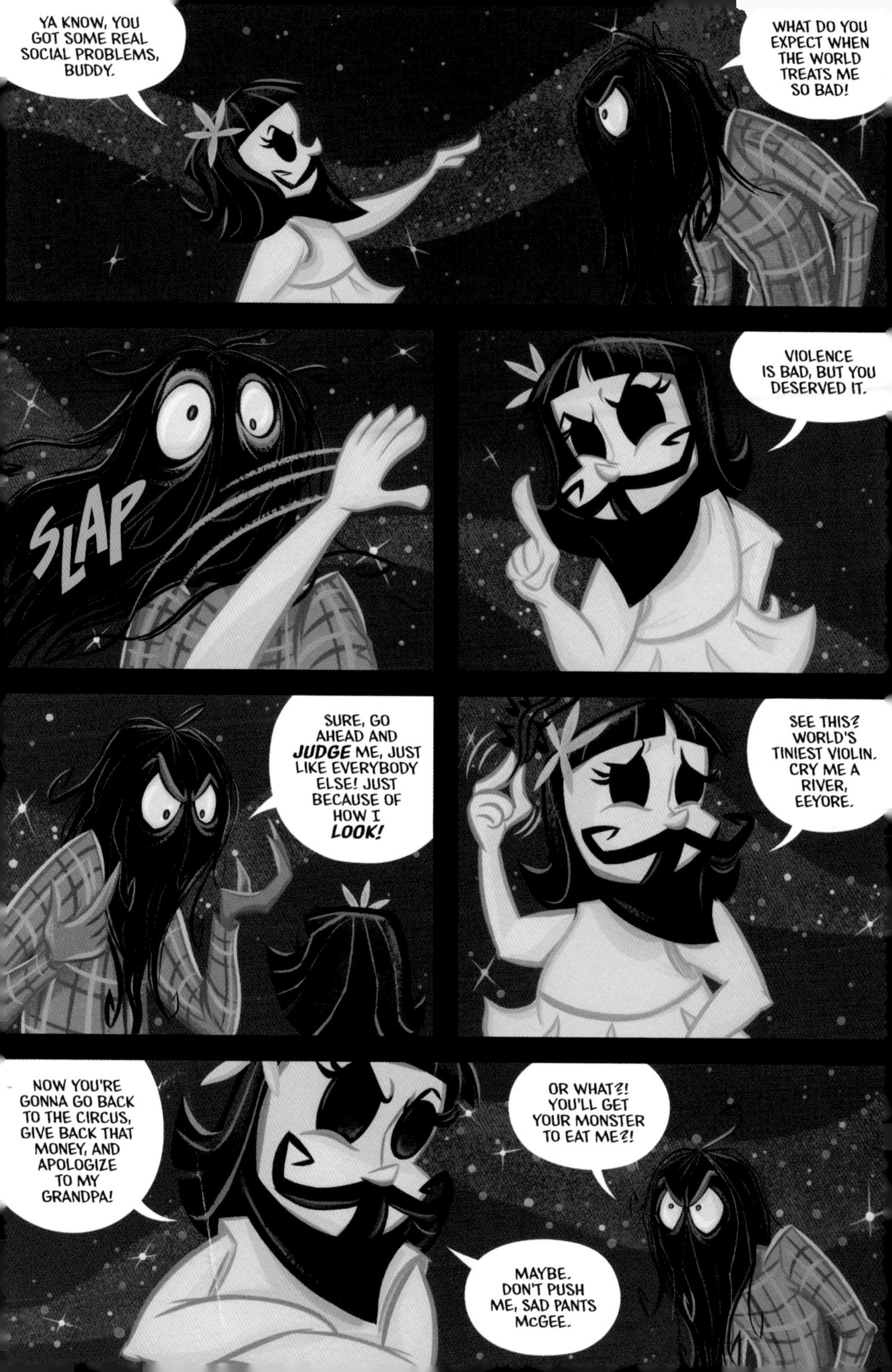
YA KNOW, YOU GOT SOME REAL SOCIAL PROBLEMS, BUDDY.
WHAT DO YOU EXPECT WHEN THE WORLD TREATS ME SO BAD!
SLAP
VIOLENCE IS BAD, BUT YOU DESERVED IT.
SURE, GO AHEAD AND **JUDGE** ME, JUST LIKE EVERYBODY ELSE! JUST BECAUSE OF HOW I **LOOK!**
SEE THIS? WORLD'S TINIEST VIOLIN. CRY ME A RIVER, EEYORE.
NOW YOU'RE GONNA GO BACK TO THE CIRCUS, GIVE BACK THAT MONEY, AND APOLOGIZE TO MY GRANDPA!
OR WHAT?! YOU'LL GET YOUR MONSTER TO EAT ME?!
MAYBE. DON'T PUSH ME, SAD PANTS McGEE.

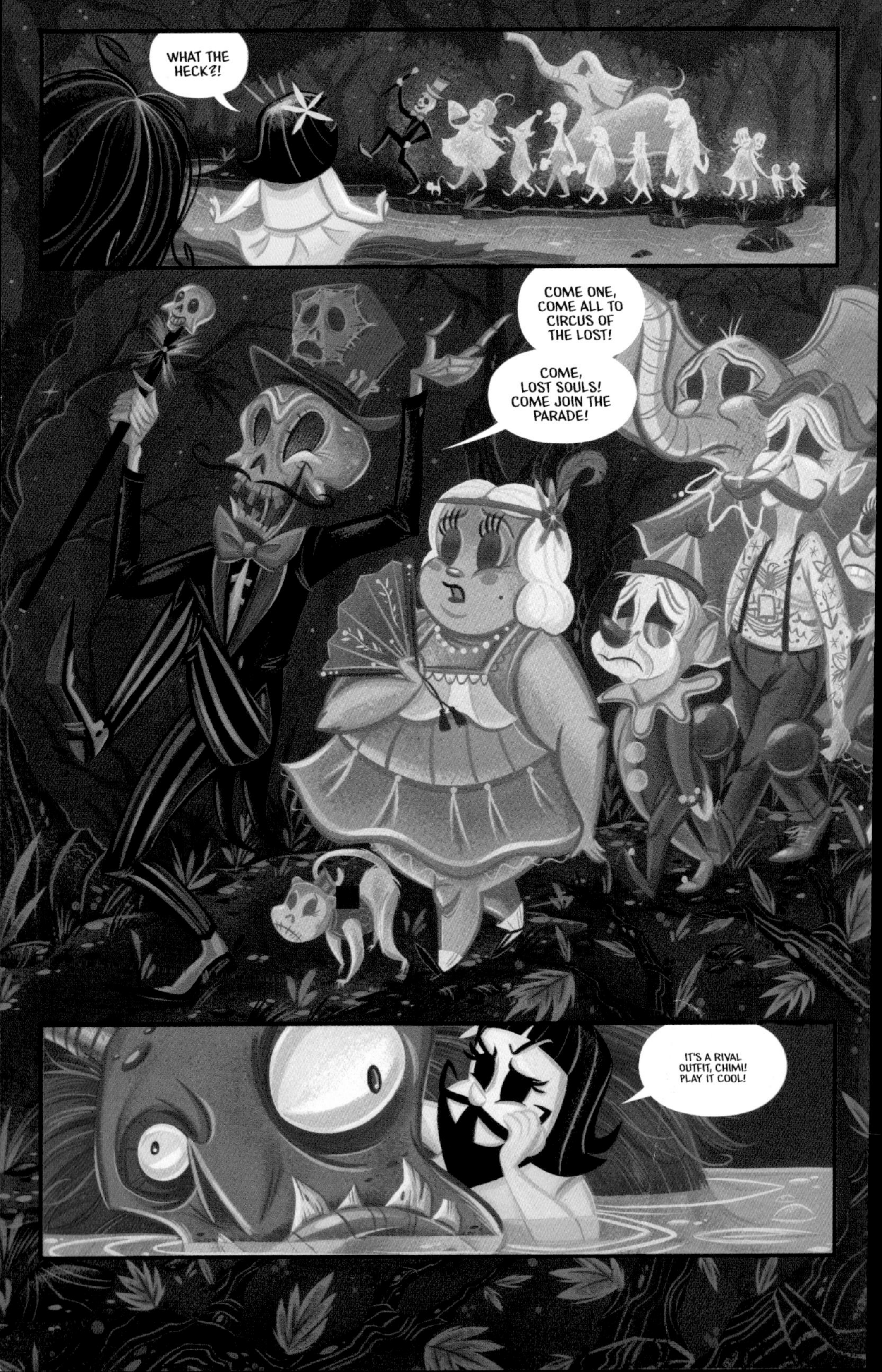
WHAT THE HECK?!
COME ONE, COME ALL TO CIRCUS OF THE LOST!
COME, LOST SOULS! COME JOIN THE PARADE!
IT'S A RIVAL OUTFIT, CHIMI! PLAY IT COOL!

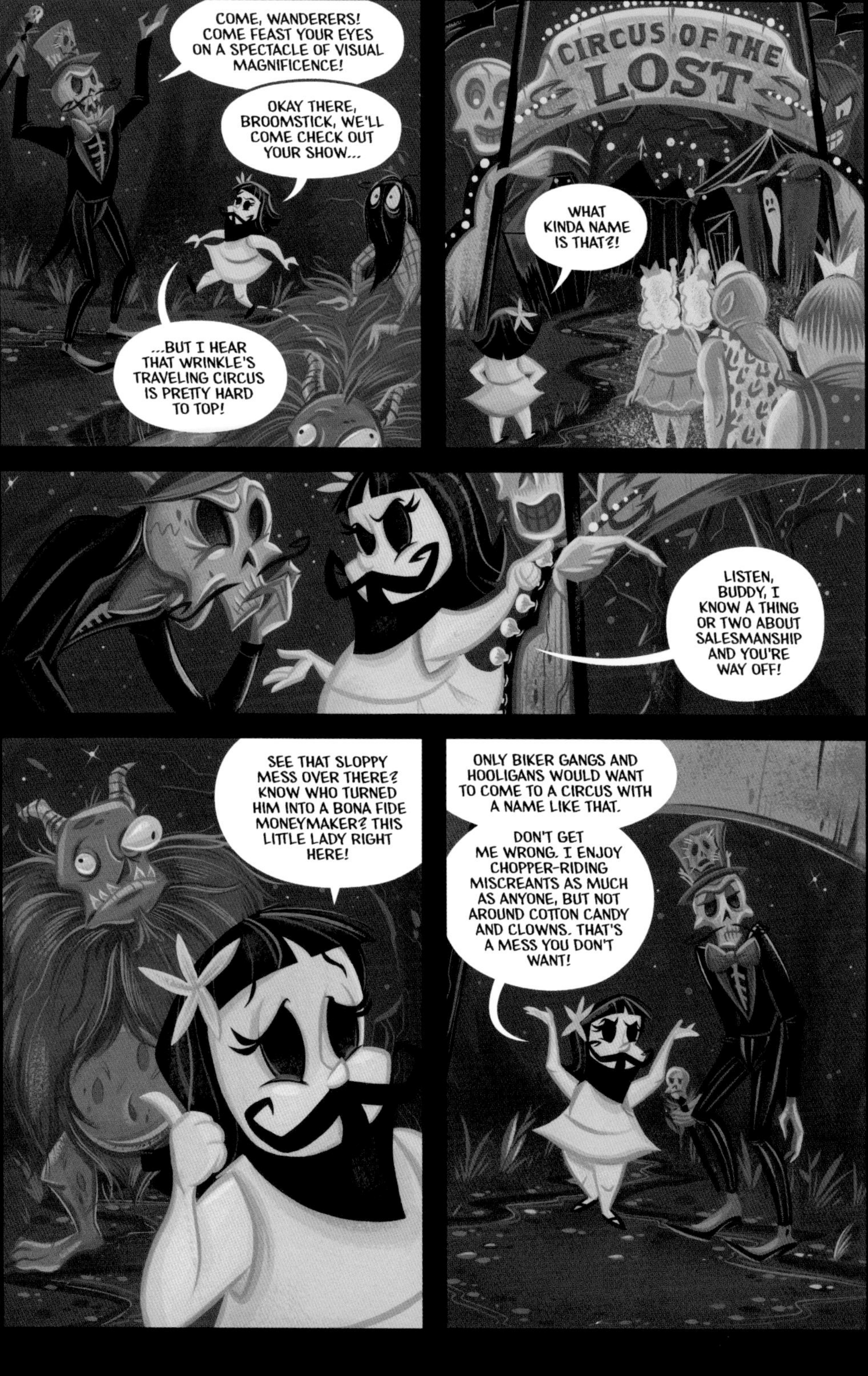
COME, WANDERERS! COME FEAST YOUR EYES ON A SPECTACLE OF VISUAL MAGNIFICENCE!
OKAY THERE, BROOMSTICK, WE'LL COME CHECK OUT YOUR SHOW...
...BUT I HEAR THAT WRINKLE'S TRAVELING CIRCUS IS PRETTY HARD TO TOP!
CIRCUS OF THE LOST
WHAT KINDA NAME IS THAT?!
LISTEN, BUDDY, I KNOW A THING OR TWO ABOUT SALESMANSHIP AND YOU'RE WAY OFF!
SEE THAT SLOPPY MESS OVER THERE? KNOW WHO TURNED HIM INTO A BONA FIDE MONEYMAKER? THIS LITTLE LADY RIGHT HERE!
ONLY BIKER GANGS AND HOOLIGANS WOULD WANT TO COME TO A CIRCUS WITH A NAME LIKE THAT.
DON'T GET ME WRONG. I ENJOY CHOPPER-RIDING MISCREANTS AS MUCH AS ANYONE, BUT NOT AROUND COTTON CANDY AND CLOWNS. THAT'S A MESS YOU DON'T WANT!

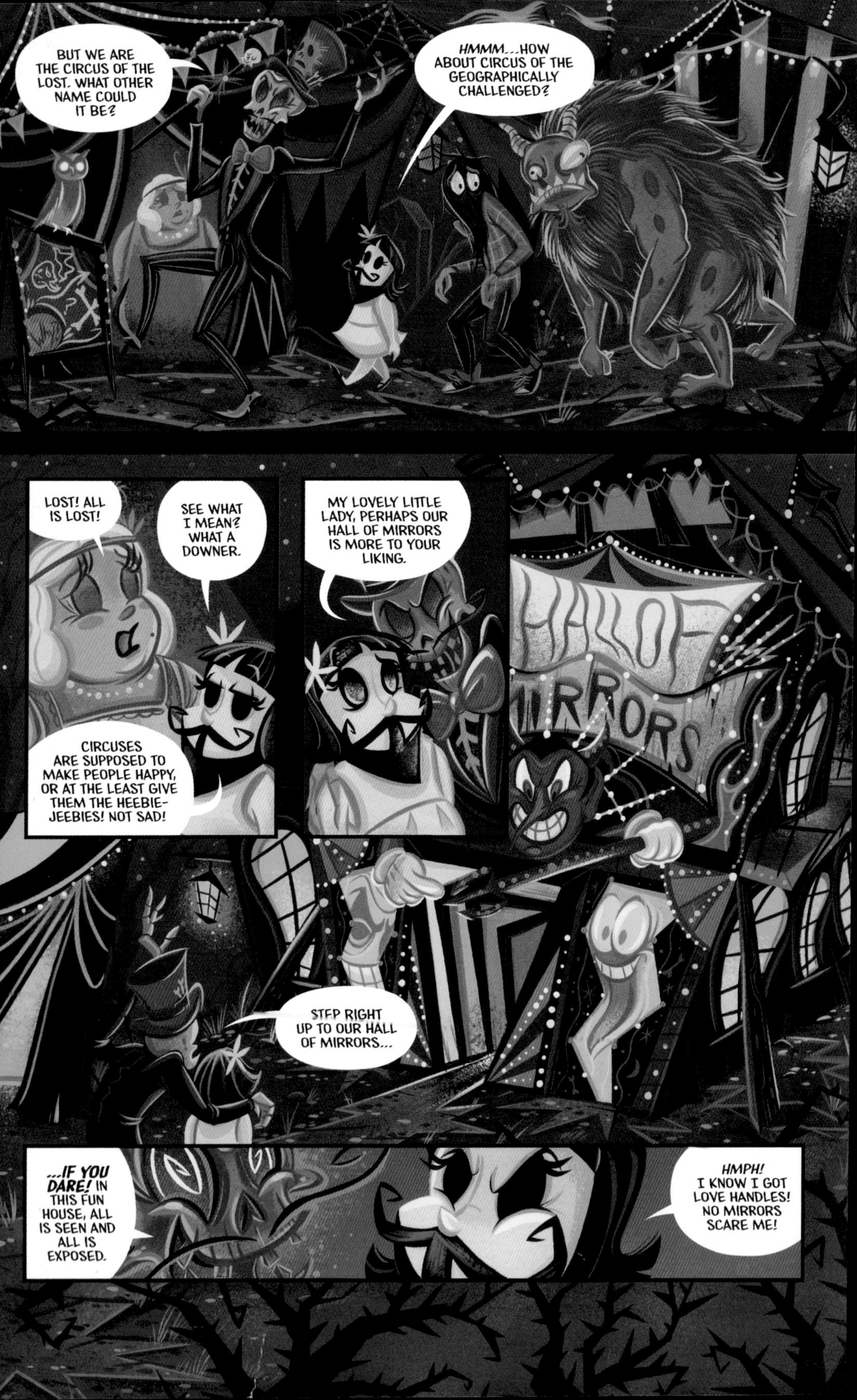
BUT WE ARE THE CIRCUS OF THE LOST. WHAT OTHER NAME COULD IT BE?
HMMM...HOW ABOUT CIRCUS OF THE GEOGRAPHICALLY CHALLENGED?
LOST! ALL IS LOST!
SEE WHAT I MEAN? WHAT A DOWNER.
CIRCUSES ARE SUPPOSED TO MAKE PEOPLE HAPPY, OR AT THE LEAST GIVE THEM THE HEEBIE-JEEBIES! NOT SAD!
MY LOVELY LITTLE LADY, PERHAPS OUR HALL OF MIRRORS IS MORE TO YOUR LIKING.
HALL OF MIRRORS
STEP RIGHT UP TO OUR HALL OF MIRRORS...
...IF YOU DARE! IN THIS FUN HOUSE, ALL IS SEEN AND ALL IS EXPOSED.
HMPH! I KNOW I GOT LOVE HANDLES! NO MIRRORS SCARE ME!

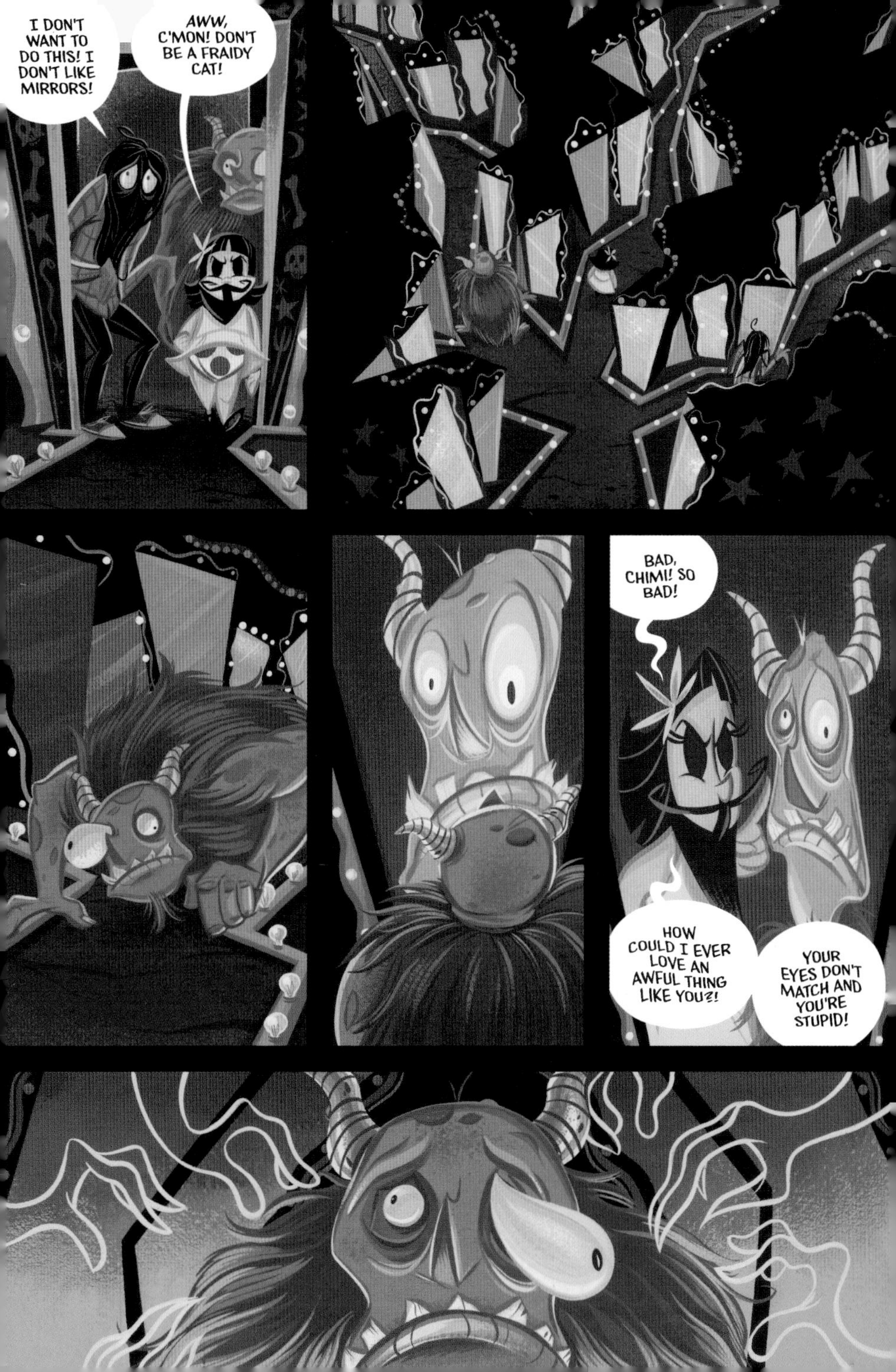
I DON'T WANT TO DO THIS! I DON'T LIKE MIRRORS!
AWW, C'MON! DON'T BE A FRAIDY CAT!
BAD, CHIMI! SO BAD!
HOW COULD I EVER LOVE AN AWFUL THING LIKE YOU?!
YOUR EYES DON'T MATCH AND YOU'RE STUPID!

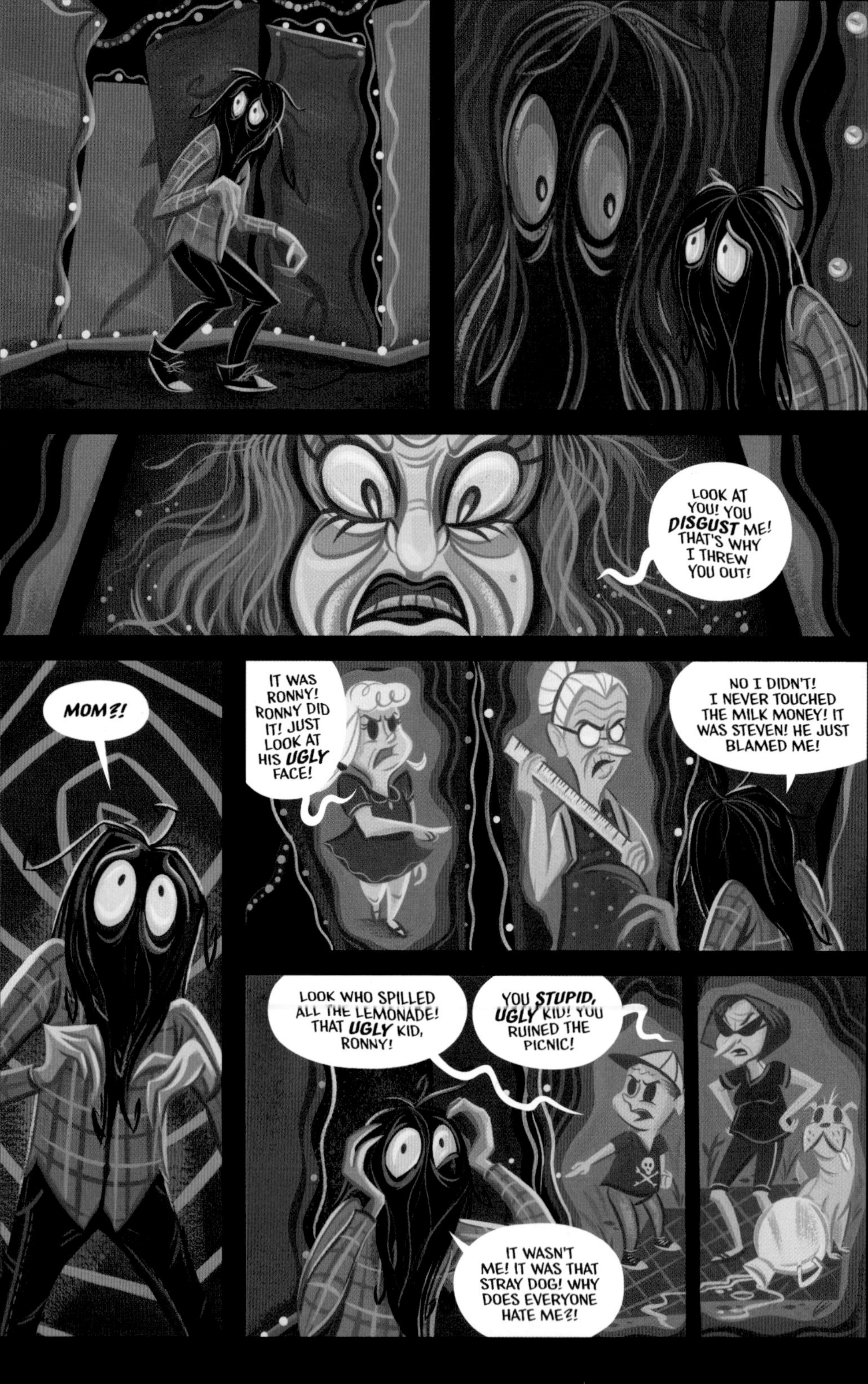
LOOK AT YOU! YOU DISGUST ME! THAT'S WHY I THREW YOU OUT!
MOM?!
IT WAS RONNY! RONNY DID IT! JUST LOOK AT HIS UGLY FACE!
NO I DIDN'T! I NEVER TOUCHED THE MILK MONEY! IT WAS STEVEN! HE JUST BLAMED ME!
LOOK WHO SPILLED ALL THE LEMONADE! THAT UGLY KID, RONNY!
YOU STUPID, UGLY KID! YOU RUINED THE PICNIC!
IT WASN'T ME! IT WAS THAT STRAY DOG! WHY DOES EVERYONE HATE ME?!

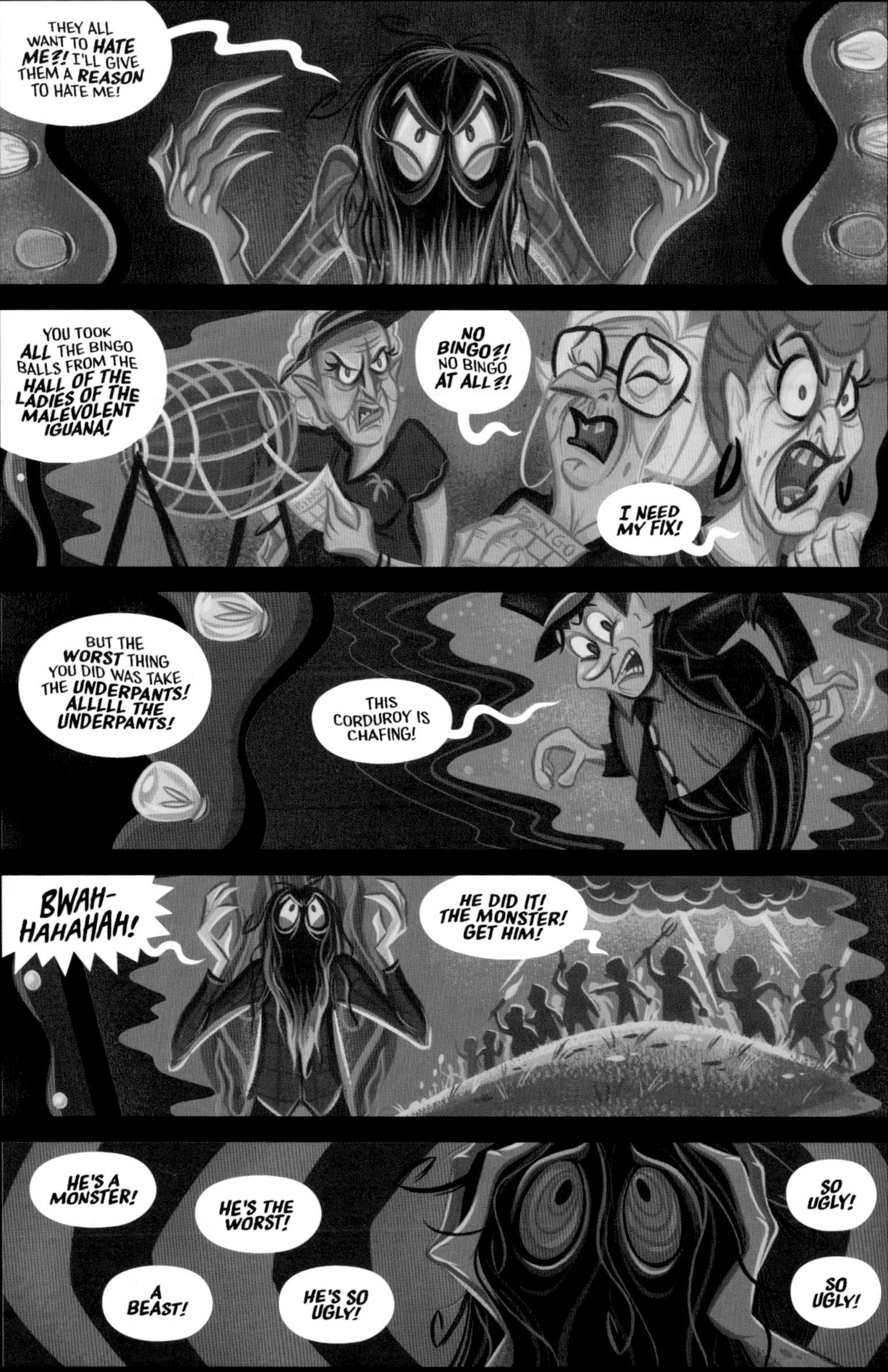
THEY ALL WANT TO HATE ME?! I'LL GIVE THEM A REASON TO HATE ME!
YOU TOOK ALL THE BINGO BALLS FROM THE HALL OF THE LADIES OF THE MALEVOLENT IGUANA!
NO BINGO?! NO BINGO AT ALL?!
I NEED MY FIX!
BUT THE WORST THING YOU DID WAS TAKE THE UNDERPANTS! ALLLLL THE UNDERPANTS!
THIS CORDUROY IS CHAFING!
BWAH-HAHAHAH!
HE DID IT! THE MONSTER! GET HIM!
HE'S A MONSTER!
HE'S THE WORST!
SO UGLY!
A BEAST!
HE'S SO UGLY!
SO UGLY!

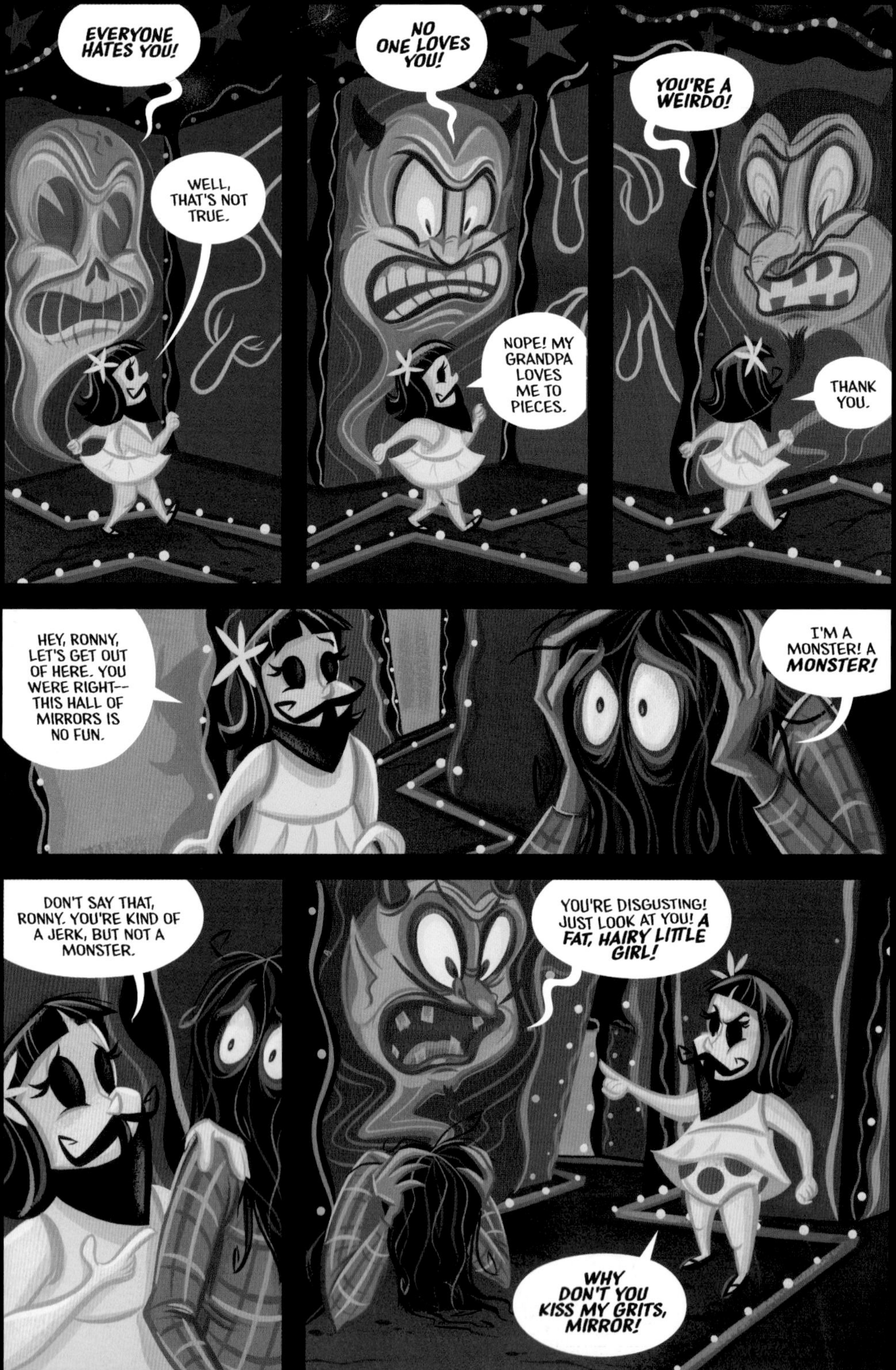
EVERYONE HATES YOU!
WELL, THAT'S NOT TRUE.
NO ONE LOVES YOU!
NOPE! MY GRANDPA LOVES ME TO PIECES.
YOU'RE A WEIRDO!
THANK YOU.
HEY, RONNY, LET'S GET OUT OF HERE. YOU WERE RIGHT-- THIS HALL OF MIRRORS IS NO FUN.
I'M A MONSTER! A MONSTER!
DON'T SAY THAT, RONNY. YOU'RE KIND OF A JERK, BUT NOT A MONSTER.
YOU'RE DISGUSTING! JUST LOOK AT YOU! A FAT, HAIRY LITTLE GIRL!
WHY DON'T YOU KISS MY GRITS, MIRROR!

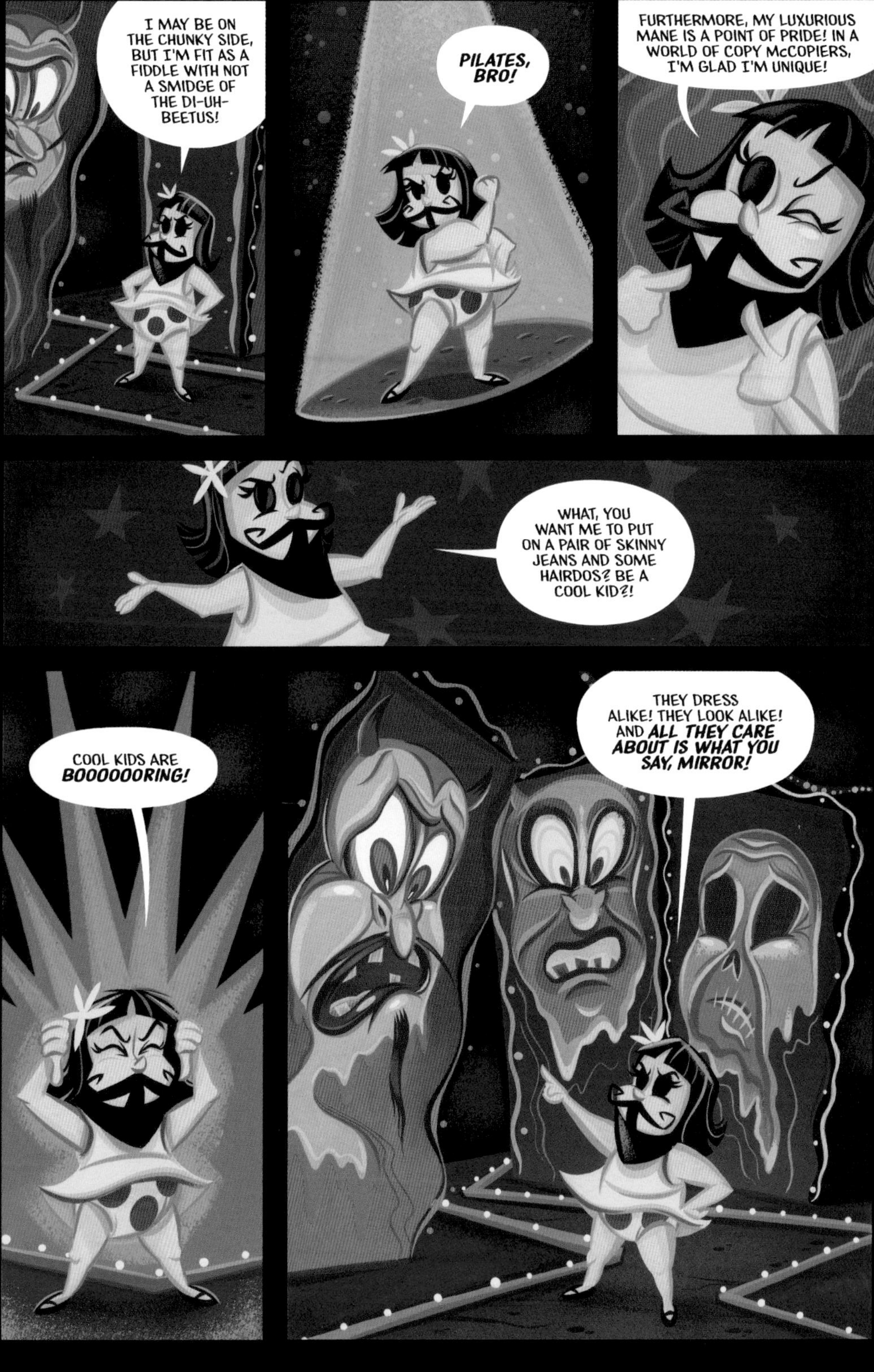
I MAY BE ON THE CHUNKY SIDE, BUT I'M FIT AS A FIDDLE WITH NOT A SMIDGE OF THE DI-UH-BEETUS!
PILATES, BRO!
FURTHERMORE, MY LUXURIOUS MANE IS A POINT OF PRIDE! IN A WORLD OF COPY McCOPIERS, I'M GLAD I'M UNIQUE!
WHAT, YOU WANT ME TO PUT ON A PAIR OF SKINNY JEANS AND SOME HAIRDOS? BE A COOL KID?!
COOL KIDS ARE BOOOOOORING!
THEY DRESS ALIKE! THEY LOOK ALIKE! AND ALL THEY CARE ABOUT IS WHAT YOU SAY, MIRROR!

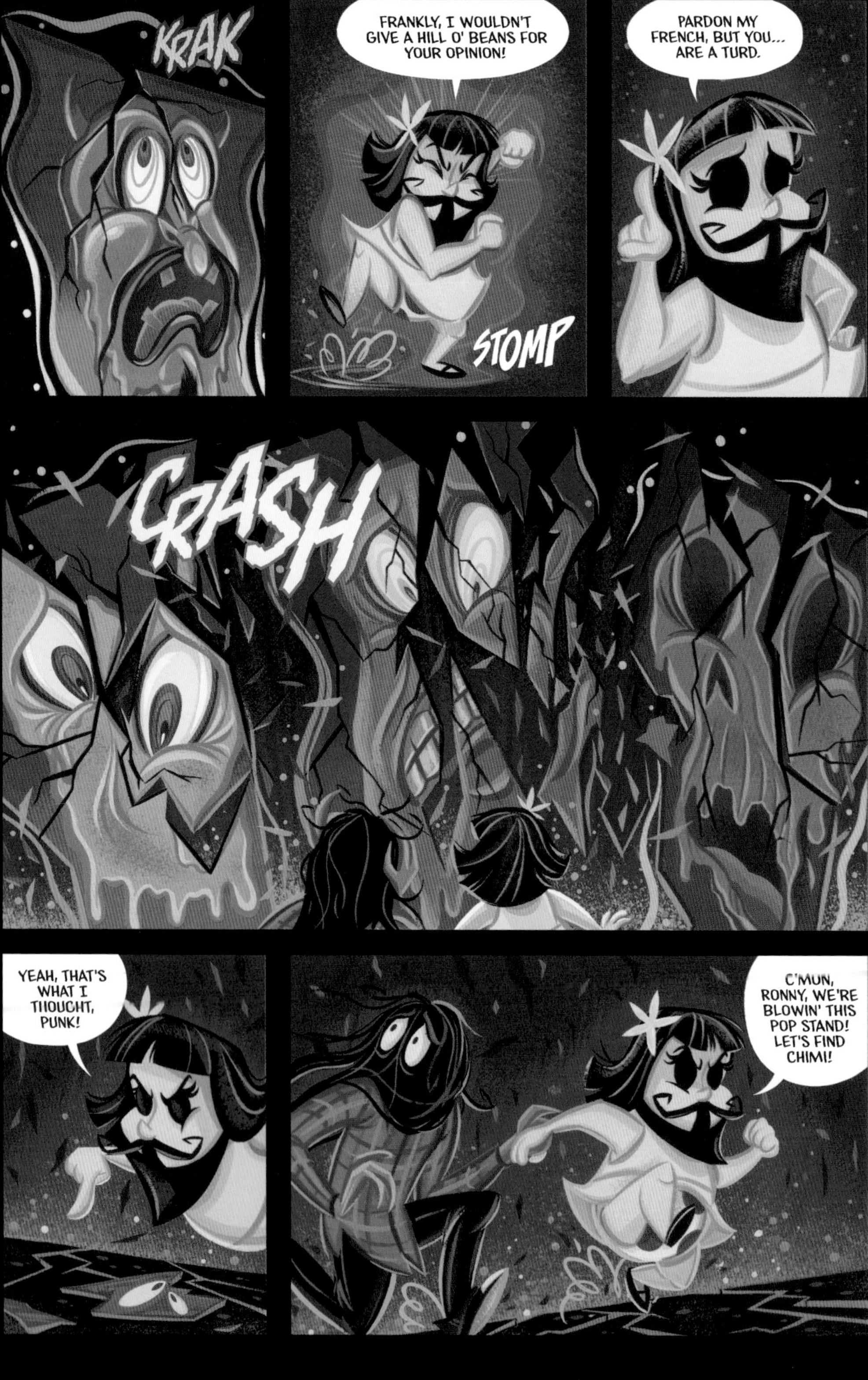
KRAK
FRANKLY, I WOULDN'T GIVE A HILL O' BEANS FOR YOUR OPINION!
STOMP
PARDON MY FRENCH, BUT YOU... ARE A TURD.
CRASH
YEAH, THAT'S WHAT I THOUGHT, PUNK!
C'MON, RONNY, WE'RE BLOWIN' THIS POP STAND! LET'S FIND CHIMI!

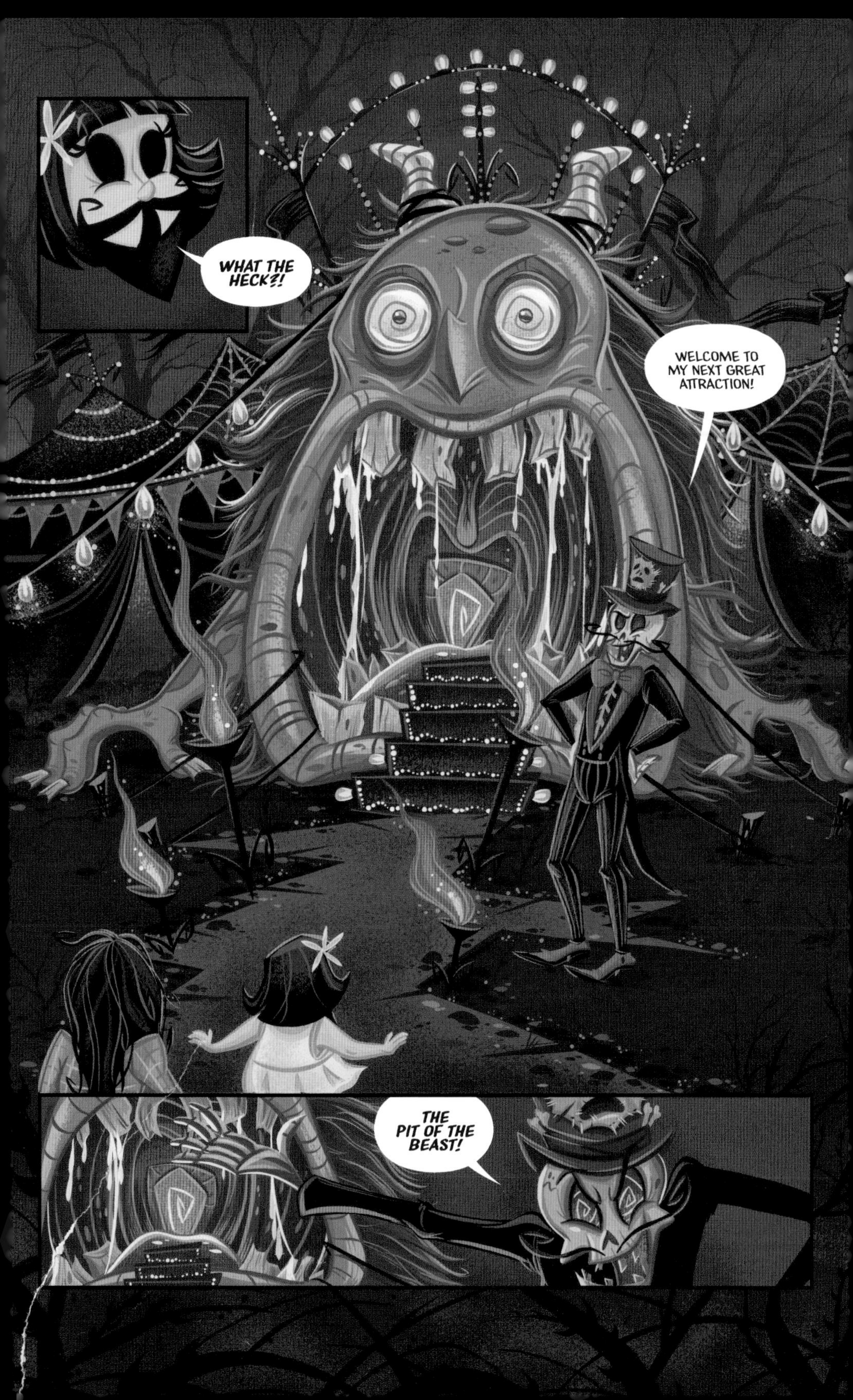
WHAT THE HECK?!
WELCOME TO MY NEXT GREAT ATTRACTION!
THE PIT OF THE BEAST!

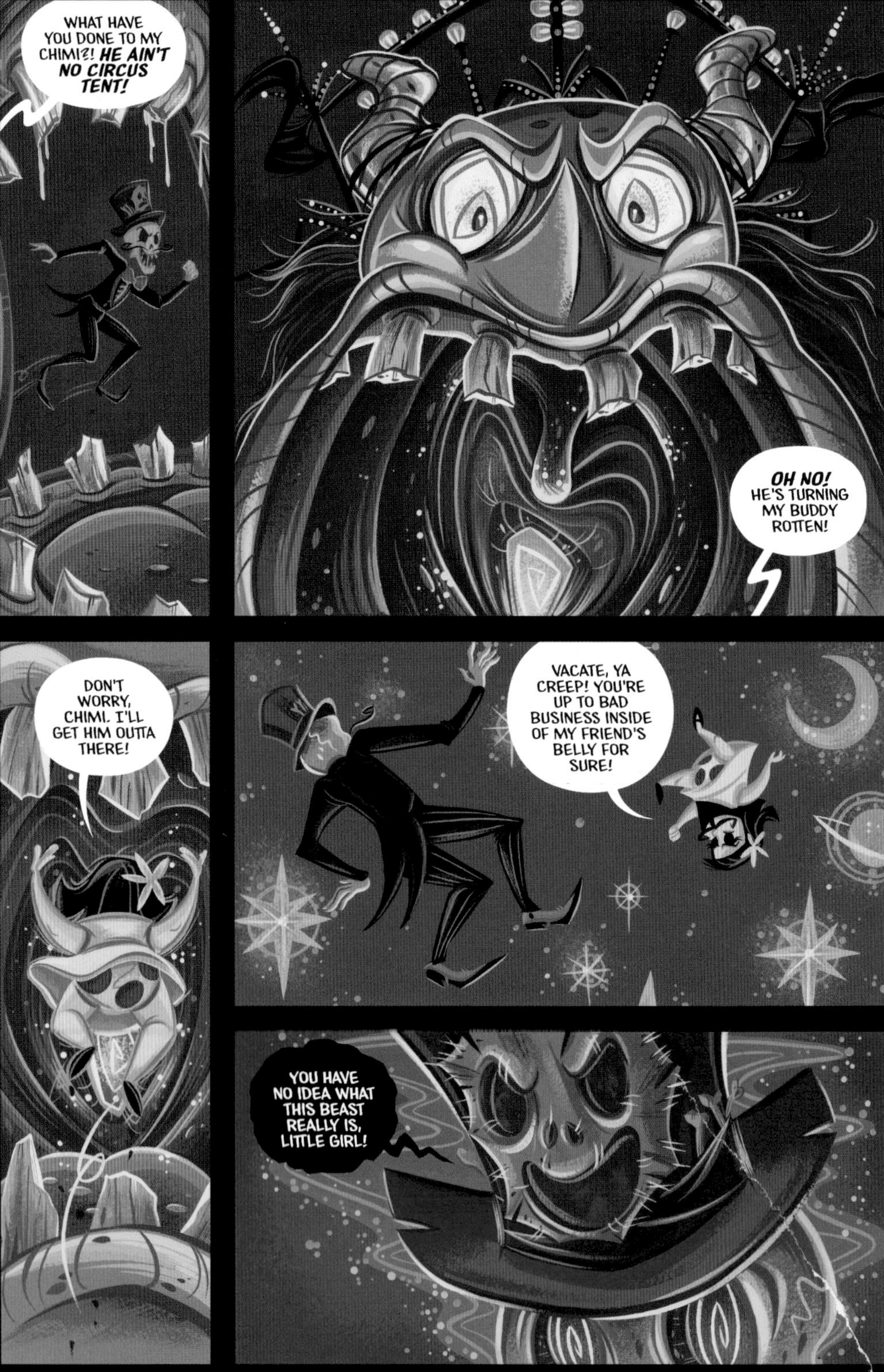
WHAT HAVE YOU DONE TO MY CHIMI?! HE AIN'T NO CIRCUS TENT!
OH NO! HE'S TURNING MY BUDDY ROTTEN!
DON'T WORRY, CHIMI. I'LL GET HIM OUTTA THERE!
VACATE, YA CREEP! YOU'RE UP TO BAD BUSINESS INSIDE OF MY FRIEND'S BELLY FOR SURE!
YOU HAVE NO IDEA WHAT THIS BEAST REALLY IS, LITTLE GIRL!

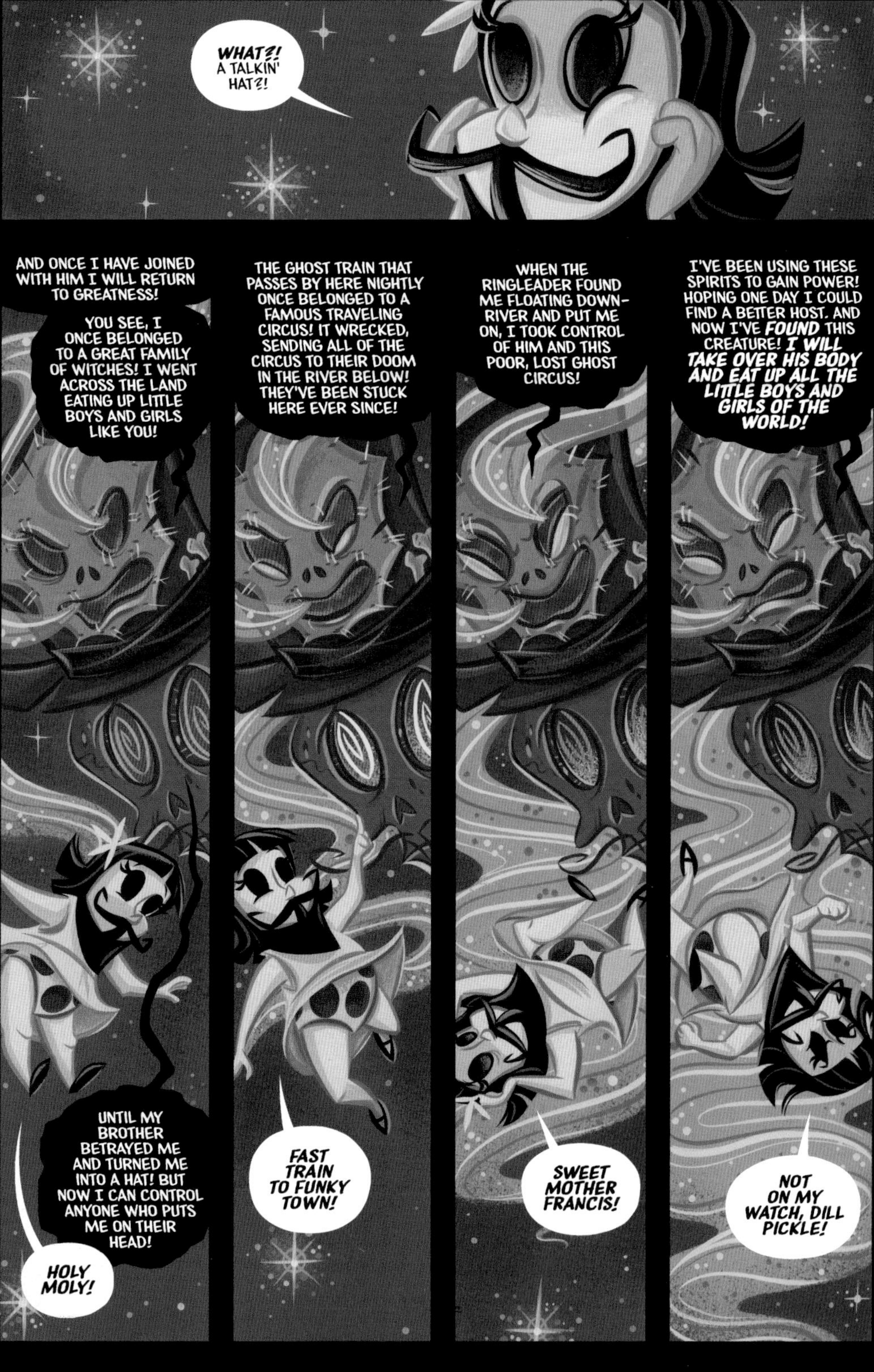
WHAT?! A TALKIN' HAT?!
AND ONCE I HAVE JOINED WITH HIM I WILL RETURN TO GREATNESS!
YOU SEE, I ONCE BELONGED TO A GREAT FAMILY OF WITCHES! I WENT ACROSS THE LAND EATING UP LITTLE BOYS AND GIRLS LIKE YOU!
UNTIL MY BROTHER BETRAYED ME AND TURNED ME INTO A HAT! BUT NOW I CAN CONTROL ANYONE WHO PUTS ME ON THEIR HEAD!
HOLY MOLY!
THE GHOST TRAIN THAT PASSES BY HERE NIGHTLY ONCE BELONGED TO A FAMOUS TRAVELING CIRCUS! IT WRECKED, SENDING ALL OF THE CIRCUS TO THEIR DOOM IN THE RIVER BELOW! THEY'VE BEEN STUCK HERE EVER SINCE!
FAST TRAIN TO FUNKY TOWN!
WHEN THE RINGLEADER FOUND ME FLOATING DOWN-RIVER AND PUT ME ON, I TOOK CONTROL OF HIM AND THIS POOR, LOST GHOST CIRCUS!
SWEET MOTHER FRANCIS!
I'VE BEEN USING THESE SPIRITS TO GAIN POWER! HOPING ONE DAY I COULD FIND A BETTER HOST. AND NOW I'VE FOUND THIS CREATURE! I WILL TAKE OVER HIS BODY AND EAT UP ALL THE LITTLE BOYS AND GIRLS OF THE WORLD!
NOT ON MY WATCH, DILL PICKLE!

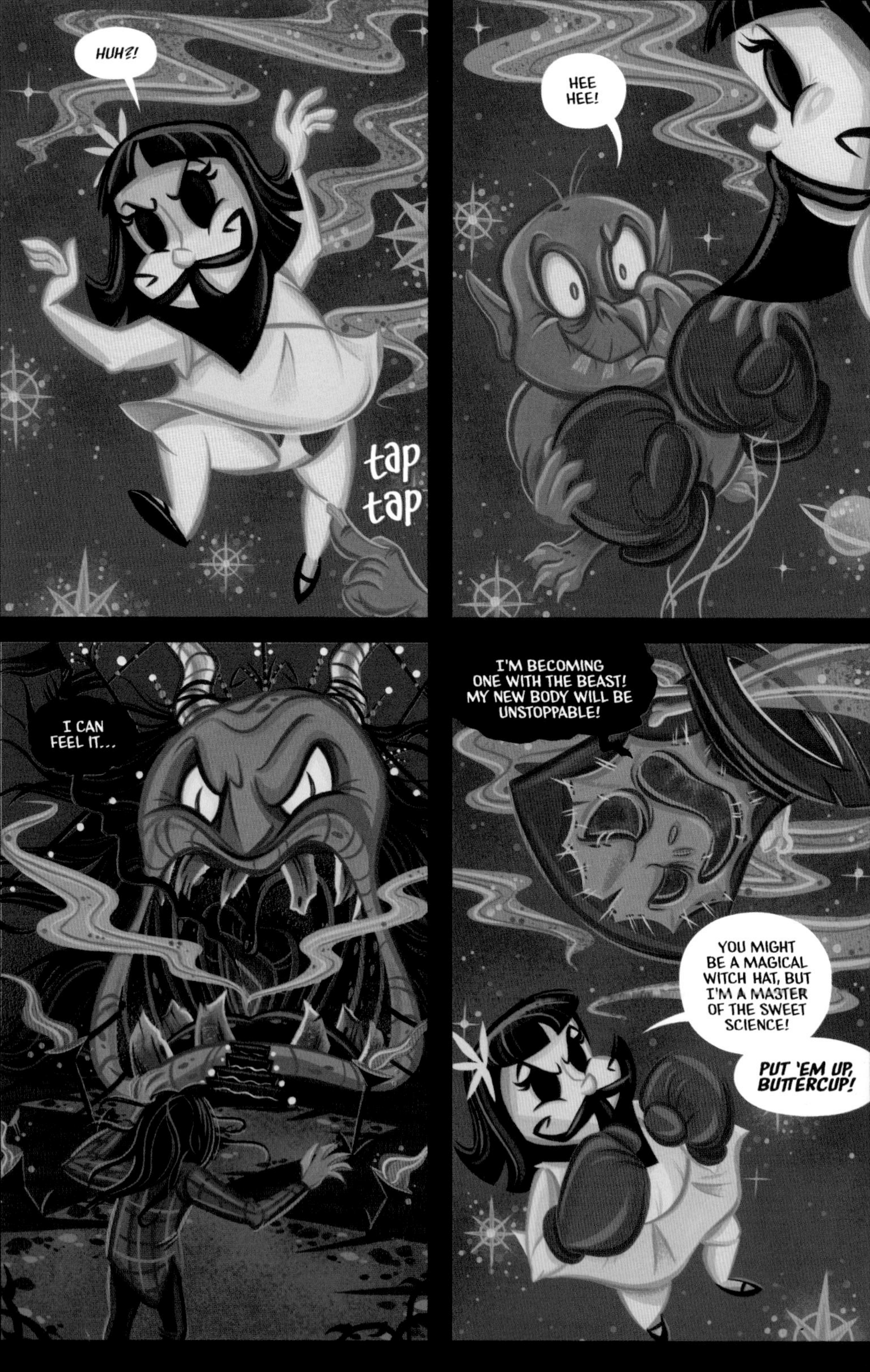
HUH?!
tap
tap
HEE
HEE!
I CAN
FEEL IT...
I'M BECOMING
ONE WITH THE BEAST!
MY NEW BODY WILL BE
UNSTOPPABLE!
YOU MIGHT
BE A MAGICAL
WITCH HAT, BUT
I'M A MASTER
OF THE SWEET
SCIENCE!
PUT 'EM UP,
BUTTERCUP!

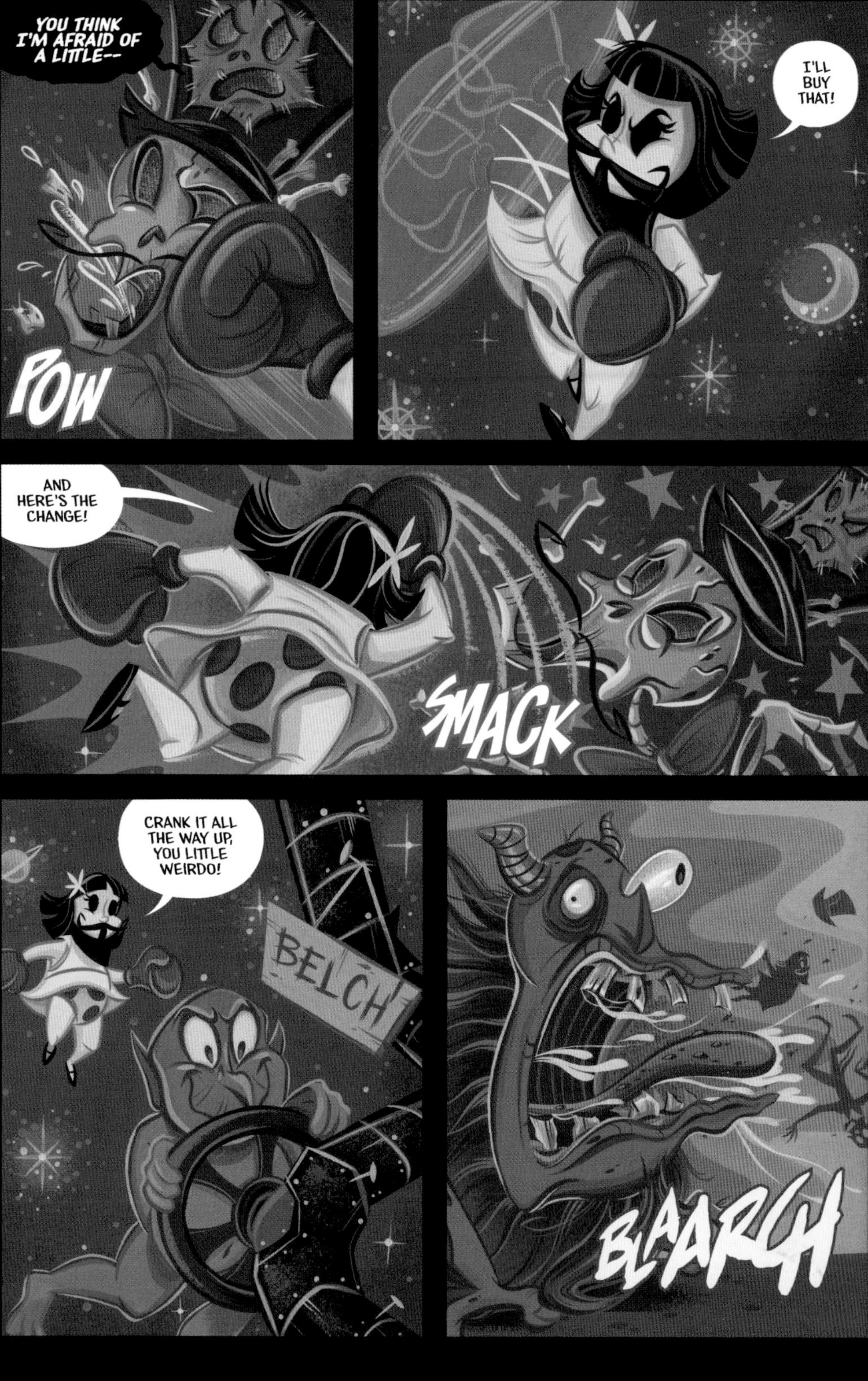
YOU THINK I'M AFRAID OF A LITTLE--
POW
I'LL BUY THAT!
AND HERE'S THE CHANGE!
SMACK
CRANK IT ALL THE WAY UP, YOU LITTLE WEIRDO!
BELCH
BLAARGH

OH, THANK YOU, LITTLE GIRL! WE ARE FINALLY FREE OF THAT AWFUL HAT!

DON'T MENTION IT!

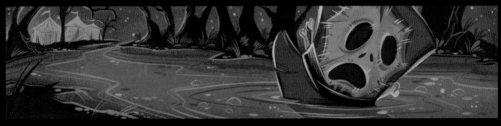

GOODBYE! AND REMEMBER, IF YOU EVER NEED ANY POINTERS, LOOK UP WRINKLE'S TRAVELING CIRCUS! IT'S KNOWN AS THE MEASURING STICK OF SHOWBIZ!

YES, COME INTO MY WOODS! RIGHT TO ME...AND MY *REVENGE!*

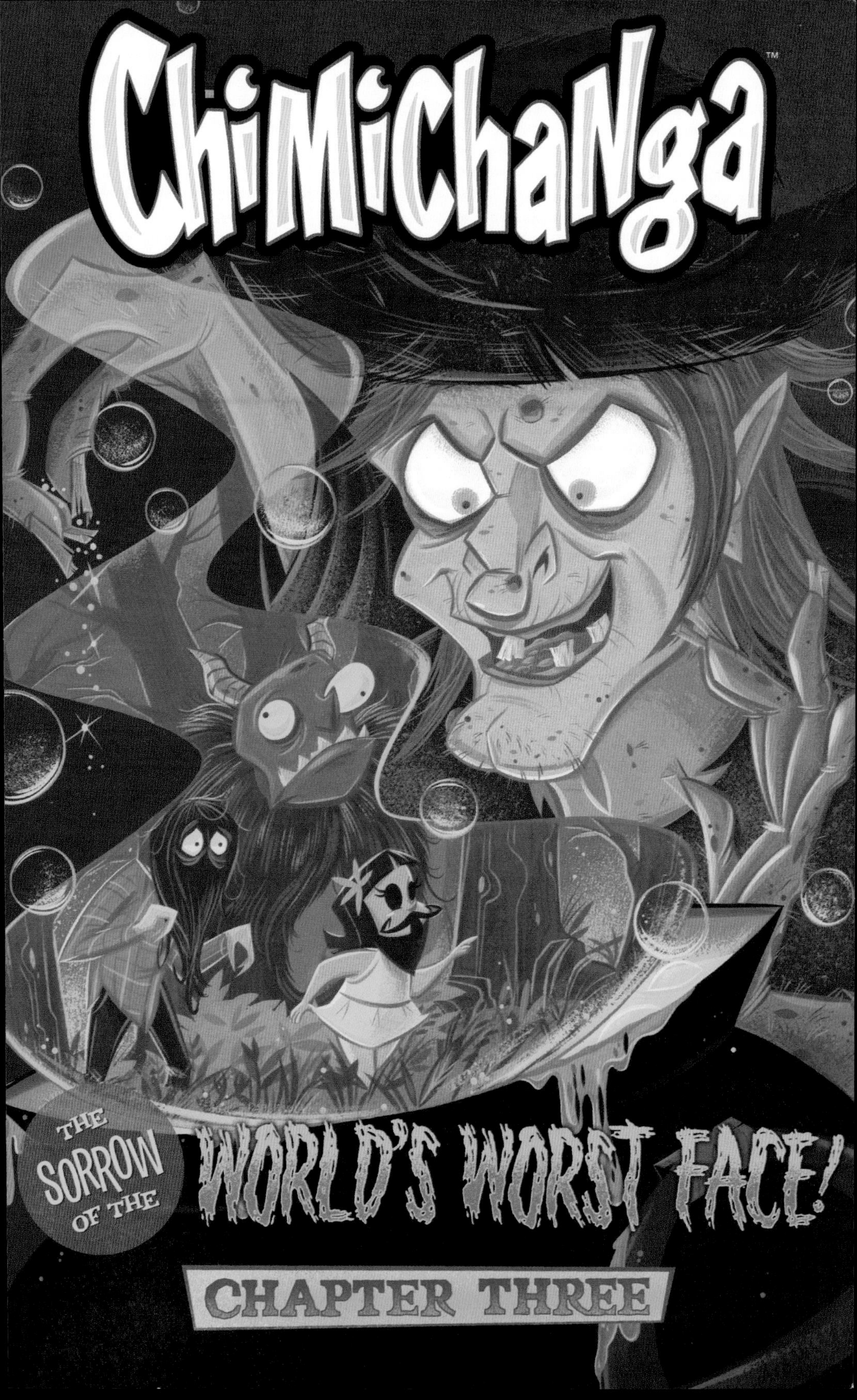
ChiMiChaNga™
THE SORROW OF THE
WORLD'S WORST FACE!
CHAPTER THREE

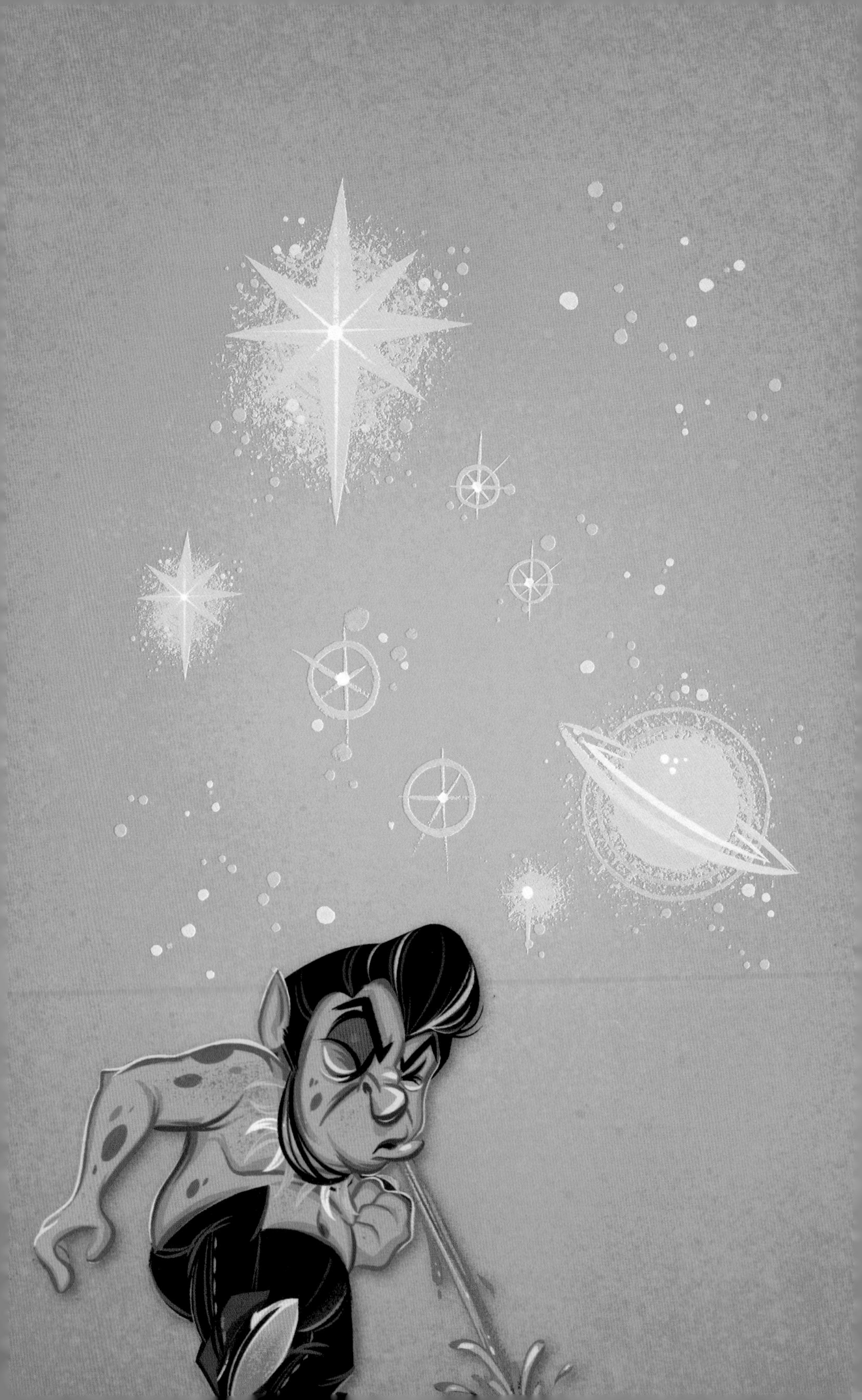

LOST in the FOREST of the FLATULENT WITCH

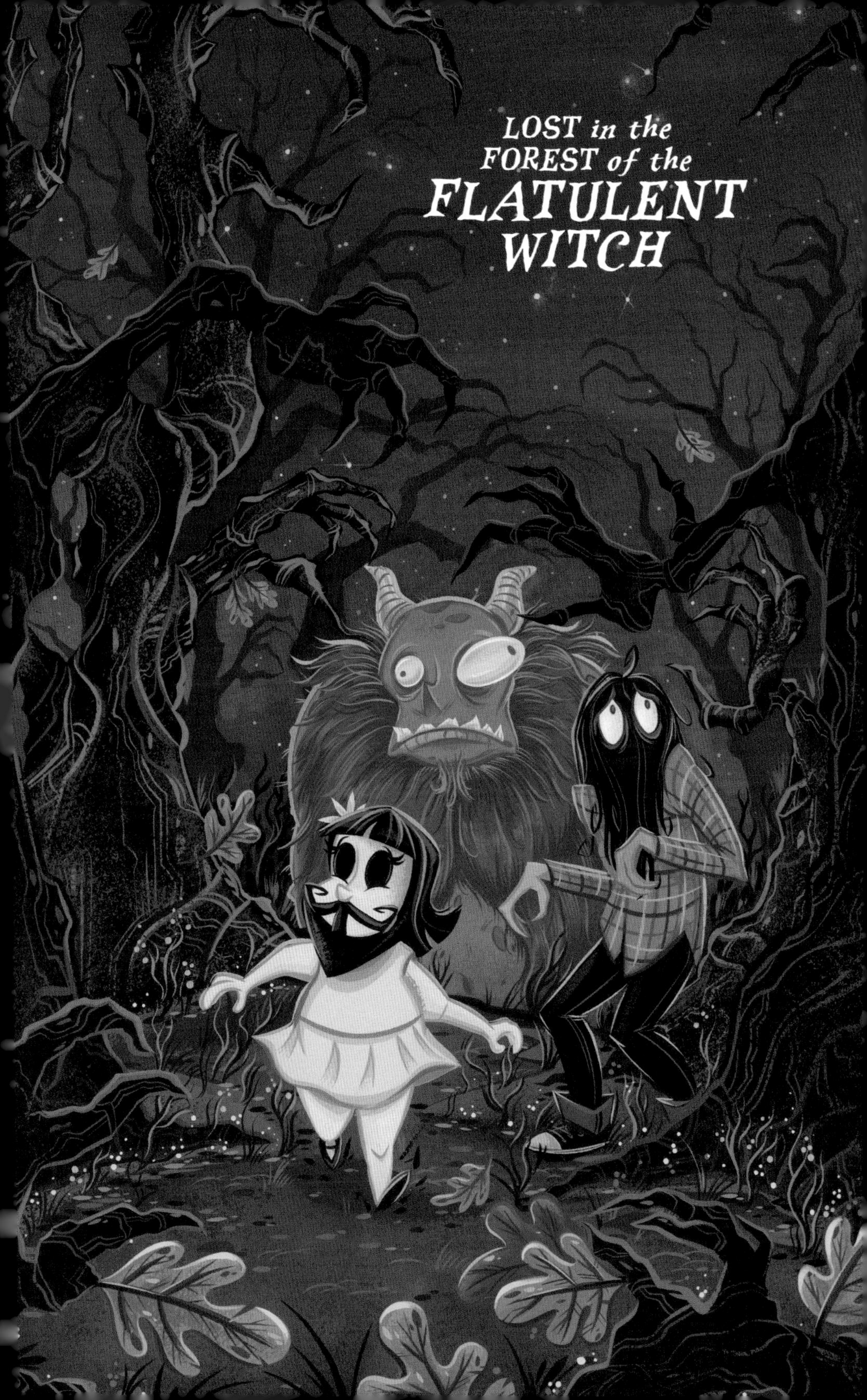

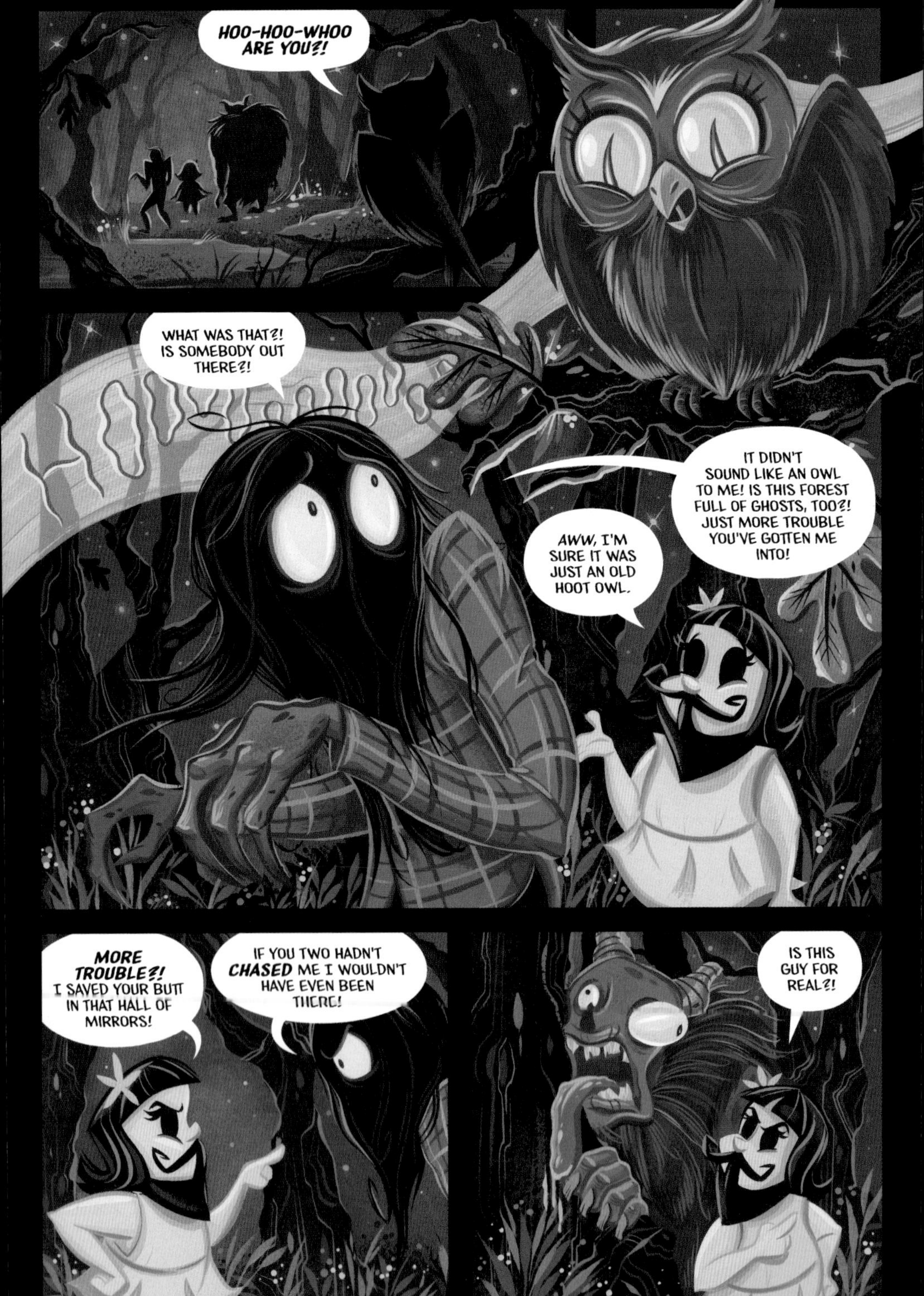

HOO-HOO-WHOO ARE YOU?!
WHAT WAS THAT?! IS SOMEBODY OUT THERE?!
HOOOoooo
AWW, I'M SURE IT WAS JUST AN OLD HOOT OWL.
IT DIDN'T SOUND LIKE AN OWL TO ME! IS THIS FOREST FULL OF GHOSTS, TOO?! JUST MORE TROUBLE YOU'VE GOTTEN ME INTO!
MORE TROUBLE?! I SAVED YOUR BUTT IN THAT HALL OF MIRRORS!
IF YOU TWO HADN'T CHASED ME I WOULDN'T HAVE EVEN BEEN THERE!
IS THIS GUY FOR REAL?!

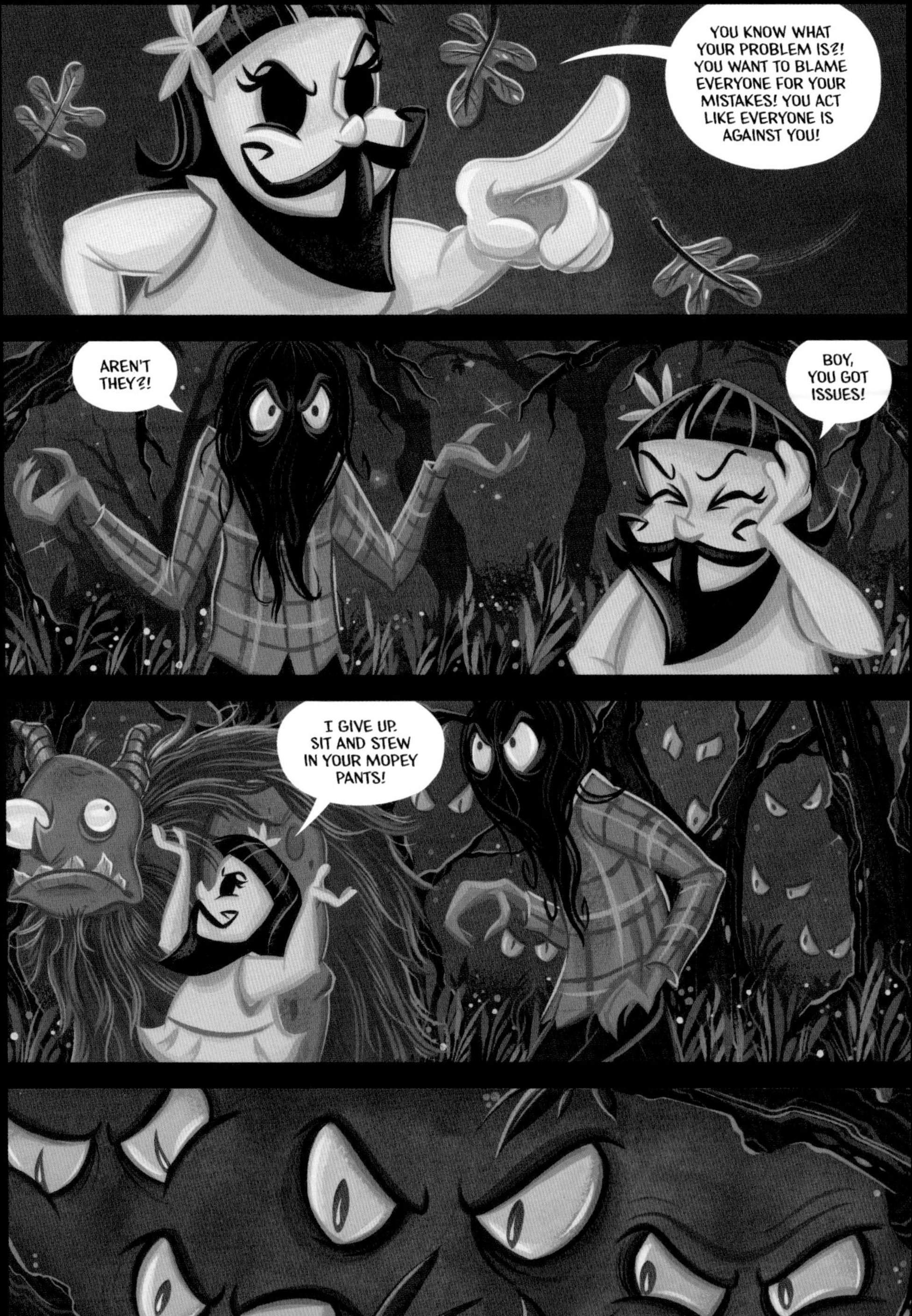
YOU KNOW WHAT YOUR PROBLEM IS?! YOU WANT TO BLAME EVERYONE FOR YOUR MISTAKES! YOU ACT LIKE EVERYONE IS AGAINST YOU!
AREN'T THEY?!
BOY, YOU GOT ISSUES!
I GIVE UP. SIT AND STEW IN YOUR MOPEY PANTS!

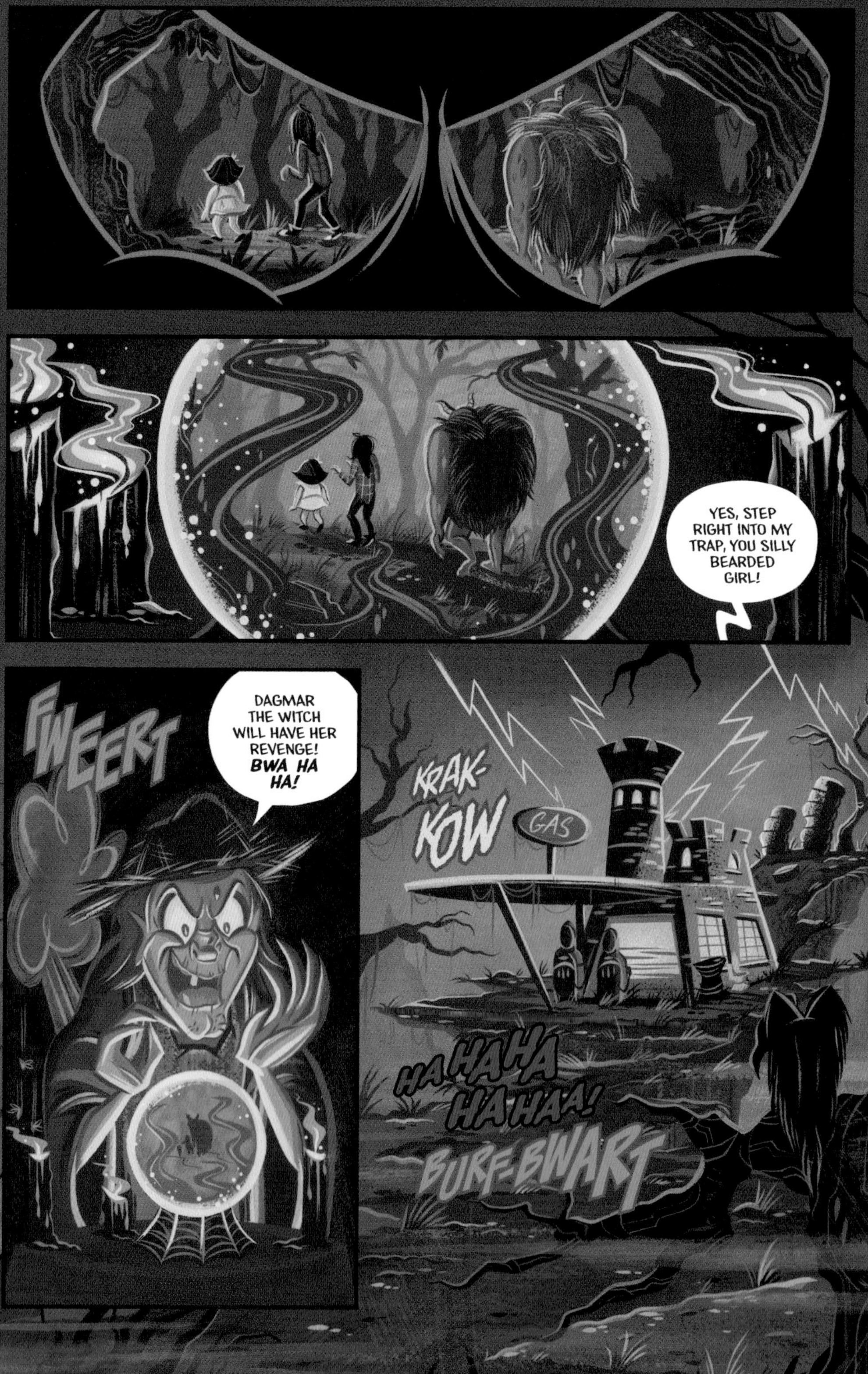
YES, STEP RIGHT INTO MY TRAP, YOU SILLY BEARDED GIRL!
FWEERT
DAGMAR THE WITCH WILL HAVE HER REVENGE! BWA HA HA!
KRAK-KOW
GAS
HA HAHA HAHAA!
BURF-BWART

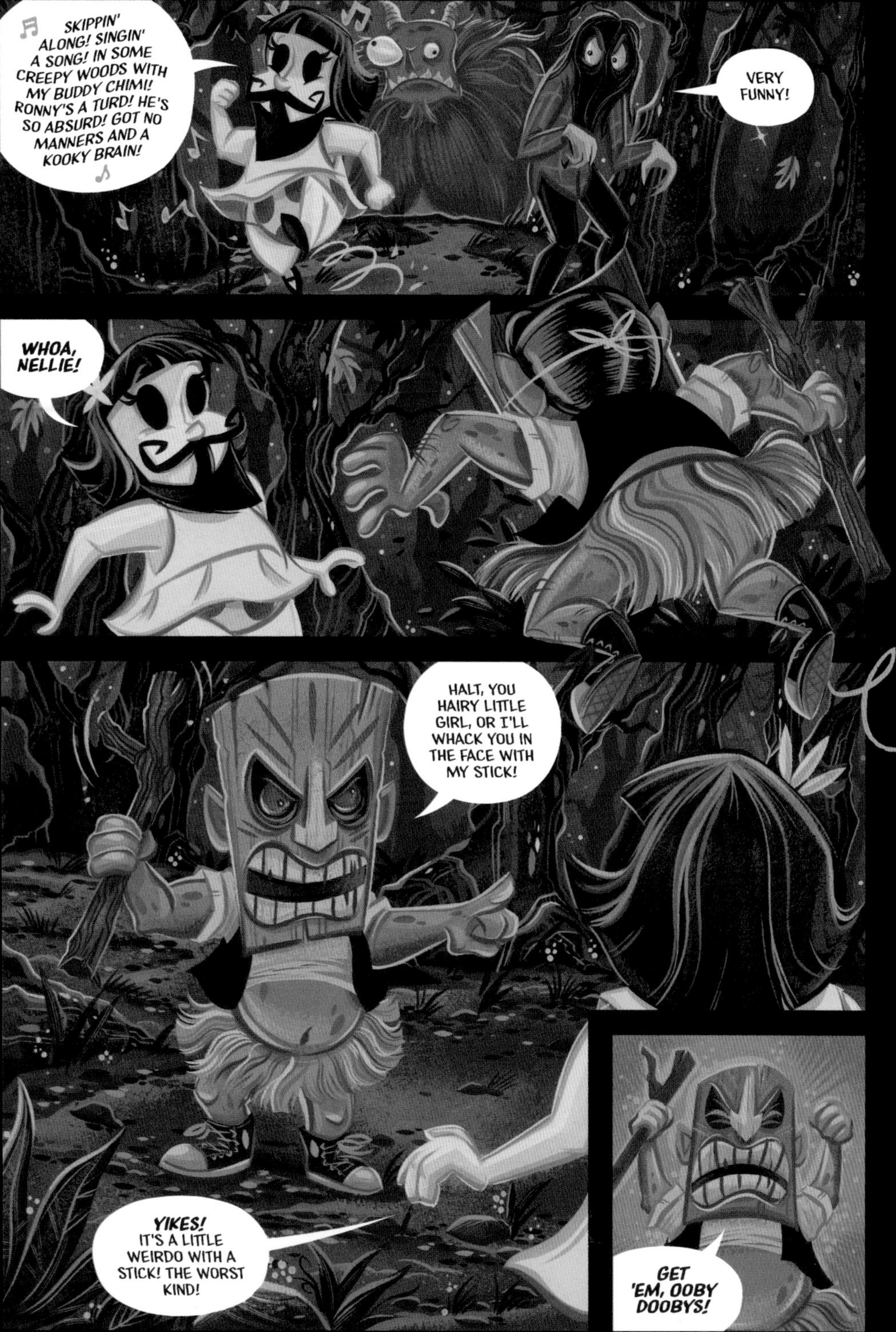
SKIPPIN' ALONG! SINGIN' A SONG! IN SOME CREEPY WOODS WITH MY BUDDY CHIMI! RONNY'S A TURD! HE'S SO ABSURD! GOT NO MANNERS AND A KOOKY BRAIN!
VERY FUNNY!
WHOA, NELLIE!
HALT, YOU HAIRY LITTLE GIRL, OR I'LL WHACK YOU IN THE FACE WITH MY STICK!
YIKES! IT'S A LITTLE WEIRDO WITH A STICK! THE WORST KIND!
GET 'EM, OOBY DOOBYS!

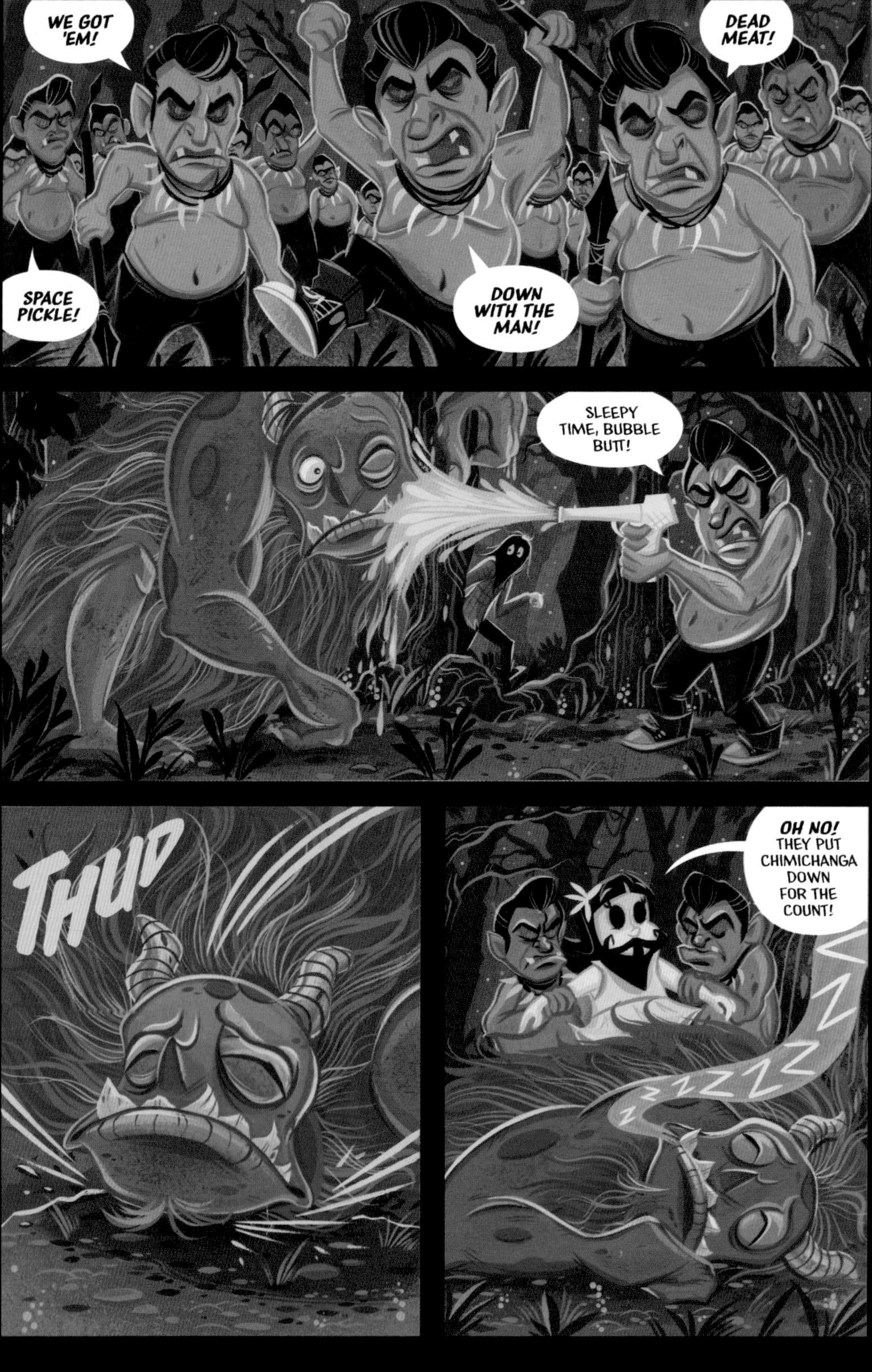
WE GOT 'EM!
DEAD MEAT!
SPACE PICKLE!
DOWN WITH THE MAN!
SLEEPY TIME, BUBBLE BUTT!
THUD
OH NO! THEY PUT CHIMICHANGA DOWN FOR THE COUNT!
ZZZZZZZZ

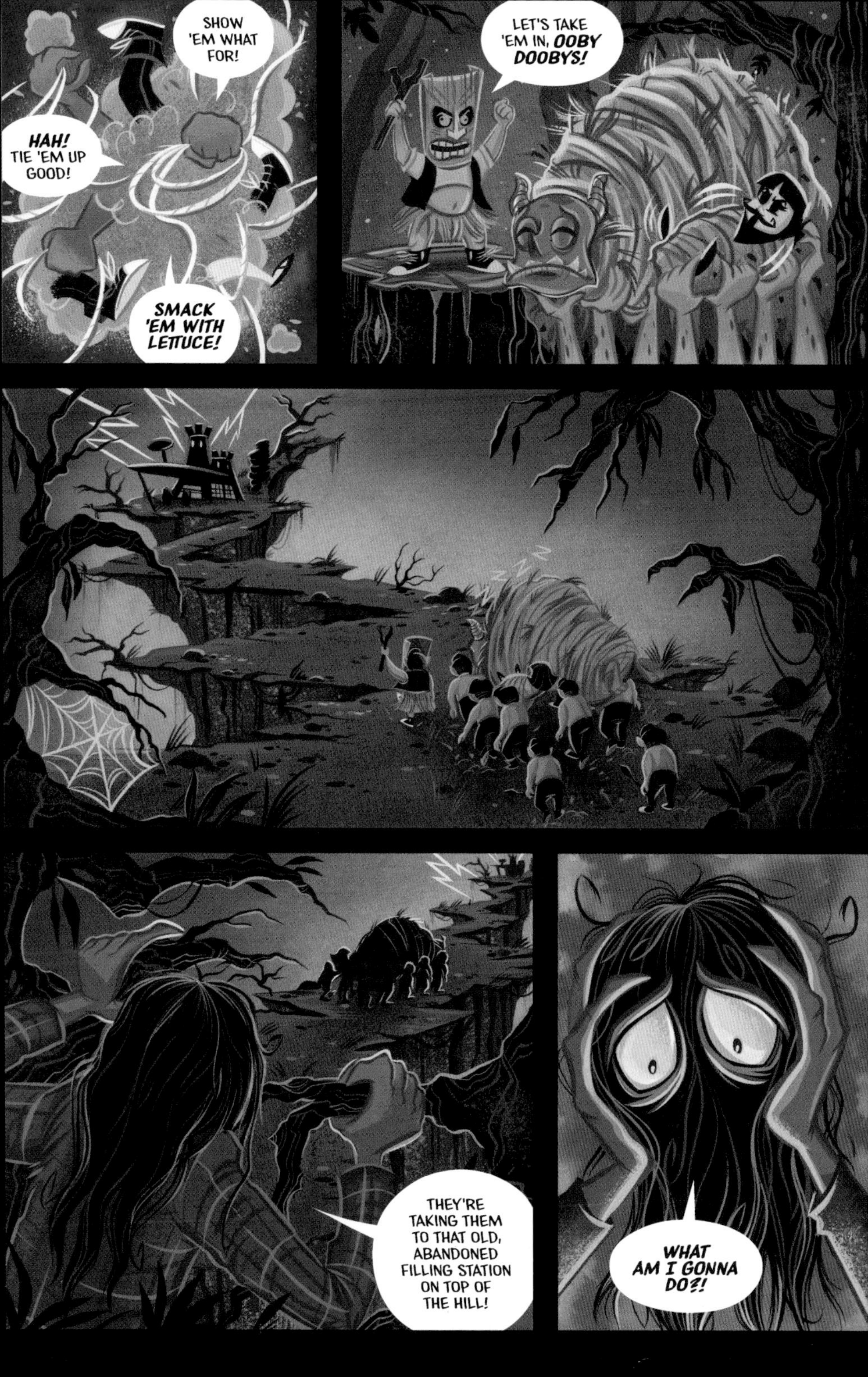
SHOW 'EM WHAT FOR!
HAH! TIE 'EM UP GOOD!
SMACK 'EM WITH LETTUCE!
LET'S TAKE 'EM IN, OOBY DOOBYS!
THEY'RE TAKING THEM TO THAT OLD, ABANDONED FILLING STATION ON TOP OF THE HILL!
WHAT AM I GONNA DO?!

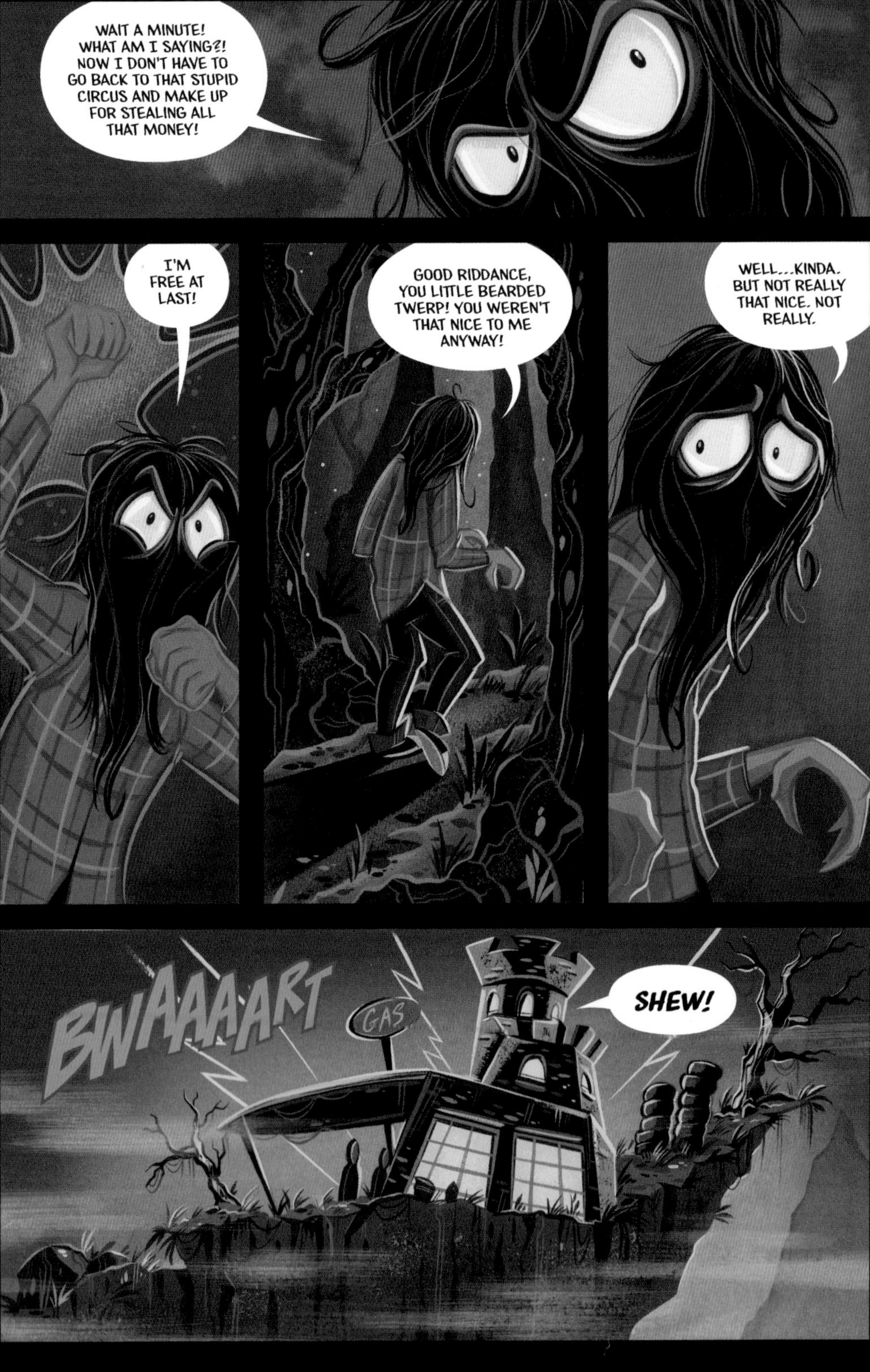
WAIT A MINUTE! WHAT AM I SAYING?! NOW I DON'T HAVE TO GO BACK TO THAT STUPID CIRCUS AND MAKE UP FOR STEALING ALL THAT MONEY!
I'M FREE AT LAST!
GOOD RIDDANCE, YOU LITTLE BEARDED TWERP! YOU WEREN'T THAT NICE TO ME ANYWAY!
WELL...KINDA. BUT NOT REALLY THAT NICE. NOT REALLY.
BWAAAART
GAS
SHEW!

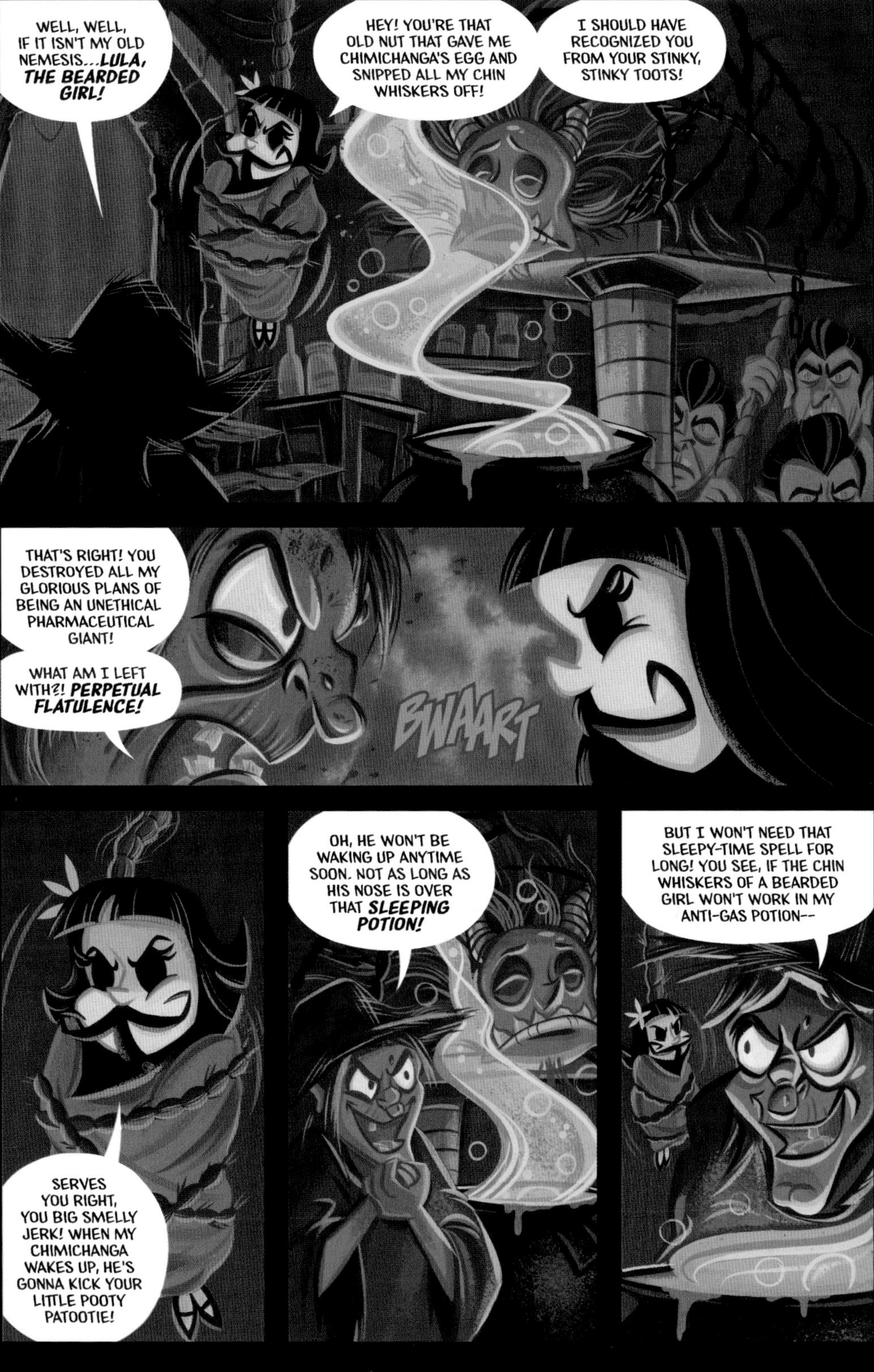
WELL, WELL, IF IT ISN'T MY OLD NEMESIS...LULA, THE BEARDED GIRL!
HEY! YOU'RE THAT OLD NUT THAT GAVE ME CHIMICHANGA'S EGG AND SNIPPED ALL MY CHIN WHISKERS OFF!
I SHOULD HAVE RECOGNIZED YOU FROM YOUR STINKY, STINKY TOOTS!
THAT'S RIGHT! YOU DESTROYED ALL MY GLORIOUS PLANS OF BEING AN UNETHICAL PHARMACEUTICAL GIANT!
WHAT AM I LEFT WITH?! PERPETUAL FLATULENCE!
BWAART
SERVES YOU RIGHT, YOU BIG SMELLY JERK! WHEN MY CHIMICHANGA WAKES UP, HE'S GONNA KICK YOUR LITTLE POOTY PATOOTIE!
OH, HE WON'T BE WAKING UP ANYTIME SOON. NOT AS LONG AS HIS NOSE IS OVER THAT SLEEPING POTION!
BUT I WON'T NEED THAT SLEEPY-TIME SPELL FOR LONG! YOU SEE, IF THE CHIN WHISKERS OF A BEARDED GIRL WON'T WORK IN MY ANTI-GAS POTION--

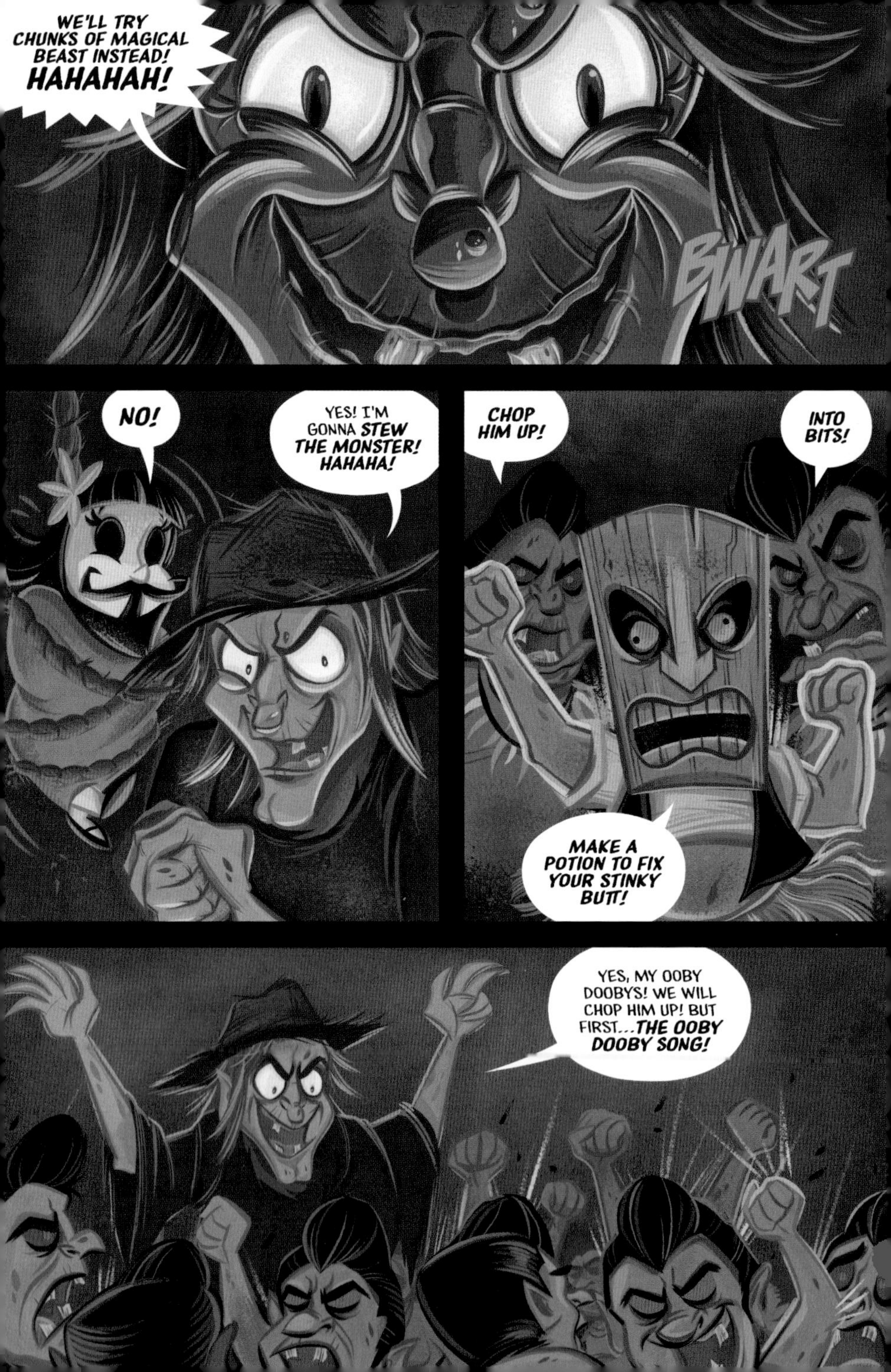
WE'LL TRY CHUNKS OF MAGICAL BEAST INSTEAD! HAHAHAH!
BWART
NO!
YES! I'M GONNA STEW THE MONSTER! HAHAHA!
CHOP HIM UP!
INTO BITS!
MAKE A POTION TO FIX YOUR STINKY BUTT!
YES, MY OOBY DOOBYS! WE WILL CHOP HIM UP! BUT FIRST...THE OOBY DOOBY SONG!

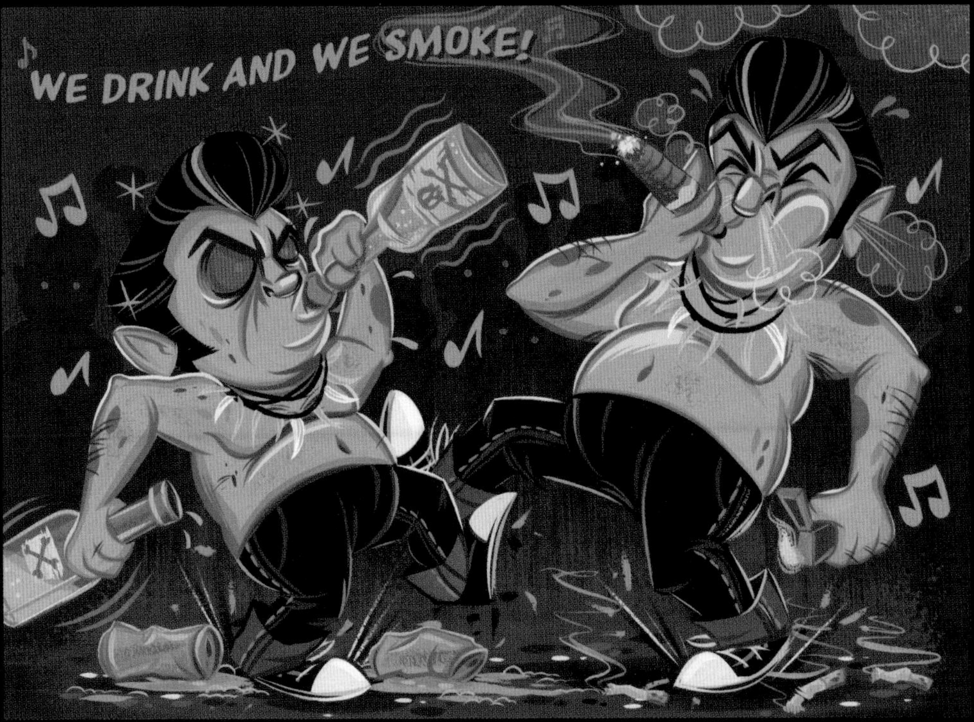
WE DRINK AND WE SMOKE!

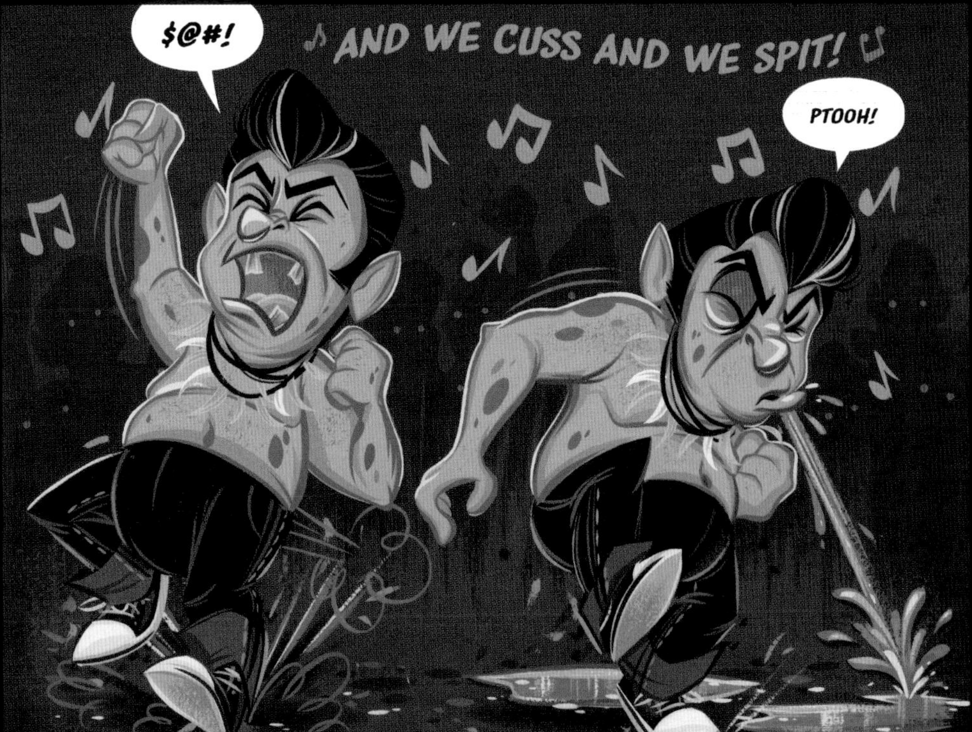
$@#!
AND WE CUSS AND WE SPIT!
PTOOH!

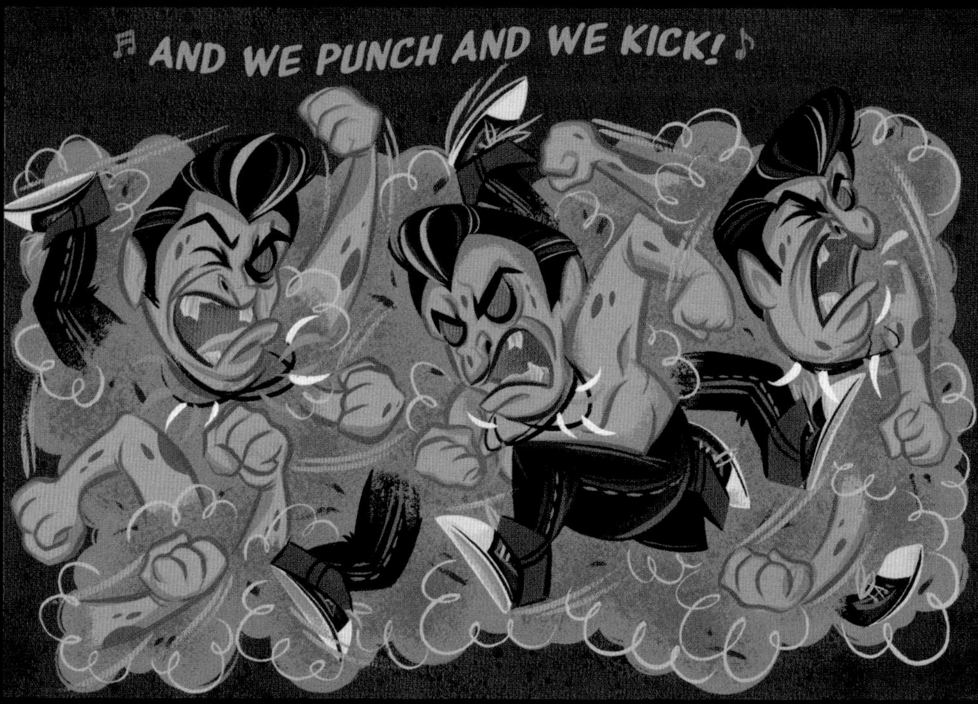
AND WE PUNCH AND WE KICK!

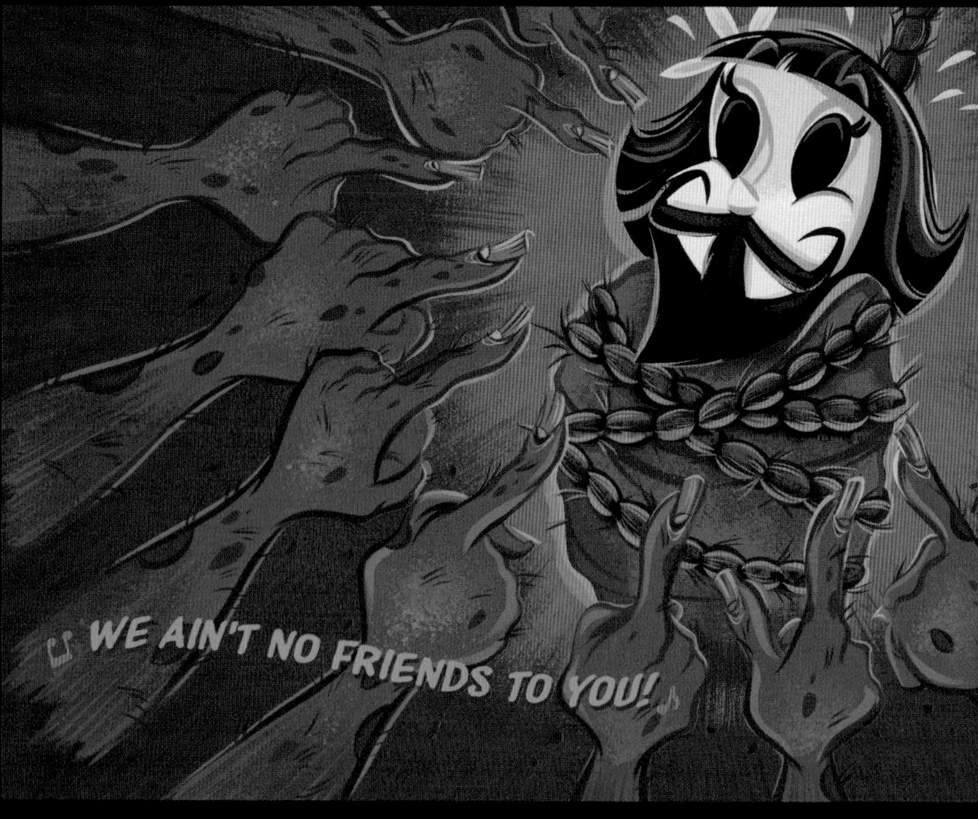
WE AIN'T NO FRIENDS TO YOU!

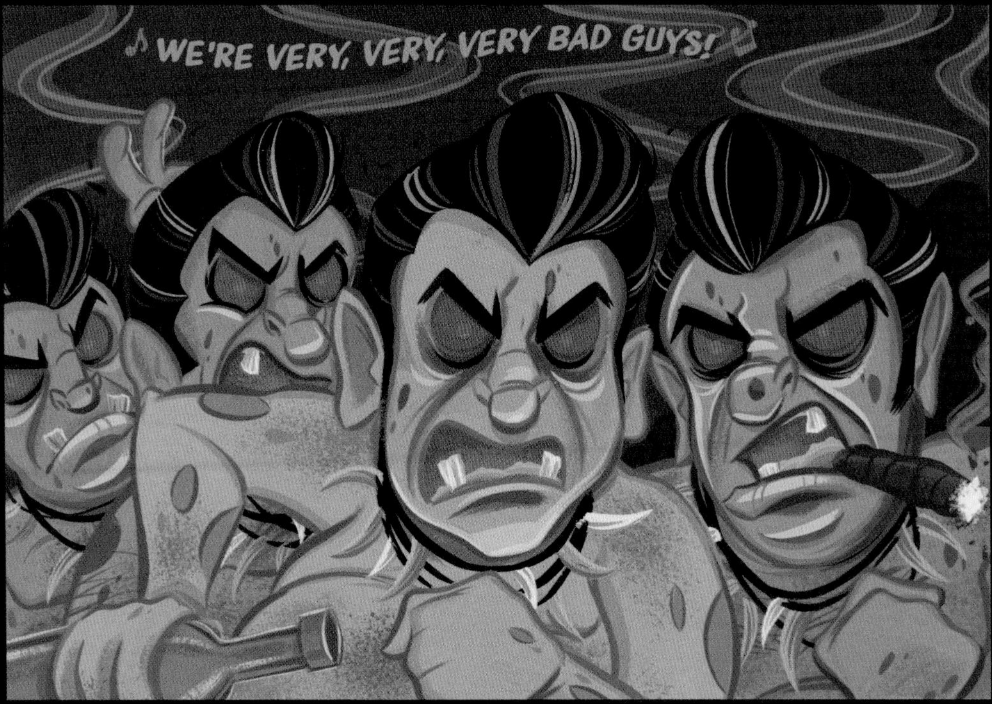
WE'RE VERY, VERY, VERY BAD GUYS!

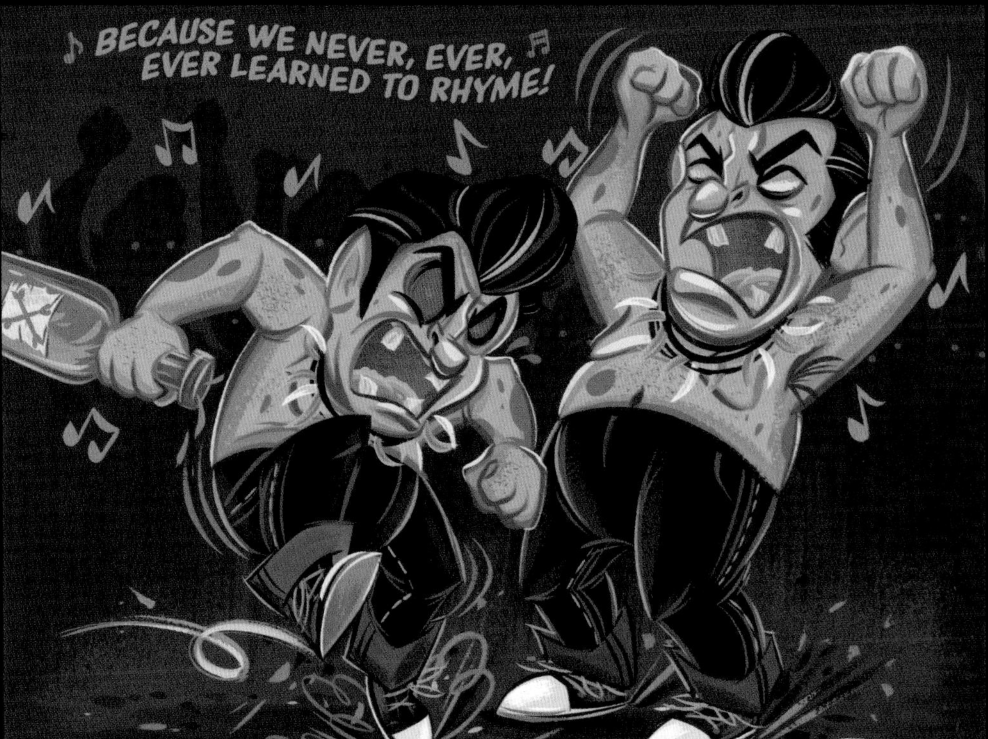
BECAUSE WE NEVER, EVER, EVER LEARNED TO RHYME!

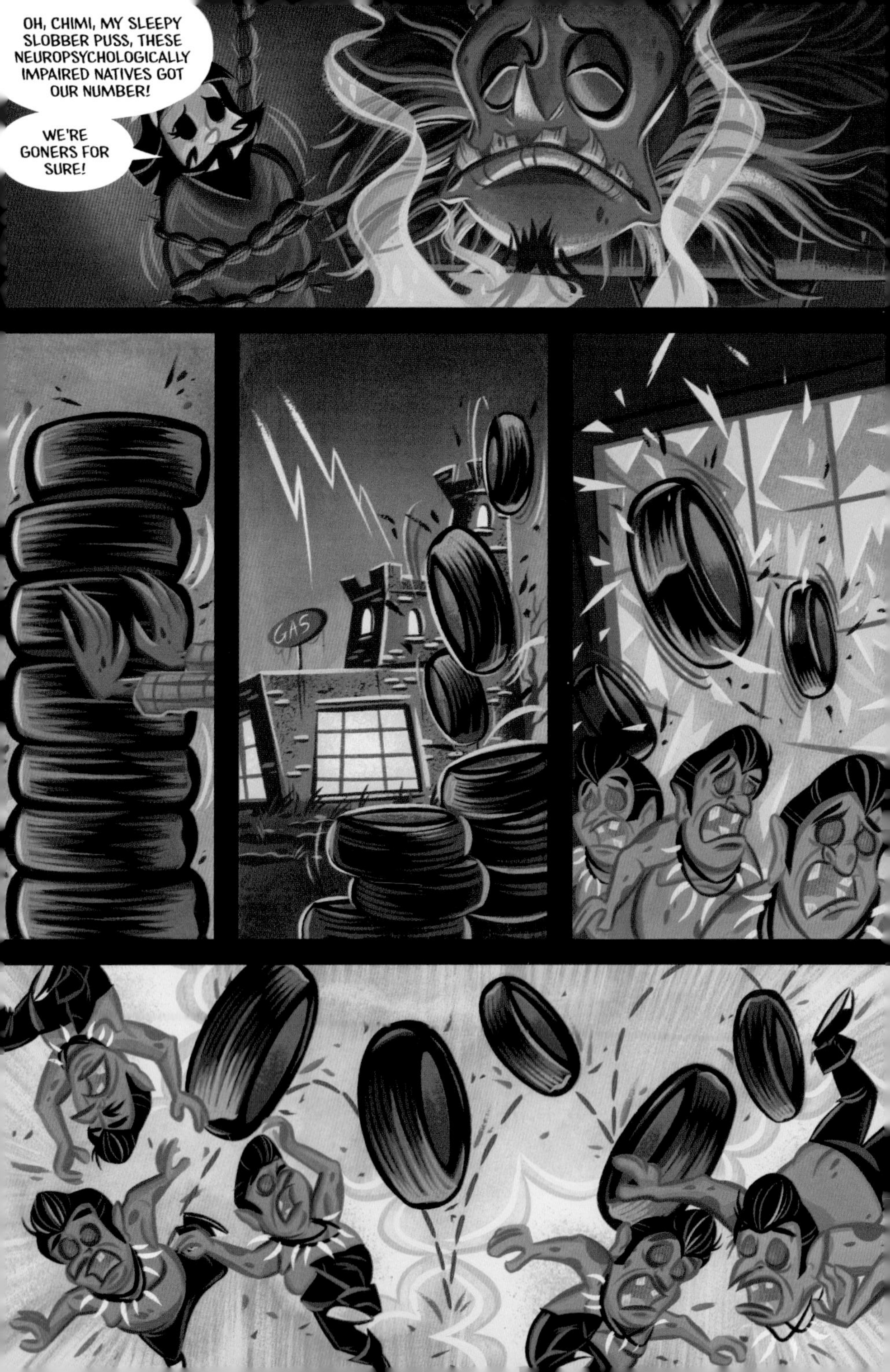
OH, CHIMI, MY SLEEPY SLOBBER PUSS, THESE NEUROPSYCHOLOGICALLY IMPAIRED NATIVES GOT OUR NUMBER!
WE'RE GONERS FOR SURE!
GAS

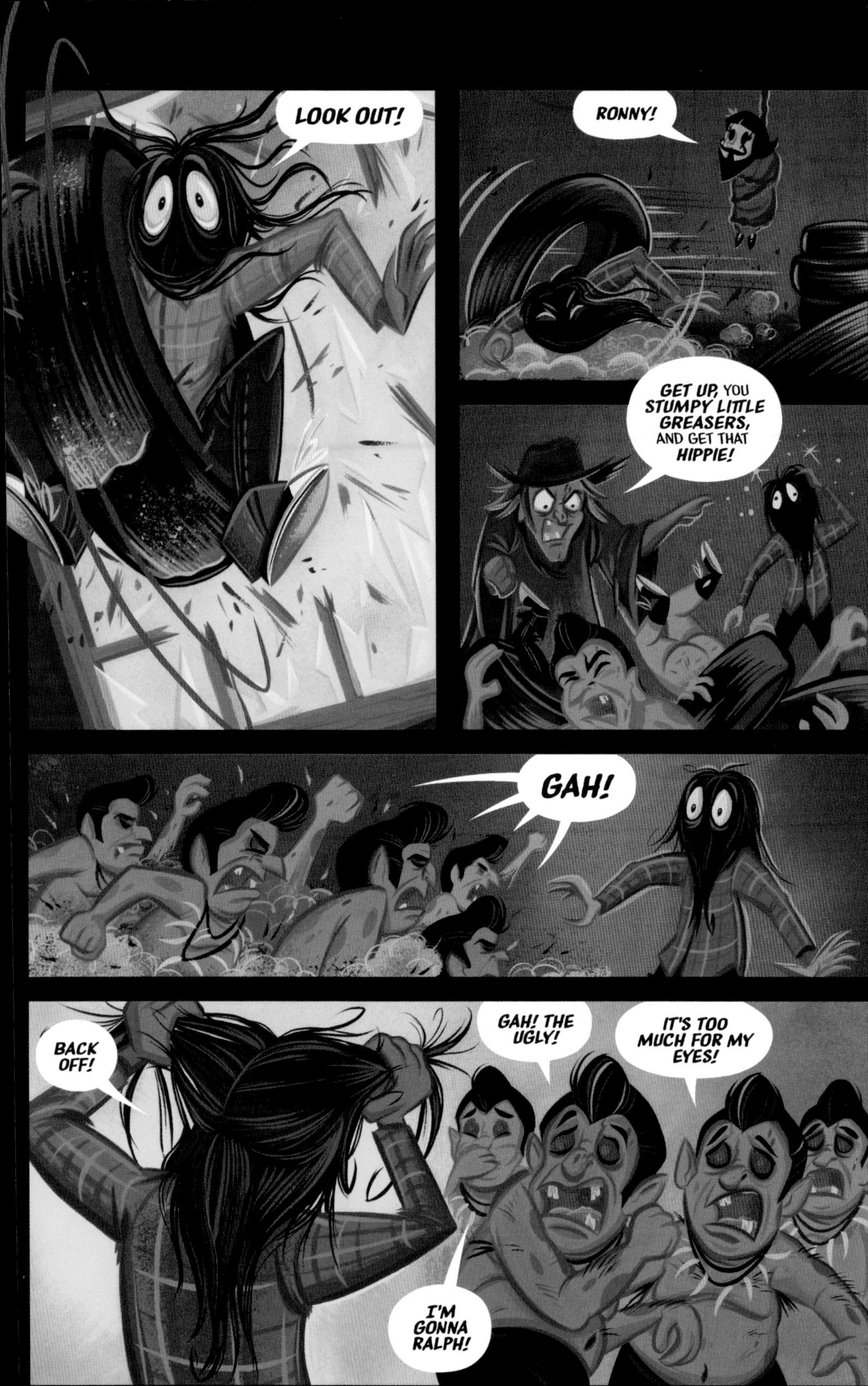
LOOK OUT!
RONNY!
GET UP, YOU STUMPY LITTLE GREASERS, AND GET THAT HIPPIE!
GAH!
BACK OFF!
GAH! THE UGLY!
IT'S TOO MUCH FOR MY EYES!
I'M GONNA RALPH!

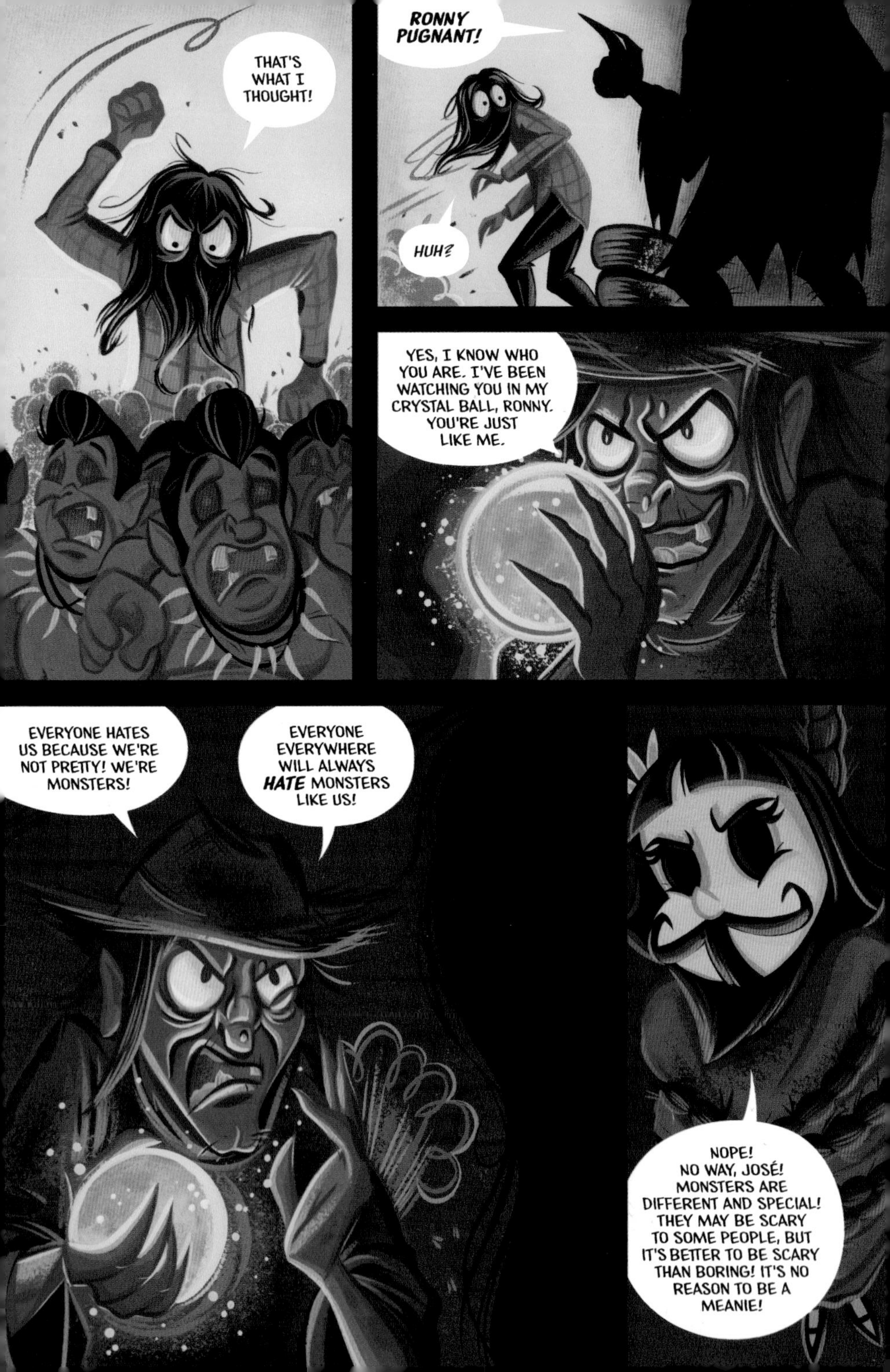
THAT'S WHAT I THOUGHT!
RONNY PUGNANT!
HUH?
YES, I KNOW WHO YOU ARE. I'VE BEEN WATCHING YOU IN MY CRYSTAL BALL, RONNY. YOU'RE JUST LIKE ME.
EVERYONE HATES US BECAUSE WE'RE NOT PRETTY! WE'RE MONSTERS!
EVERYONE EVERYWHERE WILL ALWAYS HATE MONSTERS LIKE US!
NOPE! NO WAY, JOSÉ! MONSTERS ARE DIFFERENT AND SPECIAL! THEY MAY BE SCARY TO SOME PEOPLE, BUT IT'S BETTER TO BE SCARY THAN BORING! IT'S NO REASON TO BE A MEANIE!

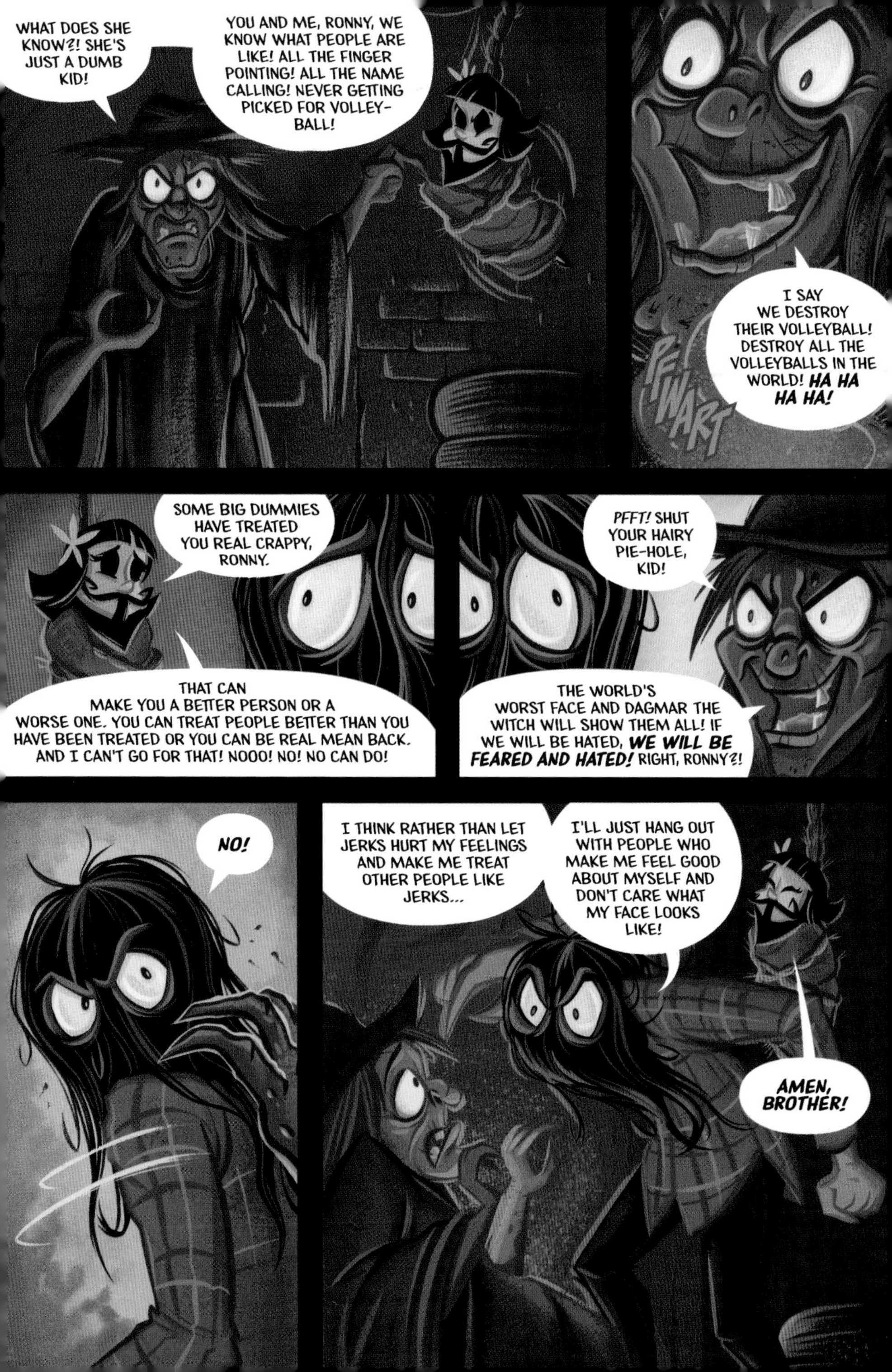
WHAT DOES SHE KNOW?! SHE'S JUST A DUMB KID!
YOU AND ME, RONNY, WE KNOW WHAT PEOPLE ARE LIKE! ALL THE FINGER POINTING! ALL THE NAME CALLING! NEVER GETTING PICKED FOR VOLLEY-BALL!
PFFWART
I SAY WE DESTROY THEIR VOLLEYBALL! DESTROY ALL THE VOLLEYBALLS IN THE WORLD! HA HA HA HA!
SOME BIG DUMMIES HAVE TREATED YOU REAL CRAPPY, RONNY.
THAT CAN MAKE YOU A BETTER PERSON OR A WORSE ONE. YOU CAN TREAT PEOPLE BETTER THAN YOU HAVE BEEN TREATED OR YOU CAN BE REAL MEAN BACK. AND I CAN'T GO FOR THAT! NOOO! NO! NO CAN DO!
PFFT! SHUT YOUR HAIRY PIE-HOLE, KID!
THE WORLD'S WORST FACE AND DAGMAR THE WITCH WILL SHOW THEM ALL! IF WE WILL BE HATED, WE WILL BE FEARED AND HATED! RIGHT, RONNY?!
NO!
I THINK RATHER THAN LET JERKS HURT MY FEELINGS AND MAKE ME TREAT OTHER PEOPLE LIKE JERKS...
I'LL JUST HANG OUT WITH PEOPLE WHO MAKE ME FEEL GOOD ABOUT MYSELF AND DON'T CARE WHAT MY FACE LOOKS LIKE!
AMEN, BROTHER!

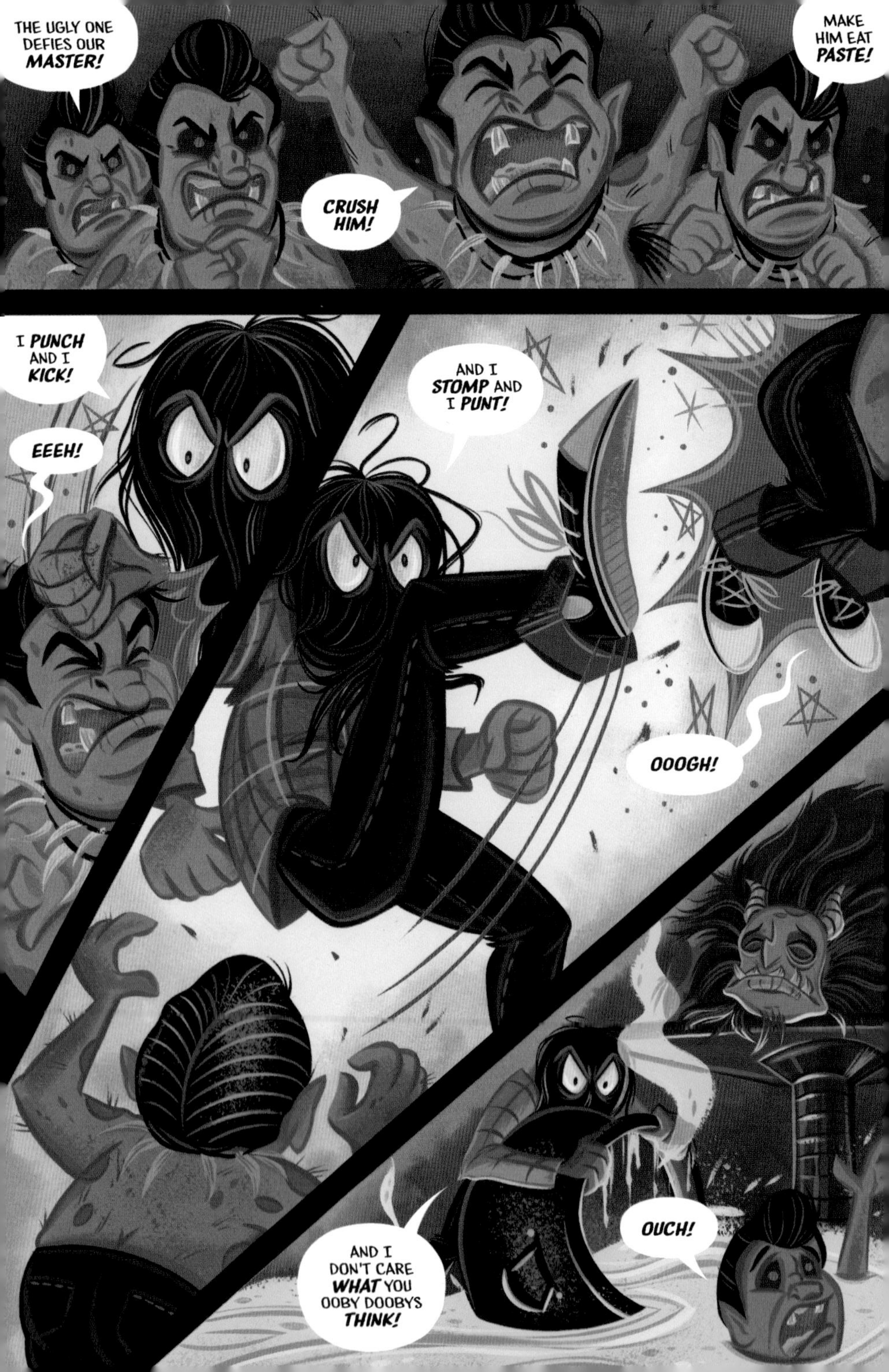
THE UGLY ONE DEFIES OUR MASTER!
CRUSH HIM!
MAKE HIM EAT PASTE!
I PUNCH AND I KICK!
EEEH!
AND I STOMP AND I PUNT!
OOOGH!
AND I DON'T CARE WHAT YOU OOBY DOOBYS THINK!
OUCH!

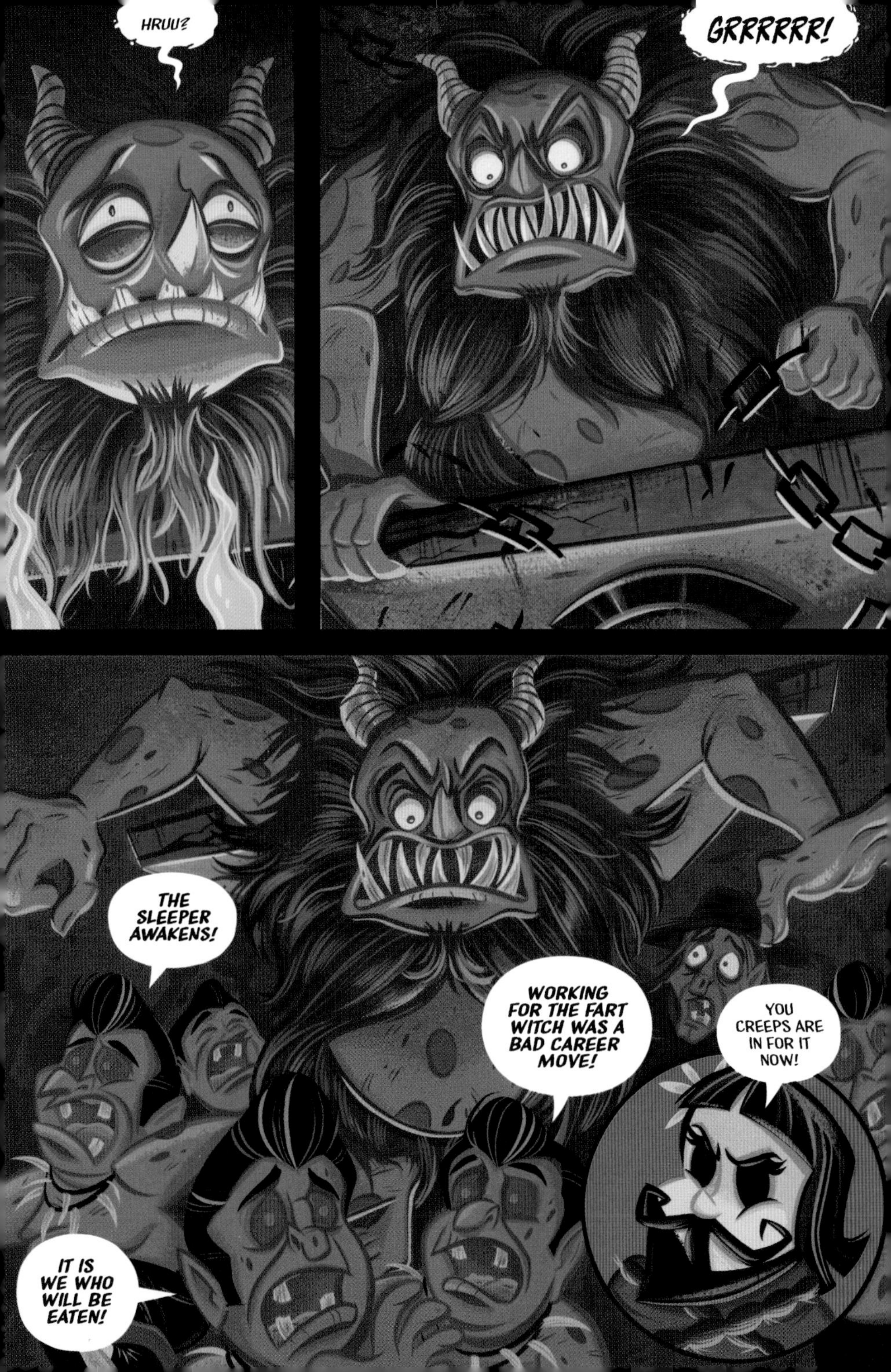
HRUU?
GRRRRRR!
THE SLEEPER AWAKENS!
WORKING FOR THE FART WITCH WAS A BAD CAREER MOVE!
YOU CREEPS ARE IN FOR IT NOW!
IT IS WE WHO WILL BE EATEN!

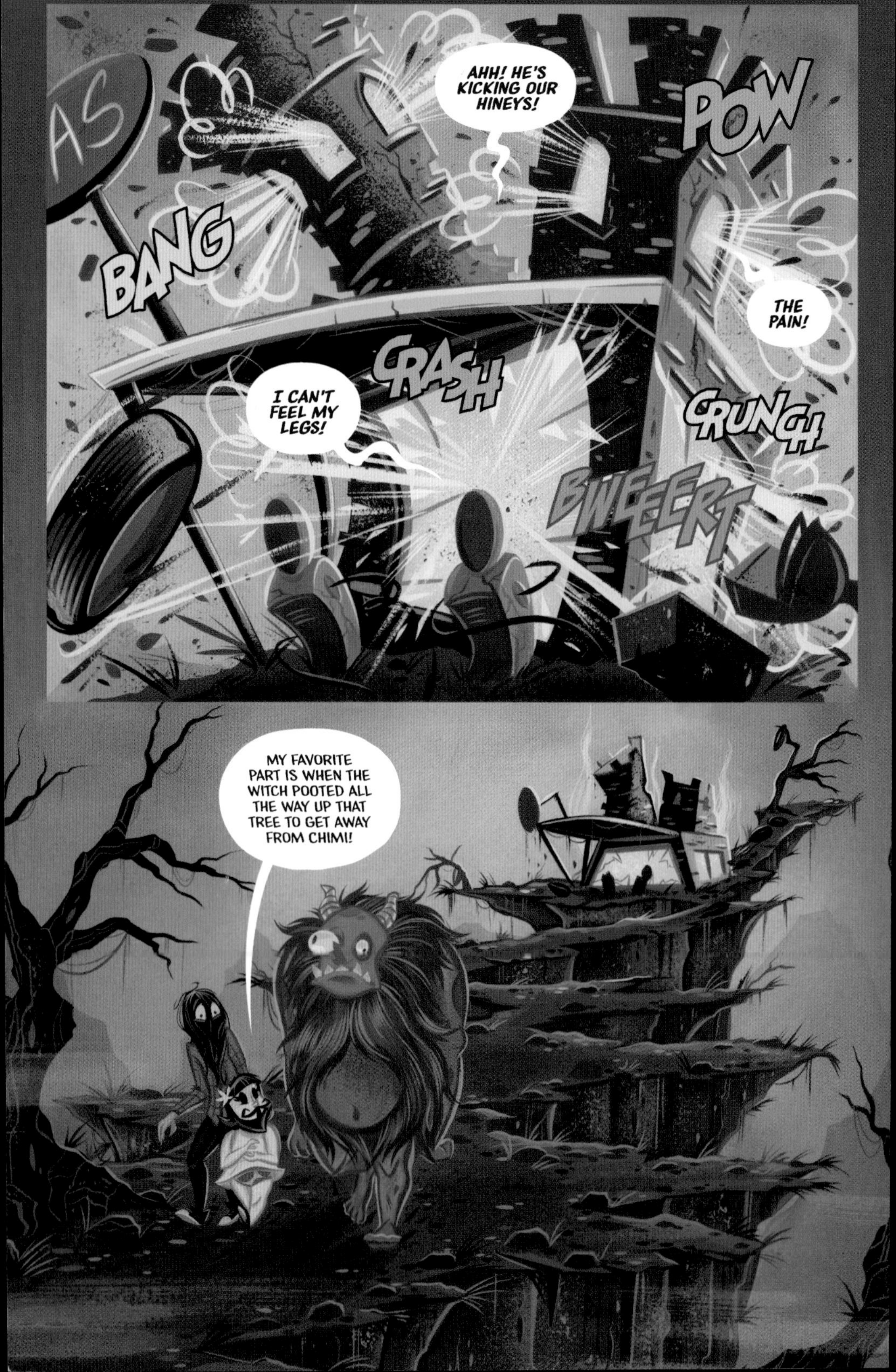
AHH! HE'S KICKING OUR HINEYS!
POW
BANG
THE PAIN!
CRASH
I CAN'T FEEL MY LEGS!
CRUNCH
BWEEERT
MY FAVORITE PART IS WHEN THE WITCH POOTED ALL THE WAY UP THAT TREE TO GET AWAY FROM CHIMI!

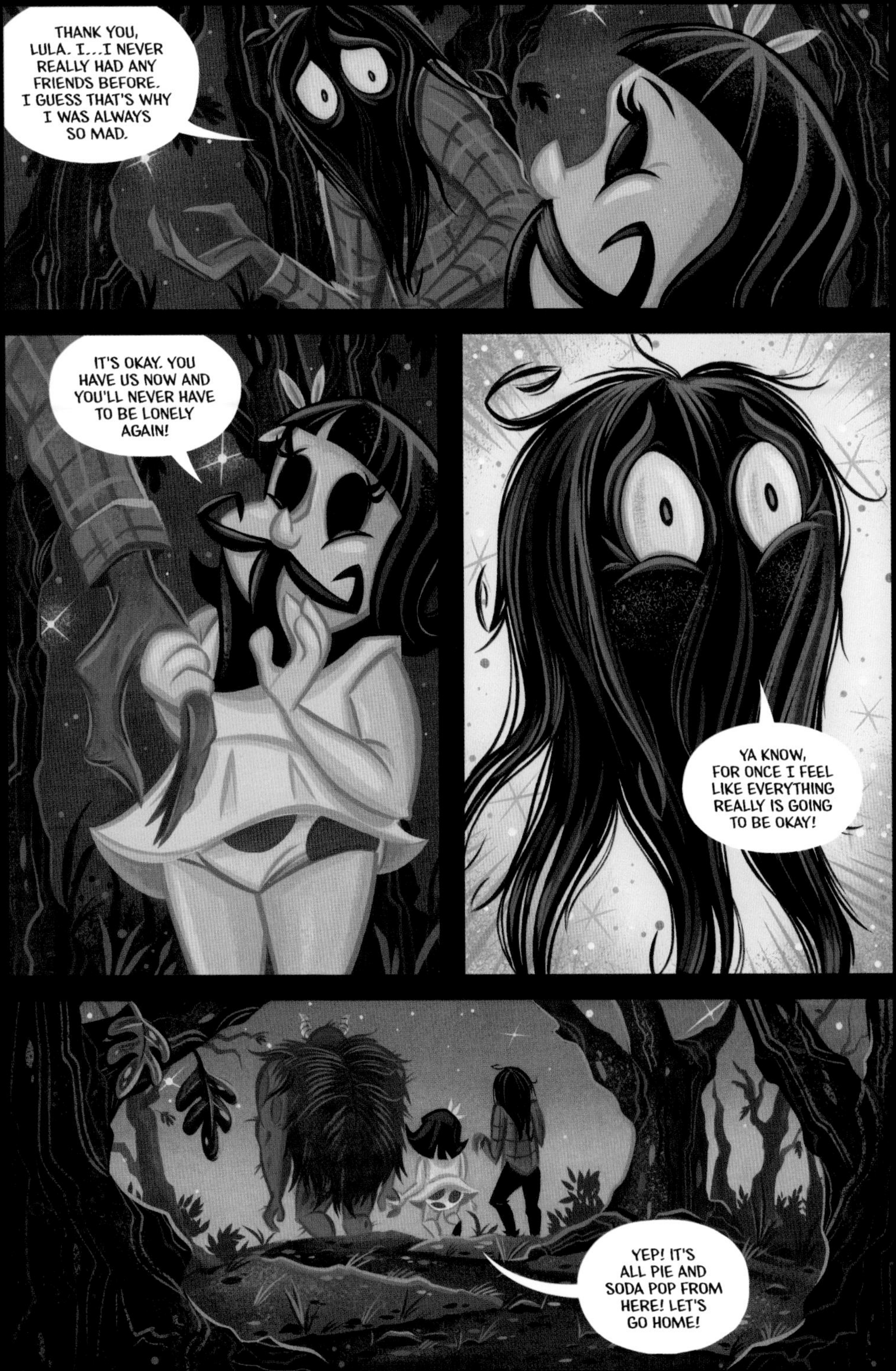
THANK YOU, LULA. I...I NEVER REALLY HAD ANY FRIENDS BEFORE. I GUESS THAT'S WHY I WAS ALWAYS SO MAD.
IT'S OKAY. YOU HAVE US NOW AND YOU'LL NEVER HAVE TO BE LONELY AGAIN!
YA KNOW, FOR ONCE I FEEL LIKE EVERYTHING REALLY IS GOING TO BE OKAY!
YEP! IT'S ALL PIE AND SODA POP FROM HERE! LET'S GO HOME!

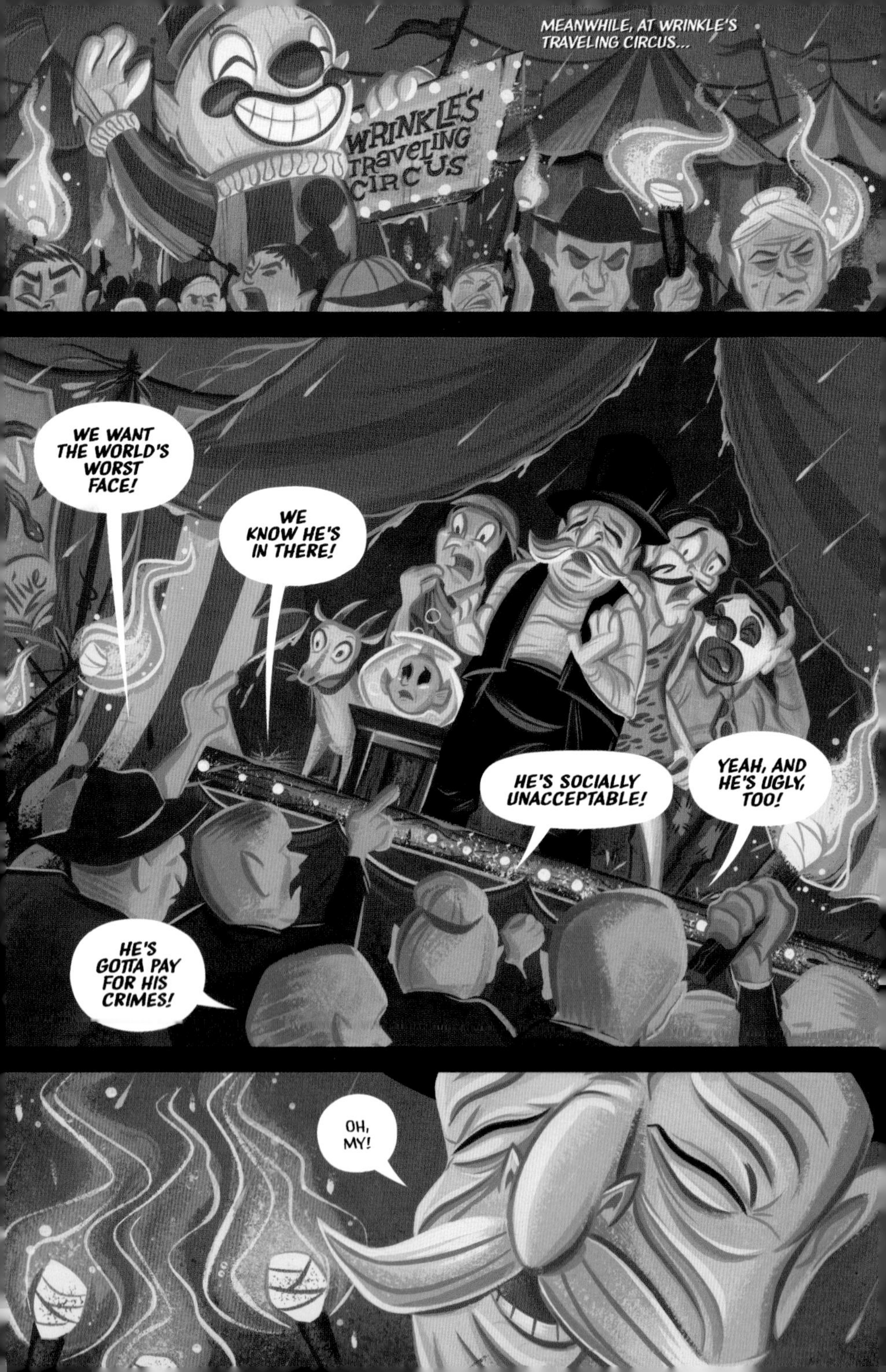
MEANWHILE, AT WRINKLE'S TRAVELING CIRCUS...
WRINKLE'S TRAVELING CIRCUS
WE WANT THE WORLD'S WORST FACE!
WE KNOW HE'S IN THERE!
HE'S SOCIALLY UNACCEPTABLE!
YEAH, AND HE'S UGLY, TOO!
HE'S GOTTA PAY FOR HIS CRIMES!
OH, MY!

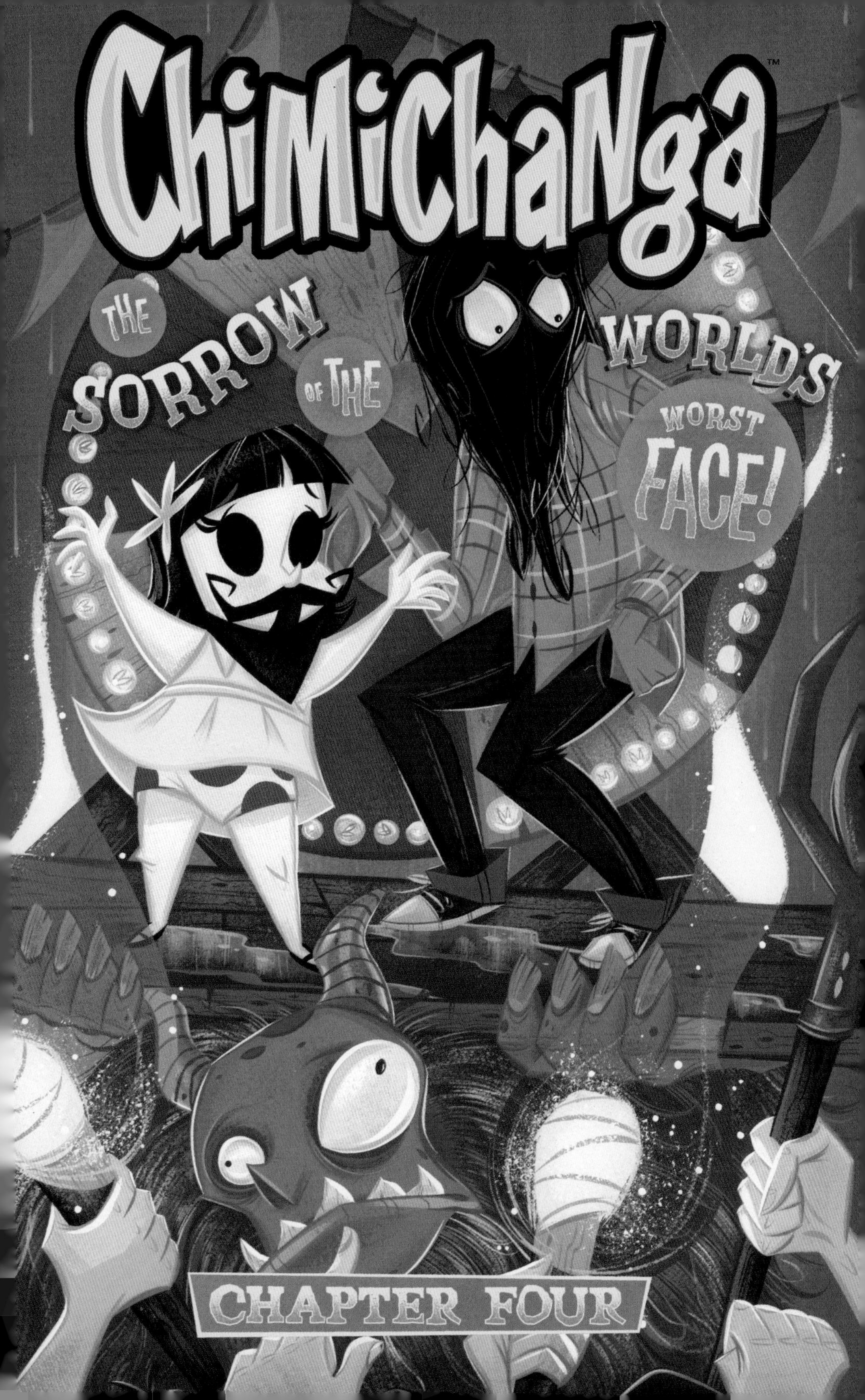
Chimichanga™
THE SORROW OF THE WORLD'S WORST FACE!
CHAPTER FOUR

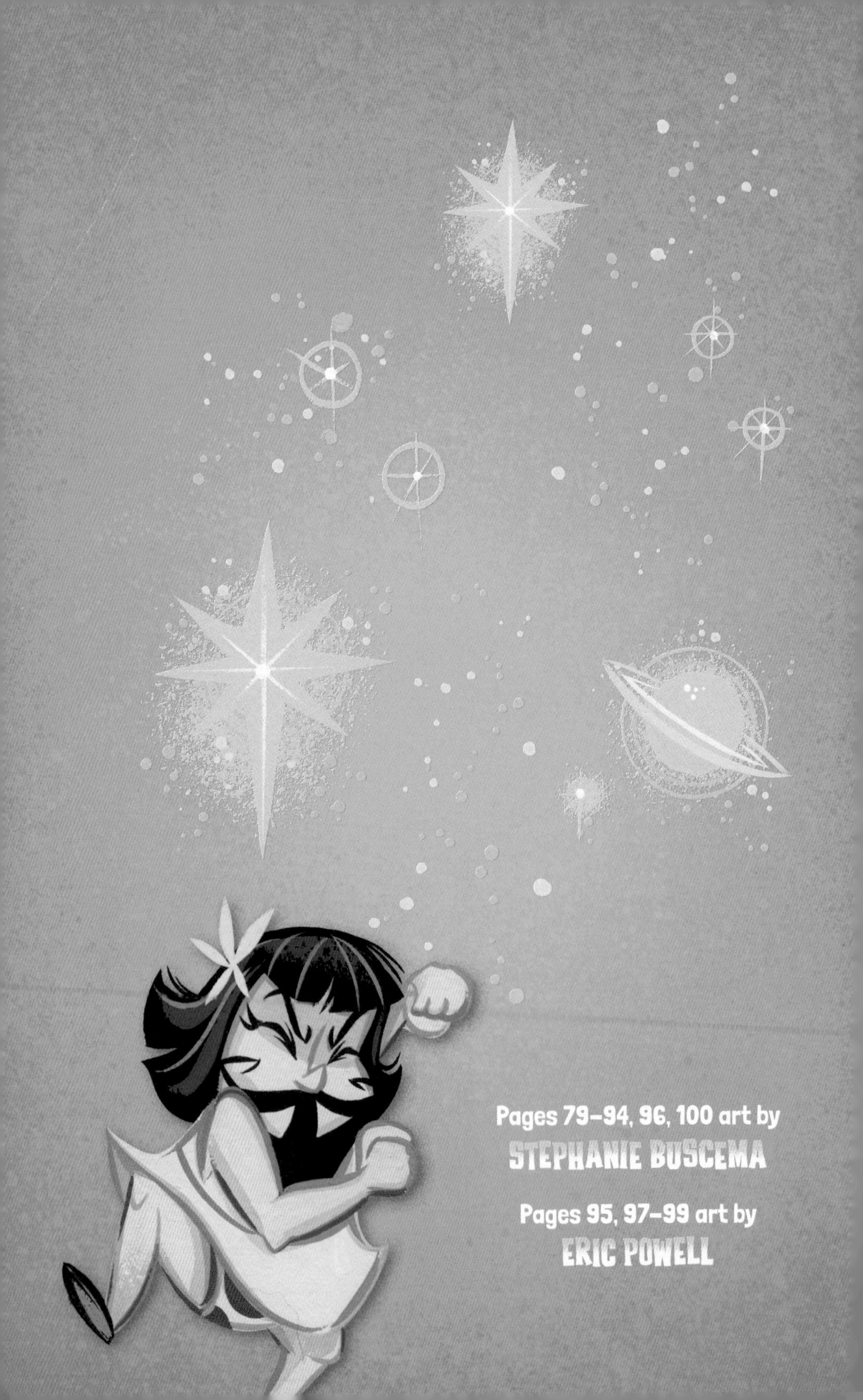

Pages 79–94, 96, 100 art by

STEPHANIE BUSCEMA

Pages 95, 97–99 art by

ERIC POWELL

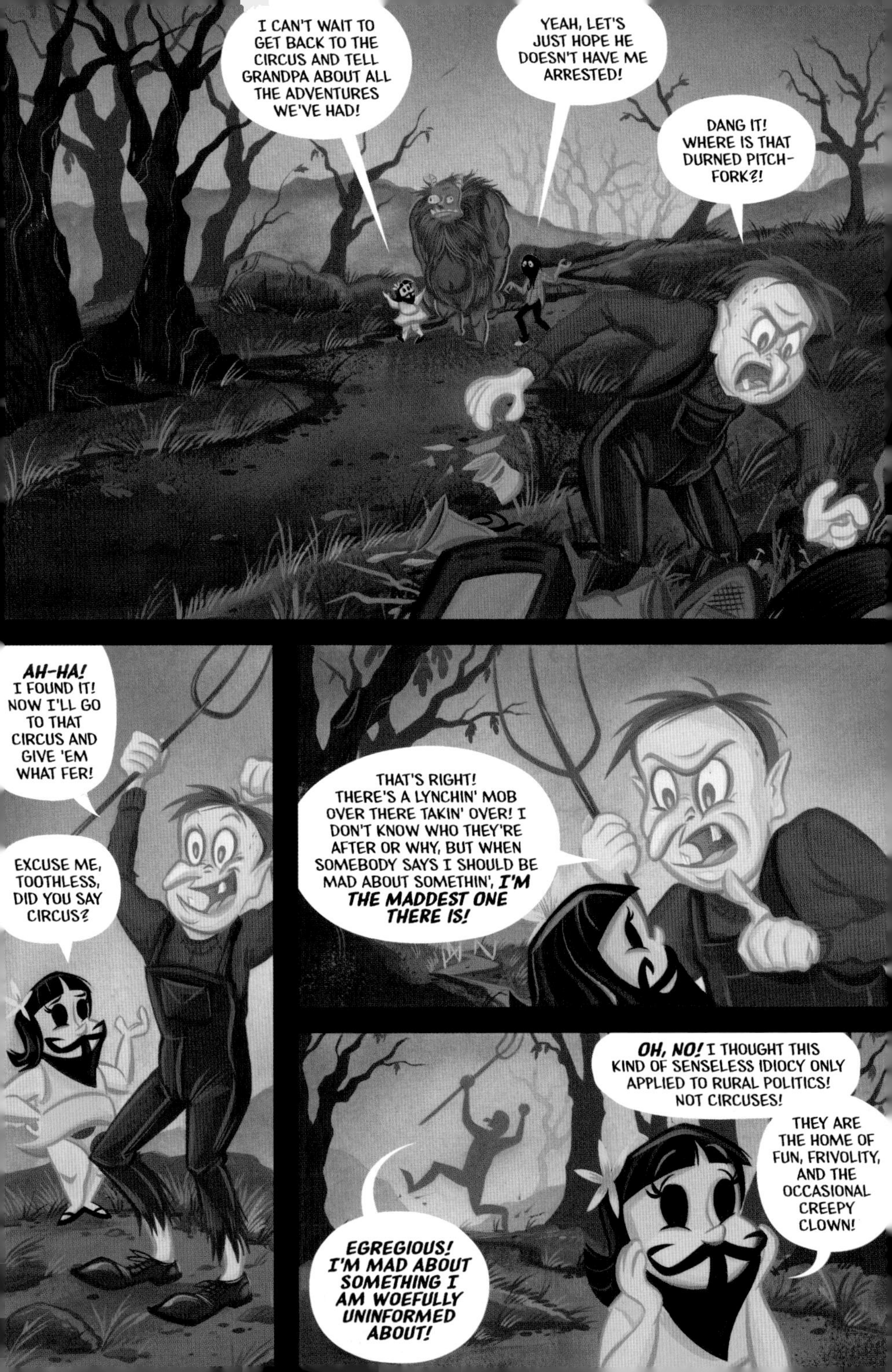
I CAN'T WAIT TO GET BACK TO THE CIRCUS AND TELL GRANDPA ABOUT ALL THE ADVENTURES WE'VE HAD!
YEAH, LET'S JUST HOPE HE DOESN'T HAVE ME ARRESTED!
DANG IT! WHERE IS THAT DURNED PITCH-FORK?!
AH-HA! I FOUND IT! NOW I'LL GO TO THAT CIRCUS AND GIVE 'EM WHAT FER!
EXCUSE ME, TOOTHLESS, DID YOU SAY CIRCUS?
THAT'S RIGHT! THERE'S A LYNCHIN' MOB OVER THERE TAKIN' OVER! I DON'T KNOW WHO THEY'RE AFTER OR WHY, BUT WHEN SOMEBODY SAYS I SHOULD BE MAD ABOUT SOMETHIN', I'M THE MADDEST ONE THERE IS!
OH, NO! I THOUGHT THIS KIND OF SENSELESS IDIOCY ONLY APPLIED TO RURAL POLITICS! NOT CIRCUSES!
THEY ARE THE HOME OF FUN, FRIVOLITY, AND THE OCCASIONAL CREEPY CLOWN!
EGREGIOUS! I'M MAD ABOUT SOMETHING I AM WOEFULLY UNINFORMED ABOUT!

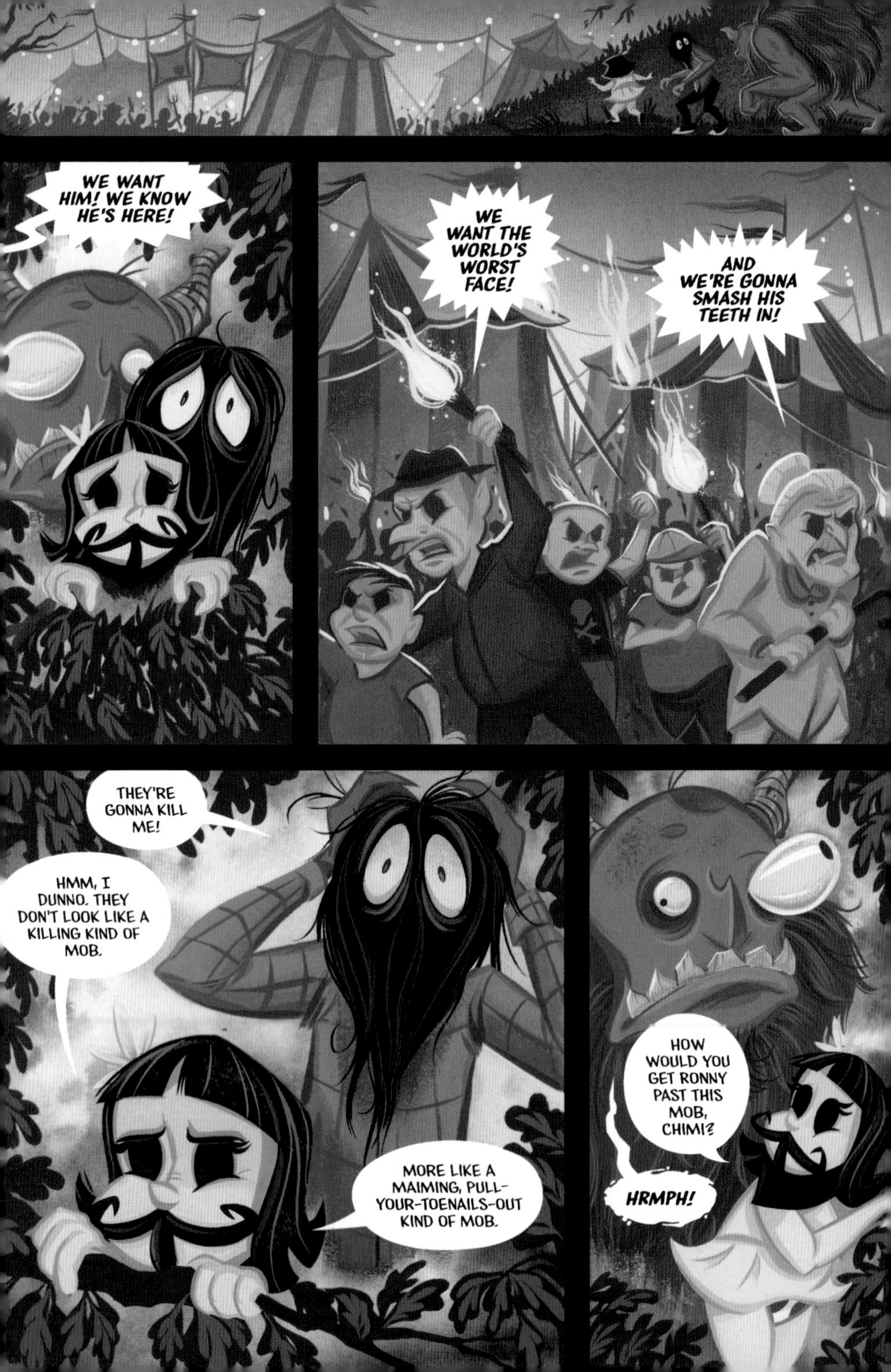
WE WANT HIM! WE KNOW HE'S HERE!
WE WANT THE WORLD'S WORST FACE!
AND WE'RE GONNA SMASH HIS TEETH IN!
THEY'RE GONNA KILL ME!
HMM, I DUNNO. THEY DON'T LOOK LIKE A KILLING KIND OF MOB.
MORE LIKE A MAIMING, PULL-YOUR-TOENAILS-OUT KIND OF MOB.
HOW WOULD YOU GET RONNY PAST THIS MOB, CHIMI?
HRMPH!

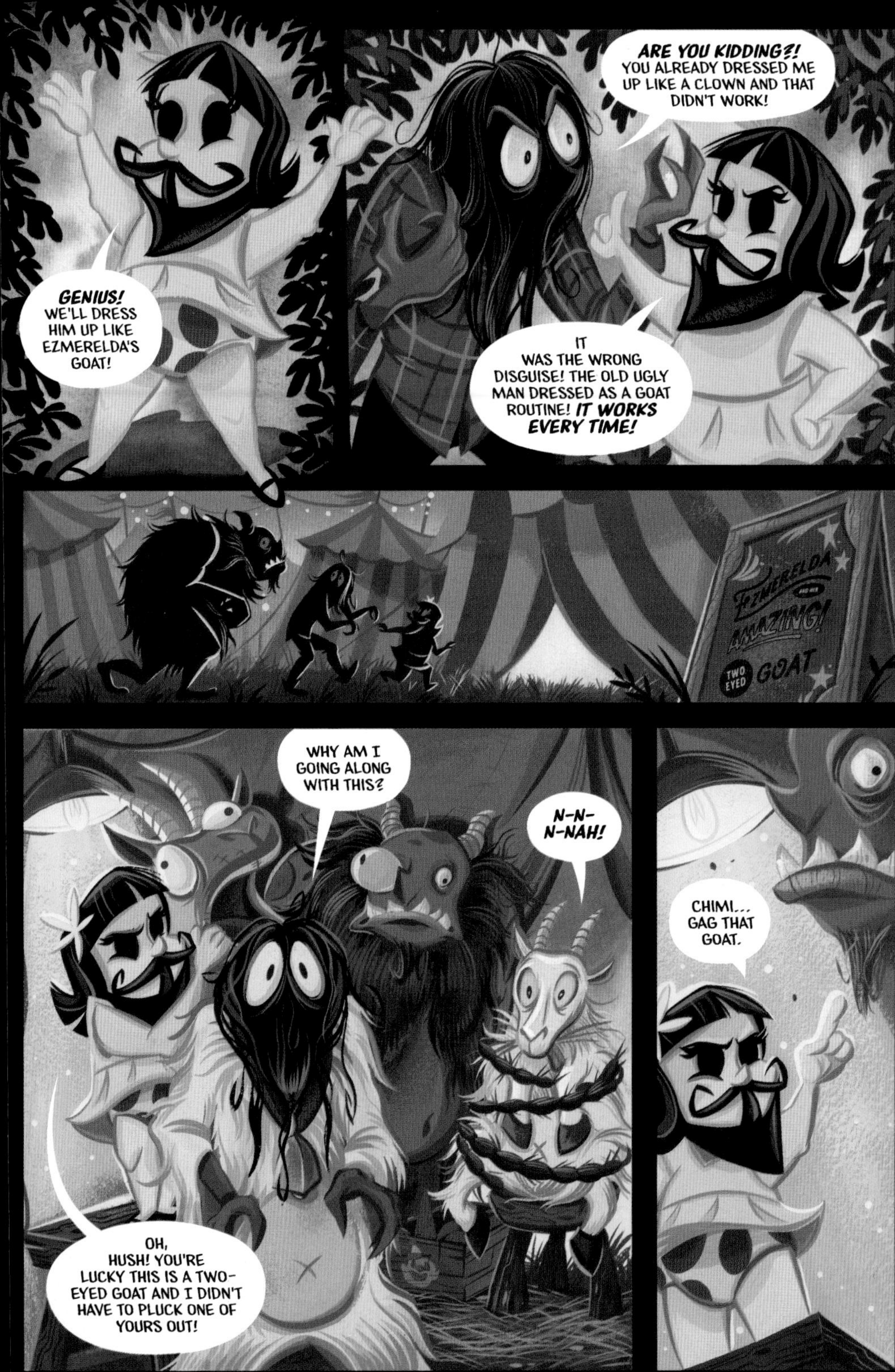
GENIUS! WE'LL DRESS HIM UP LIKE EZMERELDA'S GOAT!
ARE YOU KIDDING?! YOU ALREADY DRESSED ME UP LIKE A CLOWN AND THAT DIDN'T WORK!
IT WAS THE WRONG DISGUISE! THE OLD UGLY MAN DRESSED AS A GOAT ROUTINE! IT WORKS EVERY TIME!
EZMERELDA
AMAZING!
TWO EYED GOAT
WHY AM I GOING ALONG WITH THIS?
N-N-N-NAH!
OH, HUSH! YOU'RE LUCKY THIS IS A TWO-EYED GOAT AND I DIDN'T HAVE TO PLUCK ONE OF YOURS OUT!
CHIMI... GAG THAT GOAT.

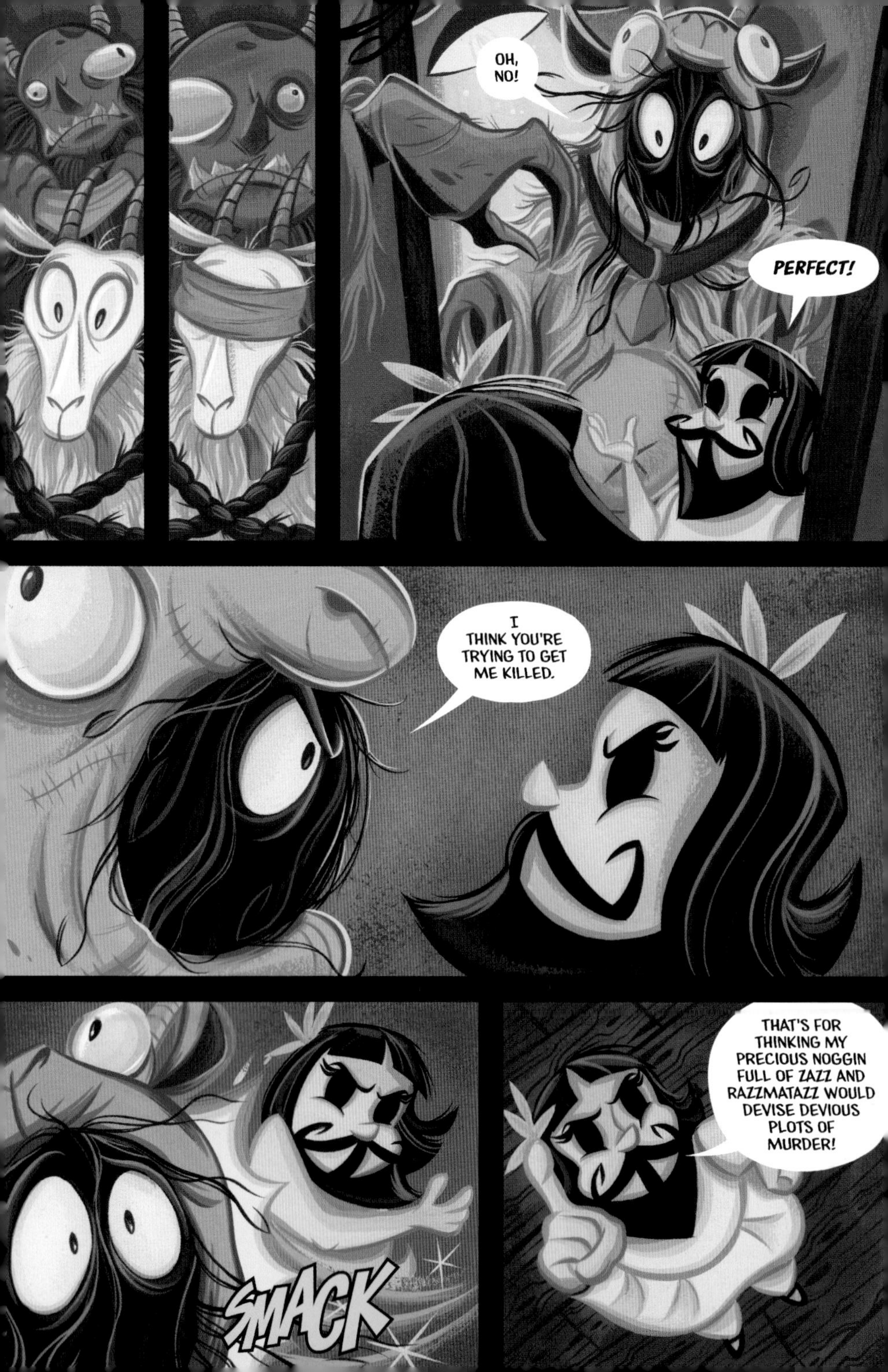
OH, NO!
PERFECT!
I THINK YOU'RE TRYING TO GET ME KILLED.
SMACK
THAT'S FOR THINKING MY PRECIOUS NOGGIN FULL OF ZAZZ AND RAZZMATAZZ WOULD DEVISE DEVIOUS PLOTS OF MURDER!

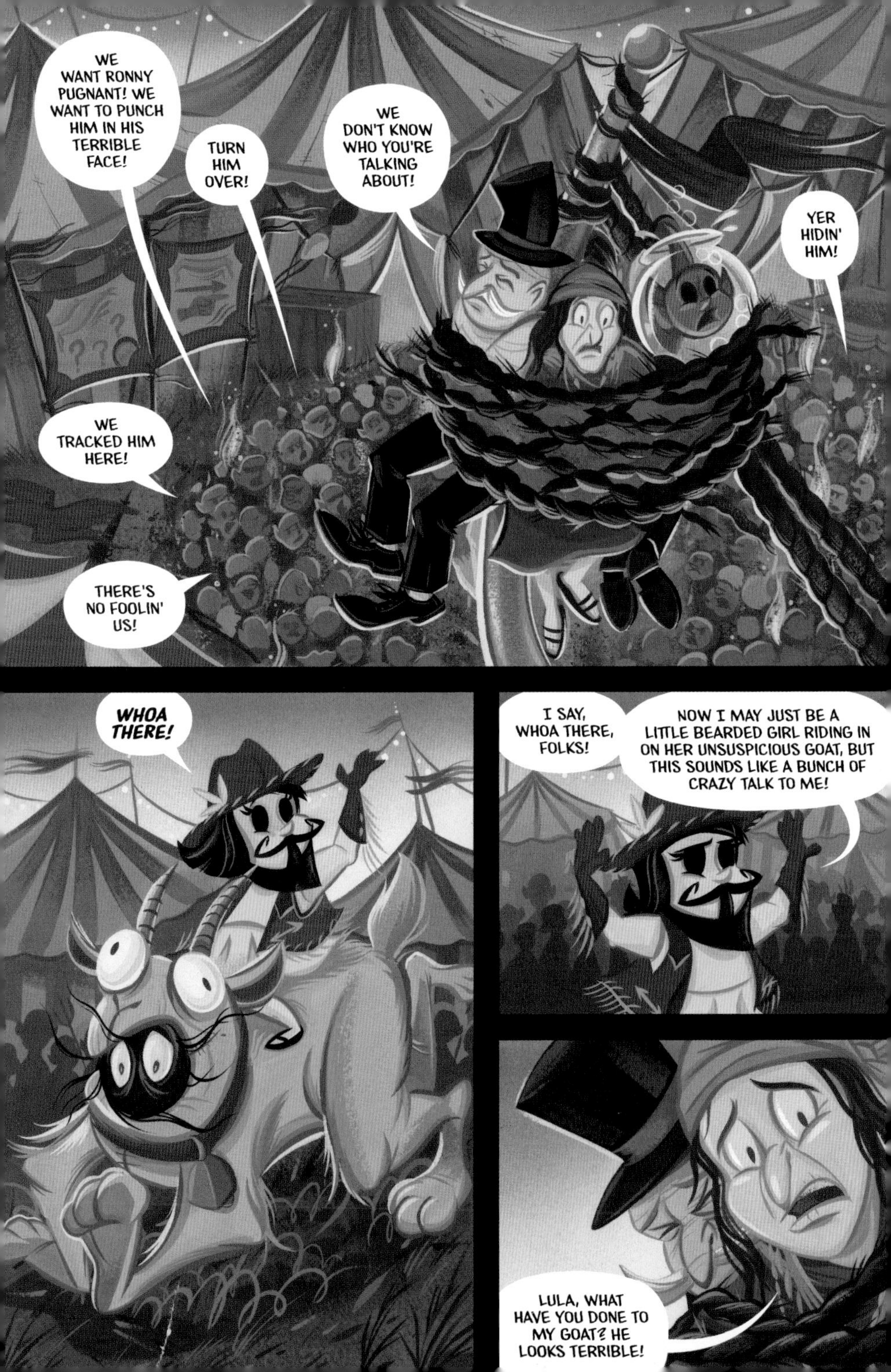
WE WANT RONNY PUGNANT! WE WANT TO PUNCH HIM IN HIS TERRIBLE FACE!
TURN HIM OVER!
WE DON'T KNOW WHO YOU'RE TALKING ABOUT!
YER HIDIN' HIM!
WE TRACKED HIM HERE!
THERE'S NO FOOLIN' US!
WHOA THERE!
I SAY, WHOA THERE, FOLKS!
NOW I MAY JUST BE A LITTLE BEARDED GIRL RIDING IN ON HER UNSUSPICIOUS GOAT, BUT THIS SOUNDS LIKE A BUNCH OF CRAZY TALK TO ME!
LULA, WHAT HAVE YOU DONE TO MY GOAT? HE LOOKS TERRIBLE!

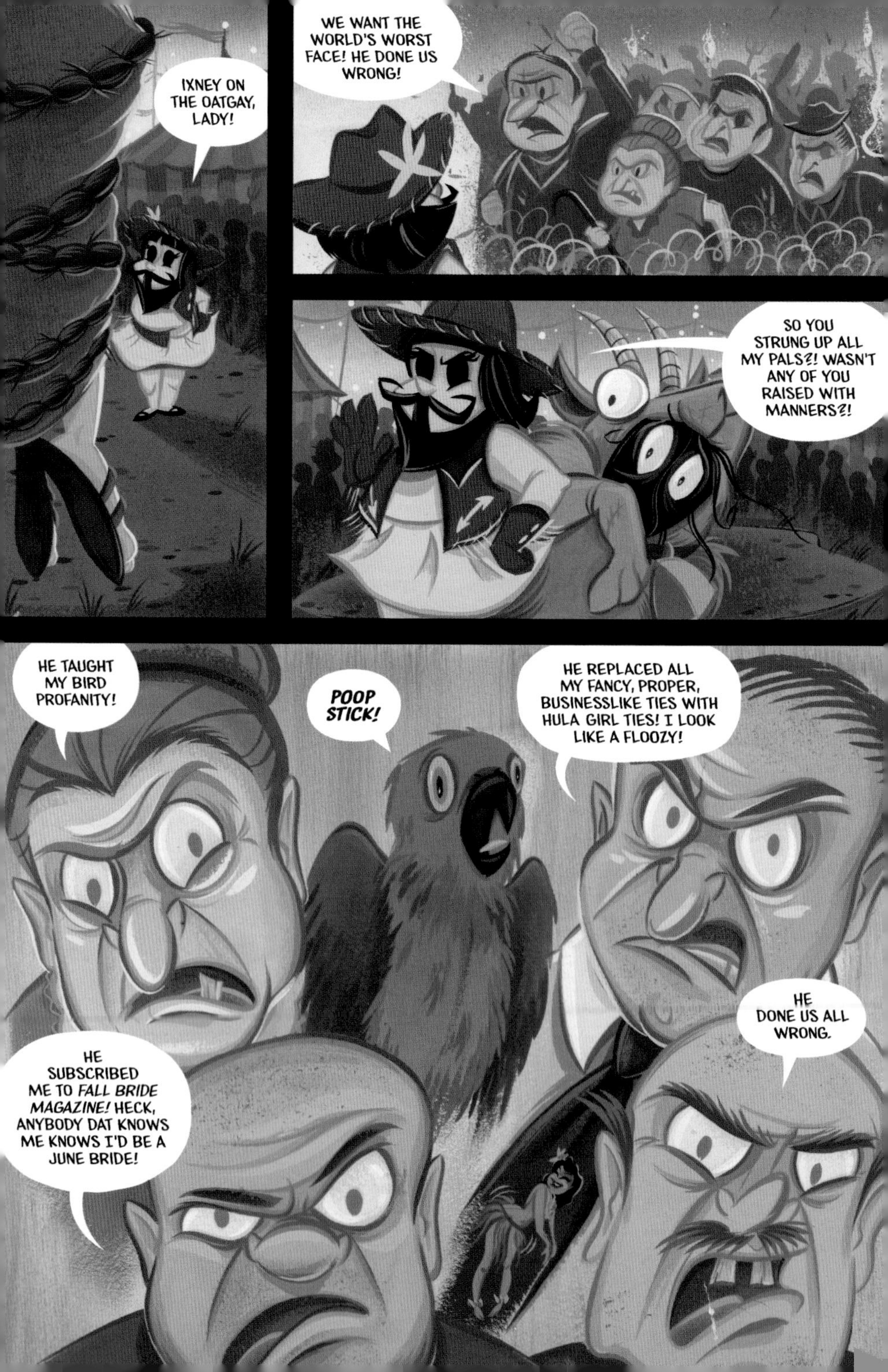
IXNEY ON THE OATGAY, LADY!
WE WANT THE WORLD'S WORST FACE! HE DONE US WRONG!
SO YOU STRUNG UP ALL MY PALS?! WASN'T ANY OF YOU RAISED WITH MANNERS?!
HE TAUGHT MY BIRD PROFANITY!
POOP STICK!
HE REPLACED ALL MY FANCY, PROPER, BUSINESSLIKE TIES WITH HULA GIRL TIES! I LOOK LIKE A FLOOZY!
HE SUBSCRIBED ME TO FALL BRIDE MAGAZINE! HECK, ANYBODY DAT KNOWS ME KNOWS I'D BE A JUNE BRIDE!
HE DONE US ALL WRONG.

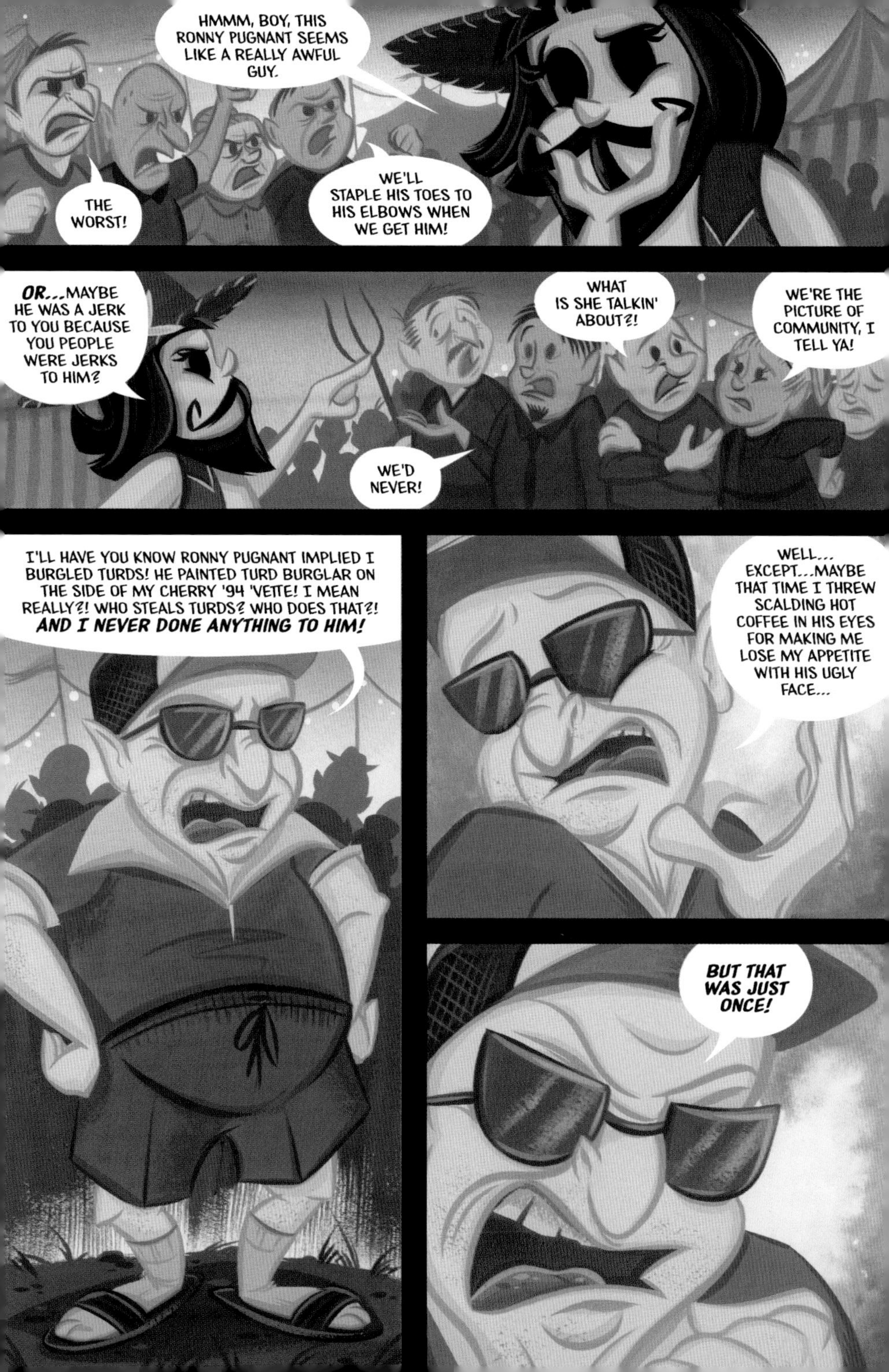
HMMM, BOY, THIS RONNY PUGNANT SEEMS LIKE A REALLY AWFUL GUY.
THE WORST!
WE'LL STAPLE HIS TOES TO HIS ELBOWS WHEN WE GET HIM!
OR...MAYBE HE WAS A JERK TO YOU BECAUSE YOU PEOPLE WERE JERKS TO HIM?
WE'D NEVER!
WHAT IS SHE TALKIN' ABOUT?!
WE'RE THE PICTURE OF COMMUNITY, I TELL YA!
I'LL HAVE YOU KNOW RONNY PUGNANT IMPLIED I BURGLED TURDS! HE PAINTED TURD BURGLAR ON THE SIDE OF MY CHERRY '94 'VETTE! I MEAN REALLY?! WHO STEALS TURDS? WHO DOES THAT?! AND I NEVER DONE ANYTHING TO HIM!
WELL... EXCEPT...MAYBE THAT TIME I THREW SCALDING HOT COFFEE IN HIS EYES FOR MAKING ME LOSE MY APPETITE WITH HIS UGLY FACE...
BUT THAT WAS JUST ONCE!

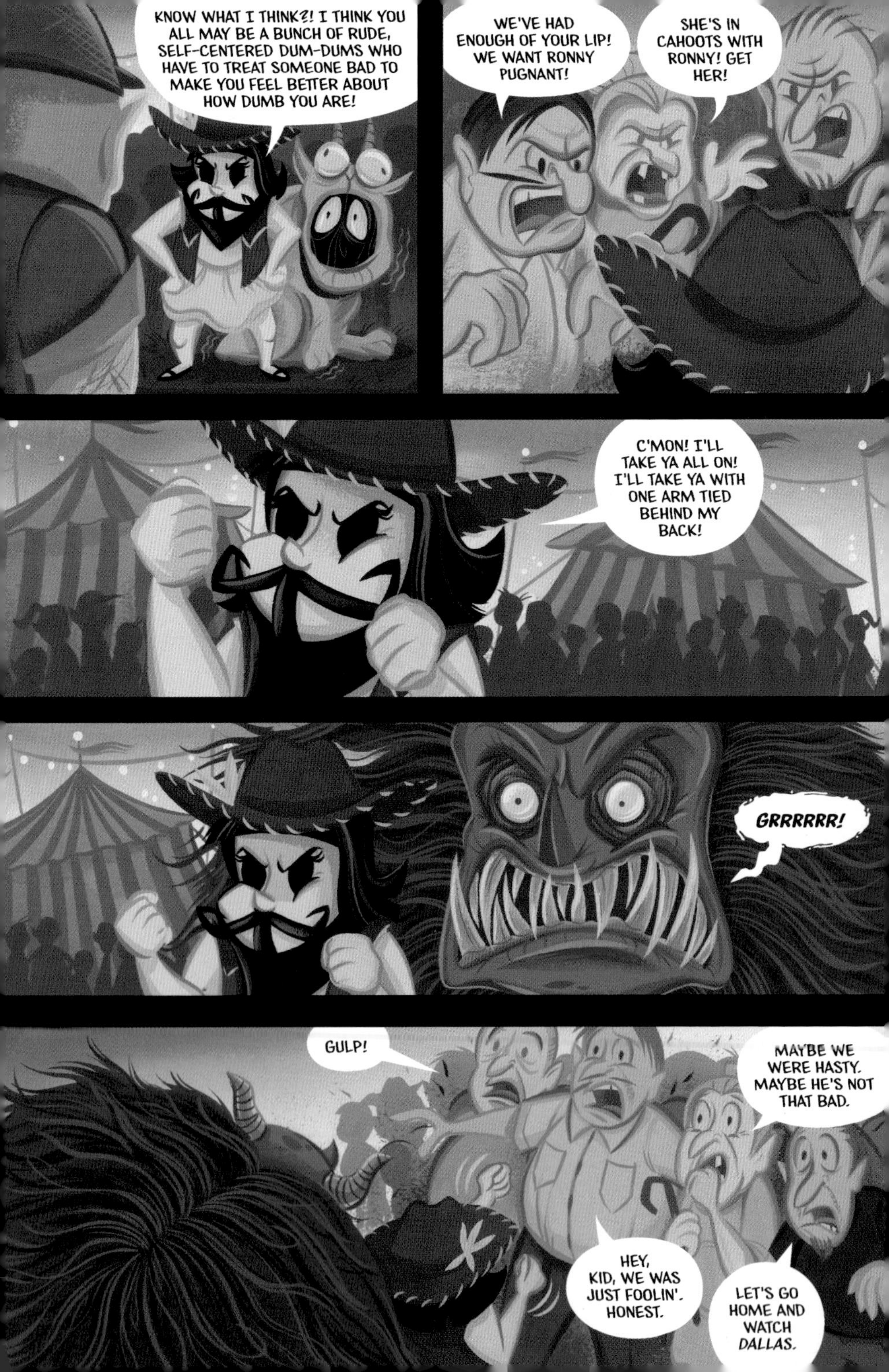
KNOW WHAT I THINK?! I THINK YOU ALL MAY BE A BUNCH OF RUDE, SELF-CENTERED DUM-DUMS WHO HAVE TO TREAT SOMEONE BAD TO MAKE YOU FEEL BETTER ABOUT HOW DUMB YOU ARE!
WE'VE HAD ENOUGH OF YOUR LIP! WE WANT RONNY PUGNANT!
SHE'S IN CAHOOTS WITH RONNY! GET HER!
C'MON! I'LL TAKE YA ALL ON! I'LL TAKE YA WITH ONE ARM TIED BEHIND MY BACK!
GRRRRRR!
GULP!
MAYBE WE WERE HASTY. MAYBE HE'S NOT THAT BAD.
HEY, KID, WE WAS JUST FOOLIN'. HONEST.
LET'S GO HOME AND WATCH *DALLAS*.

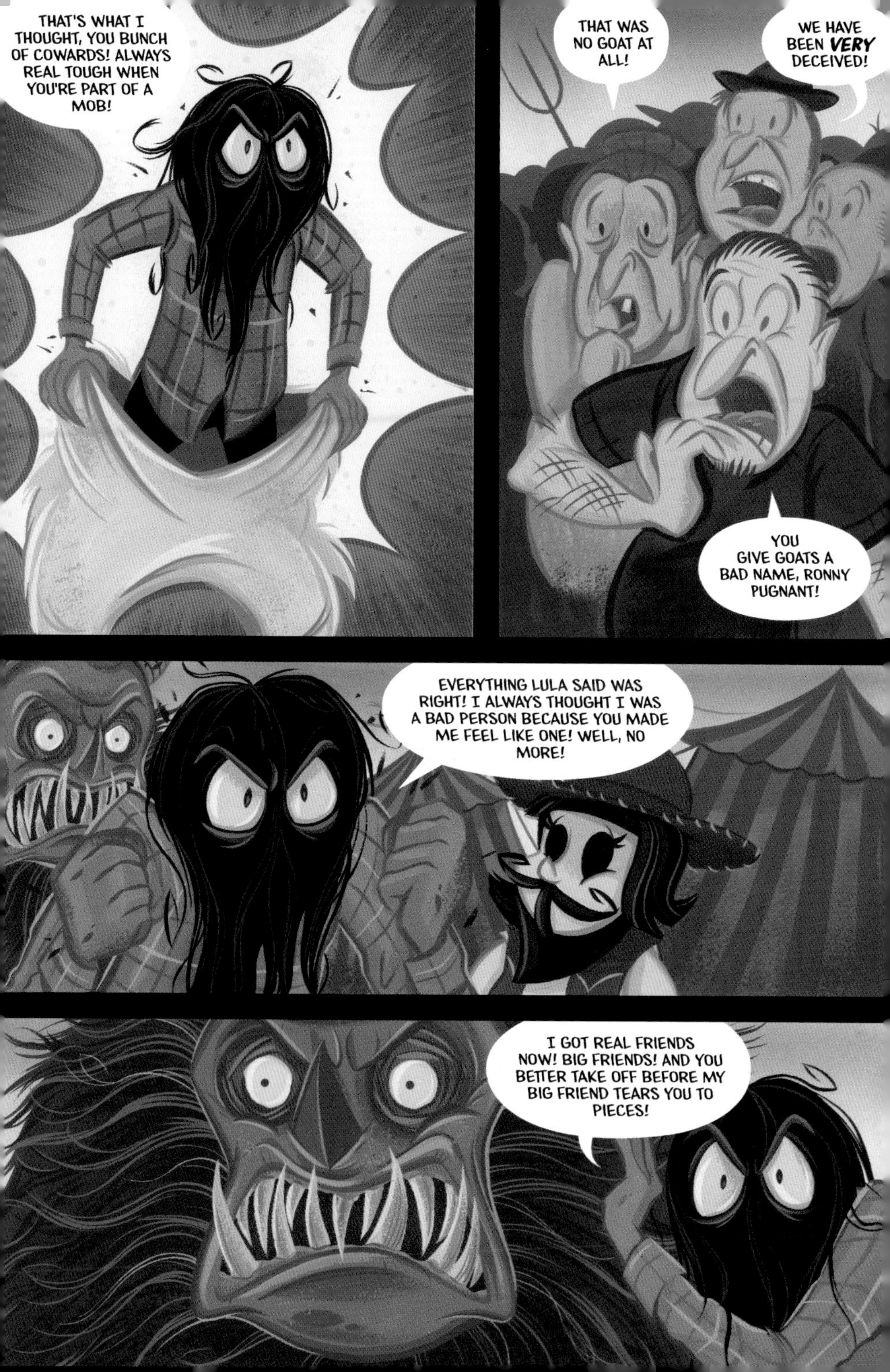
THAT'S WHAT I THOUGHT, YOU BUNCH OF COWARDS! ALWAYS REAL TOUGH WHEN YOU'RE PART OF A MOB!
THAT WAS NO GOAT AT ALL!
WE HAVE BEEN **VERY** DECEIVED!
YOU GIVE GOATS A BAD NAME, RONNY PUGNANT!
EVERYTHING LULA SAID WAS RIGHT! I ALWAYS THOUGHT I WAS A BAD PERSON BECAUSE YOU MADE ME FEEL LIKE ONE! WELL, NO MORE!
I GOT REAL FRIENDS NOW! BIG FRIENDS! AND YOU BETTER TAKE OFF BEFORE MY BIG FRIEND TEARS YOU TO PIECES!

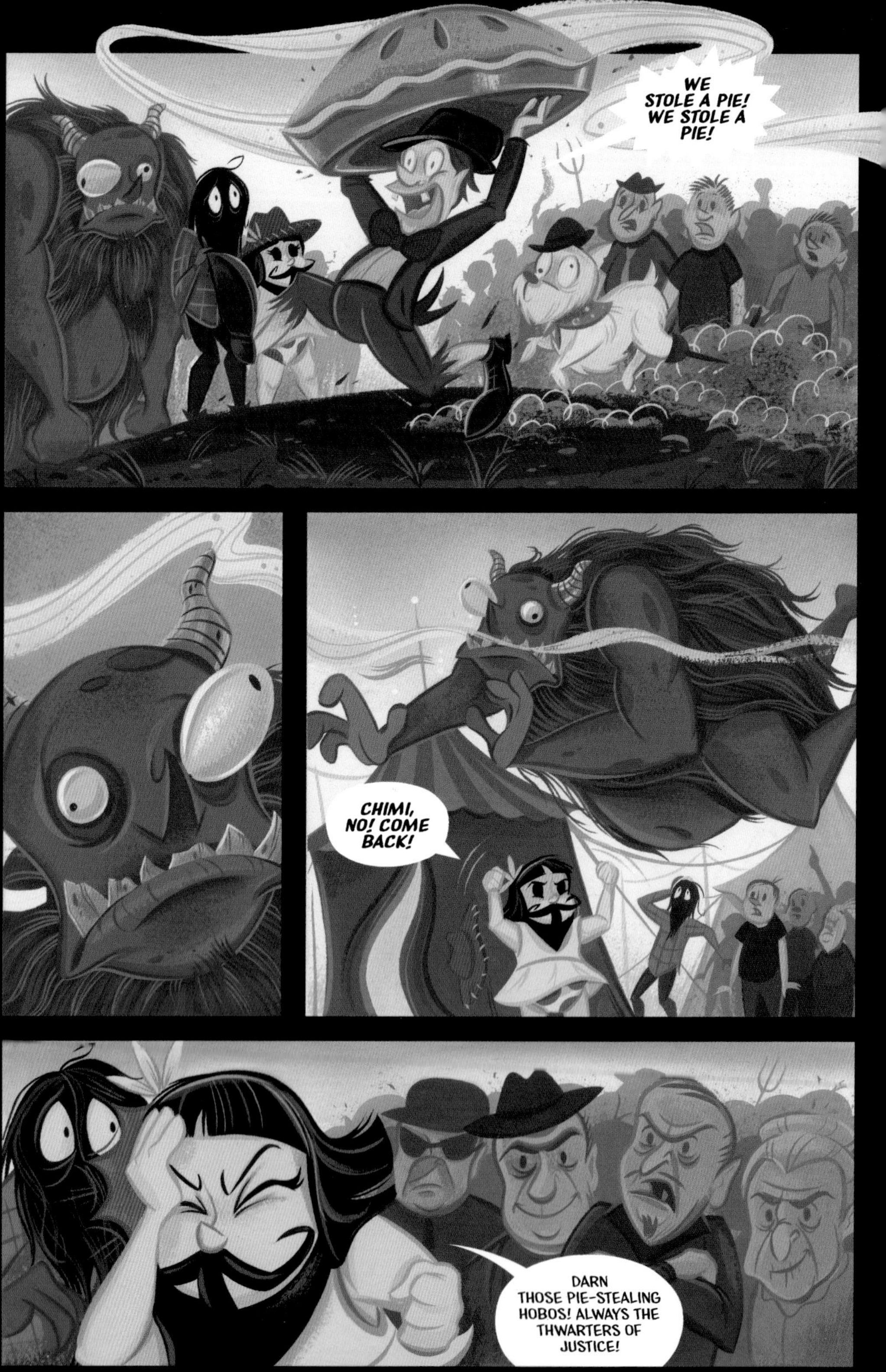
WE STOLE A PIE! WE STOLE A PIE!
CHIMI, NO! COME BACK!
DARN THOSE PIE-STEALING HOBOS! ALWAYS THE THWARTERS OF JUSTICE!

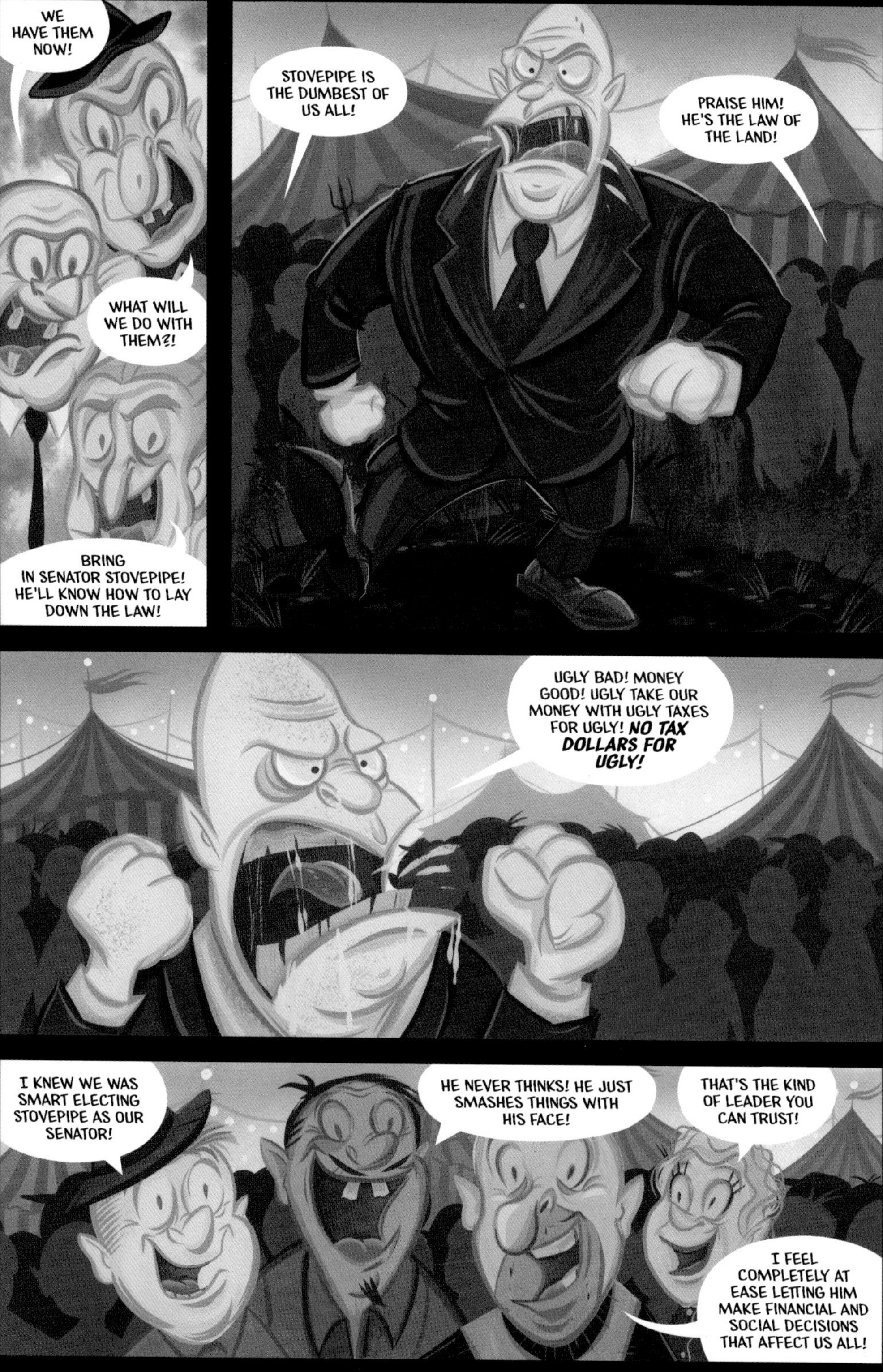
WE HAVE THEM NOW!
WHAT WILL WE DO WITH THEM?!
BRING IN SENATOR STOVEPIPE! HE'LL KNOW HOW TO LAY DOWN THE LAW!
STOVEPIPE IS THE DUMBEST OF US ALL!
PRAISE HIM! HE'S THE LAW OF THE LAND!
UGLY BAD! MONEY GOOD! UGLY TAKE OUR MONEY WITH UGLY TAXES FOR UGLY! ***NO TAX DOLLARS FOR UGLY!***
I KNEW WE WAS SMART ELECTING STOVEPIPE AS OUR SENATOR!
HE NEVER THINKS! HE JUST SMASHES THINGS WITH HIS FACE!
THAT'S THE KIND OF LEADER YOU CAN TRUST!
I FEEL COMPLETELY AT EASE LETTING HIM MAKE FINANCIAL AND SOCIAL DECISIONS THAT AFFECT US ALL!

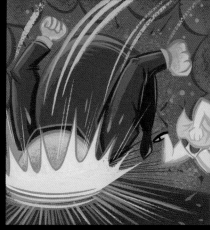

THEY DIFFERENT! NOW I SMASH WITH MY FACE! FREEEEDOM!

OW! THEY GONE! I ONLY HIT FACE ON GROUND!

WE'LL GET 'EM!

SLIPPED AWAY!

THEY CAN'T HAVE GONE FAR!

WE'RE DONE FOR!

WE GOTTA HELP GRANDPA AND THE REST OF THE PERFORMERS!

WHAT ARE YOU TALKING ABOUT?! WE GOTTA GET OUTTA HERE! THAT MOB IS OUT FOR BLOOD!

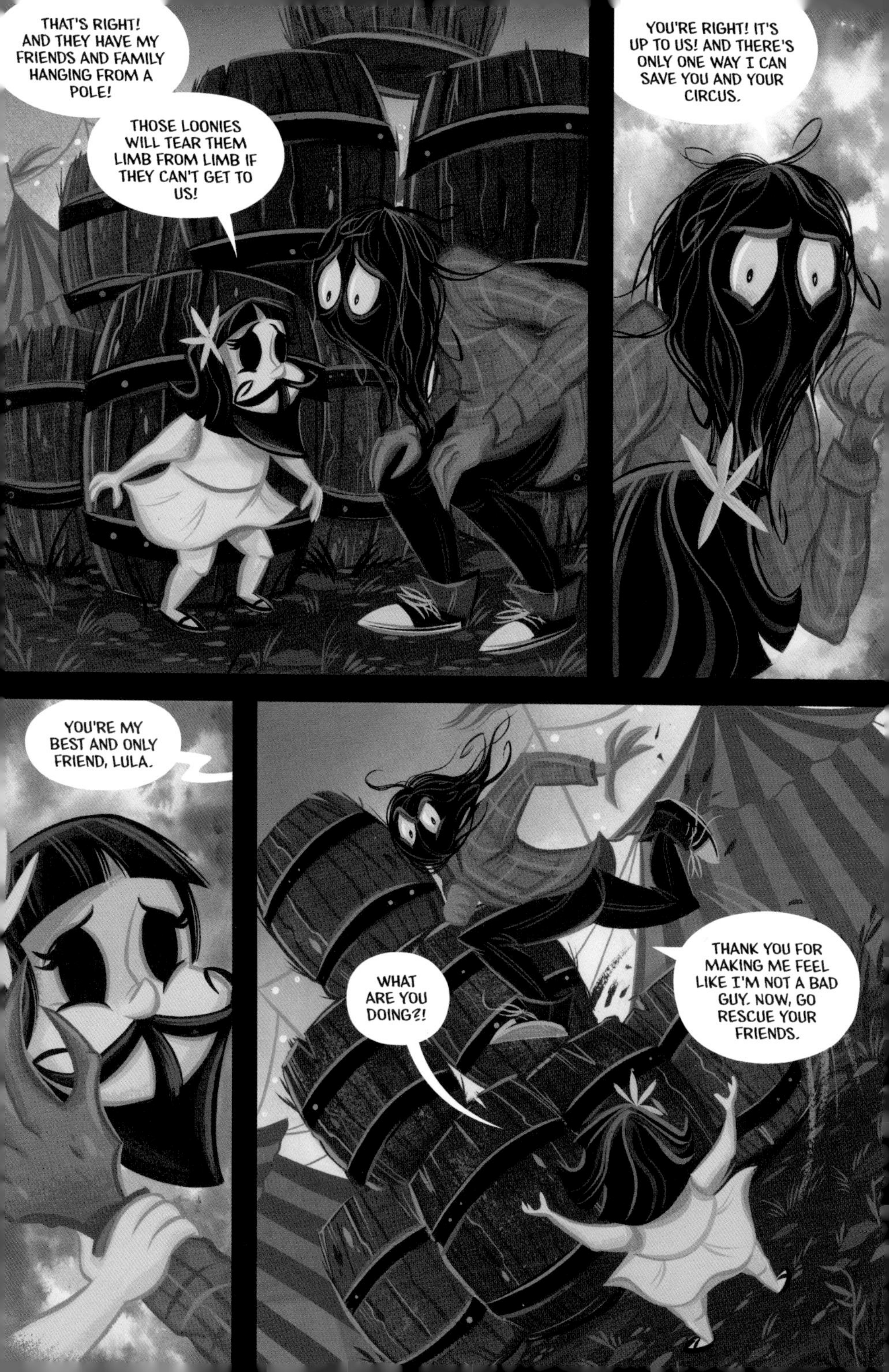
THAT'S RIGHT! AND THEY HAVE MY FRIENDS AND FAMILY HANGING FROM A POLE!
THOSE LOONIES WILL TEAR THEM LIMB FROM LIMB IF THEY CAN'T GET TO US!
YOU'RE RIGHT! IT'S UP TO US! AND THERE'S ONLY ONE WAY I CAN SAVE YOU AND YOUR CIRCUS.
YOU'RE MY BEST AND ONLY FRIEND, LULA.
THANK YOU FOR MAKING ME FEEL LIKE I'M NOT A BAD GUY. NOW, GO RESCUE YOUR FRIENDS.
WHAT ARE YOU DOING?!

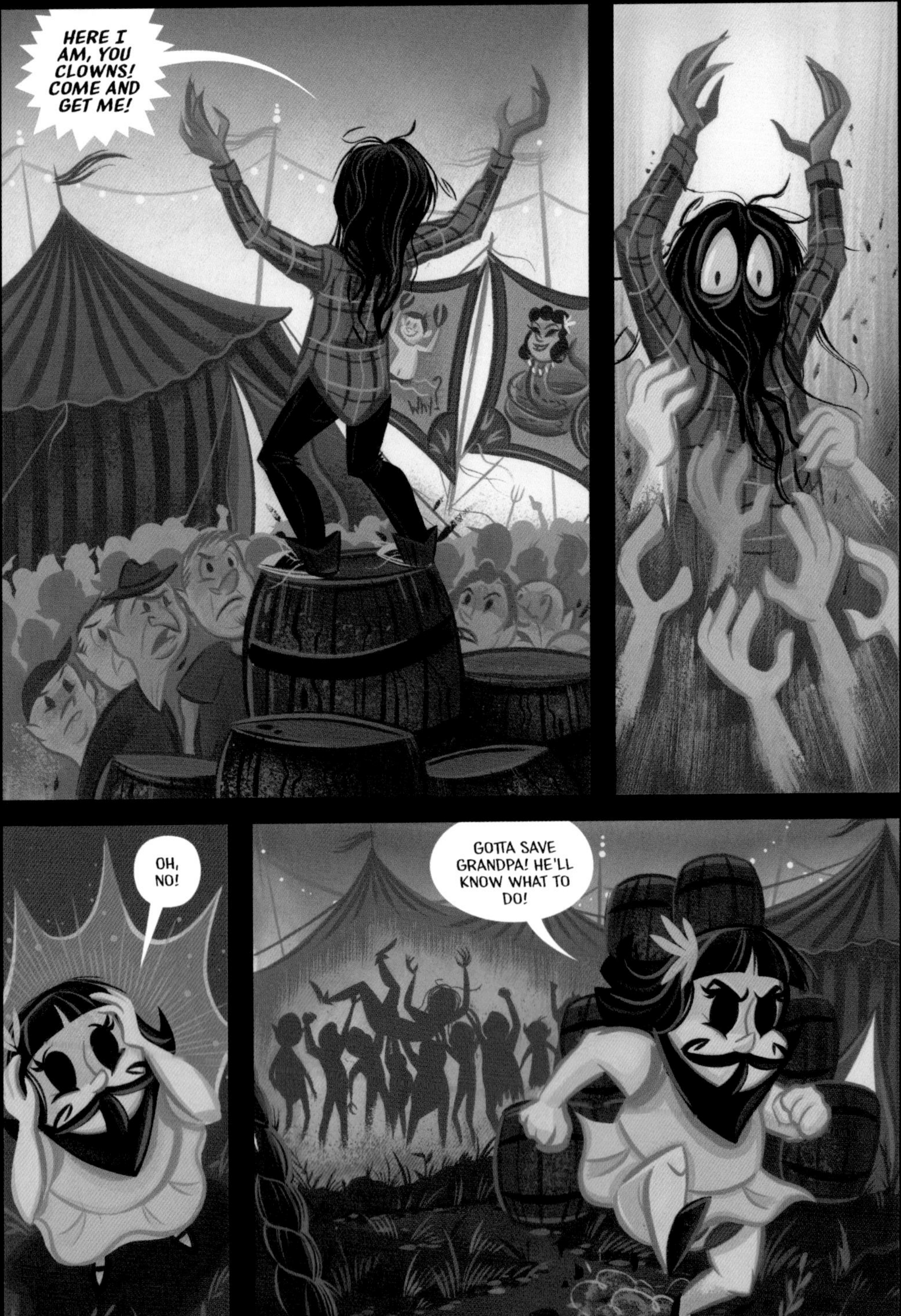
HERE I AM, YOU CLOWNS! COME AND GET ME!
OH, NO!
GOTTA SAVE GRANDPA! HE'LL KNOW WHAT TO DO!

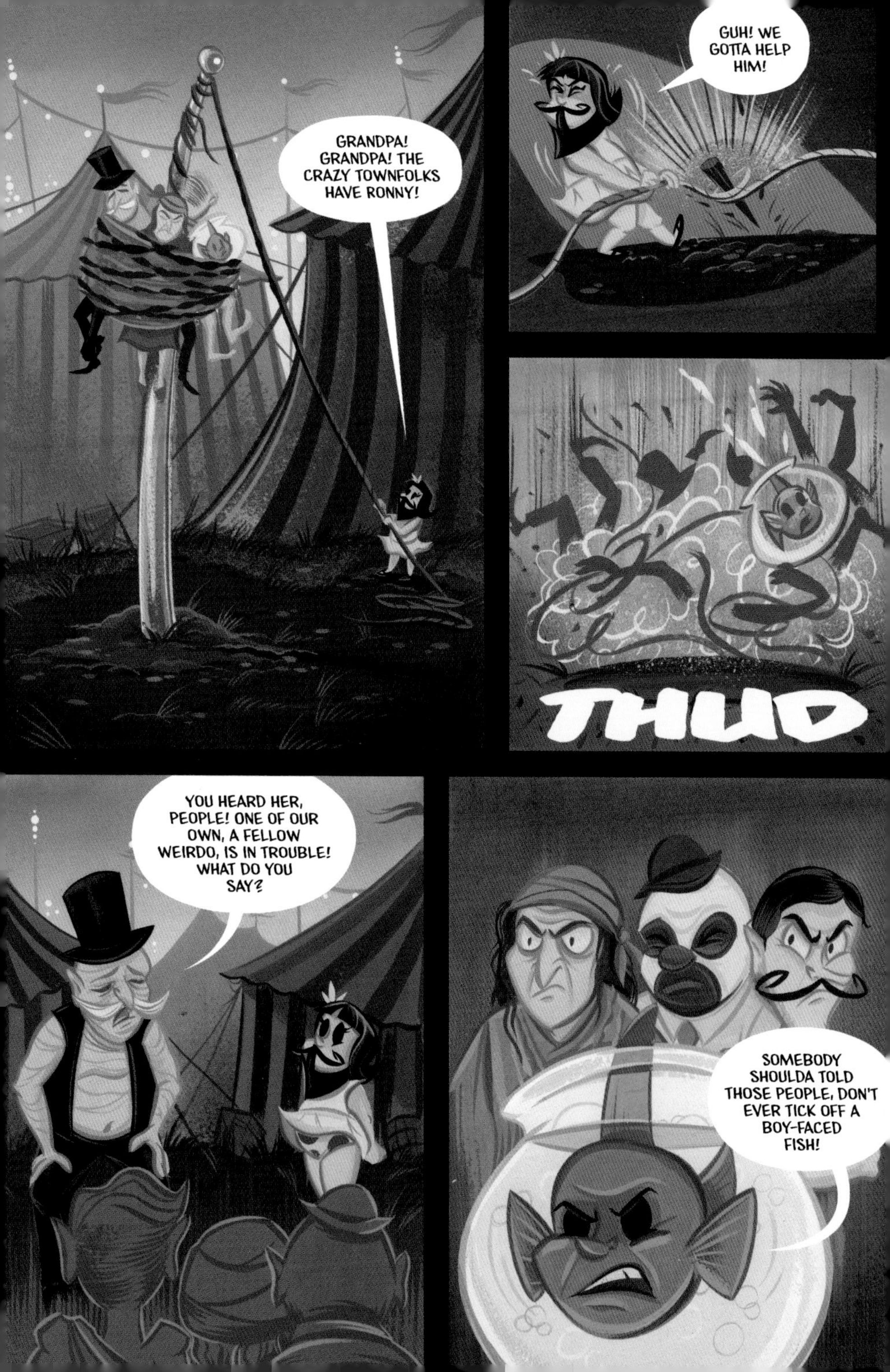
GRANDPA! GRANDPA! THE CRAZY TOWNFOLKS HAVE RONNY!
GUH! WE GOTTA HELP HIM!
THUD
YOU HEARD HER, PEOPLE! ONE OF OUR OWN, A FELLOW WEIRDO, IS IN TROUBLE! WHAT DO YOU SAY?
SOMEBODY SHOULDA TOLD THOSE PEOPLE, DON'T EVER TICK OFF A BOY-FACED FISH!

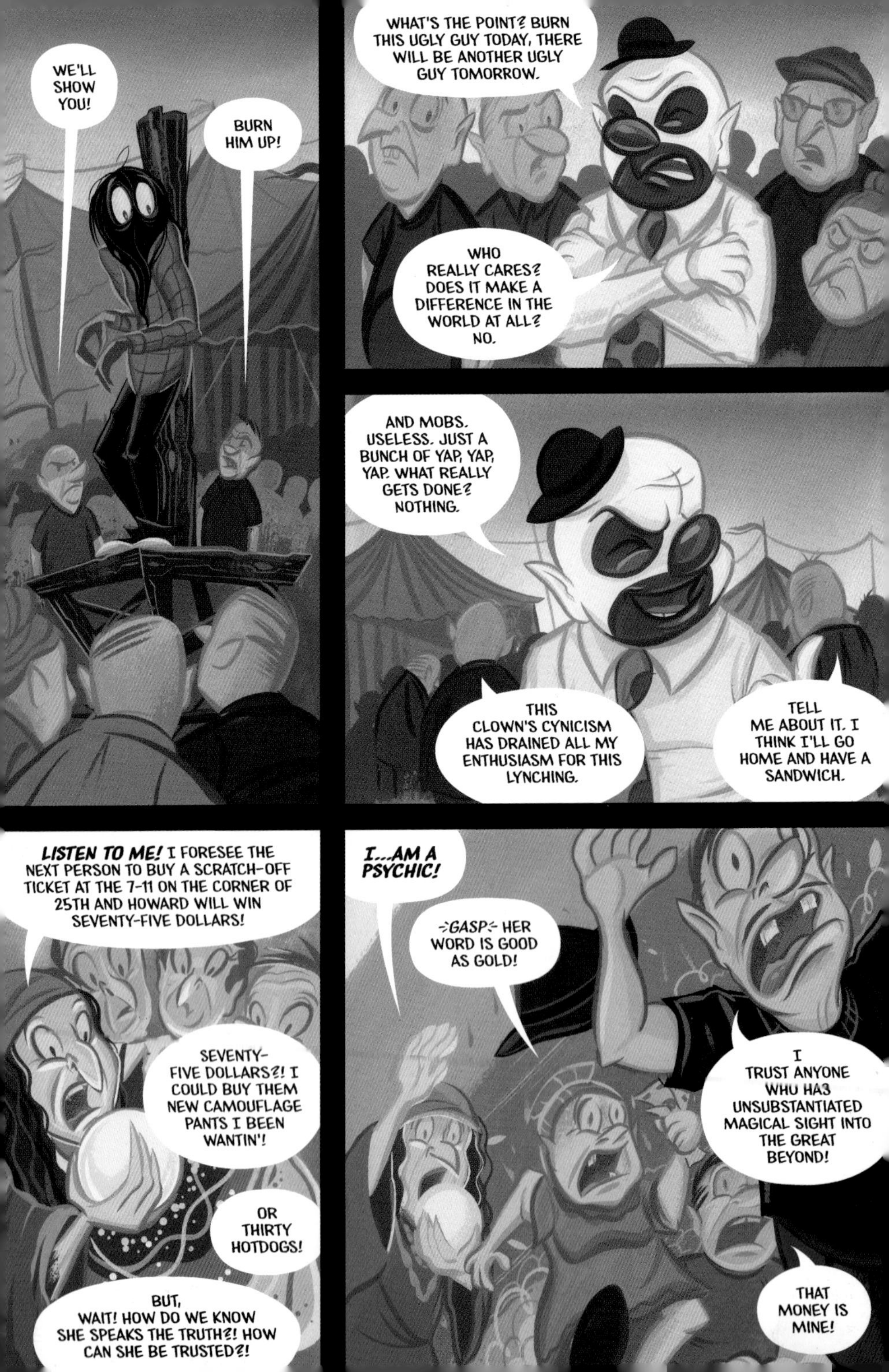

WE'LL SHOW YOU!
BURN HIM UP!
WHAT'S THE POINT? BURN THIS UGLY GUY TODAY, THERE WILL BE ANOTHER UGLY GUY TOMORROW.
WHO REALLY CARES? DOES IT MAKE A DIFFERENCE IN THE WORLD AT ALL? NO.
AND MOBS. USELESS. JUST A BUNCH OF YAP, YAP, YAP. WHAT REALLY GETS DONE? NOTHING.
THIS CLOWN'S CYNICISM HAS DRAINED ALL MY ENTHUSIASM FOR THIS LYNCHING.
TELL ME ABOUT IT. I THINK I'LL GO HOME AND HAVE A SANDWICH.
LISTEN TO ME! I FORESEE THE NEXT PERSON TO BUY A SCRATCH-OFF TICKET AT THE 7-11 ON THE CORNER OF 25TH AND HOWARD WILL WIN SEVENTY-FIVE DOLLARS!
SEVENTY-FIVE DOLLARS?! I COULD BUY THEM NEW CAMOUFLAGE PANTS I BEEN WANTIN'!
OR THIRTY HOTDOGS!
BUT, WAIT! HOW DO WE KNOW SHE SPEAKS THE TRUTH?! HOW CAN SHE BE TRUSTED?!
I...AM A PSYCHIC!
-GASP- HER WORD IS GOOD AS GOLD!
I TRUST ANYONE WHO HAS UNSUBSTANTIATED MAGICAL SIGHT INTO THE GREAT BEYOND!
THAT MONEY IS MINE!

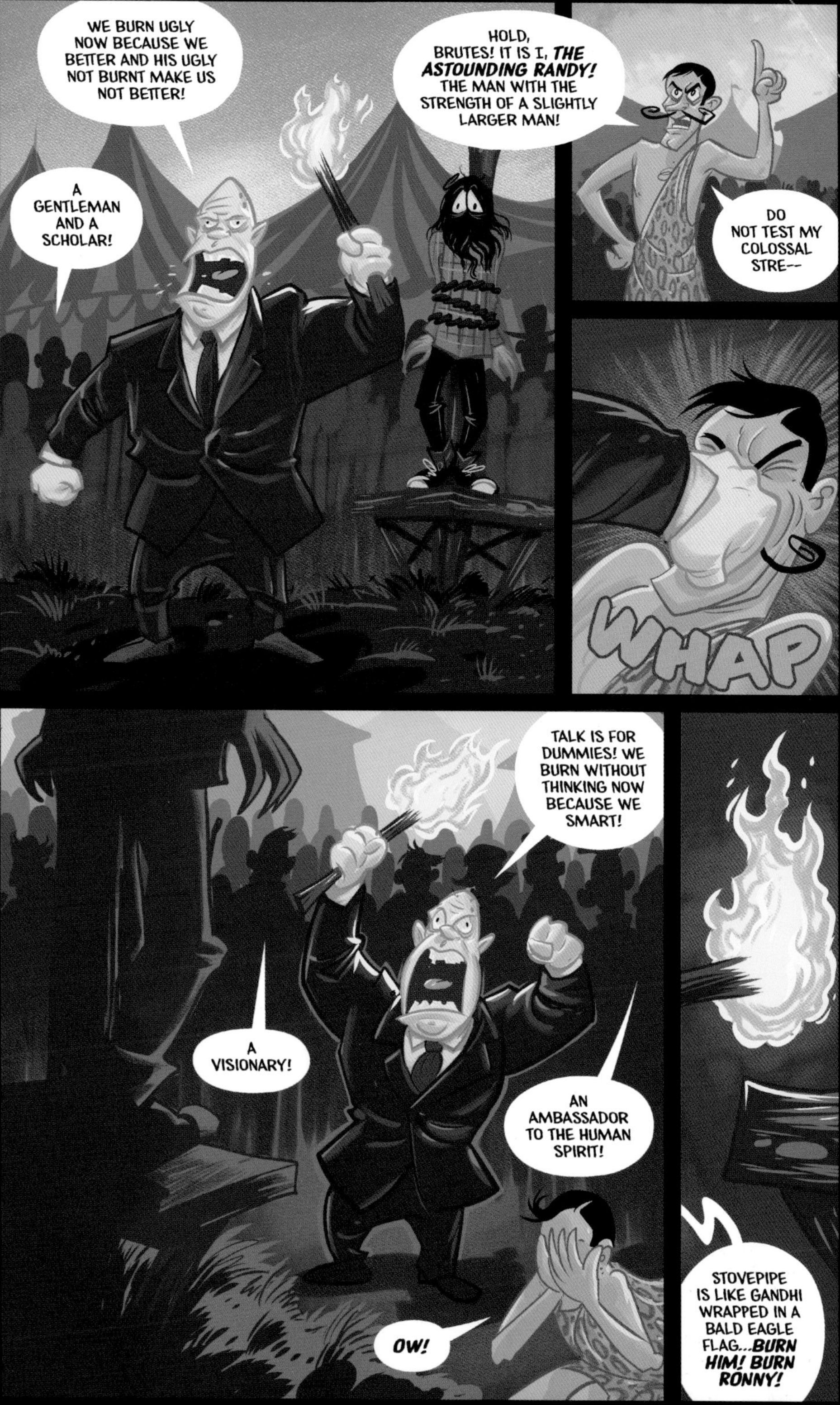
WE BURN UGLY NOW BECAUSE WE BETTER AND HIS UGLY NOT BURNT MAKE US NOT BETTER!
A GENTLEMAN AND A SCHOLAR!
HOLD, BRUTES! IT IS I, THE ASTOUNDING RANDY! THE MAN WITH THE STRENGTH OF A SLIGHTLY LARGER MAN!
DO NOT TEST MY COLOSSAL STRE--
WHAP
TALK IS FOR DUMMIES! WE BURN WITHOUT THINKING NOW BECAUSE WE SMART!
A VISIONARY!
AN AMBASSADOR TO THE HUMAN SPIRIT!
OW!
STOVEPIPE IS LIKE GANDHI WRAPPED IN A BALD EAGLE FLAG...BURN HIM! BURN RONNY!

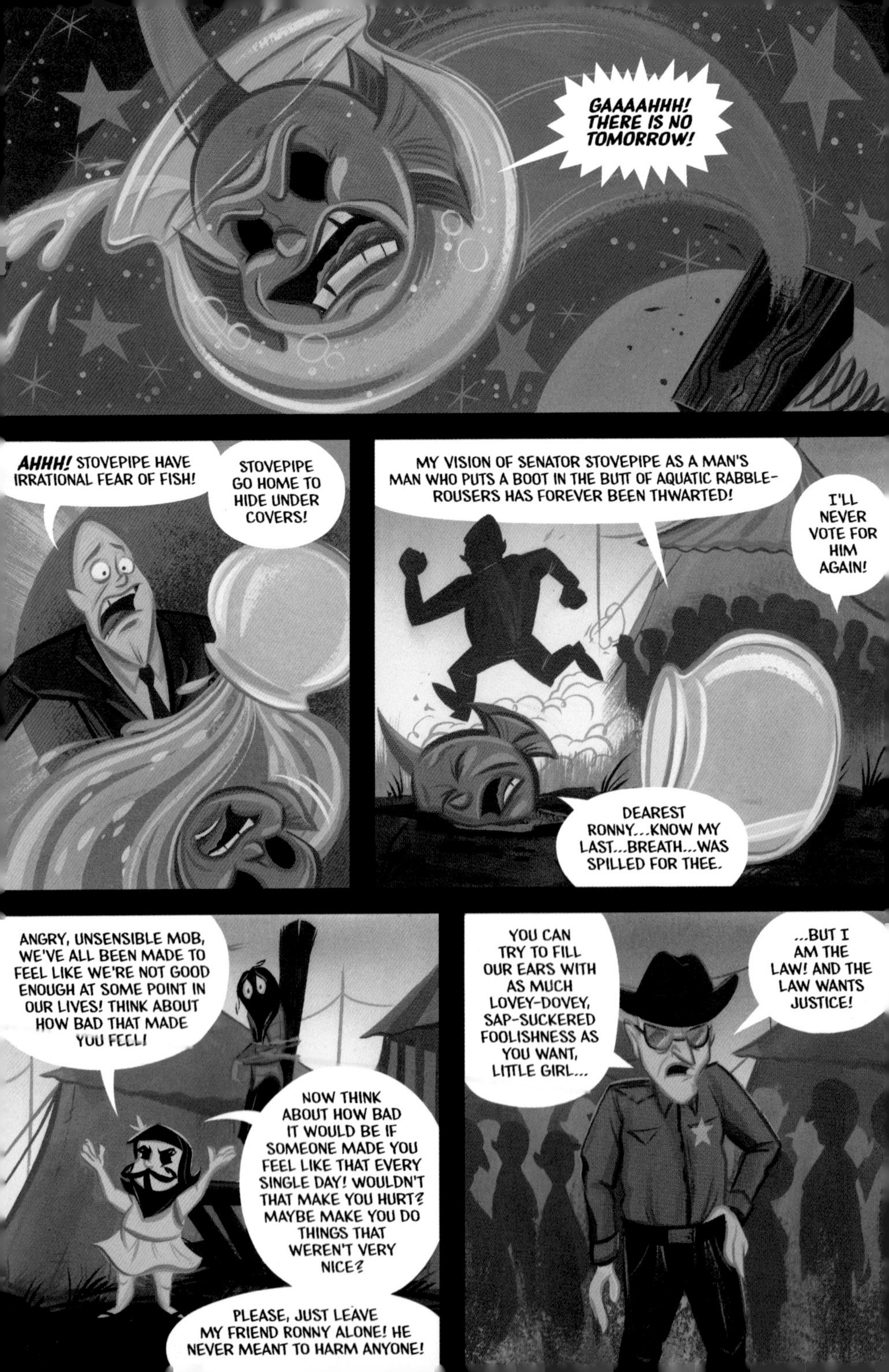
GAAAAHHH! THERE IS NO TOMORROW!
AHHH! STOVEPIPE HAVE IRRATIONAL FEAR OF FISH!
STOVEPIPE GO HOME TO HIDE UNDER COVERS!
MY VISION OF SENATOR STOVEPIPE AS A MAN'S MAN WHO PUTS A BOOT IN THE BUTT OF AQUATIC RABBLE-ROUSERS HAS FOREVER BEEN THWARTED!
I'LL NEVER VOTE FOR HIM AGAIN!
DEAREST RONNY... KNOW MY LAST... BREATH... WAS SPILLED FOR THEE.
ANGRY, UNSENSIBLE MOB, WE'VE ALL BEEN MADE TO FEEL LIKE WE'RE NOT GOOD ENOUGH AT SOME POINT IN OUR LIVES! THINK ABOUT HOW BAD THAT MADE YOU FEEL!
NOW THINK ABOUT HOW BAD IT WOULD BE IF SOMEONE MADE YOU FEEL LIKE THAT EVERY SINGLE DAY! WOULDN'T THAT MAKE YOU HURT? MAYBE MAKE YOU DO THINGS THAT WEREN'T VERY NICE?
PLEASE, JUST LEAVE MY FRIEND RONNY ALONE! HE NEVER MEANT TO HARM ANYONE!
YOU CAN TRY TO FILL OUR EARS WITH AS MUCH LOVEY-DOVEY, SAP-SUCKERED FOOLISHNESS AS YOU WANT, LITTLE GIRL...
...BUT I AM THE LAW! AND THE LAW WANTS JUSTICE!

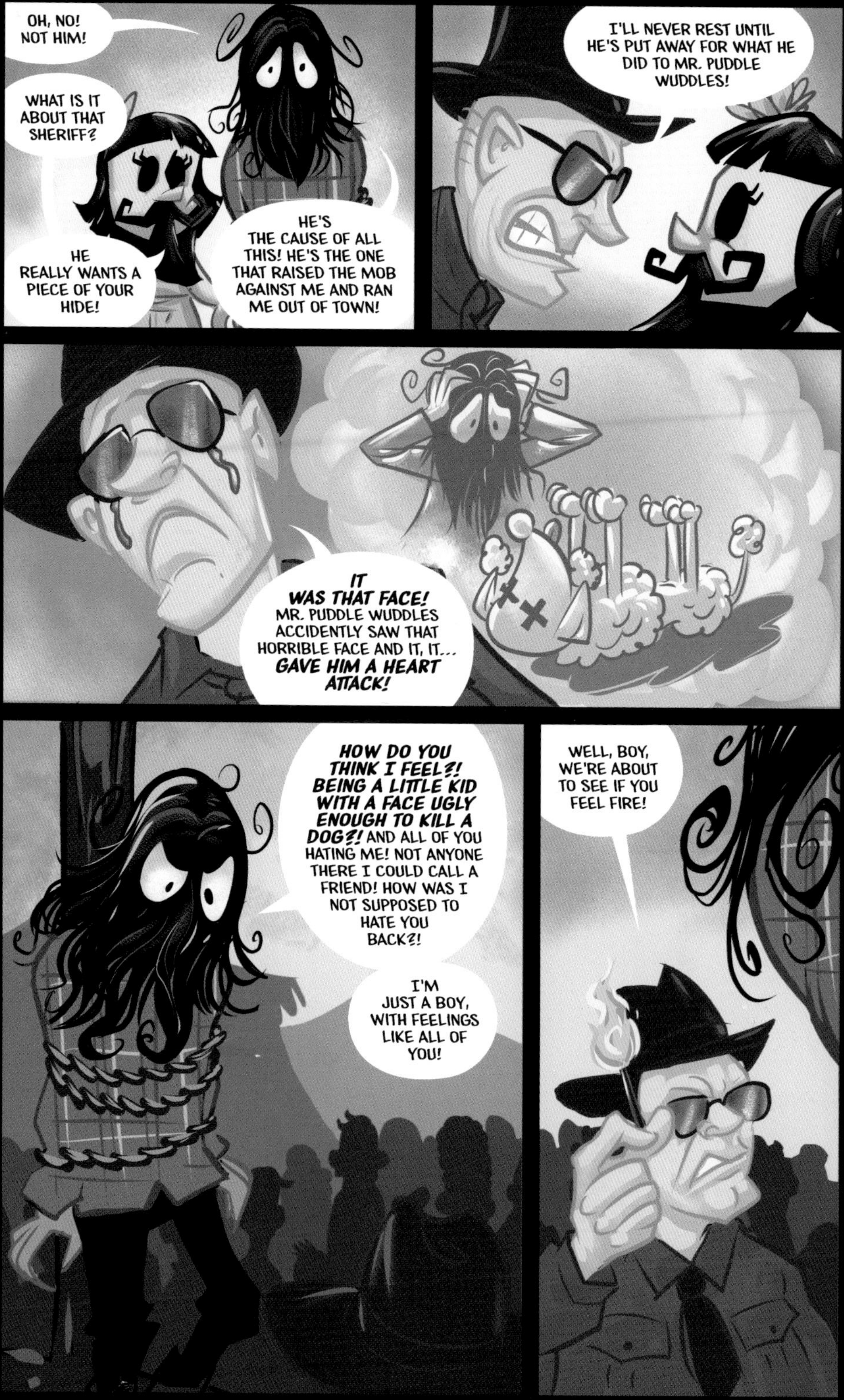
OH, NO! NOT HIM!
WHAT IS IT ABOUT THAT SHERIFF?
HE REALLY WANTS A PIECE OF YOUR HIDE!
HE'S THE CAUSE OF ALL THIS! HE'S THE ONE THAT RAISED THE MOB AGAINST ME AND RAN ME OUT OF TOWN!
I'LL NEVER REST UNTIL HE'S PUT AWAY FOR WHAT HE DID TO MR. PUDDLE WUDDLES!
IT WAS THAT FACE! MR. PUDDLE WUDDLES ACCIDENTLY SAW THAT HORRIBLE FACE AND IT, IT... GAVE HIM A HEART ATTACK!
HOW DO YOU THINK I FEEL?! BEING A LITTLE KID WITH A FACE UGLY ENOUGH TO KILL A DOG?! AND ALL OF YOU HATING ME! NOT ANYONE THERE I COULD CALL A FRIEND! HOW WAS I NOT SUPPOSED TO HATE YOU BACK?!
I'M JUST A BOY, WITH FEELINGS LIKE ALL OF YOU!
WELL, BOY, WE'RE ABOUT TO SEE IF YOU FEEL FIRE!

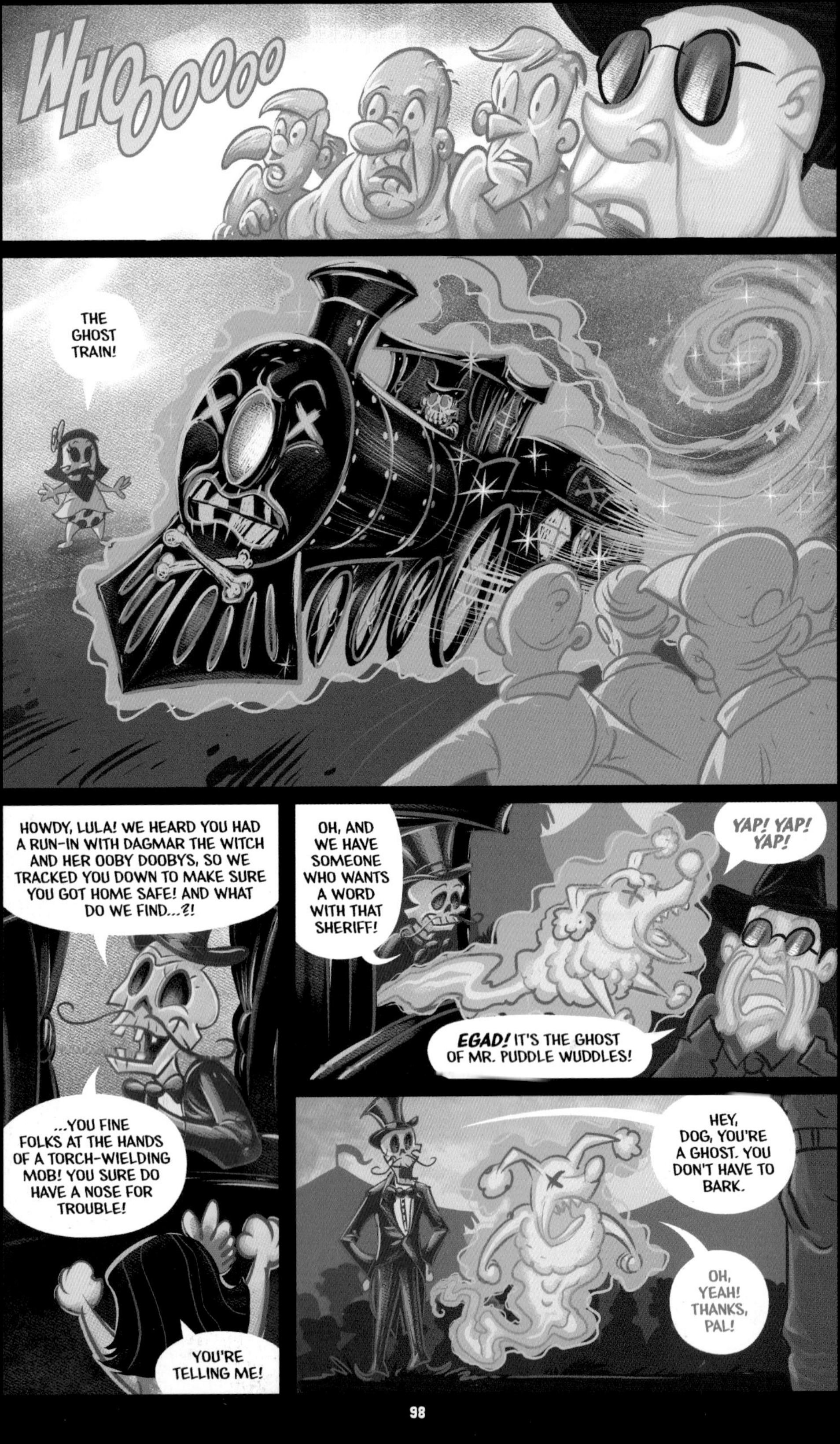
WHOOOOOO
THE GHOST TRAIN!
HOWDY, LULA! WE HEARD YOU HAD A RUN-IN WITH DAGMAR THE WITCH AND HER OOBY DOOBYS, SO WE TRACKED YOU DOWN TO MAKE SURE YOU GOT HOME SAFE! AND WHAT DO WE FIND...?!
...YOU FINE FOLKS AT THE HANDS OF A TORCH-WIELDING MOB! YOU SURE DO HAVE A NOSE FOR TROUBLE!
YOU'RE TELLING ME!
OH, AND WE HAVE SOMEONE WHO WANTS A WORD WITH THAT SHERIFF!
YAP! YAP! YAP!
EGAD! IT'S THE GHOST OF MR. PUDDLE WUDDLES!
HEY, DOG, YOU'RE A GHOST. YOU DON'T HAVE TO BARK.
OH, YEAH! THANKS, PAL!

MY DEAREST FRIEND! YOU'VE RETURNED TO ME!

B-BUT, I...I--

HE JUST STARTLED ME IS ALL! MAYBE IF YOU HADN'T FED ME NOTHIN' BUT THAT CHEAP, ARTERY-CLOGGIN' DOG FOOD, MY HEART WOULD HAVE BEEN IN BETTER CONDITION!

AWWW, STUFF IT! HOW DARE YOU BLAME THAT KID FOR MY DEATH, YOU IGNORANT PODUNK LAWMAN!

AND ANOTHER THING! I NEVER LIKED YOU THAT MUCH IN THE FIRST PLACE!

WELL, NOW THAT THE SHERIFF IS TAKEN CARE OF, HOW ABOUT WE DISPERSE THIS MOB!

HOW ARE YOU GONNA DO THAT?

MY DEAR, WE ARE GHOSTS, AFTER ALL.

AND DON'T YOU EVER TROUBLE THIS CIRCUS AGAIN!

OH, HI, CHIM! THE GHOST CIRCUS SAVED US. NEAT, HUH?!

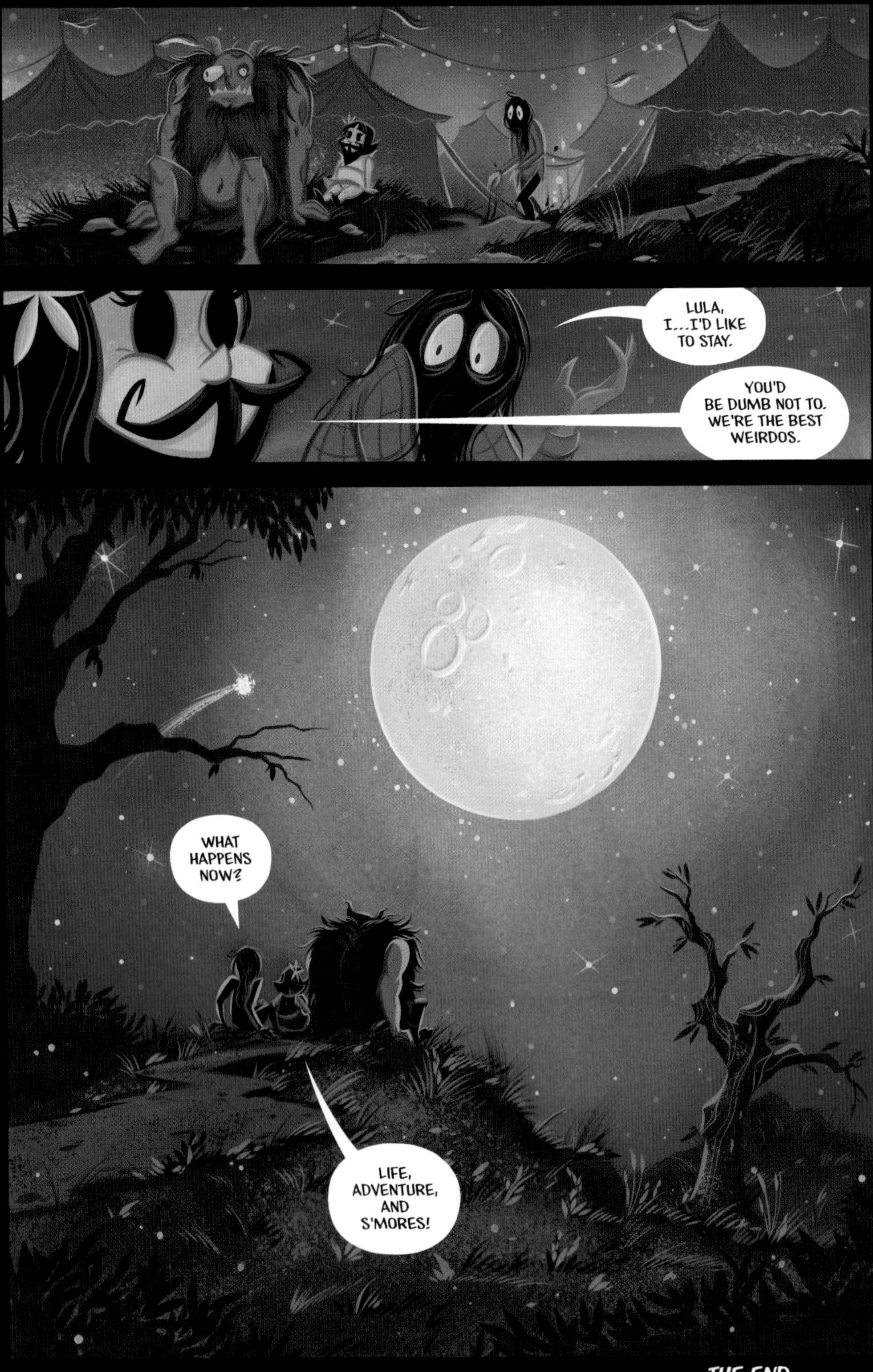
LULA, I...I'D LIKE TO STAY.
YOU'D BE DUMB NOT TO. WE'RE THE BEST WEIRDOS.
WHAT HAPPENS NOW?
LIFE, ADVENTURE, AND S'MORES!

THE END

Chimichanga ™

THE SORROW OF THE WORLD'S WORST FACE!

SKETCHBOOK

Lula character sketches by Stephanie Buscema

Color study by Stephanie

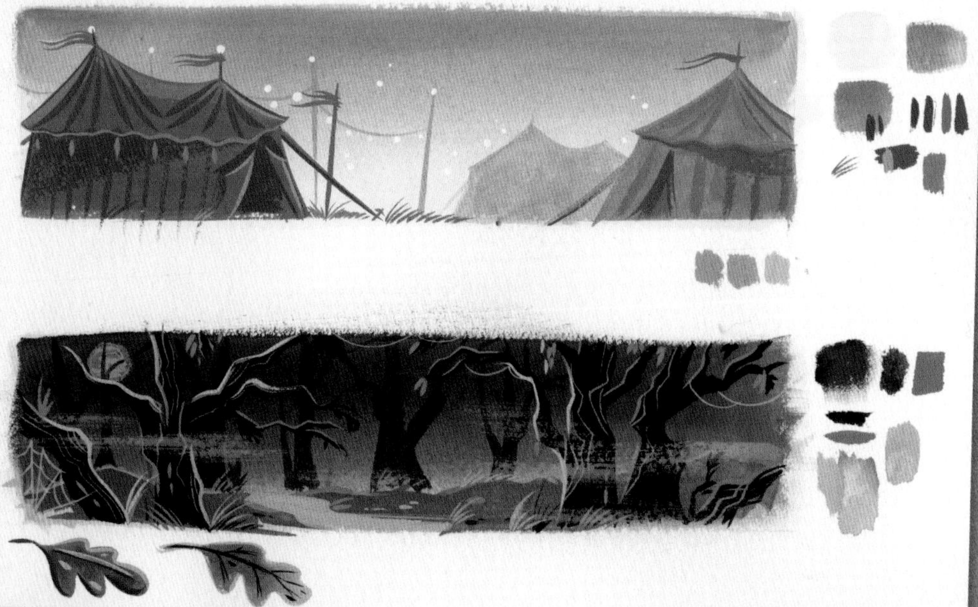

Ooby Dooby character designs by Eric Powell

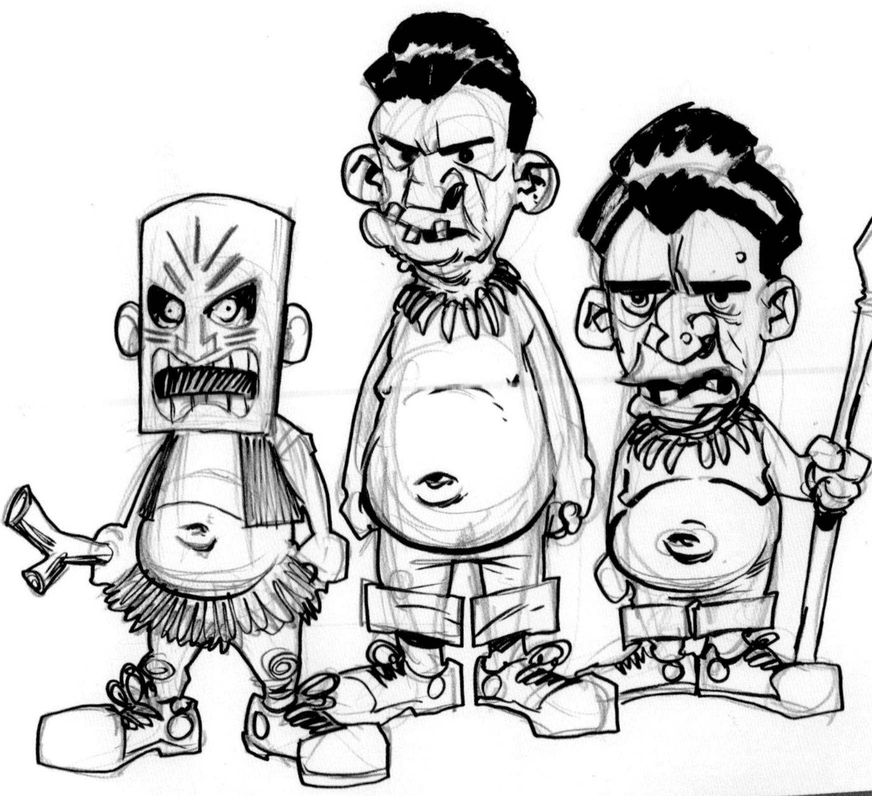

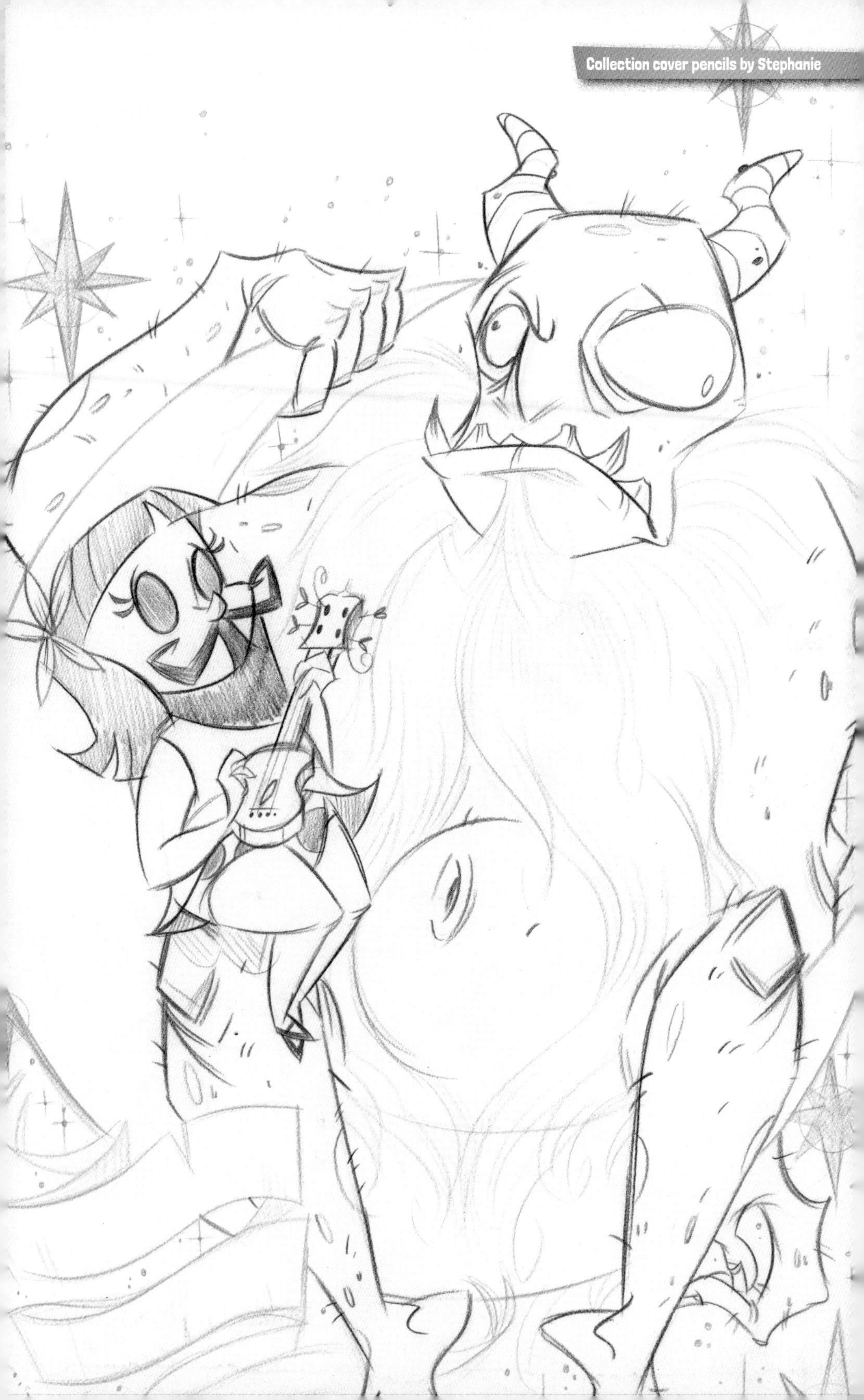

Collection cover pencils by Stephanie

Story layouts by Eric with pencils (*facing*) by Stephanie

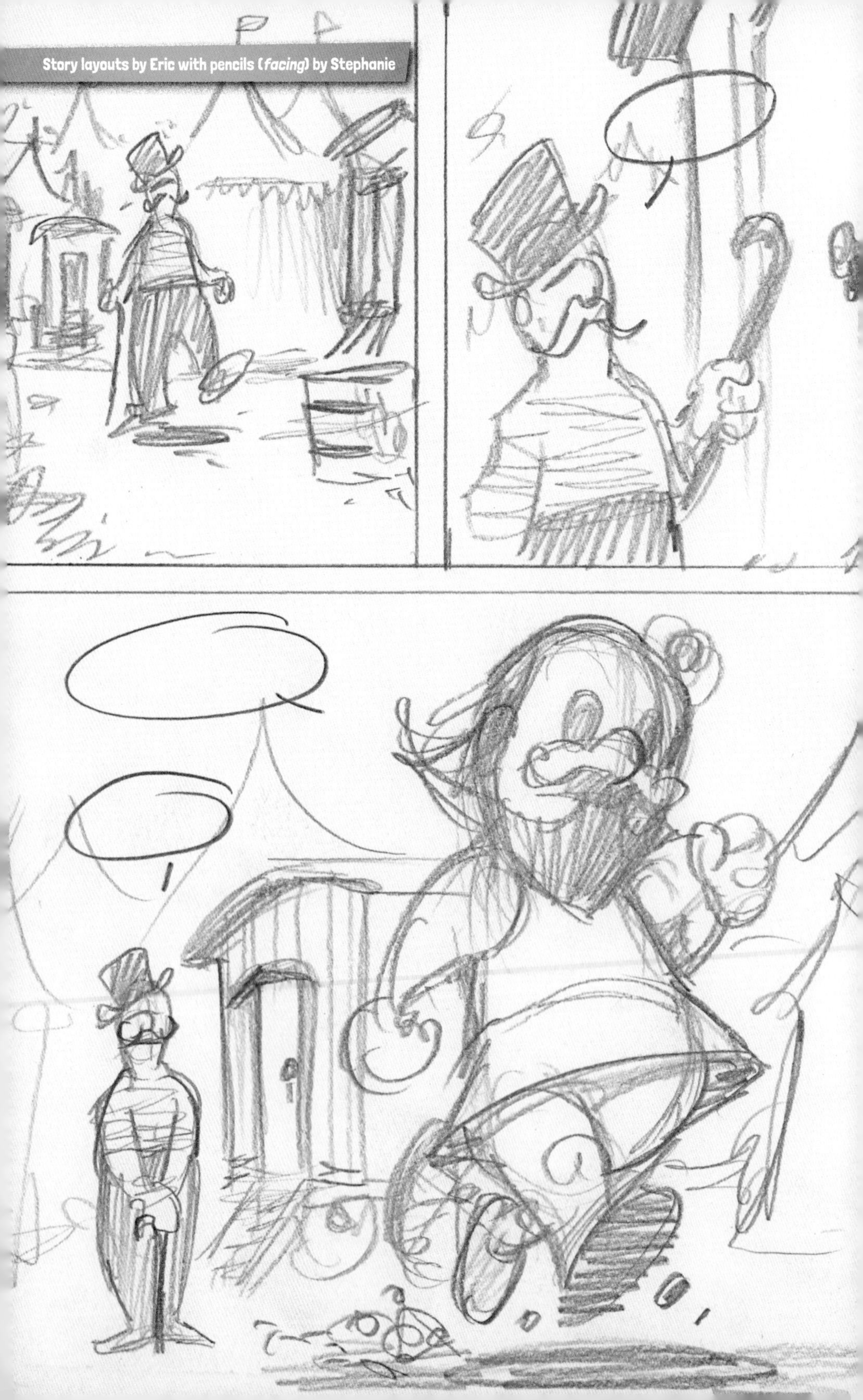

Compare to the finished image on page 9

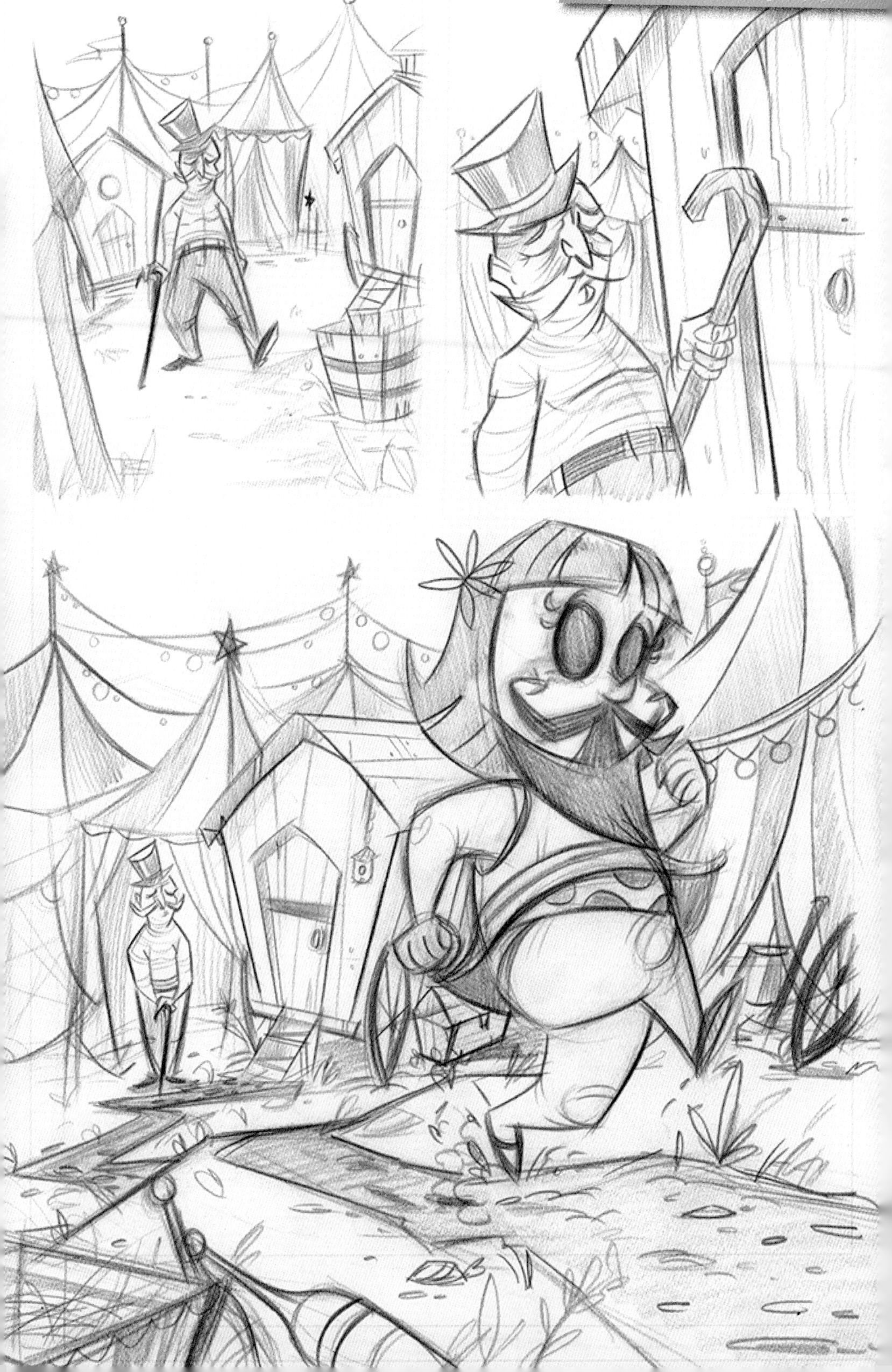

Layouts for page 21 by Eric

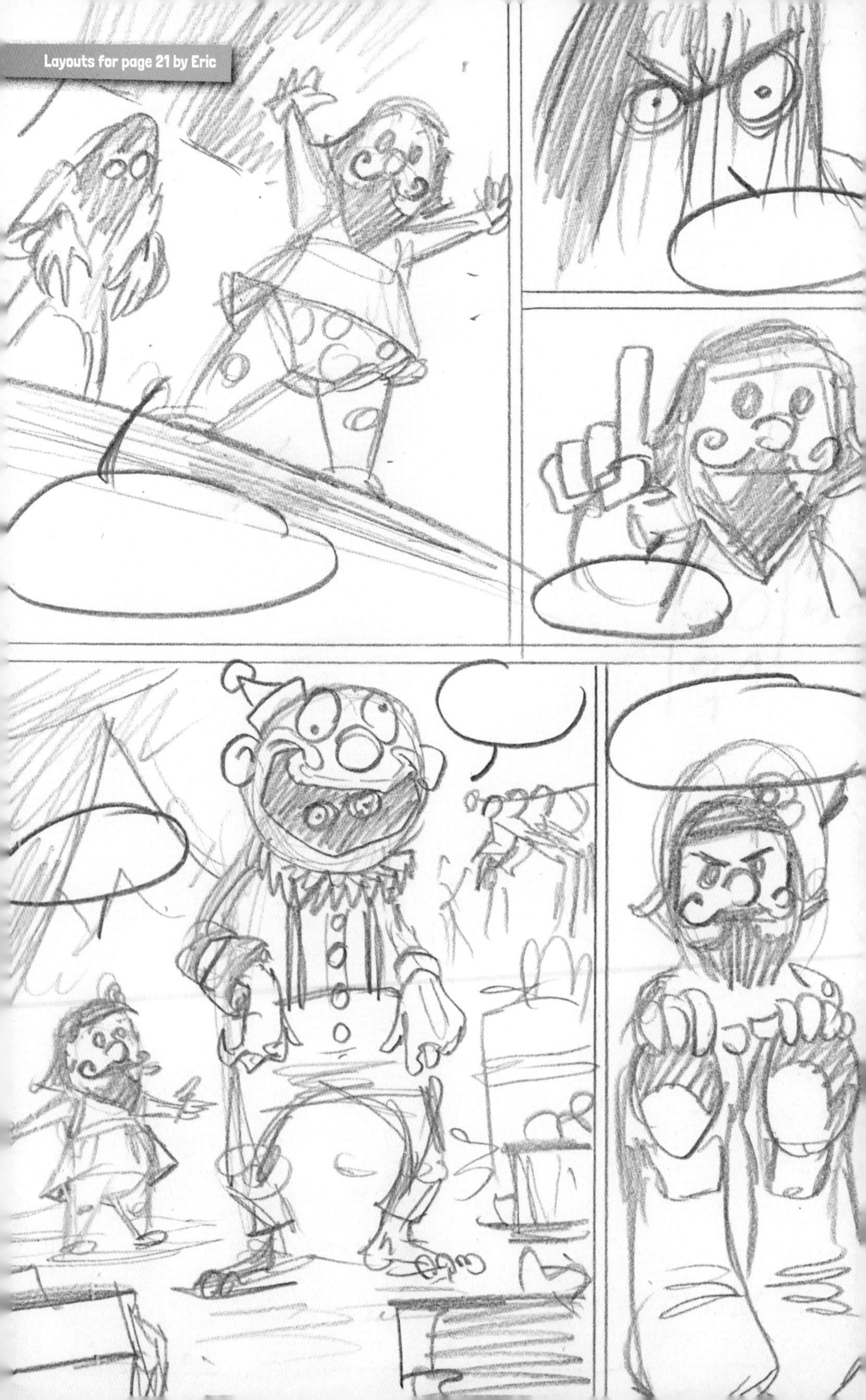

Pencils by Stephanie

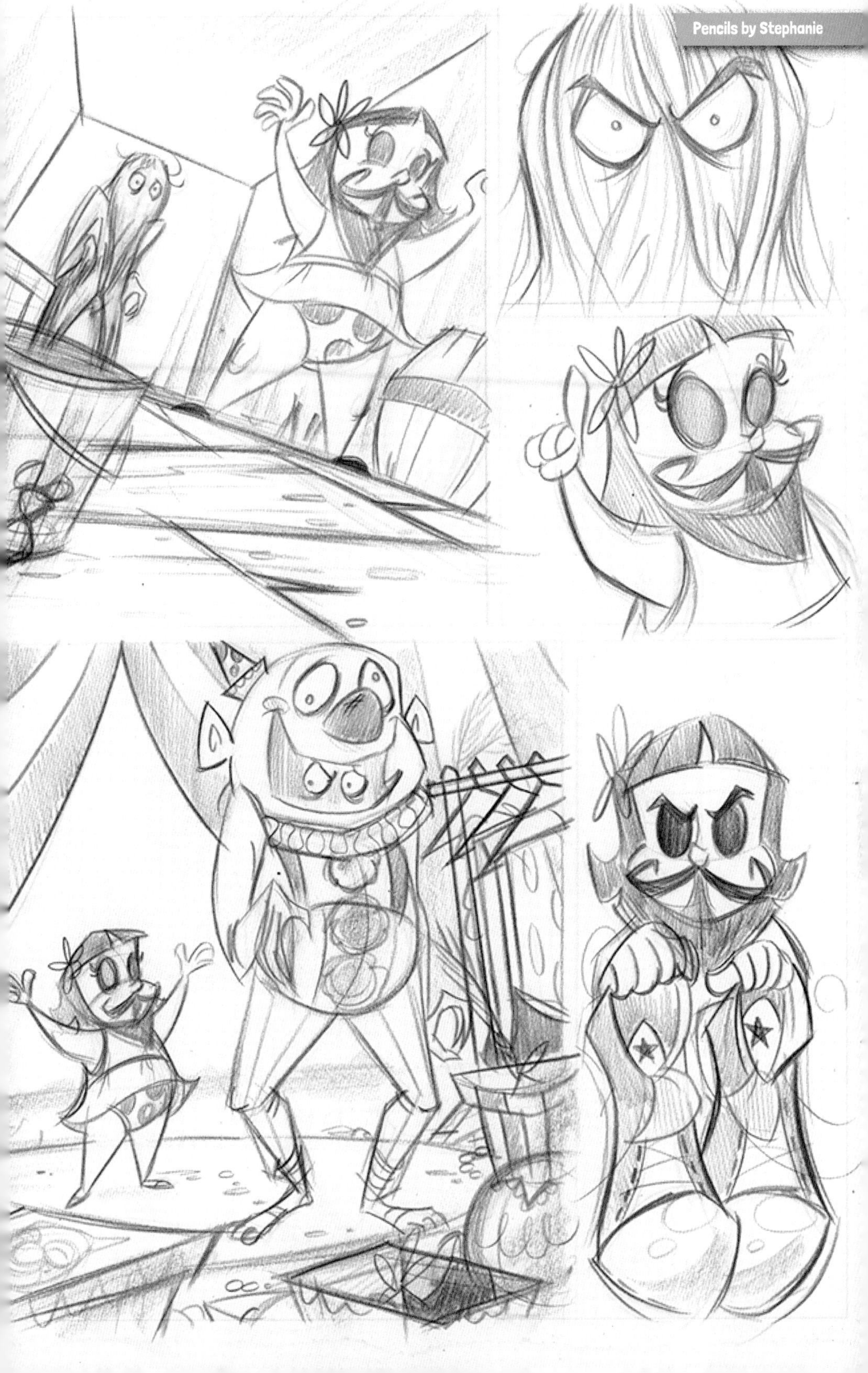

***Chimichanga: The Sorrow of the World's Worst Face!* #1 cover layouts by Eric and pencils by Stephanie; *facing*, layouts and pencils for the #2 cover**

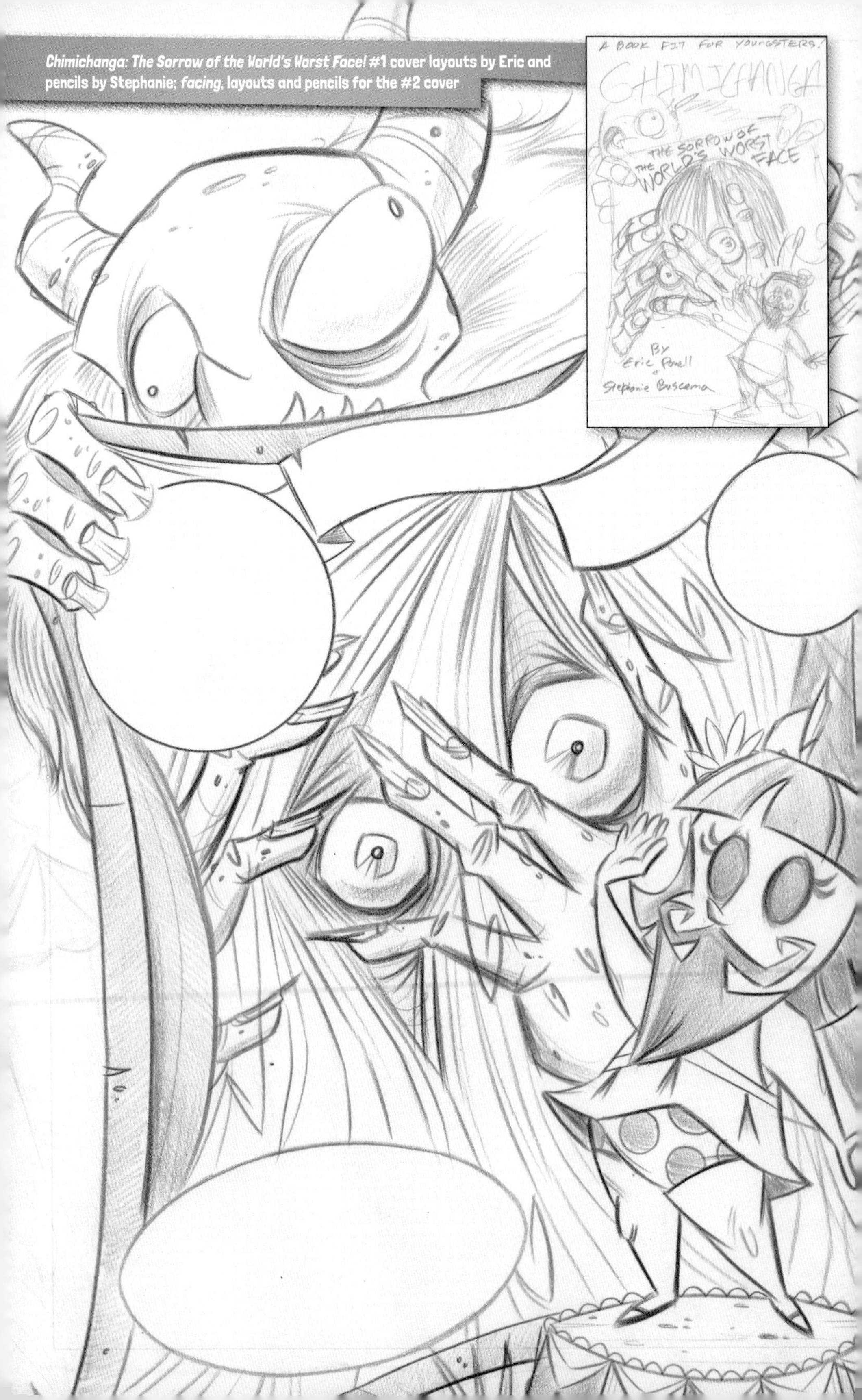
A BOOK FIT FOR YOUNGSTERS!
CHIMICHANGA
THE SORROW OF THE WORLD'S WORST FACE
By
Eric Powell
Stephanie Buscema

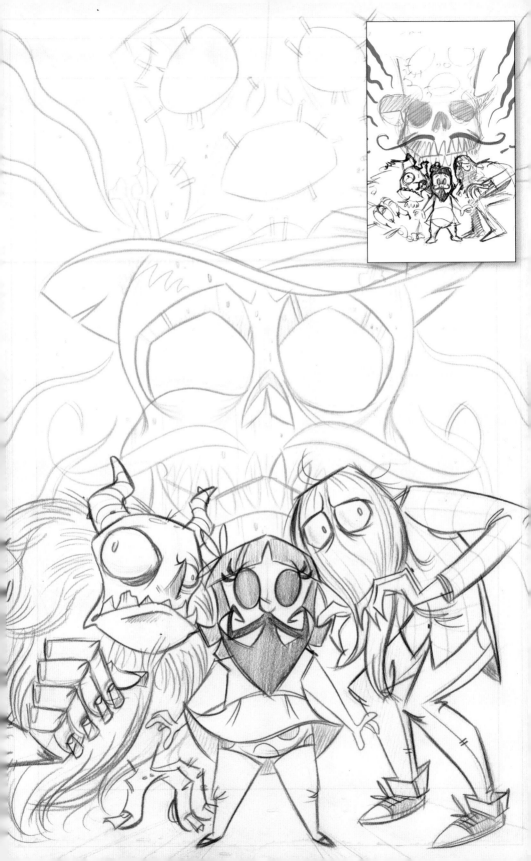

New York Comic Con exclusive cover by Eric Powell

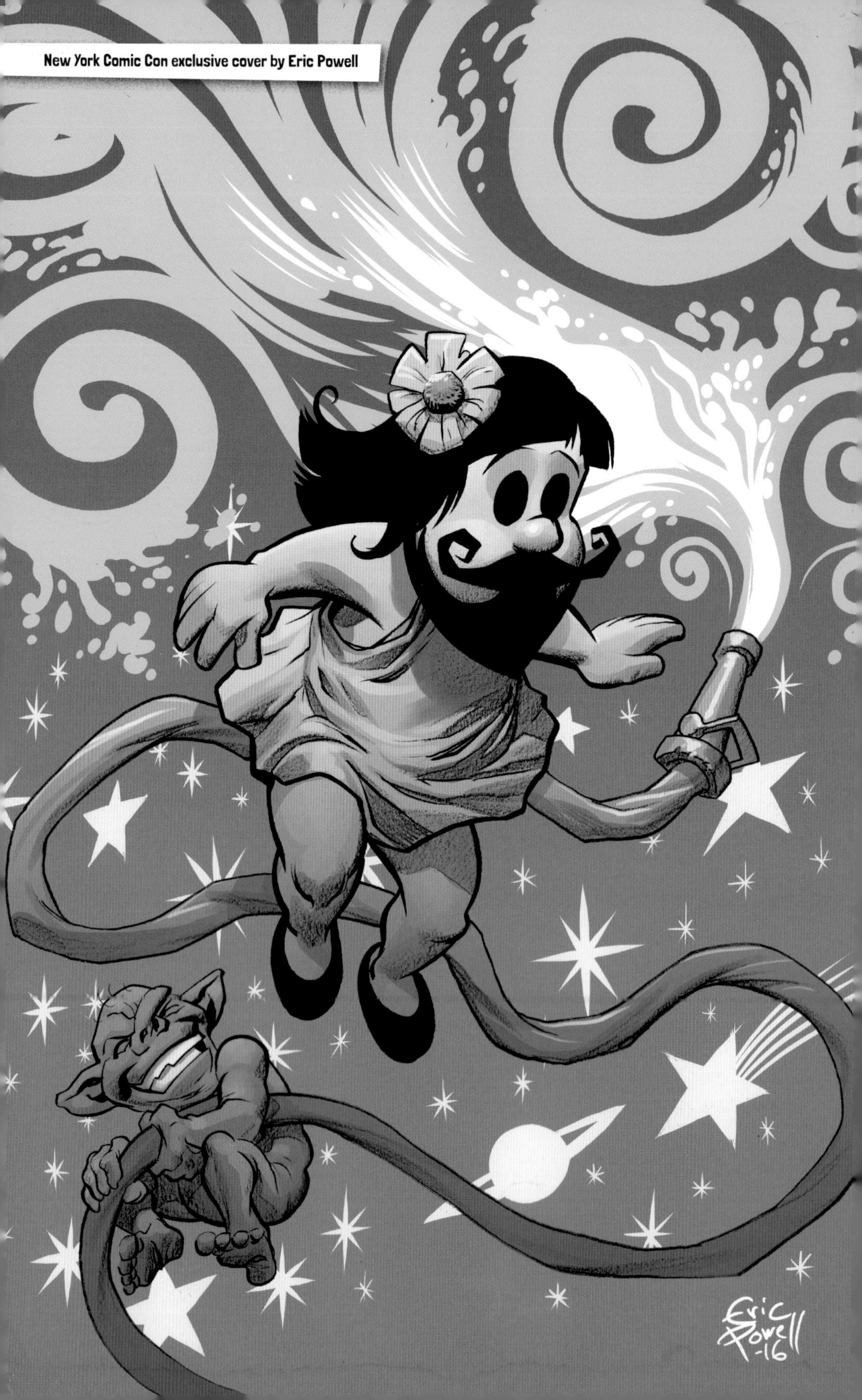
Eric Powell -16

MORE TITLES YOU MIGHT ENJOY

AXE COP

Malachai Nicolle, Ethan Nicolle

Bad guys, beware! Evil aliens, run for your lives! Axe Cop is here, and he's going to chop your head off! We live in a strange world, and our strange problems call for strange heroes. That's why Axe Cop is holding tryouts to build the greatest team of heroes ever assembled.

Volume 1	ISBN 978-1-59582-681-7	$14.99
Volume 2	ISBN 978-1-59582-825-5	$14.99
Volume 3	ISBN 978-1-59582-911-5	$14.99
Volume 4	ISBN 978-1-61655-057-8	$12.99
Volume 5	ISBN 978-1-61655-245-9	$14.99
Volume 6	ISBN 978-1-61655-424-8	$12.99

AXE COP
AXE COP GETS MARRIED AND OTHER STORIES

THE ADVENTURES OF DR. MCNINJA OMNIBUS

Christopher Hastings

He's a doctor! He's a ninja! And now, his earliest exploits are collected in one mighty omnibus volume! Featuring stories from the very beginnings of the Dr. McNinja web comic, this book offers a hefty dose of science, action, and outrageous comedy.

$24.99 | ISBN 978-1-61655-112-4

BREATH OF BONES: A TALE OF THE GOLEM

Steve Niles, Matt Santoro, Dave Wachter

A British plane crashes in a Jewish village, sparking a Nazi invasion. Using clay and mud from the river, the villagers bring to life a giant monster to battle for their freedom and future.

$14.99 | ISBN 978-1-61655-344-9

HARROW COUNTY

Cullen Bunn, Tyler Crook

Emmy always knew that the woods surrounding her home crawled with ghosts and monsters. But on the eve of her eighteenth birthday, she learns that she is connected to these creatures—and to the land itself—in a way she never imagined.

$14.99 each

Volume 1: Countless Haints	ISBN 978-1-61655-780-5
Volume 2: Twice Told	ISBN 978-1-61655-900-7
Volume 3: Snake Doctor	ISBN 978-1-50670-071-7
Volume 4: Family Tree	ISBN 978-1-50670-141-7
Volume 5: Abandoned	ISBN 978-1-50670-190-5

SPACE-MULLET!

Daniel Warren Johnson

Ex–Space Marine Jonah and his copilot Alphius rove the galaxy, trying to get by. Drawn into one crazy adventure after another, they forge a crew of misfits into a family and face the darkest parts of the universe together.

$17.99 | ISBN 978-1-61655-912-0

EI8HT

Mike Johnson, Rafael Albuquerque

Welcome to the Meld, an inhospitable dimension in time where a chrononaut finds himself trapped. With no memory or feedback from the team of scientists that sent him, he can't count on anything but his heart and a stranger's voice to guide him to his destiny.

$17.99 | ISBN 978-1-61655-637-2

NANJING THE BURNING CITY
ETHAN YOUNG
REBELS
BREATH OF BONES
HARROW COUNTY
bridget lee
ei8ht
MUHAMMAD ALI
THE FIFTH BEATLE
THE BRIAN EPSTEIN STORY

REBELS

Brian Wood, Andrea Mutti, Matthew Woodson, Ariela Kristantina, Tristan Jones

This is 1775. With the War for Independence playing out across the colonies, Seth and Mercy Abbott find their new marriage tested at every turn as the demands of the frontlines and the home front collide.

Volume 1: A Well-Regulated Militia
$24.99 | ISBN 978-1-61655-908-3

HOW TO TALK TO GIRLS AT PARTIES

Neil Gaiman, Gabriel Bá, Fábio Moon

Two teenage boys are in for a tremendous shock when they crash a party where the girls are far more than they appear!

$17.99 | ISBN 978-1-61655-955-7

NANJING: THE BURNING CITY

Ethan Young

After the bombs fell, the Imperial Japanese Army seized the Chinese capital of Nanjing. Two abandoned Chinese soldiers try to escape the city and what they'll encounter will haunt them. But in the face of horror, they'll learn that resistance and bravery cannot be destroyed.

$24.99 | ISBN 978-1-61655-752-2

THE BATTLES OF BRIDGET LEE: INVASION OF FARFALL

Ethan Young

There is no longer a generation that remembers a time before the Marauders invaded Earth. Bridget Lee, an ex–combat medic now residing at the outpost Farfall, may be the world's last hope. But Bridget will need to overcome her own fears before she can save her people.

$10.99 | ISBN 978-1-50670-012-0

MUHAMMAD ALI

Sybille Titeux, Amazing Ameziane

Celebrating the life of the glorious athlete who metamorphosed from Cassius Clay to become a three-time heavyweight boxing legend, activist, and provocateur, Muhammad Ali is not only a titan in the world of sports but in the world itself, he dared to be different and to challenge and defy. Witness what made Ali different, what made him cool, what made him the Greatest.

$19.99 | ISBN 978-1-50670-318-3

THE FIFTH BEATLE: THE BRIAN EPSTEIN STORY

Vivek J. Tiwary, Andrew C. Robinson, Kyle Baker

The untold true story of Brian Epstein, the visionary manager who discovered and guided the Beatles to unprecedented international stardom. *The Fifth Beatle* is an uplifting, tragic, and ultimately inspirational human story about the struggle to overcome the odds..

$19.99 | ISBN 978-1-61655-256-5
Expanded Edition $14.99 | ISBN 978-1-61655-835-2

THE USAGI YOJIMBO SAGA

Stan Sakai

When a peace came upon Japan and samurai warriors found themselves suddenly unemployed and many of these ronin turned to banditry, found work, or traveled the musha shugyo to hone their spiritual and martial skills. Whether they took the honest road or the crooked path, the ronin were less than welcome. Such is the tale of Usagi Yojimbo.

$24.99 each

Volume 1	ISBN 978-1-61655-609-9
Volume 2	ISBN 978-1-61655-610-5
Volume 3	ISBN 978-1-61655-611-2
Volume 4	ISBN 978-1-61655-612-9
Volume 5	ISBN 978-1-61655-613-6
Volume 6	ISBN 978-1-61655-614-3
Volume 7	ISBN 978-1-61655-615-0
Legends	ISBN 978-1-50670-323-7

USAGI YOJIMBO SAGA
USAGI YOJIMBO SAGA

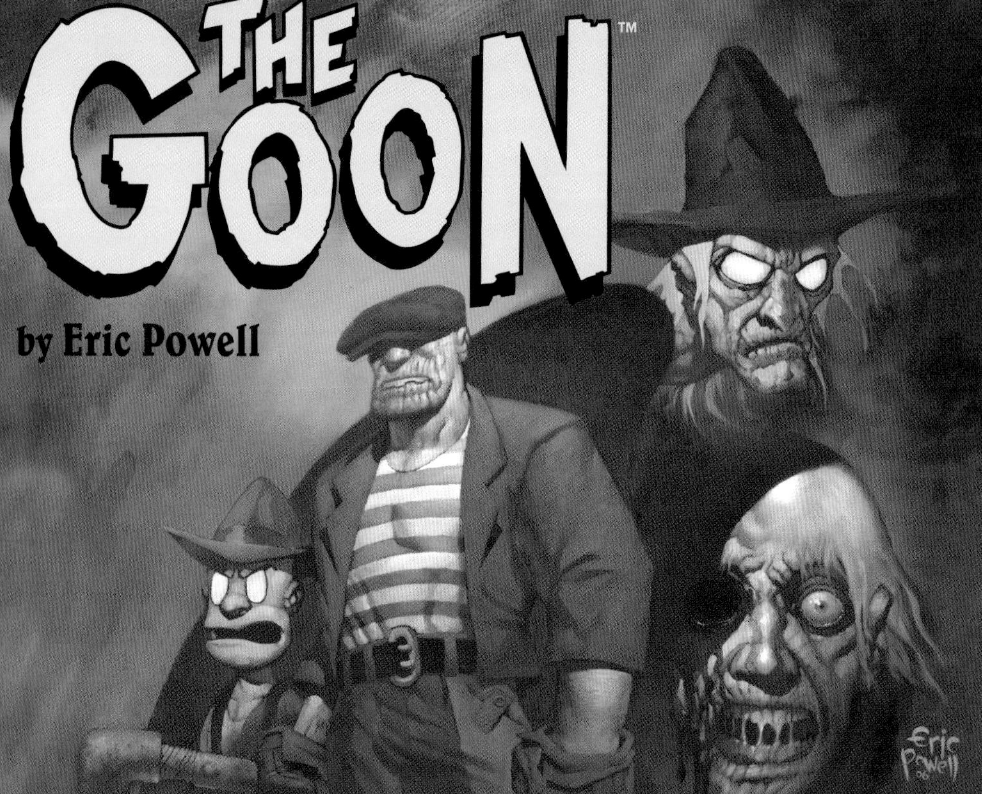
THE GOON™
by Eric Powell

THE GOON LIBRARY VOLUME 1
ISBN 978-1-61655-842-0
$39.99

THE GOON LIBRARY VOLUME 2
ISBN 978-1-61655-843-7
$39.99

THE GOON LIBRARY VOLUME 3
ISBN 978-1-61655-986-1
$39.99

THE GOON LIBRARY VOLUME 4
ISBN 978-1-50670-018-2
$39.99

THE GOON LIBRARY VOLUME 5
ISBN 978-1-50670-401-2
$49.99

Volume 0: ROUGH STUFF
ISBN 978-1-59582-468-4
$13.99

Volume 1: NOTHIN' BUT MISERY
ISBN 978-1-59582-624-4
$16.99

Volume 2: MY MURDEROUS CHILDHOOD (AND OTHER GRIEVOUS YARNS)
ISBN 978-1-59582-616-9
$16.99

Volume 3: HEAPS OF RUINATION
ISBN 978-1-59582-625-1
$16.99

Volume 4: VIRTUE AND THE GRIM CONSEQUENCES THEREOF
ISBN 978-1-59582-617-6
$16.99

Volume 5: WICKED INCLINATIONS
ISBN 978-1-59582-626-8
$16.99

Volume 6: CHINATOWN hardcover
ISBN 978-1-59307-833-1
$19.99

CHINATOWN trade paperback
ISBN 978-1-59582-406-6
$15.99

Volume 7: A PLACE OF HEARTACHE AND GRIEF
ISBN 978-1-59582-311-3
$15.99

Volume 8: THOSE THAT IS DAMNED
ISBN 978-1-59582-324-3
$15.99

Volume 9: CALAMITY OF CONSCIENCE
ISBN 978-1-59582-346-5
$15.99

Volume 10: DEATH'S GREEDY COMEUPPANCE
ISBN 978-1-59582-643-5
$16.99

Volume 11: THE DEFORMED OF BODY AND THE DEVIOUS OF MIND
ISBN 978-1-59582-881-1
$16.99

Volume 12: THEM THAT RAISED US LAMENT
ISBN 978-1-61655-006-6
$16.99

Volume 13: FOR WANT OF WHISKEY AND BLOOD
ISBN 978-1-61655-101-8
$16.99

Volume 14: OCCASION OF REVENGE
ISBN 978-1-61655-596-2
$16.99

Volume 15: ONCE UPON A HARD TIME
ISBN 978-1-50670-098-4
$16.99

FANCY PANTS VOLUME 2: THE RISE AND FALL OF THE DIABOLICAL DR. ALLOY
Limited-edition hardcover
ISBN 978-1-59307-918-5
$24.99

FANCY PANTS VOLUME 3: THE RETURN OF LABRAZIO
ISBN 978-1-59582-503-2
$34.99

THE AUTHENTIC ACCOUNTS OF BILLY THE KID'S OLD TIMEY ODDITIES
with Kyle Hotz
ISBN 978-1-61655-470-5
$24.99

CHIMICHANGA
ISBN 978-1-59582-755-5
$14.99

CHIMICHANGA: SORROW OF THE WORLD'S WORST FACE
with Stephanie Buscema
ISBN 978-1-61655-902-1
$14.99

DARK HORSE BOOKS®
DarkHorse.com

To find a comics shop in your area, call 1-888-266-4226 For more information or to order direct: • On the web: DarkHorse.com • E-mail: mailorder@DarkHorse.com • Phone: 1-800-862-0052 Mon.–Fri. 9 AM to 5 PM Pacific Time